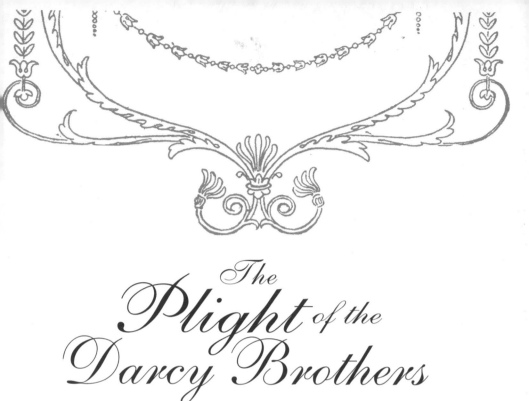

The Plight of the Darcy Brothers

A Tale of Siblings and Surprises

The Plight of the Darcy Brothers

A Tale of Siblings and Surprises

Marsha Altman

Sourcebooks Landmark™
An Imprint of Sourcebooks, Inc.®
Naperville, Illinois

Published by Sourcebooks Landmark, an imprint of Sourcebooks, Inc.
P.O. Box 4410, Naperville, Illinois 60567–4410
(630) 961–3900
FAX: (630) 961–2168
www.sourcebooks.com

Library of Congress Cataloging-in-Publication Data

Altman, Marsha.
  The plight of the Darcy brothers / Marsha Altman.
    p. cm.
  I. Austen, Jane, 1775-1817. Pride and prejudice. II. Title.
  PS3601.L853P57 2009
  813'.6--dc22
                        2009017531

Printed and bound in the United States of America
VP 10 9 8 7 6 5 4 3 2 1

Dedication

To Mary Anne Dietrich, my sixth grade English teacher,
for believing in me.

And

To Kelly, Madison, and Hannah Scott,
for being really understanding when their mother disappears
behind the computer to edit for me.

THE MASTER OF HIS REALM

LOOKING OUT ON THE lands of Pemberley and surrounding Derbyshire as a king would his kingdom, and surveying all that was within his grasp, Fitzwilliam Darcy would normally breathe in a deep sigh of relief that all was under his control. He was the master of his own fate. He had been a loyal son, a diligent student, an excellent outdoorsman, a suitable gentleman, a good friend, a loving husband and brother, and now was a caring father as well. He handled every situation that had arisen, no matter how trying, usually with the utmost civility and control—not always, but usually.

Darcy supposed, with what little emotional distance he had left in him, he could look back on the matter and say that one who tempted God forced the Lord's hand to prove that Mr. Darcy of Pemberley and Derbyshire was *not*, in fact, the master of his own fate. He just wished it could have been done in a manner that was a bit more... subtle.

"Brother?"

He didn't turn to address Georgiana properly when he heard

her voice. That would have required him standing, and he did not have the inclination to move. Manners would just have to suffer. Manners were gone from him entirely. "Yes?"

"Do you want something?" she stammered. "I mean, may I get you something? You've—you've just been out here a long time."

Her, *serving* him? Didn't he have a well-paid staff for that? *No*, he remembered, he'd shooed them all away. "No, thank you. Is she awake?"

"No."

Good. "I'm fine. Thank you for inquiring."

She took that as a dismissal, which was good enough for him; he was not interested in having a conversation with his sister, or anyone for that matter besides Elizabeth, and then he had no idea of what to say. There hadn't been a course for this at Cambridge. *What a waste of time; studying literature when it all amounted to nothing.* He should have gone to medical school. He should have had a profession as a doctor and not been a uselessly idle gentleman who could do nothing of any worth in a crisis.

Georgiana had returned, because he felt her soft touch as she put a blanket over his shoulders. There was a chill in the evening air, but so far his mind had been elsewhere. "Just so you don't catch cold," she said, and disappeared again. Maybe she didn't know what to say *either*. Not that the situation didn't merit excessive confusion or sorrow. That it had been unexpected, however, just proved fools of them all.

Elizabeth's courses had descended on her when they shouldn't have, four months into her term. He could only think "courses" because that seemed a less vulgar way to describe it than just bleeding, which was what it was. And pain. She had been a little stoic at first, but she did nothing to hide her alarm and rang for the most knowledgeable woman on these matters on the grounds, which was Mrs. Reynolds. Elizabeth was dismissive of his worries, perhaps fearing they would eclipse her own, and might have tried to ignore her condition entirely if it hadn't continued, and if pain hadn't set in. By the time the doctor arrived, their child was gone, though the doctor insisted on not calling it that, or having them call it that.

This was not the first time, but it was drastically more pain-ful. Elizabeth's first term after giving birth to Geoffrey had also ended quite abruptly, and though that was startling, they had remained upbeat about her future prospects. The second term proceeded further along, so much so that Darcy would swear to her he could see a difference in her, even if she could detect none, and would whisper encouraging words to her at night.

That the Darcys' hopes for a second child had disappeared again for no apparent reason and in a chamber pot hit them both at a level they hadn't expected. Elizabeth was a normal woman and, in the course of their marriage, could expect to miscarry, perhaps as often as she carried to term. That her mother had never done so was a wonder unto itself, with all of the emphasis on the lack of sons in the Bennet family, Elizabeth admitted, between sobbing and being forced into bed from exhaustion.

This was not a formal mourning; no one had died, and there was every temptation to close ranks, at least for the moment. Nonetheless, from the very first look he had at the amount of blood she was losing (and where she was losing it from), Darcy had called for Dr. Maddox, who very unfortunately lived in Town and, therefore, could not appear in Derbyshire at a moment's notice. They had to settle for the local doctor, who was perfectly competent and on whom they had relied in the past, but Daniel Maddox still seemed a magical wonder who could save everyone and do no wrong. He had, in the space of three months, saved both Darcy's and his own brother's lives. But no, Dr. Maddox was in the south, and the message would not have reached him before all was over and done. If he did apply to Pemberley, it would only be to give his regrets as a relative for the unhappy circumstances.

Elizabeth had to tell Jane; of course, everyone would have to be told, because everyone had been told Elizabeth was with child some time before, but there was an order to imparting the news, and letters could not be formally set out like party invitations. It was more that Elizabeth demanded no one see her and then finally cried for her sister, leaving Darcy to fill in the order of the correspondences. In the shortest note and with his most precise and ordered handwriting, betraying nothing of what he felt, he wrote to Longbourn with the unhappy news and left it entirely to the Bennets' discretion as to who would come. Mary Bennet was still on the Continent, and Lydia was still the wife of George Wickham and, therefore, did not enter into his thinking.

He wrote to the Gardiners even more briefly, barely more than a line. The Hursts he would leave to Bingley, to whom he had applied by courier. The Bingleys had arrived within the hour. The only reason Darcy was willing to leave Elizabeth's side was because her sister had joined her. Whether they were talking or not was none of his business.

He was genuinely both happy Bingley was there and not in the mood to have a conversation with him, something he had made known mainly (he hoped) by inflection when he addressed Bingley, and then by disappearing onto the balcony outside his rarely used bedroom. He remembered through a haze that gentlemen did not show their tears, and that much stuck with him enough that he took the privacy afforded to him by Jane's arrival to disappear.

When he finally came inside, it was nearing midnight. His wife was sound asleep, so he only kissed her on the cheek, but he could not find the lack of energy required for his own retire-ment. Instead he went to the nursery, where his son was also asleep. Darcy began to conjure what he was to say to him in the morning, but nothing came, and Geoffrey Darcy slept on. All he could think of, and that he said out of earshot as to not wake his son, was, "You have no idea, the burden on your shoulders someday." To be Master of Pemberley was to inflict a horrible circumstance on his wife, however unintentionally. Everything was colored by the circumstance; Darcy had in him still enough sense to see that.

Georgiana, again, found him first. "The Bingleys are staying the night."

He just nodded numbly.

"Mr. Bingley is in the drawing room, but he said he doesn't require anything. Jane went to her room, and the dogs are still outside." *Because how they'd howled; it was unnerving when they knew something was wrong.* "I'm sorry, Brother."

"I am, too," was all he could think to say as Georgiana embraced him.

"As much as I love my sister, I am so sorry someone as nice as Elizabeth has the fate of being *Mrs.* Darcy," she said, and then added quickly, "Oh, I didn't mean—"

"It's fine."

"No, I meant Mrs. Darcy. As in our mother."

This lowered his guilt and self-pity and raised his curiosity enough for him to say, "What do you mean?"

"Well, I mean, you know—surely you know."

"No," he said. "I don't know."

She put her hand over her mouth. "Then maybe I shouldn't have said. Certainly now isn't the time."

"Actually, you haven't said anything," he said, "as to what this is about. What do you know about our mother that I do not?" After all, Lady Anne Darcy had died shortly after giving birth to Georgiana. "Please. I insist."

"I suppose you should know. It's just—ill-timed," Georgiana whispered. "Our mother lost more babies than she bore, Brother."

She gave him the time to properly sort it out. She was nearly thirteen years his junior, and he had no other siblings. So, with the years of marriage between his parents, who as far as he remembered cared for each other at least decently, either periods of barrenness or failed pregnancies made some sense. But the subject had never been openly discussed with *him*. "How did—"

"Mrs. Reynolds. Before I was to go *out*, she thought it prudent for me to know what to expect. Oh, please do not blame her."

"Not in the least." Mrs. Reynolds had been in the employ of his father since his own childhood and had been head of the household since his adolescence. It was no surprise that she knew more of the personal family history of the Darcys than he did—when it came to women's issues, at least. "Thank you for telling me."

"I hope it was… some comfort."

He smiled sadly at her, which was enough of an assurance

that it was; she said her good-nights and disappeared. Most of his staff had retired, and he was inclined to wander for a bit. The halls had always given him comfort, even though now they just seemed empty and... barren.

The lights were still lit in the sitting room. Bingley was reading by the fire. Darcy took a seat by his side, and his friend nodded but said nothing. One of the things that Darcy valued very highly about their friendship was that, despite Bingley's reputation for being oblivious and talkative, he knew precisely when to be quiet—at least around Darcy. He was there, but he did not puncture the silence for a very long time, as his friend and brother stared numbly into the fire.

It was only after Darcy had began to play with it using the poker and made some noise that Bingley said softly, "It was never a competition."

"I know," Darcy replied.

And that was all that needed to be said.

⁓✦⁓

The letter posted to the Maddox townhouse in exceedingly good time, but the doctor knew from the description that his arrival would be too late, and shrugged sadly. When his wife inquired as to the letter's contents, he told her the unhappy news. Even though he would never hold back from Caroline Maddox (neé Bingley) unless absolutely necessary, especially on family matters, Elizabeth was not her favorite person, and it could have been concluded at one time that she had wished Elizabeth ill. He doubted that was still true, but he still found himself surprised at Caroline's emotions, as she did seem saddened by the news.

They were in bed when the letter came, but he knew he would be getting up and racing to Pemberley. He ordered the carriage ready but stayed in bed nonetheless, at least for the moment.

"I suppose there's no reason to rush," Caroline said.

"No," he said. "I mean, I will go, but not this instant. By now, she may well be fully recovered physically, though not fully emotionally." He sighed. "Mr. Darcy wants me to work a miracle, I suppose. Or he did when he was writing this letter. Mr. Darcy does not seem likely to remain insensible for an entire day. I doubt I could have done anything, even if I was standing there. I am not an expert on womanly issues, but I know that much."

"Perhaps you should become an expert."

He smiled, but then he looked at her in the lamplight and realized she hadn't meant her comment to be a joke. He took her hand and found it trembling. While he was processing what he was going to say to Darcy, he hadn't even considered... He kissed her palm, as if that would placate her fears. "Everything will be all right."

"And if it's not?"

"These things are not of our control," he said. "Perhaps something is wrong, and the body just... rejects it. Instinctually." He cracked a weak smile. "I tend to be one for trusting a woman's instincts." His hand strayed to her stomach, feeling under the bed robe.

"It's what makes you a good doctor," she said, kissing him on the cheek. "That and your skill with a needle. If we have a daughter, you can teach her how to embroider cushions and tablecloths, and turn her into a proper little lady."

"I do believe I've just been insulted," he said. "And I think I am going to ignore it." He eventually heaved himself up off the bed and began to stumble around for his clothing.

"I want to come. I mean, to Chatton, where I imagine you'll be staying. Unless you think—"

"Not at all. You could ride to France if you wanted."

"Darling, you *can't ride* to France."

"I meant it *metaphorically*," he said. He leaned over and kissed her again. "You will be fine if you come along."

She needed reassuring.

⁕

On the pretense of visiting Jane, the three available Bennets made their way to Derbyshire. Since officially nothing had happened, or nothing to be spoken of except in privacy, the only family gathering was at Chatton, the Bingleys' home, and those who were wont to visit Elizabeth could easily do so.

Mrs. Bennet was the first to appear, fortunately with Jane. Darcy took Mrs. Bingley aside and said quite quietly and clearly, "If she says something that upsets Elizabeth, I will cast her out of Pemberley. Not to be rude to my mother-in-law, but you understand?"

"Perfectly," said Jane, and followed her mother.

Elizabeth Darcy was still in bed. She had not left her chambers in several days and was rarely upright. The shades were drawn even though it was past noon, putting the room further into stupor right along with her.

"This... this won't do," said Mrs. Bennet nervously, as if she didn't know how to act around her own daughter, and she pulled open the curtains, filling the room with light. "Two hundred servants, and you can't have someone opening your own curtains?"

To this, her shocked daughter had no response. Mrs. Bennet ran around the bed again and sat beside her daughter, embracing her, and with this, she was silent. Jane sat down on the chaise, somewhat bemused.

"Now, now, Lizzy, we're all very sorry, and I am sorry to be the first one to tell you this, but as mothers we are to suffer some unhappiness in our lives."

"Mama," Elizabeth said incredulously, "I do know *that*."

"No, nothing compares, then, to the trials of motherhood. No matter how happy or well settled or loved we are, we will all suffer a bit in our turn. I spent far too many years wracking myself with guilt to watch you do it. Do you wish your wonderful Mr. Darcy to have suddenly married someone like *me*?"

"Mama," Jane said in Elizabeth's place, "what do you mean?"

"You know precisely what I mean. You're both women with children. But you had the great ability to bear sons, and I did not. So you have already succeeded where I failed, and that itself is cause for joy, no?" She stroked her second daughter's hair. "It may not feel this way now—we women have a tendency to lose perspective, even *you*, Lizzy, but you have all the treasures of the world in front of you—a loving husband, a wonderful home, and a beautiful son."

"Are you telling me to cheer up?"

"No, I'm barely in control of my own nerves… I hardly see how I could give advice about other people's." And yet, Mrs. Bennet seemed perfectly calm, if appropriately sad at the situation, and that left her two daughters utterly put off. "You will be your old self in no time. You will see."

Darcy did not invade the privacy of his wife's bedroom, usually very much his own domain as well as hers, until his mother-in-law and sister were done and gone, and by then it was getting late. Elizabeth did not eat with the rest of them, her appetite being sparse, and so he did not see her again until he could be properly excused from his guests.

"Lizzy," he said as he entered, surprised to find her sitting up and reading, something he hadn't seen in a while. He kissed her and climbed into bed beside her. She had never shooed him away since the incident, as would have been her right, certainly, and he had not been at all desirous to be apart from her. "What are you reading?"

"*A Midsummer Night's Dream.*"

"You have not read it?"

"It was my first Bard, actually. I haven't read it since childhood. At the time, I thought a man with the head of an ass was the most amusing thing in the world."

"And now?"

"And now, what?"

"What do you think is the most amusing thing the world?"

"I could tell you, but it might insult your considerable dignity."

"So you mean *me*, with the head of a donkey. Perhaps opiated, saying ridiculous things, or drunk and punching people."

His wife laughed. He could not remember when the sound had made him feel better, like a weight lifting off his chest. "I love you," he said, "and I might venture a strange guess that your mother did not say anything too terrible."

"On the contrary. She might even have been encouraging.

It was so bizarre… it was hard to tell. You may have to get Jane's opinion for any perspective."

"Your mother? Are you sure it wasn't Mrs. Reynolds in Mrs. Bennet's dress?"

Lizzy giggled again. "Stop insulting my mother. She was very comforting."

"Then I owe her a great debt. Perhaps I should marry one of her daughters."

Despite all of the attention, despite her husband's loving diligence, Elizabeth did not return to her old self and only seemed to brighten in private, in front of her sister Jane and in playing with Geoffrey. Darcy could not admit that the wind had also been knocked from his own emotions, but society dictated that they recover and move on. Unfortunately, he privately suspected that would only happen when Elizabeth was with child again, or something happened to distract her. Despite his best efforts, he could not provide the first.

Providence provided the second, when a letter from Mary Bennet arrived a month later.

Chapter 2

DARK CLOUDS AT BRIGHTON

DARCY HAPPENED TO BE coming down the main steps when the doors opened for Jane Bingley, and though she did not look particularly distressed, he crossed by the servants and bowed to her himself. "Mrs. Bingley."

"Mr. Darcy," she curtseyed. "I've come to speak with my sister."

"She's in her study. I assume all is well?"

"Yes. It's merely some conversation," she said, which struck him as a bit odd, but he would not inquire as to what the subject was.

He did not have time to do so anyway, with his son bounding down the steps and nearly sliding across the marble, so that Darcy had to catch him by his jacket before he slammed into Jane entirely, which was probably his intent. "What did I tell you about running down the stairs?"

"Don't!" his son simply said, squirreling out of his grasp and running to grab his aunt by her leg, which was about as high as he could reach. "Auntie!"

"My darling nephew," she said. "I fear you're getting too heavy for your poor aunt to pick up. You should listen to your father more often. You might hurt yourself."

"He should," said Darcy with a mock-indignant posture, but his son simply giggled at him and put his hand in his mouth. "But he doesn't. He takes after his mother."

"I've no doubt of that. Oh, I should have brought Georgie, but the business is too quick, and she was asleep. Well, you will see her at church on Sunday, won't you, Geoffrey?"

"Kirk!" he said, and looked at his father, almost hiding behind Jane's dress as he did so.

"Yes, yes, I'm so thrilled at your love of Scottish vocabulary. Now, Mrs. Bingley, unless you would like Geoffrey to accompany you, he and I have an appointment—"

"No!" Geoffrey clung to his aunt's legs. "Scary face."

"It's a wart, and there is nothing you can do about it," Darcy said, and then clarified for his sister-in-law. "His tailor. Has a bump on his nose. And it's *very improper to say anything about it.*"

"That's very right," she said, looking down at Geoffrey's scowl. "You shouldn't judge people by their appearances. Looking at you now, someone might think you a dour man with a permanent scowl who doesn't like balls very much."

"I fear I'll never live down Meryton," Darcy said, scooping up his son and still managing to bow. "Mrs. Bingley."

"Mr. Darcy."

He did not inquire unto her further; other things were on his mind, like keeping his son's mouth shut during the whole fitting. Maybe some sort of glue was the answer.

Elizabeth Darcy's "study" was impressive, beyond just the idea that she had one, and it was not simply a sitting or drawing room. It had a desk, a chair, and lots of legal books that she had not the slightest intent of perusing, but they were important to making it a proper *study*. As Mistress of Pemberley, she was not without her business. Certainly it was nothing that a writing table couldn't handle, but that was not her desire, and Mr. Darcy made sure that every one of her wants and needs was taken care of. Also, he desperately needed her out of his study.

When Jane entered the room, Elizabeth was sitting, reading an old epic with language that she could barely understand, but the tome was big and fascinating all the more and would not sit properly on her lap. "Jane! I was not expecting you."

"No." Jane didn't look harried, but she did shut the door. Something in her countenance changed when the door was firmly shut and they were in privacy. "What a lovely room."

"Yes. But not very good for chatting." Elizabeth was referring to the lack of couches, but Jane made her way to a gentleman's sitting chair and passed her a letter. "From Mary."

"For you?"

"My eyes only."

Elizabeth did not question further. She read through the letter, which was brief, before beginning to conjure the proper response. Mary, who was studying in a seminary just outside of Paris, had returned to England, or was to when the letter was written. She was traveling by means of a ship that would take her to Brighton first, where she had arranged lodgings, and where she wanted to see Jane alone. The first puzzlement was the obvious question of why she would not come home through

Town and then go straight on to Hertfordshire. The second was why she wanted Jane alone and in the strictest confidence.

"Why me, Lizzy?"

Elizabeth pondered before answering, "Perhaps because you are the most understanding of the five of us."

"Why would that make any difference?" Before Elizabeth could offer a suggestion, Jane added, "Perhaps she came home ill and is in Brighton for its healing qualities. She could stay with the Fitzwilliams."

"Then she would merely say so. Clearly she is in some sort of trouble."

"Lizzy! This is *Mary* we're talking about. Not Kitty or Lydia—"

"Nonetheless."

Jane could not find the words to contradict her. "Please, you must go with me."

"That would be directly contrary to our sister's request, I believe."

"I do not think it unreasonable that you accompany me to Brighton. She only specifies that I meet with her first. That you happen to be in town with me will only be a happy coincidence," Jane said. "She must see us all in turn, eventually. So it will be most convenient."

"Jane," Lizzy smiled, "you can be very devious when you wish to be."

"Lizzy!"

"But I will say no more on the subject," she said, standing up. "I simply must tell my husband that I am absconding to Brighton, perhaps to see the Fitzwilliams, whom I have been very lax in visiting despite them being my cousins."

"And he will believe it?"

"Hardly, but he will not put up a fuss." She closed the letter. "Besides, now that we are safely married, we can finally go to Brighton without any fear of great disaster."

It took Elizabeth a long while before she was sure she had misspoken in her assumption of safety from disaster.

A gruff Darcy, reluctant to part with his wife, and an over-eager son, reluctant to part with his mother, made getting into the carriage unbelievably difficult. "For the last time, you cannot go *this time*," Elizabeth said to her son, who was kicking the dust up around her in frustration. "There will be many times for us to travel to Brighton, if you are so eager to go." Not that Brighton had anything to do with it.

Geoffrey Darcy huffed and looked up for help at his father, who replied with a shrug, "She won't let me go, either. It seems she is the master of us both." Knowing his son would not catch the subtlety, he merely patted him on head.

Jane's parting was easier, mainly because Georgiana Bingley did not say anything. Georgiana had not yet spoken her first words, although she seemed to understand everyone properly. Several doctors had been called to test her hearing, which was fine, but for whatever reason, she was holding back her words. She did cry a bit when she was taken out of her mother's arms, but Bingley managed to shush her as he kissed his wife good-bye. "Write us."

"I doubt we will be there long enough to pen a letter," she assured him, "and don't forget her cough medicine."

"Right."

"And her nighttime story."

"Of course."

"And the little blanket she likes, even though it's too small for her now. I brought it from Chatton, didn't I?"

"Yes, dear."

She kissed her daughter on the cheek. This was her first major separation from her children. The twins were staying at Chatton while Bingley and Georgie kept Darcy company at Pemberley. "Don't let your father and uncle destroy the house while we're gone."

"I did manage to keep Pemberley up as a bachelor for some years," Darcy said defensively.

"But you didn't have Geoffrey to chase around," Elizabeth said, and she did mean *chase*. Her son was good-natured, but no one was going to deny that he was a bit on the wild side. That brought Mr. Bennet no end of amusement, and he would go on about how she had been as a child. "I think he shall keep you quite busy, Husband."

It was time to be going, if they were to reach a decent destination by nightfall. As they waved good-bye from the path in front of Pemberley's great steps, Darcy said, "I don't know why I have the riotous one. You're the wild Irishman."

"I'm going to ignore that insult and say just one thing to you—*karma*."

Darcy looked blank. "I have no idea what you mean."

"Because your knowledge of Eastern literature is restricted to two books," Bingley said, and walked into the house.

"Bingley? Bingley, you get back here and explain what you just said!"

The carriage ride was not a lovely discussion of sisterly things, because it was long, stuffy, and bumpy. By the time they arrived in Brighton, both sisters were tired and the sun was going down. Their first disconcerting discovery was that, despite their announced intentions to be guests at the Fitzwilliams and their explanation by letter of their sudden presence, Mary Bennet had made no call upon the Fitzwilliams, if she was in Brighton at all.

Granted, Mary did not know the Fitzwilliams well, being only a distant relation, but that meant she was staying elsewhere, and they could not imagine whom else she would call on. This concern was expressed when they were finally settled in the parlor and given tea and snacks. Both sisters were nauseous from the ride and not eager for the grand meal that was offered by their hosts.

It was most eagerly offered. Colonel Fitzwilliam had always been a bright and kind fellow, but marriage had been good to him, because his face had an ever-present shine. More striking, though, was Mrs. Anne Fitzwilliam (née de Bourgh), who looked—by her own set of standards—radiant, and by a normal person's standards, healthy and almost normal. The sea air (and perhaps being out from under her own mother's stifling presence, though Elizabeth held her tongue on that) had done wonders for Anne as it had so many other people. While she was not a robust woman by any means, she was not the trembling mouse of a girl that Elizabeth Bennet had met at Rosings nearly five years prior.

"Our only regret," Anne said as tea was poured, "is that we are so terribly far from everyone. You must tell us everything—of course, if you have time. Though perhaps I do not fully understand the matter at hand."

"Neither do we," Elizabeth fully admitted. "And now, it seems, we must go searching about the town for word of Mary, because she has not called on you or given us her address, and we have no other relatives here."

"You cannot go out tonight," Colonel Fitzwilliam said with some amount of male authority. "It is already late and you are exhausted, and you do not know Brighton's streets. Surely, your search must wait until morning."

"I fear I do not have the energy to contradict you, Colonel," Elizabeth said. "Four days of traveling has taken it right out of me."

"And yet I heard once you challenged Darcy's record by riding all the way from Scotland to Town," he countered.

"Oh God, yes," she said, the memory painful at its ridiculousness and the days she had been laid up because of that ride, excluding all of the events surrounding it. "But I have no wish to speak of *that*."

"Then you are just like your husband. And I am one to judge."

"You are three years older than Darcy, correct?" Jane asked.

"Yes, and it seems I was charged with keeping Darcy and Wickham in line when we played together, or preventing them from doing stupid things. I failed on all accounts except for the fact that they are at least both alive and have all their limbs."

"Maybe it's not all from your side after all," Jane whispered to her sister, who giggled.

The doorbell cut off Elizabeth's response.

"At this hour?" Colonel Fitzwilliam rose and went to the door of their modest Brighton home. Almost no one was surprised to see Mary Bennet, looking a little shabby from all the traveling and just a little ill. "Miss Bennet."

"Colonel Fitzwilliam. I hope I'm not intruding—"

"Not at all. We were sort of expecting you, actually, though perhaps not this very night—but we are all very glad to see you. Your sisters are here."

"Mary!" Jane said, running to greet her sister. "It is so good to see you."

"And you." Mary was not nearly so exuberant, but that was in her character and surprised no one. In fact, she looked half-terrified, and nodded to her other sister. "Elizabeth."

"I am sorry for intruding," Elizabeth said. "Jane was intending to seek you out on her own, but I insisted on accompanying her."

"Of course," was all Mary could say, "I—I am not at all surprised."

This was not the Mary they knew. Though lacking the confidence of her elder sister, Mary was not without her own self-esteem and was usually at the ready to sermonize about something. But now she was not, shifting her weight around and looking very much as if she was at a tribunal—which was honestly not far from the truth, as she could not expect to explain her circumstances.

"Mary," Jane said, in her usual warm tones, "I am very happy to see you safely home, but I would kindly inquire what I am doing in Brighton. If Papa knew you were in England—"

"Papa will know I'm in England," Mary said. "We will tell him at once. But you will understand why I did not want to see him first when I explain the circumstances. For I know he sent me to the Continent unattended expecting only the most pious behavior of me—"

The elder sisters exchanged glances, and Jane continued, "Yes. Now, what has happened?"

"Nothing. I mean, to say, nothing *can* happen, and it was an awful, awful thing for me to have been distracted from my studies so—"

"—but you met a man," Elizabeth said, because she could not think of anything else, with Mary standing before them unharmed. If Mary had been somehow expelled from school—and there was no reason to believe she had been, as all of the reports were most excellent—then Mr. Bennet would have gotten a letter from the Dean and that would have been the end of the matter.

Mary covered her mouth with her hands, as if to muffle her own words, ashamed of them as she obviously was. "Yes."

"And—it was a hindrance to your studies?"

"Quite the opposite. I was—his tutor. To be a tutor, you must do some work to prepare, so actually I was learning quite a bit—"

"You were *his* tutor?" Jane said in shock.

"Yes. The Headmistress said I was doing so well, and perhaps I could do some tutoring on the side to pick up a little money—Oh, not that Papa was being ungenerous. He was being *too* generous. Surely you know what I mean?"

"Of course," Elizabeth assured. "Do go on."

"So, I tutored some girls, but there was a young man, an Italian who needed to perfect his French, and I thought, perhaps if we met only in public, this would not be a terrible impropriety—and this was in France, so—"

"So it was not," Jane said, because Mary was having trouble. Anne and her husband had long since disappeared, and she helped her sister to the couch so she could settle, because Mary was trembling. "You have feelings for him?"

"I—I do not know. Yes, I suppose," Mary said. "Giovanni's feelings for me may have been stronger. He was only there for a short while. He attends a school in his native country, but he was taken to Paris to be treated for his epilepsy, which was interfering with his studies. I am not a fool to go boundlessly declaring myself in love."

So, Mary still had it in her to be dismissive of the expressions of others. It was almost a relief to see the old Mary, instead of the person before them, who was so remarkably different, so ashamed of her own feelings.

"But the situation is untenable. I cannot marry him. Papa would never approve, and Giovanni is promised to the church. His family expects nothing less of him than a red hat. They may already have promised him a bishopric, if he could only complete his studies and take Holy Orders."

Admittedly, the idea of Mary living in Italy with this man—Giovanni—was not ideal to either sister present, and Mr. Bennet would not settle for anyone but a son-in-law from the British Isles, for any number of reasons. Jane and Elizabeth would likely not attend the wedding or see Mary again, unless their husbands decided to travel abroad and take them with them, and with one of them constantly with child or nursing, that was unlikely. So Mary was right that her situation was problematic. If Mary was truly in love, it was hard to tell, but she was right that she was not one to go bounding about and announcing it, so they could only guess how she truly felt about this man.

"Mary," Jane said, with a hand on her shoulder. "Where is he now, this—"

"Giovanni. Mr. Mastai, if I am to be formal and English about it. He has gone back to school, with no intention to return to France."

"So he rejected you?"

"No, hardly. But as I said—he is studying for the priesthood."

Elizabeth sighed. Jane was quicker, not in wit but in finding something comforting to say. "Then there is nothing you can do. I know it seems impossible now, but surely some other man, who is English, will find the same qualities in you as Giovanni did. This man will find you so special that he will propose to you and you will be married, and this all forgotten."

Mary responded by breaking into wracking sobs, and her sisters sat protectively on each side and rubbed her shoulders. "Mary—"

"No," she said between sobs. "It is so much worse than that."

"To be sorely in love—"

"Again, no, you are wrong," Mary said. "That is not all. I am carrying his child."

THE SAD TALE OF MARY BENNET

IT WAS A LONG time before anyone could say anything. Jane, ever trusting and ever thinking the very best of everyone's actions and intentions, finally blurted out, "You are sure?"

"Quite. So very sure." Mary sniffled, trying to compose herself. "All of my supposed piety was for nothing, because I am nothing but a whore."

"Mary!" Elizabeth said. "You are no such thing. You are an innocent, and he seduced you."

"I will not lie to myself or anyone else. As… persuasive… as he may or may not have been, he did not force himself upon me, and had I known, I could have refused to see him except in public or refused outright the offer, as I should have done—"

"We can only think the best of our sister and the worst of him," Jane said, some curtness in her voice, not necessarily directed at Mary. "Did you tell him?"

"Yes."

"And he still left you?"

"What was he to do? Take me home as his bride? He offered some money, but I did not accept."

"Then you are not a whore," Elizabeth said. "You do not fit the definition. You were—are—an innocent girl, who was cruelly taken advantage of—"

"No! I will not absolve myself of my own failings or allow anyone else to do so!" Mary replied with surprising indignation. "The problem is mine. I called on you, Jane, because I had to see someone before I saw Papa. Surely now you understand, because he will cast me out—"

"He will not cast you out—"

"He cast Lydia out!"

"Lydia did not—," but suddenly even Elizabeth found it very hard to argue that Lydia had done anything as scandalous as Mary, or at the very least, presented obvious evidence of it. Lydia quite publicly ran off with the charming young soldier Mr. Wickham, and he would never have married her and saved the family's reputation if Darcy had not forced the issue. Elizabeth set that aside and found her words. "Lydia did what she did wantonly—and made a fool of herself in the process. You are trying to do precisely the opposite."

"You are being kind," Mary said, "but I cannot right this wrong. Papa has every right to send me to a nunnery and put the baby on an orphanage doorstep!"

She leaned on Jane's shoulder, and her sister replied with urgency, "How far are you along?"

"Two months."

"Are you sure?"

"Yes."

The gravity of the situation—already in high evidence—came down like a weight upon them. "Two months?"

"I didn't know—how was I to know? And then we debated what to do about it, and we tried going to a doctor—"

"*You didn't*," Elizabeth said, but was forced to imagine the desperation of her sister, all alone in France with a probably unhelpful companion. If Mary had found a doctor—could they really have ended the pregnancy? *There* was a question she would never ask Dr. Maddox.

"I did. I mean, the most horrible deed was already done, or so it seemed, and I could not wait out my term in France—not when I was expected home in the summer." Mary was crying again. "Please tell me at least one of you will take me in when Papa refuses ever to see me again."

"He will not," Jane said. "He will be very cross at first, but he will recover, and we will sort this out."

"But Jane," Mary said, "there is nothing to sort!"

Unfortunately, no one could find a way to tell her she was wrong.

⋯✦⋯

The Darcys had very good mattresses, properly lined with down and cotton. Unfortunately, the mattresses provided ample soft surfaces on which to bounce—something Darcy found his son quite ready to take advantage of. He rolled over, squinting in the (undoubtedly very) early morning light, as his eyes focused on the image of Geoffrey Darcy, still in his nightclothes, jumping up and down on Lizzy's side of the mattress with such ferocity as to shake the whole bed. Whether Geoffrey intended to wake his father—or even cared if he did—was not obvious from his expression.

"Geoffrey," Darcy said in the most commanding voice he could muster, which, at that particular moment, was not very commanding. "Come here."

His son finally stopped jumping and crawled over to his father as if he expected a joyous celebration of his achievement.

"Now, Son, allow me to explain this to you in the best way that I can at this hour in the morning—and while I hold back my desire to thrash you," Darcy said. "It is considered *very improper* to enter your father's private chambers uncalled."

"*Mother* sleeps here!"

Darcy put his head back into the pillow and groaned. His son was technically correct. Darcy was so used to sleeping in Elizabeth's chambers that the habit tended to continue even in her very seldom absences. "While you are technically correct, I will say that the same holds true for your mother's chambers. In fact, *especially* for your mother's chambers."

His son cocked his head and said curiously, "Why *improper?*"

"Because a gentleman is expected always to act with the most proper of manners. Believe it or not—and at this moment, I do find it a bit hard to believe—one day you will be a gentleman, and that behavior will be expected of you."

"Do I havta be a gentleman?"

"Yes."

"Why?"

Darcy sighed because he knew already where this would lead—down the endless road of whys. He would have to think of something very clever to avoid that, and he was not in the mood to be clever. He was in the mood to call for Nurse to take his son out of the room by his collar so he himself could go back to sleep. "Because."

This was thoroughly confusing to Geoffrey, who stood towering over his father. In fact, he actively climbed onto his chest and said, "Because?"

"Yes. Because. See, I can give one-word answers, too!" He grabbed his son to lift him up. "Now stop vexing your father so early in the morning!" He added, as he set Geoffrey down, "And don't ask if you can do it any other time of day. See, I knew you were going to say that. Your father is very wise."

Geoffrey did sit down on the bed, at least temporarily. "Are you smarter than me?" he asked his father.

Darcy sighed. Geoffrey was a rather precocious two-year-old, and while the family marveled at his early speaking ability, Darcy found this to be more trouble than it was worth at the moment. "I hope not. Perhaps you will not make all of the stupid mistakes I've made in my life. None of which you are old enough to hear about, so don't ask."

"Are you smarter than Mother?"

"No," Darcy said. "Definitely, definitely not. I think my whole life will consist of her outwitting me."

"Are you smarter than Uncle Bingley?"

"Are you going to go down the list of everyone you know and ask how I compare myself to them?"

"Yes."

"Then do you want to sit inside all day and practice your reading instead of going outside and playing with Georgiana?"

His son was horrified. "No!"

"Then I suggest you cease this line of conversation and let me sleep!"

Geoffrey hopped off the bed and scurried out of the room with exceptional speed, even for him. Darcy let out a contented sigh and stared at Elizabeth's empty pillow. "It's from your side of the family, you know," he said, and turned back on his other side.

But he did not, in fact, go back to sleep. Before long the rooster crowed, and Darcy slowly drifted in and out until his regular time for waking. Since his marriage, the servants no longer came in and opened the curtains for him, especially when he slept in his wife's room, so he had to do it himself and ring the bell for his manservant.

Pemberley was quiet—uncomfortably quiet. It was still quite early, and there was no sign of his only two guests or his son, although that was to be expected. Darcy took his regular breakfast and was lost in the morning paper when Nurse came in screaming. "Oh God! I promise... I promise... I'll get it off!"

"What?" he said, thoroughly confused, and still in the middle of his food.

"Mr. Bingley—he's not awake. I'll get it all off before he wakes, I promise!"

Darcy swallowed and said calmly, "*What* off?"

She could not explain; she was too flummoxed. Instead, she insisted that he follow her quickly and quietly to the nursery, so as to not wake Mr. Bingley. And there he found little Georgiana Bingley, giggling happily.

In a tub full of ink.

"I—I don't know how it happened, Mr. Darcy, I swear!"

Darcy already had a fair idea of what had occurred and was busy mentally debating how to maneuver the situation so that he was in full view of Bingley's face when he saw his daughter.

By morning, the three Bennet sisters—former and current—had come to one conclusion. The discretion of the Fitzwilliams, who had hosted them, could be trusted. They deserved an explanation for all of the disruption, and they received one. However, the sisters did not return to their carriage until they had received the Fitzwilliams' solemn promise that not a word of this would be uttered to anyone. Obviously, time was of the essence. The only question was if Mary should ride in her "condition," but they decided that she had no other option. For the moment, they would go to Pemberley and decide on a course of action from there.

Mary said almost nothing. She had had the ground pulled out from under her, having always stood on a high moral ground. Mary's chances for a good marriage—or a marriage at all—were utterly ruined. Kitty's chances could be salvaged, but not until the scandal blew over. After all, Longbourn had suffered one scandal and emerged with two extremely advantageous marriages. But surely now Mary would have to be satisfied with being a lonely mother, provided something drastic wasn't done.

"You don't think—with all due respect—that Mr. Darcy will say anything about this, do you?" Jane whispered when Mary was out of earshot.

Elizabeth sighed. True, her husband was a severely proper man, averse to any scandal. However, he was also intolerably good at covering them up. "If he does, I will make it known that I am *severely* disappointed in him, and that will be enough to quiet him about this entire affair."

But her husband was not disapproving. Not at first, when

they climbed out of the carriage at the grand doorstep of Pemberley. After all, Darcy and Bingley did not know the story, and Mary was not showing. But the two men, holding their children, also had the most adorably hapless look on their faces that Elizabeth had no doubt was well-practiced.

"So there is a very good explanation—"

"—a perfectly, *perfectly* good explanation—" Bingley broke in.

"—as to why our children are blue."

For indeed they were.

Geoffrey Darcy and Georgiana Bingley were properly dressed to greet their parents, looking scrubbed and proper, except for the fact that their skin and hair were soundly a deep shade of blue. They looked like members of some unknown species, and they offered no explanation as they broke free and ran to their mothers. After Elizabeth and Jane were done laughing, they were able to greet their children properly. It felt so good to be happy at something ridiculous, after the torturous ride of worries, that Elizabeth had to recover some before she could properly approach her husband with a look that demanded everything.

"Well, since it happened first to—"

"Darcy, *your* son started it. Don't you dare try to implicate me in this!" Bingley demanded.

"Charles," Jane said in her very patient, loving, and deadly voice. "Where were you when… this occurred?"

"Sleeping."

"Only the first time," Darcy corrected. "Not the second."

"How was I to know there would be a second time?"

"Will someone *please* provide your promised explanation?" Elizabeth said. "Oh, and my sister, of course," she said, nodding to Mary.

Their husbands bowed. "Miss Bennet."

"Mr. Darcy. Mr. Bingley," she said shyly.

"How was your—"

"Don't try to distract us," Elizabeth cut in. "I will go as far as to say I am, for the moment, more concerned with my son than my sister."

"We did try to scrub them," Bingley offered. "I mean, *really* tried."

"It hurt," said Geoffrey, pointing to his father. "He hurt me. And made me sit in the corner."

Darcy shrugged unapologetically at his son's comments.

The whole story came out after much questioning and demanding of specifics. Geoffrey had crept into Georgiana's early morning bath and dumped a bottle of ink in the water. Georgie had been most amused at the concept and had gotten it all over the top half of her body before Nurse returned. All the while, Bingley enjoyed the sound sleep that could only be enjoyed by the father of two toddlers who had yet to sleep fully through the night and were now three miles away. If that hadn't been enough, Georgie had gotten her revenge the next day by adding ink to the bucket of water to be dumped on Geoffrey in his tub. After so much panicked scrubbing by their fathers that the children cried that their skin was raw and pained, Mrs. Reynolds intervened and said the ink would fade—in time.

"A few weeks," Darcy said.

"Oh goodness," was all Jane could say.

Bingley and Darcy exchanged confused glances. Why their wives found the predicament more amusing and delightful than horrifying was beyond them. They were both taken aside and told the more pressing situation, in private, so Mary did not have to endure the disclosure. After all, she had to be handled most carefully now as an expectant woman.

Darcy listened to the tale in his study, as Mary sat with the children outside. He said nothing during the whole recitation, though his face did go through a series of expressions, none of them particularly unexpected.

"So," Elizabeth said at last, announcing she was finished.

"And—he's in Italy, this Mr.—"

"His proper name is Mr. Mastai-Ferretti, I believe. Or, I suppose, Signore Mastai."

"He's younger than she?"

"Yes."

Clearly pondering, Darcy asked, "From where in Italy does he hail?"

"Sin—Senigallia. But Mary believes him to be elsewhere in Italy now, finishing his education." Elizabeth made her own logical conclusions. "He is surely unreachable."

"Mr. Bennet can write, if he wishes, but our Mr. Mastai could simply choose not to respond. Considering his actions forthwith, I would not see that as beyond the range of possibility."

"Then there is nothing to be done."

Darcy said nothing.

"Darcy, she's my sister."

"That I know," he said, not uncaringly. "But there is an order for things. Her father cannot be unknowing in this."

"Then you *do* have a plan."

"There is only one I can think of, Lizzy. Surely you have thought of it yourself."

"It is out of the realm of possibility, surely."

"As far as family is concerned, nothing is out of the realm of possibility." But that was all he was willing to say for the moment.

~❦~

The five of them now had the first obstacle in front of them: they could go to Longbourn and give Mr. Bennet the news in his own home, as he deserved when his daughter disgraced his family. Or they could keep Mary in Derbyshire and invite her father there in an effort to avoid the scandal for some time, as might be possible if she stayed there instead of returning to Hertfordshire. Bingley immediately offered up Chatton as a permanent residence for Mary, and Darcy, who was his usual quiet self, did not challenge him, though he did mention in passing that she could stay at Pemberley if she wished. Mary declared no preference, so Chatton it was to be.

"Perhaps we should call on Maddox," Bingley said to Darcy in confidence. "To... I don't know, assess things."

"He is not the only doctor in England, Bingley! And he would undoubtedly come with Caroline."

"So what if he does? We cannot avoid the extended family knowing the whole of it for long, and as she is now related to Miss Bennet, Caroline has almost as much interest in avoiding the scandal as we do. So no harm done there."

Bingley had a point. Besides, if Mary was to see a doctor, it had best be the one least likely to gossip. "Fine. But first, Mr. Bennet."

"Oh dear God, never did I fear our father-in-law so."

"He has no reason to be cross with us. That is, provided we hide the children from him, and even if we don't, he'll hardly be concerned. Might even find it amusing. In fact, it might put him in good humor for the very bad news."

"You have a point."

"So that is the plan, then. He will see his grandchildren. And *then* Miss Bennet."

"Poor Mary."

Darcy gave him a look.

"How can you be so hard on her, even in private? It's not *her* fault."

"Unlike your own Calvinist leanings, I *do* believe in free will, Bingley."

"That is not to say she wasn't taken advantage of. Even if she thinks she wasn't, with… cultural differences and such. You've been to the Continent—you know they all think we're stuck-up Englishmen with no romantic nature whatsoever, and for good reason."

"I never said I had no romantic nature."

"But people have thought it of you. I've *said* it to you, in so many words."

"On that, I will relent," Darcy grumbled.

"What are we to do, Darcy?"

"Simple," he said, as if it was. "I am to save yet another Bennet sister."

"How do you propose to—*oh*. Well, I'm willing to help. She's my sister as well."

"You have two small toddlers and a daughter who hasn't said her first words."

Bingley frowned. "Point taken. I do feel useless then."

"You will be sheltering a young woman with child from considerable scandal. That is hardly the definition of 'useless.' In fact, I believe you will be quite busy for the next seven months."

"Plus your child. Who, I imagine, will have us all ink-skinned when the matter is done."

To that, Darcy had to hold back his response, as he decided that, with all of the serious goings-on, hitting his brother-in-law in the face would not be proper. Not again, anyway.

STORM AT CHATTON

FORTUNATELY, AS THEY WERE able to travel at greater speeds than the elderly Bennets, who had not been informed of the cause for their invitation, Dr. and Mrs. Maddox arrived at Chatton first. This was their first journey there in several months, as the doctor's schedule kept him in London, and he seemed reluctant to take whatever salary was offered from Bingley. Dr. Maddox had a townhouse, small but still far beyond his own means, that Bingley had given the couple as a gift.

Dr. Maddox insisted that he would provide for his wife, though privately Charles wrote to his sister and said that if the doctor worked himself ragged, she would start receiving checks from Chatton anyway. So Caroline Maddox had two dedicated men trying to satisfy her every want and need, and she never looked more radiant, aside from being a bit worn from the traveling. Upon their arrival, the doctor was quickly taken aside and informed they rather selfishly needed him to see Mary Bennet.

"Is she ill?"

They shrugged and pushed him in a room with Mary Bennet, a person whom he had never met, but to whom he was related by marriage. On the other side of the door, the Bingleys and the Darcys waited. He took only a few minutes to reappear.

"What do you want me to say? She's with child," Maddox shrugged, apparently unhappy with the stares he was receiving. No, he knew the situation well enough. They wanted a magic answer—that she was wrong or that he could, God forbid, *do something* about it. "About two months. Or, if you want to go by her own recollection, two months and six days, and I am inclined to believe her."

He swallowed, wanting to avoid any further questioning of how close the inspection had been. It hadn't been very close; it didn't need to be. He merely looked at the size of Mary's belly and believed her on everything else. There was no reason to do otherwise. "I suppose the father is—"

"Gone."

"French?"

"Italian."

"He has run away to his home soil," Darcy said, not hiding his repulsion at the idea.

"He is promised to the church," Elizabeth said, partially countering it.

"Oh, dear," Maddox said. "Well, I'm sorry I can't be much help in this matter. I am not familiar with Derbyshire's offerings of midwives, but I am sure you are." He added, "I am very sorry for the circumstances, but there is nothing I can do, beyond being a supportive relation, if you wish the support."

That was not the answer they were looking for, and he knew it. So he did what he thought was best, which was to flee the room and let them think it over. He went to his chambers, which were now the same as Caroline's, and found her already there.

"I know," she said, as he put his bag down and shooed the servant away. "Horrible, is it not?"

She did not say horrible in the way that Caroline Bingley would normally say *horrible*. There was, instead, a hint of sadness. Pangs of sympathy, perhaps? He could not imagine. He was just beginning to understand the whole of the situation himself. Clearly, the Darcys and Bingleys hadn't told Mr. Bennet yet and were still devising their strategy to lessen the blow to Mary. There was a great amount of love in this family, even for one who had so soundly ruined her life when she was entrusted with it by being sent to study abroad.

It was best to assume this Italian, whoever he was, had just taken advantage of Mary, but the Maddoxes knew love was more complicated than that. Mary, as pious as she obviously was, refused to implicate the man, taking the blame all unto herself—and that was bad for her health and the health of the baby. Maybe that was the real reason Dr. Maddox had been called—to be a buffer between Mary and her father. This musing he expressed out loud.

"You really think so?" Caroline asked him.

"I have no idea, honestly. They are keeping her here perhaps because she is too ill to travel, or because they want to avoid the scandal as long as possible. Doesn't she have a younger sister still unmarried?"

"Catherine. They call her Kitty. A flirtatious girl, if ever I met one."

"So, like you."

She smiled severely at him. "I did not know you considered me a girl."

"Hardly. But—and I mean this in the most positive way— you were flirtatious. So much so, you could not avoid the habit even around Mr. Hurst's poor servant."

"And how lucky I was in that. But I cannot imagine the same for Mary. Poor girl."

Was this the same Caroline he had courted and married? He had to wonder. There was something almost *motherly* in her tone.

Maybe this wouldn't turn out so badly after all.

* * *

The three Bennets were called to Derbyshire without any knowledge of what they were to encounter. Even though they arrived hot from an early spring heat wave and exhausted from the bump of a long carriage ride, they had to cock their heads at the sight of two wild African-painted children running to greet them. "Grandfather!" said the boy who, from his proper dress and general disposition, was undoubtedly Geoffrey Darcy, despite his coloration.

He raised his arms with the expectation of being lifted, to which a very patient and confounded Mr. Bennet said, "I'm afraid you are getting a bit big and your grandfather is getting a bit old in the back for that." Geoffrey frowned but still grabbed Mr. Bennet's legs enough to make him stumble a bit, only to be caught by Kitty. Mrs. Bennet was no help, because she was busy attempting to pick up the child she assumed was the silent Georgiana Bingley.

"My goodness! How did we raise our children, Mr. Bennet?"

"I'm not quite sure who is responsible for this, but I may venture that our grandchildren may, in fact, shoulder some of the blame. Or all of it." He looked at Geoffrey sternly, but it was a very hard composure to maintain when facing off with a boy whose skin was the shade of berries.

"Lizzy?" His daughter had appeared at the front door, chasing the children, who had run out at the sight of the carriage. Her own expression was not so pleasant. He immediately patted his grandson on the head and turned his attention to his favorite daughter. "Lizzy, whatever is the matter?"

Despite all of their advice otherwise, Mary insisted on telling Mr. Bennet herself, with him sitting down in Bingley's study and receiving her properly as if at Longbourn. Darcy shrugged privately at Elizabeth's harsh look at this turn of events, saying only in a hushed voice, "It is only right. I would expect nothing less of my own children."

So, behind closed doors, Mary Bennet told the entire story. Or, she could have told him complete hogwash, because no one would venture close enough to the door to listen in. Bingley tried, but his wife held him back. The Maddoxes, their presence for the moment unannounced, had remained above stairs. So Elizabeth and Jane were left to tell their mother, along with Kitty, in the sitting room.

"Ruined! She is ruined!" Mrs. Bennet cried, and they said nothing, because it was an accurate assessment. "Oh, we never should have sent her to that dreadful country. All of that time—only to be taken advantage of by some—some papal rogue! And now he cannot be found!" She called for another handkerchief, having used up her current stash of them. "Kitty, you are ruined as well! Oh, we should have married you to that officer!"

"Mama!" Kitty looked to her sisters for help.

"Kitty," Jane said, sitting down next to her sister protectively. "All is not lost."

"For Mary, it is. She will die an old maid now. No man in England will have her," Mrs. Bennet said, adding, "Oh, Mary!" even though her daughter wasn't in the room—but that was irrelevant. Surely Mary was, at the moment, enduring Mr. Bennet's rarely used but considerable censure. "Oh, thank goodness, this did not happen at Longbourn, or all the neighbors would be talking. Oh, but they will soon enough! Oh, Mary!"

The last time Mrs. Bennet had wept over a daughter had been when Lydia ran off with Wickham. But Mary, by all appearances, had not acted wantonly, despite the obvious results. Her self-admonishments only made her a more pathetic and helpless figure, one that they could not help but be protective of—even Mrs. Bennet, who was crying out for her daughter's desperate situation.

Her sobbing was only interrupted by the arrival of Mr. Darcy, who was not noticed until he tapped on Lizzy's shoulder and whispered in her ear, "The door is open."

"Does Papa want to see anyone?"

"I believe it would be best if you were to see him. I've—called in the doctor."

"The doctor?"

He let her make her own assessment, as she ran into Bingley's study, where Dr. Maddox was taking Mr. Bennet's pulse. Her father was full of barely contained indignation as Mary slipped out of the room.

"Papa," Lizzy said, kneeling before him and taking his hands, which were shaking with rage.

"I do not need a doctor!" he said. "I have every reason to be furious."

Elizabeth looked at Dr. Maddox, who was looking at his pocket watch. When he was done with his count, he pulled away from his patient and said, "He is in a very agitated state."

"That I know!" said Mr. Bennet.

"Mr. Bennet, please do listen to Mrs. Darcy and take some deep breaths." With that, Dr. Maddox bowed to him and took his leave, shutting the door behind him.

Mr. Bennet did not respond, but he did take a deep breath. There was silence in the room as he visibly regained his composure, or attempted to do so. "I have every right as a father to make myself ill over this."

"As a father to Mary, perhaps. But not to the rest of us," she said gently. "Papa, please."

Mr. Bennet took one of his hands out of hers and used it to hold up his head. "What am I to do? I have ruined one of my daughters by sending her to France." He added quickly, "And don't bother me with the business of it being of her own volition, because Mary tried to assign as much blame to herself as possible. She may be out, but she is my responsibility until the day she is married, and now it seems she never will be." When he looked up, there were tears in his eyes. "I have ruined her."

"Papa, you have not."

"If only I'd not let her go to France—"

"She took liberties there you did not know of—"

"But she seemed so sensible! Well, perhaps not sensible, but so religious! I thought the worst of it would be she might end up in a nunnery, and if that would make her happy, then… so be it. I only wanted to see her happy." He gave a sad smile. "I only wanted to see you all happy. I put you *out* one after another, when it wasn't proper to do so. I sent Lydia to Brighton. Oh god, if Darcy hadn't saved us all—"

"Papa, that is in the past."

"I know. I know." For once, he seemed very old and bumbling and somewhat out of his senses. "Even Darcy cannot save us now. Though, I thank God, Lizzy, you and Jane do not need saving, and Lydia is at least settled, and perhaps Kitty will survive— what with two older sisters who did well—and we shall not lose Longbourn. I have that solace, but so little it is. Even if I forgive Mary, as I will eventually manage to do, she will not forgive herself." He was now openly crying. "Lizzy, what am I to do?"

"I do not know," was her honest answer as she embraced him.

"I suppose," he said, after trying to regain his composure again, this time in a different way, "that Mr. Bingley will take her in for the rest of her term and shelter us all, for a time, from the scandal. That may be enough time to marry off Kitty, or perhaps something else will come up. I find myself without an answer to our question. But now—I must discuss it with my sons-in-law, and I must be the properly angry father again. So, please, give me a moment and send them in, will you, darling?"

"Of course, Papa." She kissed him on his forehead and left the room. She needed a moment herself, before she could face the waiting crowd in the next room.

"I'm quite well now," Mr. Bennet announced as his two

sons-in-law and the physician entered the room. He shooed Maddox's attentions away, though he clearly was calmer now, if still not considerably angry. "This is a situation with only one obvious remedy."

There was a long silence.

"I'm very sorry, but I can't go," Maddox announced.

"Daniel," Bingley said, "You had never even met Mary until this day. You can hardly be expected—"

"But I am the only one here beyond Mr. Bennet with a proficiency in Italian, and I spent a month of my life in Rome itself. So I would be the most logical choice, and Caroline would love to see France. But she cannot travel... right now."

"I don't see—," Darcy said, and then stopped. "Were you ever going to tell us?"

"I left that up to her. After all, she has to do most of the work."

"My sister. With child." Bingley was stupefied. "I don't know whether to throttle you or shake your hand, Doctor."

"They *are* married, Bingley," Darcy reminded him. "Out of curiosity, when does her confinement begin?"

"In four months."

"In four..." Bingley had to sit down. "You bastard. You didn't tell us."

"I told you—I left it up to her, and you know how she likes grand announcements. The only reason I tell you now is out of necessity."

"So we will have two confinements at once," Mr. Bennet said, his mood not lifted. "Congratulations, Doctor. Under different circumstances, I would be more generous in my compliments, but it seems I must go to Italy now."

"Mr. Bennet, with all due respect, you know you cannot," Darcy said.

"I am not dead yet, Mr. Darcy! Despite arrangements being made otherwise."

Darcy turned to Maddox. "Please tell Mr. Bennet he cannot go."

"I am not sick!" Mr. Bennet shouted, nearly deafening them all from the shock. They had never heard him shout before or raise his voice, even when he was being stern.

After an appropriate silence, Maddox ventured, "With respect, Mr. Bennet, I would not advise such a journey."

"I do not recall asking you!"

"I cannot go," Bingley said. "For… obvious reasons. I can hardly leave Jane with three small children."

"Of course," Darcy said, "I will be going." He made the statement as if his journey was an already known fact that they had merely overlooked.

"Mr. Darcy!" Mr. Bennet said indignantly.

"Darcy, I have to inquire how your languages are," Bingley said.

"My French is inexcusably abominable, and my Italian is nonexistent, but that's what a translator is for, and I'm sure there's at least one in the entire Continent for hire. Besides, I am clearly the only one available. Geoffrey is old enough to be on his own for a few months, and Elizabeth has never had the pleasure of seeing the Continent. So it is decided."

"It is hardly decided!" Mr. Bennet said. "I have decided on nothing. It seems all the decisions are being made without me, and this is *my* daughter, Mr. Darcy, not yours."

Darcy motioned to the others for privacy. He then sat down

next to the infuriated Mr. Bennet, who seemed to be calming down as the room became quieter and he was able to digest all of the information they had thrown at him.

"I will confess something to you, Mr. Bennet, if you would hear it."

"Is it about my grandchildren being blue?"

"Well, there is that, but this is more pertinent. One of the reasons I am making the offer of this considerable journey is for Elizabeth's sake. I think it would be good for her to get out after…" Even after these months, he could not bring himself to say it, and Mr. Bennet laid a hand on his.

"I had not even considered. You show a great deal of concern for Lizzy, Darcy. You have always impressed me with that. I admit that perhaps my gallivanting across the Continent would not be ideal to my health. But I still cannot ask this of you."

"You do not have to ask."

Mr. Bennet sighed. He seemed to be coming to his senses, his fury exhausted, and now was sinking into a depression. "Is there any way I can repay you for all you have done for my family, Mr. Darcy?"

"Yes," Darcy said, rising to leave and tell the others the news. "You can do me the favor of marrying your remaining daughter off without my help."

THE D'ARCYS OF NORMANDY

PREPARATIONS BEGAN IMMEDIATELY FOR the Darcys' departure. Time was of the essence, as they might need two months to find Mr. Mastai and then even more time to either drag him back to England (unlikely) or to send a letter with the news of finding him and await its response. All in all, the Darcys imagined that they could be gone for several months, back hopefully in time for the births, which would probably be within weeks of each other.

"I will be honest with you," Darcy said to his father-in-law. "The best we can hope for is a considerable settlement, if his family is so inclined. If he is already a priest, the discussion will be even more complicated."

"That I have already realized," Mr. Bennet said. "Whether you wish to tell Lizzy this or not is at your own discretion. I have no intention of telling anyone else the expected outcome."

So it was decided. Elizabeth loathed to be separated from Geoffrey, who obviously could not travel with them without slowing them down considerably. Darcy assured her that, at two, Geoffrey was quite old enough to be on his own for a bit, and that their absence might even do him some good. "We do have a general tendency to spoil him."

"And you think Bingley will not?"

Darcy only smiled at her from behind his desk, where he was gathering the papers he thought he would need.

"You don't think there's any chance of having Mr. Mastai return to England with us, do you?" she said.

"No," he answered. "I will not encourage unreasonable expectations. If we can even locate him in time, he will probably either have taken vows or be so intent on taking them that our best hope is a settlement."

"He did offer her something in France."

"I imagine now that he is faced with her family, perhaps even willing to throttle his collared neck, he will offer more," he said. "How much, I have no idea. The point is, we will not let this injustice pass by."

Elizabeth seemed satisfied by this answer and left him for the moment to return to her own packing. Darcy had no further intrusions until there was a knock on the open door. "Come."

It was Mrs. Reynolds, not an unexpected face in the hurry of packing, as the Master and Mistress of Pemberley were to go on a long and unexpected journey. "Mr. Darcy."

"Mrs. Reynolds."

"I seem to recall—it's been some time since you've been to the Continent."

"Yes," he said. "I went only once, after college and before my father's death. I was not particularly enamored of it. Why do you ask?"

"I was just wondering—do you intend to stop at the mansion in Valognes?"

"The Hôtel des Capuchins?" Generations back, it had been the old d'Arcy estate, or so the history went, and had been held by very distant relatives of his until the Revolution, when they fled their home. Now an imported English family owned the mansion and ran it as a hotel. The head of the family was a military officer who had taken a liking to the mansion while stationed there to fight Napoleon. Darcy had stayed there for a few days in their company during his journey to the Continent, and the family held him in esteem.

"I suppose we would shelter there for a night or two," he replied. "I admit to not having a formal itinerary at the moment, but if Valognes is on the way, then yes." He thought about it. "Why do you ask?"

"Well—it's probably nothing, Sir, but I do recall your father mentioning to senior Mr. Wickham that he had some financial papers there of some import. They may have been burned in the Revolution... I don't know. I was just askin' if you know anything about them."

Darcy stopped his work for a second and looked up at her. "No. I mean, yes, there are piles and piles of old papers there going back centuries, because the mansion itself was not burned when my relatives fled. But I did not peruse them while I was there, nor was I told to do so by my father." But come to think of it, that had been before his father's illness and death, and young Master Fitzwilliam had been given a year to explore and have fun before settling down to the serious matters of learning to be the real Master of Pemberley and Derbyshire. His father might not have mentioned the need to view the financial papers, or Darcy might have simply forgotten about it and so had his father. "I suppose, if there is time, I will look into it. Thank you, Mrs. Reynolds."

She curtseyed and let herself out. It was not until he was returned to his sorting that the oddity of the conversation descended on him.

⟿✦⟾

"I don't understand," Elizabeth said later that night in their bedchamber—or, properly, *her* bedchamber. "Why do you find that so odd?"

"Despite being the housekeeper, Mrs. Reynolds is not involved in the financials of Pemberley," he explained. "Her knowledge extends to a certain idea of how much the servants beneath her in the house are paid. At times, I have asked her advice in deciding on the salary of a new employee, as she is given the task of choosing certain ones herself, but I always make the final decision and do not always tell her.

"The only way she would even know about these financial papers in France is if she happened upon a conversation between my father and his steward, or if my father specifically told her for some reason that I cannot imagine. More to the point, Mrs. Reynolds has never, in my life, approached me about anything pertaining to my family's personal finances. About hiring and firing hands, yes. But my father's personal accounts?" He shook his head. "It was just an odd thing for her to do."

"Are you saying there may be more to it?"

He smiled. "You are always a step ahead of me."

"In some countries, wives walk two steps behind their husbands, I think."

"Thank God, then, that we are not in one of those countries."

He climbed into bed with her, still temporarily dressed.

"Do you think it will be all right with Geoffrey? To leave him now?"

"We will not be gone so terribly long," he assured. "And he is certainly old enough. Who knows? It may do him some good."

"Are you implying something is wrong with our son?"

"It could hardly be from my side."

"I thought we had established that it was." She kissed him on the head. "Colonel Fitzwilliam implied that Geoffrey's behavior was not, in fact, from the Bennet lineage, and that you were quite the savage in your days as a child."

"Clearly, then, I cannot allow you to visit my cousins again, because Richard is spreading bad rumors about me that are entirely untrue." He swallowed. "Or may be true, to some extent. Perhaps."

"*Perhaps?*"

"Perhaps. And that is all I will say on the matter."

As she settled down on her side of the bed, Elizabeth added, "You do not have to do this. Just because of your history of saving the Bennet family reputation, you are not obligated to save Mary from her own stupidity."

"She is my sister, and therefore, I do feel the obligation. I doubt I can 'save her,' if that is what you mean. But this is for you as well, Lizzy. Surely you realize that. Since you have never been out of England—"

"I *have* been to Scotland."

He smiled. "—Never been out of *Britain* and are available to travel, so why not? When will we have this opportunity again, even if our travels will be a bit rushed? I should think you would like to see some of the glorious sites—" But that was when he noticed the shift in mood, and the tears slipping out her eyes like stray water over glass. "Lizzy—"

But she leaned over and could not hold back from sobbing into his nightshirt. When others had cried over the situation with Mary, she had not. She had held it in, perhaps feeling some obligation to do so. But he knew, very well, it was not entirely Mary she was crying over. "I love you."

"That does not change it. It does not change why... why I am so *available*."

He frowned, but she didn't see it, leaning on his shoulder as she was. He frowned because he didn't know how to answer her. "Lizzy, you have already given me everything I could ever want in my life. No more is required of you."

"Very well then. So my life is about giving to you? What about what *I* want?"

That he could not give her.

"We both—we both know you are perfectly fine," he said. "And that—it is only a matter of time. The traveling will be good for everyone, I believe. Good for us, good for Mary, good for Geoffrey... Can you not see that? That is why we are going— not to get money from some Italian priest and his family."

This seemed at least to appease her, because she pulled away from their tight embrace and was no longer sobbing. "I'm sorry. I'm being a foolish girl."

"No, you are being a heartbroken woman, which is a very mature position to be in. This is something all mothers must suffer, while all husbands have to sit by helplessly and wish we could mend it, but we can't. On this, I cannot help—though I am willing to try very hard." He kissed her hand. "Lizzy."

She laughed, and the mood in the room changed. The

heaviness was gone, at least for a time, as she wiped her eyes and kissed him. "And we have the added benefit that upon our return, our son will be his normal color."

"Or another one entirely."

Packed and ready as they would be, the Darcys returned from Pemberley carrying Geoffrey's things, as he would be staying with his aunt and uncle, if very reluctantly. Normally happy to visit them, he had to be dragged out of Pemberley quite physically this time by his father and his nurse. At last they arrived at Chatton, and the final preparations were made, so they could depart to Town and then take a ship to France from Dover. The route would vary, based on information collected on the road, and a guide would need to be hired, so Darcy had his steward free up a good amount of cash.

They also needed to learn all of the specifics of this man— Giovanni Maria Mastai-Ferretti—from Mary, as she knew them. He would likely be in school or visiting extended family in Rome. Dr. Maddox noted that Rome was a hot, unpleasant city in the summer months, and that most wealthy people retreated to villas elsewhere, often including the Pope himself.

Mr. Bennet was not willing to let Mary out of his sight, so the Bennets also would stay at Chatton. The Maddoxes would be in Town until Caroline's own confinement, and possibly during, as the good doctor was tied to London by his work.

"Oh, Mr. Darcy, you are so good to us," Mrs. Bennet said. "And to Lizzy. Keep her safe on those roads."

"It will be my first duty, Mrs. Bennet."

Mary had one last thing for them—a Catholic rosary. "From

him; if you need to prove who you are. I didn't ask for it—I don't use it—but he gave it to me." It was a fine item, too, with a tiny, silver figure of Jesus on the cross, and the beads were a beautiful red.

"Thank you, Miss Bennet," Darcy said, and bowed to Mary.

Three couples and two children waited for the carriage that would take the Darcys on the first leg of the journey, as the Bingleys insisted on seeing them off. With many tearful good-byes, they were finally off, on the way to say good-bye to one last person—Georgiana Darcy.

"You will take care," Darcy said to his sister, standing in their townhouse, as the last vestiges of business had taken some two days to contract. "And if anyone—"

"We will wait for your consent."

"Good girl." He kissed her on the head.

"So you have finally agreed that I may *eventually* get married? Maybe Elizabeth has softened you, Brother."

He smiled. "No, I just decided that I would not want your beautiful hair hidden under the veil of one of those horrible black nuns' habits."

"Now you are toying with me!"

"Perhaps. Do you wish me to get out my sword and have my manservant hold it up in front of you in my absence instead?"

"It would be more familiar, but no, Brother."

It was then that Mrs. Maddox appeared. "Daniel will be on his way in a moment. We wish to give you this, Darcy." She handed him a book, very small and old, with its title worn off from obvious use. He flipped it open and found a stamp of the seal of the earldom of Maddox on the inside cover. It was a travel-sized book of Italian words and phrases, very light and usable. "He says he can no longer read the print, so it is as good as yours."

"I am honored," he said, knowing full well how much Dr. Maddox treasured his books and his eyesight, the latter of which was—as Darcy had been told privately—in slow deterioration.

The doctor appeared quickly to wish them well and give them a paper full of various contacts they could use and places they could stay in France and Italy. "I don't know how good they'll be. They're a bit out of date. But if you use even one..." He shrugged. "I wish to be of more help than that."

"I think you are needed more here," Darcy said, patting him on the shoulder. "Good luck, Doctor."

"I would say the same to you."

"But we mean it for different things. Now if you will excuse us, our ship leaves at noon."

"Brother! Must you go *today?*" Georgiana begged.

"The sooner we leave, the sooner we will be home."

They said their good-byes and joined the Bingleys at the awaiting carriage. "I expect you to be a proper gentleman when I return," Darcy said to his son. "But I will not hold my breath, for my own sake."

His blue son scowled at him. "I wanna go!"

"One day, you will, but not today. It's not safe."

"Is it safe for Mother?"

"Yes. Your mother is a hardy woman," he said, and noticed the resulting glare from Elizabeth. "I meant it as a compliment!"

Elizabeth shook her head and shooed him away, kneeling so she was at eye level with her son. "Be a good boy to your aunt and uncle. I know you have it in you, and they will be so worried for us that you should not tax them. Look at you," she said, straightening his hair, which was a slightly darker hue of blue than the rest of his body. "All grown up. And... blue." She hugged him. "Keep an eye on Georgie. She... we worry about her."

"Why?" Geoffrey said.

"Because—she doesn't talk."

Her son's expression was bemused. "She talks to *me*."

They were out of earshot of the Bingleys, who were talking to Darcy. Elizabeth looked up at them and back at her son, and then whispered, "She does? Like normal people?"

He squirmed in her grasp. "She tol' me not to tell."

"Why would she do that?"

Geoffrey shrugged.

"Well, when someone makes you promise something... I suppose you ought to keep it," she said. "So it will be our secret for now. But do tell her to say something to her parents. Will you promise me that?"

He nodded. He was so adorable when he did that. He was so adorable when he did everything, and she would miss... She could not imagine it. It was too painful.

"Mummy," he said. "Don't cry."

"I promise," she said, and kissed him on the cheek again. "Not too much, at least. I love you."

She had to part from him. She stood up, and hand-in-hand, they walked to the others. "Such a long journey," Jane said.

"Well, the Continent is not actually very far. I hear you can swim to it," Bingley said. But for the Bingleys, it was worlds away. He turned towards Darcy, who took him aside, as the sisters said their good-byes.

"Best of luck," Bingley said, offering his hand, into which Darcy placed a set of keys. "What are these?"

"The master keys to Pemberley. I know *you* don't need them to get in, but do put them somewhere safe." Darcy looked uncomfortable, almost as if he was at a ball or something. "Bingley, I'm sorry for dragging you to Town to sign the papers for my will—"

"I'm honored," Bingley said, leaving out at least vocally that Geoffrey Darcy would go to his care until he reached the age of majority, should something happen to his parents. These arrangements, which had to be formalized on paper with signatures and witnesses, had been done in some secrecy the day before in a small office in the city.

"I would say, 'Don't be too hard on the boy,' but I know that it is an impossibility. So I would say, 'Don't be too *easy* on him.'"

"Are you saying something about my parenting abilities?"

"I'm saying more about my son," he assured his brother-in-law with a slap on the back.

Their departure could not be put off any longer. There were hugs, and Georgie waved and Geoffrey pouted, but finally Mr. and Mrs. Darcy were able to climb into the carriage, bound for Dover, where the ship would take them to France. They waved, and between their son's skin hue and Bingley's red hair, they could get a good view of their beloved family until the London smog blocked their vision.

"Five shillings says we return and they're all blue," Darcy said.

"Red," his wife said. "I'll put five shillings on red."

As London disappeared behind them, they shook on it.

THE ACCOUNT IN QUESTION

THE TRIP TO THE Continent—the physical landmass that was the continent of Europe—was mercifully short, with their arrival in Calais coming shortly before nightfall. Elizabeth was shocked to discover that the people on the other side of the Channel looked much the same as she did, at least in that major port town, and spoke English and *were* English—either stationed soldiers or English gentlemen fleeing their debts for the financial refuge Calais' laws offered.

"Did you expect them all to have green skin?" Darcy said, watching her face.

"No, we would have to be in Derbyshire for that."

But this was not Derbyshire, or even London. It was Calais, a bustling but war-torn city. The streets and buildings were in disrepair, and even the best hotel was below Darcy's reasonable but meticulous standards.

It was terribly hard to procure a carriage to take them to Valognes, in Normandy. The roads were not clear, though the Darcys would have more to risk from the mud than from the

French soldiers fighting counterrevolutionaries in the country-side. Darcy finally arranged for their travel. "We have to go west anyway. If the Hôtel des Capuchins is still under the same owner and has not been let, then there will be people I know there to aid us," he said, and took her hand.

The trip to Normandy was uneventful. The roads were bad, but not at their worst (or so their driver said), and the land was quiet, its people exhausted by three decades of political and social turmoil. Elizabeth spent most of the trip watching the French countryside go by, while Darcy kept his head in a book of French phrases. "Don't worry, my dear. You will be quite sick of the countryside by the end of this and will not miss it one bit."

"Perhaps our trip back will be more leisurely."

"Perhaps."

He had sent his card ahead, so there was some reception at the ancient manor that was now Hôtel des Capuchins. The stone building had once been a modest noble estate but had since fallen into a state of some disrepair. The man who greeted them was a soldier, probably a colonel, who seemed to be in his mid-thirties. "Mr. Darcy. And I assume, Mrs. Darcy." He had a smile and a vaguely southern English accent. He was quickly joined by a modestly dressed woman with a young child at her side; there were bows and curtseys all around. "Mrs. Darcy, I am Colonel Audley, and this is my wife, Mrs. Audley, and my son, Robert."

"Pleased to meet you all," Elizabeth said.

"It is good to see you again, though our stay will be brief, as we have pressing business in the south," Darcy said. "Is that old room where I used to stay still intact? The one that contained some family artifacts?"

"Of course, though I would say it's too small for you now," the soldier said with a wink. "We have done some personal renovations, but not in that part of the house, and we would never throw anything out without inquiring first. I believe your father was here some years ago."

"Yes I do recall he made a trip to France before he passed on."

"I heard about that. My condolences, Mr. Darcy."

"It is the way of things."

They were welcomed in and found a quiet sort of charm about the wing that was in use. After the Darcys were served refreshments, Colonel Audley gave them a tour of the manor, pointing out many pictures and items he admitted being unable to identify, but that probably had belonged to the d'Arcy family. The Darcys were then released, shown suitable quarters, and told that dinner would be at six. The colonel's wife was French, from her accent, and spoke little to them.

Darcy went to the room he wanted to visit: a bedroom with a small bed, a desk, and a chest of drawers. He immediately sat down at the desk, opened its drawers, and began sifting through the contents.

"This is where you stayed?" Elizabeth said. With the lavish way Darcy lived at Pemberley, she could not imagine him living in such a cramped apartment. Clearly the d'Arcy family had come up in the world by moving to England and marrying into families there like the Fitzwilliams.

"Yes. At the time, Thomas—the Colonel—and I believe her is name is Arlette—were newly married, and he had been released from the army because of a nobly won wound. Because her family was here and he liked the country, he decided to settle down; the house was let by whatever local person had control of it. I was here only a short while. I believe my father would stay here sometimes on business. See, here are some papers of his." He pulled a sheet out and lit the candle next to it. "Some letter about shipping prices to the senior Mr. Wickham."

Left to her own devices, Elizabeth began opening the drawers. They were mainly filled with clothing, laundered but unused for some time. A layer of dust was in the room, but nothing too bad. The third drawer, however, was entirely different. "Darcy!"

He looked up from his papers and joined her. "Look at that."

It was a vast collection of various personal artifacts, hastily stuffed into the drawer. She picked up one of the many small portraits. "Is this you? As a child?"

"It seems so. Not a very good likeness, though."

"Yes, the nose is off. Or you've changed, perhaps."

"Perhaps." He scooped another one out. "I believe this is… Mrs. Isabella Wickham."

"Did you know her?"

"No, but I've seen her in portrait. She died when I was too small to remember her." He put it aside. "And Mr. Wickham. Our Mr. Wickham." For it did look like George, but as a little boy. "Yes, definitely him." He put it away with distaste.

"This one?" she said, holding up yet another, slightly larger one of a bejeweled woman.

"My mother." He took that one out of the drawer and put it into the pocket of his waistcoat.

There were other things in the drawer, too, including a lot of jewelry. "Would you like it?" Darcy said to his wife.

"Oh, I have so much already," Elizabeth said. "And I feel as though we are looting the place."

"Hardly. These are my father's possessions, or a relative's.

They don't belong to Colonel Audley, certainly." He plucked one up that interested him, a gold bracelet with an inscription. "'To my darling Anne.'"

"For your mother."

"Yes. Either he never had a chance to give it to her, or he took it around with him after she died and left it here for whatever reason." This, he took out of the drawer and also put in his waistcoat. "If you see anything you like… I doubt we will be back here. We should take at least some if it." He returned to the desk and opened up the drawer on the left, which was full of files and papers. He pulled one out at random. "Oh God."

"What?"

"'My dearest'—I think this is a love letter my mother wrote to my father." He stashed it away as if it was on fire and would burn him. Elizabeth laughed at the spectacle. "What? Would you like to read letters your father might have written while courting Mrs. Bennet?"

"No! What an awful idea!"

"Exactly."

He returned to his scouring and she to the drawer. The items in it were all very lovely, but she could not imagine taking them, at least not the ones not clearly marked as belonging to his parents or relatives. She picked up the portrait of the young Darcy again and flipped it over. Upon closer inspection, she noticed a name scribbled hastily on the wooden back—and it was not Fitzwilliam Darcy.

She slipped it into the pocket of her coat without a word.

"Here it is," her husband announced, startling her, but she hid her surprise as she turned around. "Some financial notations from a local bank where, according to the date, my father set up an account shortly before his death. It should still be there, and I should be the benefactor. If you wouldn't mind, I'll inquire with our hosts as to its precise location."

"Since when did you become so money-hungry, Darcy?"

"It is not that, and you know it. I am the financial head of the Darcy fortunes, and I should at least take the time to know where they are. It may be nothing, some charitable fund. But as long as we are here…" he trailed off as he passed her, giving her a quick kiss.

Elizabeth had little understanding of the Darcy fortunes beyond what he had taught her that she would need to know upon his death. She had never studied economics, but she prided herself on having a keen sense of when her husband had some kind of scheme or plan running through his head that he did not want to share with her. Well, that was fine. She had one, too.

The bank turned out to be but a half hour's ride away, giving them enough time to be back for dinner, if their inquiries took a reasonable amount of time, and Darcy was fairly sure that they would.

The bank itself was an old, crumbling building but very much still in service and full of guards like any proper bank that had survived the Revolution. Unfortunately, as he had warned on the way, Darcy had to leave Elizabeth at the door to the office of the bank manager, because they were to discuss an account to which she had no rights. So she walked around a bit outside, admiring the wonderful fountain in the center of town, while Darcy was called into a stuffy office where an exceptionally fat man was struggling to seat himself behind his desk.

The bovine banker before him put on his reading glasses, looked briefly at the note, and then finally turned to his visitor. "So you are here to inquire about the account of Geoffrey Darcy. May I assume you are the executor of his estate?"

"I am his son, and yes, I am."

The banker squinted at the records before him again. "Fitzwilliam Darcy."

"Yes. Do you require proof of my identity?"

"No, Mr. Darcy, I do not, unless you wish to alter the nature of the account. Which, according to Geoffrey Darcy's own specifications, only you may do, and in person."

"I admit to not knowing his specifications. I was only recently informed that he had an account here. It is not in the record books in England."

The banker grunted or possibly snorted. "Yes, well, if you wish to alter the arrangements, you may do so, but I must require the proper papers for that."

"Arrangements?"

"Yes." The banker glanced over the records again, which he shared with Darcy. "Three thousand pounds are sent to Mont Claire annually, drawing on a reserve of some fifty thousand."

"Mont Claire?" Darcy did his best to hide his surprise at the staggering sum.

"Yes. It is, I believe, in the west."

"The money goes to an estate?"

"No, it goes to a person. Grégoire Bellamont. As the account specifies, he is permitted to do as he pleases with it, with the exception of redepositing it in the same account. What I mean to say is, Monsieur Darcy would not allow him to refuse it."

Darcy was trying to stay focused on the bizarre information being thrown at him. "I am not familiar with this man. Have you met him?"

"No, Monsieur. The account was set up in the presence only of your father and a Mademoiselle Bellamont."

Now with the blood rushing to his head and the pounding in his ears, Darcy could barely manage his last question, "And the date of that event?"

The banker squinted again. "February 7, 1797. Do you have any—"

"I wish all of the records to be made available in copy form at once," Darcy said, standing up. "I will return tomorrow for them. Thank you for your time."

The banker nodded, and Darcy left, rejoining his wife, who was waiting for him on a bench. "Darcy? Are you all right?"

How would he explain this to her? How could he possibly— "I don't know. This has become complicated. Please, I'll explain back at the manor."

The ride back was brief, and Elizabeth stroking his hair did nothing to relieve his frustration. In fact, it made him feel down-right guilty. They retired to their own quarters, and he spelled out what he had heard at the banker's.

"1797," Elizabeth said. "Your father died—"

"In November of 1797. He was ill for about a year before."

"And you were at Cambridge?"

"No. I had graduated two years prior and…" But he had already done the calculations when he heard the sum granted and that a woman was involved. He just didn't want to hand those calculations over to Elizabeth. "… I had just spent a year traveling the Continent. I returned the previous fall."

"To begin your formal training? I mean, to be master of Pemberley."

"Yes."

"You did not accompany him on this trip—to set up this account?"

"No. He made mention of the trip, but to be perfectly honest, I have little recollection of it. It was brief, and I was busy with other things. I think Bingley was up from University and had come in for the shooting season. So—I took no notice, and my father did not talk much about it when he got back."

Elizabeth paced in front of him, which terrified him, because he knew she would reach the same conclusions he had if she tried hard enough, which she would. "So a year or so after your return from your year abroad, some of which you spent here—"

"—A small amount, at the beginning—"

"—Your father goes to France and sets up an extremely generous account with an anonymous woman for someone who is obviously her son."

He could not bring himself to answer her. His silence said everything anyway, and he could see the anger rising in her eyes.

"You think it's yours," she said with such a lack of emotion that it was positively frightening.

"It is within the realm of possibility."

"So you knew her?"

"The last name means nothing to me, but—"

"—That doesn't matter, does it? Do you even remember her first name?"

He softened his expression. "Elizabeth—"

She responded by slamming their bedroom door in his face.

"Elizabeth!" he shouted, pounding on the door. There was

no noise from inside, other than the door soundly locking. "I—cannot further explain myself. And we have no confirmation! She could have been a family friend!"

Still nothing. Darcy knocked his forehead against the door. "Lizzy," he said, in a whisper that he judged loud enough for her to hear. "I love you. Please."

He almost fell forward as the door came open. Elizabeth's expression was of stone. "Then we will go to Mont Claire and get confirmation that there lives an old friend of your father who deserves a generous living."

Then she shut the door again. This time, he did not have the strength to protest.

It was late in the evening when the messenger came to the Maddox townhouse, but this was no surprise. As both a doctor and a surgeon, Dr. Maddox was often called at all hours, as illness had no particular time schedule. His wife was quite used it and kissed him as he went off to work, as if he were doing so at a more proper time.

He did not tell her where he was going. His patient list was confidential, to the point of most of it being in his head. Before marrying Caroline, he had been practically destitute for years, with nothing but a shabby apartment and a collection of books he had managed to save from the people who came to collect everything that belonged to his profligate brother, and thereby, to him.

Maddox had saved many books by sneaking them out in the night. Those books were precious treasures that kept him company and were his only solace as his brother fled the country to avoid his debtors. Maddox had spent many hours reading by daylight when he worked a long night shift and spent the next day recovering. When the print on some of the pages began to blur, he had to shell out a small fortune—most of his savings—to get his glasses changed.

He took every job he had no major moral objection to, and that he was physically capable of, even the ones considered beneath proper doctors and assigned to surgeons. Surgeons, in his opinion, were not well trained, and doctors rarely put their training to use. He was also extremely discreet, partially from having no one to tell and partially from wanting the repeat business.

As a result, though his wife did not know it, he was one of the favorite people to call for every madam and pimp in Town. He did not treat the women of easy virtue unless their maladies were something that could be mended, though he was very polite to them—as he felt a gentleman should be, whatever his profession— he could not cure their diseases because there were no cures that he knew of. Yet despite explaining this at length, and many times, he still found the women throwing rather risqué and grotesque descriptions of their symptoms at him, so that he probably knew what was wrong with every fancy lady in London.

On this particular evening, when he arrived, he was ushered along to a familiar room with a woman, barely covered by a silk robe, standing at the door.

"Hullo doc," said the woman.

"Hello, Lilly," he said.

"How's the good doctor these days?"

"Married," he said quickly, and ducked into the appropriate room, which was not properly lit, but he knew his way around it. A man wearing trousers and an undershirt lay on the floor beside the bed, holding a cloth to his bloodied chest with one hand and a bottle with the other.

"I'm the doctor," Dr. Maddox said very formally, kneeling beside his patient and setting down his bag. "Do you mind if I look at the wound?"

"Go ahead," said the man, and removed the cloth. "There's been a lot of blood."

Dr. Maddox removed his glasses and held up the lamp, peering in very closely. "The wound doesn't look deep. It was mainly done for dramatic effect, I imagine, but it's more of a surface wound. I'm going to probe it, if you don't mind. There may be some discomfort, and the instrument is a little cold, but it's more sanitary than my hands."

"Goddamn it," the man said, taking a swig from his bottle. "Goddamn whore."

Dr. Maddox ignored this and opened the bag, carefully removing his instruments. The madam appeared at the doorway. "The usual water, please, in a clean bowl, and some towels."

She nodded and disappeared. He turned his attentions to his patient. The wound was indeed mostly superficial, meant to draw blood (which had a fright factor) but not do serious harm. However, the initial blow, before Lilly had dragged the knife along his chest, was deeper, and the bleeding would not cease. The fact that the man was especially fat had given Lilly more room to work with.

"If you would allow, sir, I'd like to give you a few stitches on the top, perhaps no more than three or four."

"If I would allow it?" the man said, his cultured, obviously high-class accent slurred by drunkenness. "*I bleed.* Go ahead."

"I usually prefer consenting patients when they're conscious,"

Dr. Maddox carefully explained, and went about his business. His patient rambled on as the doctor did his work, explaining that Lilly had attempted to renegotiate the price after the deed. When he refused, she had stabbed him, and she was a "crazy woman."

Actually, Dr. Maddox suspected Lilly was quite sane, if a bit in love with the knife, as this was not the first patient with a stab wound that he had been called to, but he kept that counsel to himself. He focused instead on stitching the wound while having his patient press down on the lesser wound area until the bleeding stopped. In the end, five stitches were required, more than Lilly's usual.

"These will need to be removed in about a week. I can give you my card, or you can have someone else do it," Dr. Maddox told his patient.

"I'll take your card, but I may not use it," the man said, putting his shirt back on with a grunt of pain.

"I understand completely. Keep the wound clean. I recommend boiling water and letting it cool before putting it over the wound to prevent infection. Do this at least once or twice a day until the stitches are removed, keep the area bandaged with something clean, and you should prevent infection, which, of course, would be most serious." He quickly put his instruments away, washed the blood from his hands, and stood up. "Good luck."

The patient raised his bottle in a sort of toast. "Good job, Doctor. I did not get your name."

"Dr. Maddox," he said, and doffed his hat.

He was nearly out the door when his patient said, "You have not asked my name."

Maddox turned back to him, took one look at the man in the diminished light, and said, "No." Then he left with all expediency.

When he returned to his house, his manservant was up to greet him, as these calls were not unknown, and Dr. Maddox found it convenient to drop his bag with a servant and be able to reasonably expect the instruments to be cleaned and ready in the morning. He found himself tired, probably from the hour, and inquired as to his wife. "Mrs. Maddox is retired."

Of course she was. The sky was practically lightening. He did not want to disturb her, so he took to his own bedroom, as was his custom when returning from a late call, and collapsed on the bed.

Chapter 7

THE INVITATION

"Daniel! Daniel, wake up!"

Dr. Daniel Maddox opened his eyes to the normal blurry world and a figure that was undoubtedly his wife. He knew her figure, but the red hair always gave it away, even if her voice didn't. Though her voice was not particularly piercing, it was very excited and, therefore, a little rattling to someone who was sound asleep. "What?"

"Daniel." She leaned over, and he had only the vaguest idea of what the gesture was, being unable to see it with any clarity, until she kissed him on the head. "You won't believe what I have to tell you."

"I already know you're with child."

"Stop being a doctor for once," she said. "We've been invited to a royal ball."

That made him sit up. If not for the level of pure exasperation in her voice, he would not have begun to believe it. "What?"

"I know! I cannot properly explain it, unless *you* can. Here." She handed him the invitation, which was very large in his hands.

He held it up to his face and let his eyes adjust to the morning—well, probably afternoon—light, as the letters became clear. "It seems we have. Dear, can you hand me my—" But she already had his glasses and put them in his hands. He put them on, and as the world became clear, he lay back and gazed at the invitation and then at his wife. She was dressed properly, so it must have been at least a decent hour of the morning, probably later. "I cannot explain it either."

"You are descended from nobility."

"I have never in my life spoken to the current earl of Maddox. Nor would he have the authority to invite me to a royal ball." He gave her back the invitation. "But this is—uhm, good news. This Friday, so frightfully soon."

"I know. I never thought I would say this about a ball, but I haven't a thing to wear."

"Neither do I." It would certainly cost him, but as they had no choice in the matter, and as his wife was exuberant over the idea, he was readily willing to spend every last shilling on her dress. He also had the wisdom not to share this with her at the moment. "I suppose something will have to be arranged."

"You will not admit it," she said, and kissed him as she sat down next to him, "but I know you had something to do with this."

"If you are inclined to keep rewarding me as such, I will not contradict you."

The invitation was set aside.

"Just so you know," she muttered, "the Hursts are coming to dinner, and Charles may be in town in time to be invited."

"And… and when is that, exactly?"

"In about three hours, dear."

"Oh," he said. "Good."

As it turned out, Charles Bingley was in Town, arriving at his own townhouse just in time to be ready for dinner at theirs. "Business with my steward," he explained, and nothing else was asked. "Everyone is well. I mean, nobody is sick, except from worrying."

"Have the Darcys written?" Maddox asked over the first course. He felt it odd, sitting at the head of the table with guests far above his own station, even if they were all his relatives. Georgiana Darcy was also dining with them, as Caroline had a great affection for her, and since she was in Town, finding Pemberley "too closed and empty" for her liking.

"They wrote when they arrived in Calais, and Darcy reports that they are fine. His letter was a bit brief. Elizabeth's was longer, but it was addressed to Jane," Bingley said.

"Never liked France," Mr. Hurst mumbled over his soup. "Too much rain and too many vowels."

Maddox stifled his laughter as Bingley gave him a smile, and Caroline announced the great news, which had everyone turning to the doctor, who merely shrugged.

"Isn't your uncle an earl?" said Mr. Hurst.

"He passed on long ago. I am not acquainted with the current earl. Not that that would explain it."

"Are you going to meet the king?" Georgiana whispered, though loud enough for everyone to hear.

"He's not going into public these days, is he?" Mr. Hurst said.

"I hardly think a private ball qualifies as public," Mrs. Hurst retorted.

"I heard he wasn't," Georgiana said. "I mean... being seen."

"Or they are not *letting* him be seen," Caroline said. "It must be, because we have not heard anything in the papers for a while now."

"The invitation failed to specify," was all Dr. Maddox had to offer. "The Prince of Wales is the host. I suppose he will make a decision based on his father's particular mood at the moment, if we are meant to be presented to him at all—and I have no idea if we will be."

"So you know something of his illness? I mean, beyond what we all know," Bingley said, passing a dish of vegetables to his sister. "Perhaps that would explain it."

"I sincerely hope they have no medical expectations of me," Maddox said, and when the idea sank in, it worried him even more. "I've no expertise on the mind. No one does. It's too closely connected to the soul, perhaps. I only know what I've heard from other doctors who are more closely following the reports."

"Which is?" his wife said expectedly.

"That his madness passes in and out, and sometimes he can be quite sane," he said. "But apparently not enough to rule the country, as his moods are very unpredictable. I doubt his condition has anything to do with us, because he has the best doctors in the world treating him. I hardly believe they would resort to a Town doctor."

"Terrible malady," Mr. Hurst said. "Madness."

"Is it treason to say that of His Majesty?" asked Georgiana innocently.

"Maybe *in front of* His Majesty," Caroline said, "but not in this house. You are allowed to state the obvious, Miss Darcy."

"Perhaps you will learn for yourselves," Charles said. "Well, I think you're very lucky. I can't even imagine being invited to a royal ball. Darcy, surely, has been presented, but he's Darcy of Pemberley and Derbyshire. Do you have a sword, Doctor?"

"Oh goodness, no. Am I going to have to get one?"

"I believe that is part of the appropriate dress," said Mrs. Hurst. "But perhaps not for a physician."

"You could bring that scalpel of yours," Caroline said, and Charles laughed in his seat next to her.

"Get a big enough scabbard for it, you should be fine," slurred Mr. Hurst.

Dr. Maddox smiled and kept his nervousness to himself.

Bingley's business was brief, and he quickly returned to Derbyshire before the mystery could be solved. Caroline was exceedingly happy at the prospect of a royal ball, and Bingley was exceedingly happy to see his sister content. However the doctor was managing that, it was working.

Geoffrey and Georgie were there to greet him at the door, their skin coloration beginning to fade. During the day, when they were allowed to play about, not yet being of the age to have proper lessons (though Darcy had begun his son on reading and writing, but not particularly harshly), they were free to run about and could hardly be separated.

As the servants removed Bingley's coat, he inquired after his wife and asked that his other children be brought to him in his study. Before long, Jane appeared, carrying little Charles, and passed him off to his father as she kissed her son. Nurse arrived, carrying Eliza, but Jane waited until Bingley was settled with his son in his lap before passing a letter to him. "From Darcy." It was only then that she took Eliza into her arms.

He broke open the seal and quickly scanned Darcy's elegant but precise script. He told Nurse to wait outside. When they were alone and the door soundly shut, he read it aloud.

To Charles Bingley,

Please be assured first that all is well and we are now on our way south. We have a stop of business to make in the east, but it is not terribly off course.

I have a request of you that may seem of an odd nature, and I would wish that, if you want to tell anyone of it, please restrict this conversation to your wife.

In the back right corner of my study is a small cabinet made of red oak. All of its three drawers are locked, as they contain financial records dating to my father's lifetime and possibly before. It has been years since I have been through any of them. You will find that the master key of Pemberley opens the first two drawers, but not the third. I made an attempt at opening it some years ago, but either the lock was rusted out, or I did not have the appropriate key. I could do nothing to open the drawer without destroying the cabinet, and I had no major interest in the cabinet beyond mere curiosity, so it has never been opened in my time as master of Pemberley.

Please take the keys and make some attempt to open that drawer, employing whatever methods may be necessary. In fact, I give you full permission to destroy the cabinet, but I imagine that, with your skills, it will not come to that. Please keep this task quiet, and if anyone asks, have Mrs. Reynolds called in. Inform her that I have given you the authority to do this, and that it directly relates to a matter I believe she is better informed of than I am.

If there are any documents in the drawer, please do me the additional favor of reading through them. In particular, I am looking for someone by the name of Bellamont, whether he or she was under my father's employ, and when. If you discover anything, please report it to me.

I will explain the matter in full detail when I return. I regret that the explanation is too complicated to give justice to now, as the road is very exhausting.

Many thanks,

Darcy

"What does he mean about the keys?"

"He gave me a set of the master keys of Pemberley before leaving," Bingley explained, and quickly produced his own keys, which he used to unlock the bottom drawer of his desk. "Here." He put a set of keys on the desk for display. "Oh, and these." He reached into the drawer, sifted through the various Indian books there, and retrieved a set of lock picks. "I never should have told him that story. Now I'm going to feel like a common burglar."

"Better than destroying the cabinet, I suppose. Do you think you can do it?"

"I've no idea. But if he's off saving your sister's reputation, I might as well aid him in some fashion. Are you accompanying me?"

"Let me put our children down for a nap, and then, yes."

An hour later they were at Pemberley and greeted by a surprised skeleton crew, which included Darcy's manservant, who was waved off. They quickly made their way to the study. The cabinet in question was not hard to locate. It was in the back, obviously not in regular use, and the only one with precisely three drawers. "If anyone inquires as to what we are doing," Bingley told the servant attending them, "please send in Mrs. Reynolds. Otherwise, Mr. Darcy's specifications were that we be left alone."

The servant bowed and left, closing the great doors behind him.

"First," Bingley said. He went through the ring of keys from Pemberley, but while one opened the first two drawers, Darcy was right that it did not open the bottom one. "It doesn't even fit. The lock was changed at some point."

"Surely a locksmith can handle it."

"Not without making a fuss. I think, knowing Darcy, he wishes to avoid that at all costs." When his wife did not contradict him, he sat down on the floor and placed the lower pick into the lock, inserting the other one just above it and fiddling with it. "Rusted. But not impossible, I think."

"You are quite the rogue."

"I haven't opened it yet," he pointed out. "Argh! What a difficult lock. You may wish to sit down... this may take a while."

"Charles! I'm not *currently* with child."

"That we know of."

She gave him a smirk before having to greet Mrs. Reynolds, who entered very authoritatively with a grand opening of the door and silently awaited the explanation of why someone, even Darcy's in-laws, was messing around in her master's study.

"Mrs. Reynolds," Jane said, "Mr. Darcy has written and asked Charles to retrieve some records from a particular cabinet for him. He said it pertained to a matter that you have some knowledge of, but he did not specify what that was."

Mrs. Reynolds went through several changes of expression, but she nodded obediently and said nothing. She moved around the desk and looked at the rather hapless-looking figure of Charles Bingley on the floor working at the lock.

"I think that was the first pin… or me breaking it. Either one."

"Mrs. Reynolds," Jane said very calmly. "Do you have any idea as to the contents of this cabinet?"

"Oh no, Mrs. Bingley. I imagine if he keeps it locked, it's financial records, and I remember Mr. Darcy—Mr. Darcy's father—using it occasionally, but I came to Pemberley some years after the master's birth, and it has never been my concern."

"Well, this should solve it," Bingley said. "Yes, first pin, definitely. All right, first pin is the hardest. Or is it the last pin? I forget."

Whether he remembered or not, he took some time in opening the lock. Mrs. Reynolds called for tea but brought it in herself and otherwise kept the door shut. She did, however, stay in the room and was not dismissed.

"There!" Bingley said triumphantly, as the sound of the lock very soundly turning open finally broke the silence in the room. He wiped the sweat off his brow with a handkerchief from Mrs. Reynolds and pulled the drawer open. Its hinges had rusted, so this took some work, but finally the cabinet revealed its treasure—pages and pages of documents. "Well, after all that, I was hoping for gold or something."

"You did a good job anyway," Jane said, and kissed her husband as he rose and pulled the records from the drawer, putting the huge stack on the desk. "Oh dear."

"May I help you, sir?" Mrs. Reynolds said. "If you're looking for something specific—"

"Yes. A Mr. Bellamont, or records of his employment at Pemberley, if they exist."

Mrs. Reynolds visibly paled, and the Bingleys stopped opening various folders to stare at her with the obvious intention of waiting for her to explain her reaction.

"Do save us the trouble," Bingley said.

"Well." For once, the elderly Mrs. Reynolds, usually sharp as a pin, began to look her age. "I did know her—and it is a Mrs. Bellamont. Or, properly, *Miss* Bellamont. The master seems to have forgotten, perhaps because of his age at the time, but she was his mother's lady-maid."

"What else do you remember of her? I think Darcy will require more specifics."

"Only that she was dismissed rather hastily, shortly before Mrs. Darcy's death. At the time, I was not the manager of the house, only the laundress, and so I don't remember—"

"It's fine," Bingley said. "The date of Mrs. Darcy's death?"

Mrs. Reynolds supplied it. Mrs. Darcy had died twenty years earlier, days after Georgiana's birth, when a fever had overtaken her. The whole house had been devastated, especially, of course, the young Darcy, then thirteen.

That made going through the records much easier, as they were dated very accurately and in the traditional neat script of the Master of Pemberley. Annual salary sheets were signed and dated by Mr. Geoffrey Darcy and, in the earlier years, by his steward, Mr. Wickham. Before tremendously long, with the three of them working, they located the document specifying a termination payment for Miss Alice Bellamont. Oddly, Bingley noted that the termination came during Mrs. Darcy's confinement, a few months before her death.

"An odd time to dismiss a lady-maid," he said, and no one found a proper response.

⌘

The Bingleys got into bed later than usual, as they had every night since Geoffrey Darcy had stayed at Chatton without his parents around. One look from his father was still enough to scare him into listening to Nurse, but his Uncle Bingley was not his father and had trouble making such a severe face as was appropriate. Jane had to put three small children to bed and thus was similarly exhausted when she climbed next to her husband, and they lay there for some time with the candles still lit.

"I suppose we should give more responsibilities to Nurse."

"I suppose."

"A good gentleman does not take such interest in his children until they are properly grown," Jane said.

Charles turned on his side to face her. "And who told you this? Your father?"

"Hardly! My mother."

"Of course. I should have assumed. Well, then I am not a proper gentleman. I am sorry to disappoint you, a gentleman's daughter, who deserves only the best. Surely you are disappointed in me."

"Most disappointed, Charles," she said, and kissed him. "I suppose it would be horrible of us to speculate about exactly what we did today."

"Yes."

"And to assume only the best."

"Yes. But we are both thinking the same thing, correct?"

"I am not a mentalist, Charles, so I do not know what you are thinking. In fact, the matter is entirely puzzling to me."

"Well," Bingley said. "Then it is my husbandly duty to enlighten you as to what I am thinking, which most unfortunately, is a bit gossipy. But duty is more important than gossip." He held her hand as they talked. "I do not think Mrs. Reynolds was entirely forthcoming with us today."

"That I did realize."

"It was more what she left out. Now, Miss Bellamont, whoever she was, occupied a treasured position for many years and, for her to do so, we will assume that Mrs. Darcy had some attachment to her. It is quite unlucky to upset the normality of the household during confinement. So Miss Bellamont must have done something to make Mrs. Darcy quite upset—or Mr. Darcy suitably upset to dismiss her despite his wife's protests. Now, the first thing I can think of for a servant is theft, but Mrs. Reynolds would have known about that and would have had no shame in saying it. News of a dismissal would have gone around all the servants, no doubt. But Mrs. Reynolds omitted the reason, which she surely must have known. So—I will assume the latter of the two offenses I can imagine."

Jane looked curious. "Pray?"

"She was with child."

"Not so horrible. I know the Darcys are a particularly upstanding and proper household—very proper—"

"—Very, *very* proper," Bingley said as they giggled.

"—But that sort of situation cannot be unknown with an entire retinue of servants who are all apparently expected to be celibate, despite lacking a religious vocation that requires it. Am I wrong, then, that the established rules of conduct may be broken occasionally?"

"Occasionally, yes. But to dismiss a treasured lady-maid..." he trailed off and turned on his back.

She tugged at his arm. "Charles."

"I am saying... I don't want to say what I am thinking."

It took her a moment. "That it must have been someone of some standing within the household. Mr. Wickham?"

"Already passed on. And his son too young at twelve." Charles gave her a look.

Jane covered her mouth in horror. "It *couldn't* have been—"

"It would explain everything quite neatly. The hidden records, the impromptu dismissal, the fact that Darcy is only discovering this now, and probably by circumstance. It is a terrible thing to think, especially of the dead. Darcy held his father in such high esteem—and still does, so if true, this would be a terrible blow to him."

"Did you know the elder Mr. Darcy?"

"Yes. I spent my summers at Pemberley when I was still at University, Darcy had graduated, and my father was still alive to care for my sister. Darcy's father was a kind man, very proud but not vain, the perfect gentleman, and an affectionate man nonetheless. He taught me how to fish, as I suppose his son had to best me at something. The only thing we did in competition was hunting, and I had more affection for the sport than Darcy did, so I was more accomplished. But I never became the fisherman that Darcy is. And fencing—I have no desire even to pick up a blade, much less face Darcy. Mr. Darcy was everything Darcy described him to be, or so I thought... until today."

She put a hand on his shoulder. "We may be assuming too much. We may be unkind to his legacy."

"Perhaps. Yes, let us assume that until we hear otherwise."
But he had a feeling they would be hearing otherwise.

THE LAST MONKS OF MONT CLAIRE

THE TRIP TO MONT Claire was a particularly brutal one for Darcy, not just because of the bad roads and the uphill (and at times, dangerous) climb. There was also the intolerable matter of his wife not speaking to him. After many hours of being bumped about, when bodily contact could not be avoided, she finally accepted the comfort—after rejecting it many times with a grunt—of him putting his arm around her to protect her shoulders from the jostling of the carriage, but she continued her stony silence.

They were a little surprised to discover nothing at the top of the mountain but the ruined remains of a monastery, now a winery, and a small community surrounding it. They found no inn and applied to the local tavern for information. No one in the town knew the name Bellamont, and the Darcys' poor French made the discussion worse, but they managed to scrape together that they would have to get their information from the town priest, who lived in the winery.

For a medieval structure, the monastery was small, but it had been built over the years and with great care, its gothic stone resisting the temptation of the times and the horrible mountain winds that came up from the valleys beneath. The land was relatively bare for the planting season and was being worked furiously by the peasants they passed. Though the Darcys waved with smiles, their presence was greeted with cold stares.

There was no one to greet them at the winery. Darcy rapped his walking cane against the heavy wooden doors, and an elderly monk answered. Darcy tried to explain in French what they were doing there, but the monk only shook his head and opened the door. "*L'Abbé*," he said. But he put his hand up at Elizabeth's attempt to enter. "*Aucune entrée.*"

Darcy turned helplessly to his wife. To his surprise, Elizabeth said, "I will wait in the carriage."

Those were her first words to him in three days.

He turned, somewhat angrily, to the monk at the door. "*L'Abbé.*"

The hallway Darcy was led through was impressive, with its gothic arches, but it was also incredibly drafty. He imagined that, with only a single wool robe, the old man in front of him must be cold regularly, as he himself was freezing.

"English?" the monk said.

"Yes, please."

"No, English." He did not mean the language, but Darcy's nationality as well. "The Abbot speaks."

"I thought the monasteries were dissolved."

"Revolutionaries come, Father Abbot goes to Belgium, then Ireland, and comes back for Napoleon's promise. He is allowed four monks, no more, all French." He knocked on the beaten wooden door, which had holes from where a cross must have once hung in grander days, and Darcy was shown into the Abbot's study.

"*Excusez mon intrusion. Je suis Monsieur Darcy de*—"

"*Excusez*, but I speak English," said the Abbot, through a heavy French accent.

Thank God. "May I—" And with a gesture from the Abbot, he took a seat on a very uncomfortable stool before the desk.

"You are Geoffrey Darcy?"

"No, his son, Fitzwilliam. Mr. Darcy passed on some years ago. But I see you are familiar with the name."

"Yez." The Abbot did not explain himself. "Your purpose for this visit?"

"I am looking for a boy named Grégoire Bellamont," he said, his voice wavering when he said the name. "He may have been here at some time. A banker has led me to believe so."

"Yez, yez, of course, Monsieur," said the Abbot, his rough tone not particularly welcoming but not dismissive all the same. "Brother Grégoire."

Startled, Darcy leaned on his cane. "He is a monk?"

"Yez, he is to take his final vows at Christmas. He has been with us since his mother died, but he took the cowl in 1804 when we received permission to reform a brotherhood. Before that, he was my assistant in the parish."

"So… so he is not—anymore? A little boy?"

Whatever the Abbot made of Darcy's surprise, his own expression betrayed none of it. "No, Monsieur. He is nineteen."

There was the severe temptation, when he had fully processed this information, to run out of the monastery to Elizabeth, who was undoubtedly still fuming in the carriage, and scream at the top of his lungs, "*He isn't mine!*" Not that he was cleared of all charges, but the weight of possibly discovering an unknown bastard son by chance was lifted from his shoulders.

But… for his father to have left such an impressive sum to someone who must have been almost nine or ten at the time of Mr. Darcy's trip to the Continent, a connection had to exist. *No, that could not be it.* This was Geoffrey Darcy, his excellent father, his idol and his own son's namesake. He would not—

"Forgive me," Darcy said, putting a hand on his head. "I'm just—not fully aware of the arrangements here."

"Of course." Then quite calmly, as if it was nothing, the Abbot said, "Do you wish to meet your brother?"

"Yes," Darcy spit out before his own mind could reply. It was just instinctual. "Very much." *It can't be true. It isn't true. It is all a mistake.*

The Abbot escorted him, and the long trek gave him plenty of time to sharpen his mind against the possible truth of the situation. His father, Geoffrey Darcy, a most upstanding man, had trained him to be an upstanding gentleman, to be discreet and loyal in all matters. Darcy could not imagine—it was not possible to imagine otherwise—Not until he had all of the proof before him.

But then the proof was before him, in the form of a young man bent over the spigot of a cask of wine. With great precision, the young man measured a small amount into a glass, sniffed it with obvious expertise, and then tossed the wine out to the side on the dirt floor, where cats immediately appeared to attack it and lick the dusty remains. He did not stand up until he heard the approach of his Abbot, so consumed was he in his work, but then he bowed to his master and to the other man before him.

"Brother Grégoire," the Abbot said in English, making it plain that the monk understood the language. "This is Monsieur Fitzwilliam Darcy."

The monk took off his spectacles, which were little more

than two lenses held together with rope and wood, and stood in full to look at the visitor. He did not match Darcy in height—he was shorter and smaller and considerably less well nourished, or so it appeared under his shabby robe. His brown hair, identical to Darcy's in color, was perfectly tonsured, and while there were differences in their facial appearances, the familial resemblance was undeniable. Clearly terrified, Grégoire bowed to Darcy, who quickly returned the gesture. The Abbot said something quickly in French to his charge, who nodded and bowed to the Abbot as he departed, leaving them alone.

Grégoire turned to the towering figure of "Monsieur Darcy" and said in strangely accented English, "I understand English like to tour the grounds... if you would, Monsieur."

Darcy could only reply with a "yes."

<hr />

The garden was being turned over to prepare for the seed planting, and they moved slowly to an unattended section. How Grégoire was not freezing in his poor clothing was beyond Darcy's understanding, as the winds whipped up again.

"Where did you learn English?" Darcy asked, because even though the answer was obvious, it was a conversation starter.

"My mother," Grégoire said. "She died when I was eleven, of cholera. Because I was a good student, and Father Abbot was so strapped for priests, he took me in to help with the parish. He said I was meant for the church."

"And you believed him."

"Times have been very hard—very trying in France for everyone, and for people to be without the Sacraments is even harder. Father Abbot was once a brother prior in the Cistercian monastery here, before the dissolution. He refused to sign the Civil Constitution, pledging himself to the Holy Father rather than France, and he became a refractory priest. To escape the guillotine, he had to flee.

"When Monsieur Napoleon formed his government and stopped most of the killings, Father Abbot returned and swore allegiance to him. In return, he was granted permission to open an informal brotherhood. Four monks—the other three were monks before the Revolution, all in hiding, and I am the only novice. My mother stood by the church when the soldiers came... this is what she would have wanted."

"I assume your mother was Mrs. Bellamont? She never remarried?"

"She never married," he said. "I will not deny it. I am a bastard."

"I find it very hard to call a monk a bastard, no matter what his heritage," Darcy admitted. "I do not know the formal connection..."

"And I have no wish to dishonor my father. It is a biblical commandment..." Grégoire countered.

"... But nonetheless, we are standing here, finally and only by happenstance, and it seems we are related. I think the dishonoring, if there was any, was done many years ago and involved neither of us."

Grégoire considered this before answering, keeping his head low and saying shamefully, "My mother was your mother's maid. She was dismissed and sent home to France, where she had family, despite having come to England to find work at a very early age. I do not know the arrangements, and had no idea of my—heritage until I met our father."

"You spoke with him?"

"Once, when I was ten, and the financial arrangements that brought you here were made. He was... very kind to me, very penitent. He offered me a living with the Church."

"Not this living, I assume."

"No, he offered to pay for my tutoring, then University, and then a bishopric. If he had lived—and at that point, he said he was certain he would not—he would have paid for a red hat. But I refused."

"On what grounds?"

"I wanted to join the church to get close to the Holy Spirit," he said. "Not to get rich." He quickly raised his eyes. "I mean no insult, Monsieur Darcy."

"No insult taken."

"What I mean is, I believed that he meant his offer for my well-being, and I was honored that he should treat a bastard child in such a way. But I did not want it, so I refused. And he insisted on providing the money. So we reached an agreement with the current arrangements, most of which went to provide for my mother for the extra year she lived."

"And now?" Because, considering the surroundings, Darcy had trouble imagining that this monastery swallowed up three thousand pounds a year, unless the monks were hoarding gold-plated relics somewhere.

"I receive my monies, and I donate them to various charities. The Revolution left many widows and also children filling orphanages. If you wish to change the arrangement, you may do so, but that will have no effect on my own living situation."

Darcy looked out at the empty fields of Mont Claire and said, after some contemplative silence, "Brother, do you happen to know how to speak Italian?"

※

Upon sending Grégoire to his abbot to make the appropriate request, Darcy practically broke into a run to the carriage. He pulled open the door to a very expectant Elizabeth, who appeared to have something in her hands. "Well?" she asked.

"It seems the shades of Pemberley were thoroughly polluted long before you came into the picture," he said.

"You—," Elizabeth was befuddled by her husband's expression, which was a smile.

"He's not mine," he said. "He's my brother. Half—my half-brother."

"So your father—"

"Yes." He climbed into the carriage with her. "My father was not the man I thought he was." He wanted to be close to her, now that he could, and now that her anger was dissipating. He wanted the intimacy that he had had to suffer without because of a perceived sin. Only with her securely in his arms did he notice that she was holding the portrait of himself that he did not remember taking from the old d'Arcy estate. At least, they supposed the boy pictured to be him. She flipped it over and held it so he could see the scribbled note on the back.

It read, *Grégoire Bellamont.*

"You knew?"

"I—had suspicions. But still that did not say everything, though the boy in this picture is—well, it was hard to tell."

"But the portrait does prove—well, it provides considerable proof. And I suppose Grégoire would like to see it."

"I am to meet him, then?"

"He is to go with us, with your permission. He speaks Italian, French, English, Latin, and some German. He has never seen the world outside of Mont Claire, within what he can remember."

"They will allow him to leave?"

"He is just a novice. So we will see. Here he comes now." He took her hand, which she gladly allowed, and she stepped out to greet two monks, an aged one who was obviously the abbot and a young man with an uncanny resemblance to her husband, although younger and with a gigantic, perfectly bald spot on his head. They both bowed deeply to her and Darcy.

"Monsieur Darcy," said the Abbot through a heavy accent. "Brother Grégoire will accompany you on this journey, with my permission, and see Rome. After that, he will guide you back here, and then you shall part ways again. He has instructions as to the behavior expected of him, and you would do well not to interfere."

Darcy was not cowed, but he had assessed the situation and recognized the need to appear respectful. "Of course, Father," he said. "The carriage?" he said, gesturing that Grégoire could enter it.

The Abbot threw a severe look toward Grégoire, who lowered his eyes and replied, "I cannot ride in a carriage."

"Then how exactly do you intend to travel?"

"I am told I am to walk."

Fine. If the Abbot could be severe in his looks, so could Darcy, who spared the old monk nothing in his gaze. "You cannot walk to Rome. Certainly not with our pressing matter there. It is—impractical. Impossible."

"Can he ride? On a horse?" Darcy asked.

"I… do not know how," Grégoire said shamefully.

"He shall not ride in the carriage with you and… your wife."

Darcy did not have to look at her to know that Elizabeth was horrified, and that was enough to incite his considerable ire. He reached forward, took up Grégoire's sizable hood, and put it over his head so that most of his face was blocked. "There. Now his holy robes will protect him. May we go now, Father?"

At last, the Abbot relented. He spoke some words to Grégoire in quiet Latin and handed him a small sack. "Go with God."

Grégoire finally joined them, as Darcy gave the Abbot one more cold glance. "Papist."

"Heretic." The Abbot turned away, not willing to engage him further.

"*Husband*," Elizabeth chided, pulling him into the carriage.

"You are bound to your master, Brother," Darcy said. "And I to mine. Fortunately, mine is prettier."

Formal introductions were made in the carriage. Apparently Grégoire intended to wear his hood and stumble around blindly, so Darcy sighed and reached across to pull it off. "Brother Grégoire, this is my wife, Mrs. Elizabeth Darcy."

The monk bowed to her, as much as was possible in his seat, exposing his bald top. He was clearly afraid to look at her. While arguing with the Abbot, Darcy had not been oblivious to the fact that poor, young Grégoire had been ogling his wife. Thinking about it now, he could imagine that Elizabeth was probably the only grown woman the boy had seen since puberty, and she was, in Darcy's opinion, the most beautiful woman in the world. So, since he felt the young man's interest was mainly harmless, Darcy kept his normally possessive instincts in check.

Elizabeth could not curtsey in the carriage, so she nodded her head to Grégoire. "I believe you would want this—"

"Oh no, I should have no possessions—" but he stopped when he saw what she was holding—a portrait that he was, at least, willing to inspect. Darcy recognized it instantly.

"The back, Brother Grégoire," she explained.

He flipped it over and squinted at the faded lettering. "'Grégoire Bellamont.' This... this is me." He looked at the child on the other side. "As a boy."

"You do resemble your,"—she looked to Darcy for some approval—"brother. We thought the portrait was of him when we first saw it. Then I saw the inscription."

"It was among our father's possessions," Darcy said to the monk. "You said he held you in some affection. I do not doubt it. It is yours."

"No," said Grégoire, passing it back to Elizabeth. "I do not have possessions."

"None?" said Elizabeth in disbelief.

"What I have with me is borrowed from the monastery collective." He looked away, as if she was the sun, hunching up his sizable but tattered robes.

Elizabeth gave her husband a look; he just shrugged and put an arm around her. "We are happy to have you along, Brother."

He did not say which kind of brother he meant.

Having lost time going to Mont Claire, the Darcys did not return to the estate but instead headed south, stopping at an inn at the foot of the mountain. While the Darcys were offered the best room in the house (which, despite having a quaint charm, was hardly impressive by Darcy's personal standards), his brother took the worst. Darcy happened to look in it, and found only a mat and a candle on the dirt floor. Grégoire, clearly exhausted, stayed up for Vespers, which he recited from heart, and then retired.

"Darcy," Elizabeth said, watching the sad look on his face as they returned to their cramped chambers. She put her arms around him. She knew she had been hard on him the past few days, perhaps the hardest she had been on him since their wedding day. But the situation had been difficult—almost unbearable— for her, too, not because Darcy might have unknowingly fathered a son before he met her, but because of the physical separation, itself a trial. She wanted, more than ever, for them to be in each other's arms again and not spend another night separated, thin walls of the inn be damned. "He is so hard on himself."

"He was not raised properly."

"Not every man is meant to be an English gentleman."

"Every man with some money—and he has more than *some money*—should have a clean set of clothes, should not be expected to walk the length of his country in sandals, should..." he sighed, leaning into his wife. "I don't know. This is beyond my understanding... why is he such a ready student of that life? Undoubtedly because he has been exposed to nothing else."

"Or he truly believes it."

"He is nineteen. He does not know what he believes."

She kissed him on the cheek. "You don't know that."

"I know I was a fool at nineteen. And twenty. And eight and twenty, certainly."

"Perhaps a bit stubborn, at eight and twenty," she said with a smile. "But you came around."

"I had someone to inspire me," he said. "Elizabeth, I've missed you so much."

"As have I you. It was my fault, not to make the connection and assume it of you and not your father."

"Because my father was a good man." He shook his head. "Or, I thought he was."

"While I would say to my own husband that I find the idea of an extramarital indiscretion—especially with a lady-maid— inexcusable, that is not to say your father was not generous with Grégoire, or tried to be."

"Grégoire is the richest monk I have ever met. With no entails and no family to support, he would be quite an eligible bachelor if he were not celibate." He smiled. It felt good to be in his wife's arms and to smile. "I cannot excuse my father. I cannot truly believe it, either."

"You have quite sound proof."

"I know." He leaned on her. "I know. I just... cannot. Yet, perhaps I will grow into the idea that my father was not flawless."

"All children must, at some point. Not to say you are a child, Darcy." She kissed his hand. "If you were, I would have to call you Master Fitzwilliam."

"Oh, God no," he laughed. "No, never."

"Except when you are drunk or muddled, and I think I can get away with it."

"Except for then, yes. But otherwise, no." He added, "And don't think I didn't hear everything you said to me after I was shot, even if I couldn't process it at the time. *Eliza Bennet.*" A year prior, Darcy had taken a bullet in a fight with Caroline Maddox's former suitor, and Elizabeth and Bingley had conspired to make some amusement out of his post-operative, opium-induced state, in which he mispronounced people's names, to their obvious delight.

His face, fortunately, was not as severe as his voice. In fact, it was rather playful. Her response was to kiss him, and then all conversation ceased.

Chapter 9

THE ROYAL BALL

THE FEW DAYS LEADING up to the royal ball were as busy for Dr. Maddox as those leading up to his wedding had been, mainly because he had to manage his normal patient list and wonder how he was to be dressed properly. Fortunately, Caroline was walking on air and did a lot of the work for him, procuring him a sword and setting up his haberdasher appointments. While he was busily nervous, she was busily in a sublime mood, and what little time he had left was busy taking advantage of that, which led to a lot of late nights that had nothing to do with calls for his surgical services.

When the evening arrived, he was still no closer to finding the source of his invitation. The point was that he had it, and his wife was the happiest he had seen her since their wedding day—and that alone was enough of a comfort, even if seeing Caroline walk into his chambers in her beautiful emerald gown did make him a bit weak in the knees. "You are quite dashing, Daniel." She kissed him, meanwhile straightening out his collar.

"I do hope so," he said. "I do hope I won't be called for military service of some sort," touching the sword at his waist.

"It's *ceremonial*, dear," she assured him. "But are you saying you would not lay down your life for king and country?"

"If it is to be between king and country or be a husband to a wife and father to a child, then I suppose I will opt for treason," he said, and his hand strayed to her stomach, which was hidden behind layers of gown. Fortunately she was not far along enough to make a ball an impropriety.

"I do not deserve you," she whispered, and then continued in her normal voice. "Your hands are shaking. Are you nervous?"

"I've—never been—"

"—Nor I."

"It has been quite a while since I've been to a proper ball."

"Do you remember how to dance?"

"Every good gentleman knows how to dance."

"Then you are only obligated to stand up with me, or perhaps someone else you run into that you know. So, you may do as you please. You are not an eligible bachelor whom women will be chasing after while you stupidly dance with every one, which only serves to confuse them as to your intent."

"I will assume you are speaking of your brother."

"Charles may have had blinders on to everything but the fun of dancing with a pretty girl, but he did manage to land one with a great deal of sense. Still, the process was both amusing and embarrassing to watch."

"And you?"

"And me? I was not so silly."

"I did not presume that you were. But what did you do while your brother gallivanted about?"

"Made jokes about it with Darcy. To no avail."

"Good luck for me, then."

She laughed, and that in itself put him more at ease. It was well timed, for the servant entered just then to say that their carriage was ready, and it was time to depart.

***

The Royal Ballroom was in full display and decoration, dwarfing Pemberley and everything but a vague memory from his trip to Versailles, but that had not been during a ball, when the room was filled with people dressed as opulently as the windows. This was above both of them, and their invitation was checked. But after appropriate introductions were made, Caroline quickly made herself a welcome addition to the gaggle of chatty ladies. She was in her element; there was no doubt about that. That her husband was not was irrelevant to him, so long as she was happy.

"You are Brian Maddox, no?"

He bowed to the man in front of him. "Daniel Maddox, sir."

"Ah, the doctor." The man bowed. He was wearing a gold chain and various insignia. "Excuse me—I am Lord Stephan, Earl of Maddox."

They did look a bit alike, if vaguely, and seemed to be in the same age range. "Very pleased to meet you, my lord."

"My lord! Please, we are cousins. I must be Stephan." He smiled. He sort of reminded the doctor of his brother, minus all of the debts, lying, theft, and the limp, as far as he knew.

"Daniel." They shook on it. "I must introduce you to my wife, as soon as I, uhm, find her—"

"Probably chatting away with the rest of them. Best to let them do it, yes?"

"Perhaps." Instinctively, Maddox took the glass of champagne that was offered to him—for his nerves. He knew very well that alcohol was a poor tonic, and tended to make things worse rather than better, but he saw no other options. He had to sit it out. "I am unfamiliar with these events, I admit. Is His Majesty to make an appearance?"

"He does, on occasion, but only when he's sane. But you probably know more about that than I do. Where was your degree?"

"Cambridge and the Academy in Paris," Dr. Maddox said, sipping his drink. "But I'm no mind doctor. No, it was just idle curiosity." The sudden burst of trumpets made his stomach turn. "What is that?"

"Probably the Prince of Wales arriving. Fashionably late, of course."

The doctor nodded and finished his drink, which was quickly taken from him by a near-invisible servant. The general activity in the ballroom stopped, people cleared away, and conversation died down—slowly enough—to make way for the present head and future king of England, George Augustus Frederick, the Prince of Wales. His title was announced, and combined with the music, Dr. Maddox found the sound quite deafening. Between his general nerves and the champagne, the doctor was a little light on his feet.

That was until the prince entered, and Dr. Maddox saw him clearly. The doctor was ready to swoon entirely; only grabbing onto his newfound cousin's arm kept him from doing so.

Dinner in the Bingley house was an ordinary affair with current guests in residence, so that meant a lot of talking on Mrs. Bennet's part and a lot of nodding silently while rolling his eyes on Mr. Bennet's part. Bingley was at the head of the table, with his wife at the other end and their guests between them. The Hursts and the Maddoxes were in Town, and Bingley, being used to the most unwelcome houseguests, was more than happy to welcome the Bennets to Chatton for Mary's term. That did not, however, always make their visit easy.

"Mary, you must eat something!"

"Mama! I've eaten!"

"So little!" Mrs. Bennet had eventually made the transition from a mother concerned about her daughters' future welfare to a mother concerned with the immediate issue of her daughter's pregnancy, especially now that the rest was out of their hands. "Mr. Bennet!"

"What?" he said, looking as though she had never said anything like this before, which was amusing to watch. "Oh, I'm not foolish enough to tell a woman with child what she should or should not be doing. Do you ever remember me telling you to eat more or less?"

"Then you should know to back me instead of this foolish business of always contradicting me!" said his wife. "She must eat more! I will call for a midwife, if I must, if no one here will hear sense! Mr. Bingley?"

"Hmm?" he said, attempting to imitate Mr. Bennet's exact "surprised" dinner expression. According to Jane, in private, he was getting rather good at it. "Oh yes. Midwife. I'll call for one in the morning."

"Mama, I am not unwell," Mary insisted. "I am just full."

"You always ate like a bird. Proper for a lady, I suppose, but a lot of good it has come to. Now Lydia—and Lizzy, they are eaters. Could eat a horse."

"Mama!" Jane said, as her husband broke out into laughter. "Charles!"

He mumbled an apology and covered his mouth.

Of course, Mrs. Bennet was ready to fill the uncomfortable silence. "Now perhaps Lydia can finally see Derbyshire. Mr. Bingley, would you treat your mother to finally being able to see her daughter and grandchildren without having to travel to Newcastle? Because Mr. Bennet has forbidden them to Longbourn and Mr. Darcy has forbidden them to Pemberley… and I would like to see them."

"She would talk, though, Mama." Surprisingly, this came from Kitty before anyone else could say it. "About—you know."

"Kitty! Have some respect for your sister! Who would she tell, the regimentals at Newcastle?" She turned her attention back to Bingley. "Mr. Bingley, would you please be so kind as to invite the Wickhams to Chatton? If only for a short while?"

The rest of the Bennets openly cringed at the idea. Bingley hid whatever he was thinking and merely said, "I will put it under serious consideration."

"Oh, do not be so stubborn! You have no dispute with Mr. Wickham. And when is Mr. Darcy so far from Derbyshire that we can afford to invite him?"

"My dear," Mr. Bennet said, "Mr. Bingley is the master of Chatton and can invite and not invite whomever he pleases and for whatever reason, if I need remind you."

Bingley sat back in his chair, looking a bit lost in thought. "I will consider it. I would hardly want to get in the way of you seeing your own grandchildren, Mrs. Bennet." Actually, he didn't want to get in the way of Mrs. Bennet and anything. She did have a point about neither Darcy nor Elizabeth being even on the same island as Wickham. When would they have a chance for that again?

But something else was occupying him, and he was largely silent for the rest of dinner. Bingley had only met George Wickham once, on the day of his wedding, but knew of him extensively by reputation. He had no reason to be hostile to Wickham, if he ignored the past, but that was not what bothered him.

"Charles?" came Jane's voice, shaking him out of his apparent stupor. "Are you all right?"

"Oh. Oh, yes, I'm fine," he said.

"*Tell me later*," she whispered, and dinner continued. He would not escape her. That was also on his mind as they wrapped up dinner, all through the evening, and as they got all of the children to bed.

"What was that about?" Jane said, as she helped Geoffrey put on his nightshirt. They were in the other nursery, the twins already asleep. *Thank God*, they were now sleeping through the night, because Jane refused a wet nurse and handled her children personally, which made it terribly hard to sleep at times.

"What was *what* about?"

"You were—thinking."

He placed Georgie in her cradle and tied up her nightcap. "Am I not allowed to think?"

"Was it about Wickham?"

"Should we really discuss this in front of the children?"

"Where we discuss it does not concern me. Do you have an issue with Wickham coming or not?"

"No. To be perfectly honest, aside from me once helping Darcy to toss him out a window, we've never had an uncivil conversation. We barely know each other, and I'm sure he would be on his best behavior."

"What was that about—?"

"The point," he said, briefly interrupted as he leaned over to kiss his daughter good-night, to which she giggled, "is that I was thinking of something else. But it is not for me to say."

"It is not for you to say?" Jane asked, because she had never heard him say that.

"Yes, sadly." He leaned over and kissed her. "This is a most private matter that, since it does not involve your sister and hardly involves me, I have no business in sharing, unless you insist."

"Perhaps when Wickham arrives, if he does arrive, I will insist. But until then, you may have your secret."

She kissed Geoffrey and left. Bingley heaved a sigh of relief and looked over into Geoffrey's crib. "You have *no idea*."

Thankfully, Geoffrey was too sleepy to answer. He turned over and ignored his uncle entirely.

12 Years Ago

As they approached the nineteenth century, Charles Bingley found himself at ease. His first year at Cambridge had gone quite well in every respect, and his father was pleased. As a sort of reward, he was given no obligations beyond attending his sister's marriage to Mr. Hurst in early June, and then he was free to travel about a bit.

He was overjoyed, of course, when the newly graduated

Darcy invited him to Pemberley. The shooting season had not quite begun, but there was plenty of wildlife in Derbyshire year-round, or so Bingley had heard. His father was also interested that his son had developed a friendship with the famous Darcys of Pemberley; such a social connection could only bring about good things. Bingley himself had not that intention when he traveled up north. He simply wanted to see his friend and get away from his sisters.

Darcy was less a man of leisure, as his father was continuing his education in how to be Master of Pemberley, and Darcy was to leave for a year on the Continent in the late summer, giving them only a month together. Several hours of the day, sadly, Darcy was caught up with his father, an amiable but serious gentleman. The Darcy fortune seemed to be incredibly complicated and hard to master. With so much of it coming from different marriages and stocks in overseas companies, almost the whole of Pemberley was caught up in entail, but there also was the land in Derbyshire that they rented to the peasantry and the income that brought.

Darcy remarked that he had utterly failed, until that point, to estimate his own worth, but he had decided to say it was ten thousand pounds a year, because that was "a nice, round number" and probably not terribly far from the truth. He would stick with that number for years to come, while Bingley, with a tradesman's blood, knew that Darcy was worth far more.

Clearly, becoming the head of such an estate was looming for the young Darcy, and he treasured his free time. They spent many an hour outside, to the point that the cook said she was positively out of different ways to season bird and they ought to shoot something else. Georgiana, barely in her eighth year, ran about, tried to join them, and occasionally invited "Mr. Bingley" to tea parties. Darcy informed him that if he responded positively, he would have to sit on furniture that was too small. Clearly he himself had done it many times. Bingley did say no, but he gave Georgiana enough rides on his back to make up for it.

One morning when Darcy had no standing obligations, they were setting out for a particular creek so Darcy could teach Bingley to fish. Before they could depart, Mrs. Reynolds appeared at the top of the stairs. "Master Fitzwilliam."

"Yes?"

"Mr. Darcy requests your presence in the study immediately."

That hadn't happened before during Bingley's stay. In fact, the look on Darcy's face made it obvious that the severity in her voice was alarming to him. "Bingley, you may wish to go without me."

"But I can't—Oh, forget it." Darcy was already gone in the direction of the study. Bingley managed to avoid the temptation to follow him there and listen through the too-thin door for five whole minutes consumed with furious pacing. After that, he gave in to his instincts, but only because he was busy shooing Georgiana away.

The Darcys—father and son—had voices that could, to some extent, be considered raised, as Darcy retorted, "How could you even accuse me of this? I am insulted just at the implication!"

"What you do in your spare time—"

"I have never, *ever* used my spare time at Pemberley in such a way, and you know it! Have I ever given you reason to think otherwise?"

"I've heard stories about your behavior in college," his father said coldly.

Darcy was quick to answer, "And who told you those stories? Wickham?"

"Whatever you like to be called yourself, you will show him respect and use his proper Christian name!"

"Fine! *George*. He is the person who should be in question here, not me. This is hardly the first time this has happened, and every time, he has been responsible! How many maids have you had to dismiss since he became a man?"

"You will not speak gossip about George in my house!"

"It is not gossip! It is fact! I just cannot see..." There was a pause, and Darcy's voice upon return was considerably calmed and almost upset in a different way. "I cannot see why a man of your wit and intelligence will continuously turn a blind eye to it. To even go as far as to accuse your own son over him!"

"You will not sit in judgment of me!"

He was right, at least on that account. However annoyed (or correct, from the sound of it) Darcy was, he could not call out his father. It was a biblical sin.

After some time, Darcy's voice changed again. "I... am sorry, Father. I reacted strongly to your accusation, and I had no place to do so in front of you. But I stand behind my opinion that George is the father."

"Mr. Wickham—"

"With all due respect, Father, Mr. Wickham was a saint of a man, but he died long ago and his own countenance seems to have little bearing on his son's." He added more desperately, "Why do you not see it? How much evidence must be before your eyes before you open them?"

"Would you like me to use these same harsh eyes to look at you?"

"I've—done nothing wrong! Please, Father!"

There was silence on both ends. Eventually, Mr. Darcy replied gruffly, "Excuse my accusation. Of course, you would have more propriety than that. It must have been one of the other servants. You may go."

This time, Darcy did not contradict him. He stormed out, looking not halfway surprised that Bingley was there.

Their trip to the lake was a strange one, not to be repeated in the same fashion. This time, Darcy took liberties with the bottle of wine that was in one of the baskets, and Bingley learned more about Wickham and less about fishing that afternoon as Darcy ranted on. Bingley and Wickham had only missed each other by a few weeks, it seemed, as Wickham had been in residence at Pemberley when Darcy returned from Cambridge. However, Wickham decided he had had enough of Darcy's "stuck-up attitude" and left. Not, apparently, before impregnating another servant girl.

"And my father!" Darcy said. "I do not—I don't—we don't often misunderstand each other. Please do not let me give you that impression," Darcy said through slurred speech. "I just do not understand it. I do not understand it. He treats Wickham like his own son! He has given him a home, an education, a living—all of which he has wasted away! There wouldn't be an innocent woman working at Pemberley, if he could help it!" He shook his head and took another swig from the bottle. "I just… don't understand it."

Bingley admitted that he did not. Over a decade later, he had a feeling that he did.

His Royal Highness

With the combination of the circumstance, the immense social pressures at work, and the various drinks continuously offered to him, Dr. Maddox knew he needed an escape. Fortunately his wife was thoroughly enjoying talking to the ladies of court, so he slipped out onto a balcony. Only the fresh air kept him from being ill altogether. A servant was there to attend him, but he shooed the fellow away with more anger than he normally would have. Caroline was happy, but that was because she had no idea of the noose that was around their necks, perhaps not even metaphorically. How could he ever tell her? If he were to tell her?

"Lovely evening, isn't it?"

He knew that voice, now from two different places. His intended escape had resulted in the opposite effect—he was trapped on a balcony with the prince himself. He bowed, another threat to his ready stomach, but managed to keep down all of the alcohol he had so foolishly ingested to calm himself. "Your Highness."

The prince didn't return the bow. "My God, man, you look positively spooked. I seem to have that effect on people."

"It's just—I just—I'm not accustomed to being in the presence of royalty—sir—Your Highness."

"But you are," corrected the prince.

"I—I wasn't going to say it," Dr. Maddox said. He wanted to bow again, but he was fairly *sure* he would lose his stomach if he did. Instead he removed his glasses and began to clean them with a handkerchief, even though they were perfectly clean. However, the action removed the distinctness of the world and had almost the same effect of looking away, as if looking directly at the prince would burn his eyes.

"You have a good deal of discretion, Doctor."

"Thank you."

"You really had no idea who I was?"

"I don't—I don't inquire after my patients. Not—not at—well, I'm not going to say it. And it was dark. And I had never seen you before, so... No. I saw a gold ring and you... you overpaid me, but that just meant—you were titled or—or something. I don't know."

"You could have asked someone there."

"I didn't. I don't do that sort of thing." He swallowed. "I'm just a doctor."

"You are a very good one."

"Thank you, sir," he said earnestly, very earnestly. He watched the blur that was the prince walk over to the edge of the balcony, probably facing out, not facing him. "Your Highness."

"So... the stitches. Tuesday?"

"Tuesday would be fine, yes."

"I'll send a courier. Now, I must get back to my party. Good evening, Doctor."

He bowed yet again. "Your Highness."

Somewhere in France, in a tiny, unnamed inn above a tavern, the Darcys had their first peaceful rest in days. Far north and a crossing away, the Bingleys had retired from their many guests and responsibilities with children, and the twins were giving them some peace. But between them, in a townhouse in West London, while Caroline Maddox was being freed from her complex gown and jewelry, her husband was emptying his stomach into a chamber pot by the fire downstairs. It was only after some time that she noticed his absence and appeared before him, a shawl wrapped over her nightgown. "Daniel?"

"I'm fine," he said, his voice weak. The servant had already taken the pot and covered him with a blanket. She sat next to him on the chaise and held a hand to his head.

"You are freezing! Did you catch something at the ball?"

"No. No, no, I was in trouble long before that." He swallowed. "Forgive me. It will pass. I had too much to drink." He put his hand over hers. "Go to bed."

"Look at you—you're shivering and sick, and you send me away? Do balls really bother you that much?"

"No. Just—this one."

"Are you nervous around royalty?"

"Apparently."

She looked at him quizzically, which he pretended not to catch. "Go to bed, darling."

"Only if you come with me. If it's drink, I won't catch it, will

I? Come." She was willing to drag him up, and he waddled up the stairs and was helped into bed. He was so very, very happy to have her. It would be such a shame to lose her, all because of his foolishness.

"I was going to regale you with tales of whom I met, but it seems you are not in the mood," she said. "So I will not torture you. But you will tell me why you made yourself sick."

"I did not make myself sick."

"You are so prodigiously careful with your own health that I can hardly believe anything else," she said.

Damn her, for being so intelligent!

"Who did you meet?"

"Can't tell," he mumbled into his pillow. "My patients need their privacy."

"Are you saying your wife ranks below your patients?"

"I am serious, Caroline."

"So you met one tonight. Who was it?"

"Oh God, please, let us not talk of this. It will only lead to bad things."

"What? A former lover?"

"*What?* No!" He turned over to face her. "Of course not. There is no one in England that—well, you know."

"Does this line of conversation bother you so?"

"Have I not said that? Several times, I think, at this point?"

"Fine, then! If you don't like royal balls, you never have to go to another one! I will go alone if we are invited, and you will never see any of those people again."

He considered and then said, "On the contrary. I have an appointment with the prince on Tuesday. Or, he has appointment with me."

Caroline, who was getting ready for bed, turned over in disbelief. "How did this come about?"

"I spoke to him."

"You—spoke to the prince? *When?*"

"He cornered me on the balcony. About midway through the night, just after I'd met the Earl of Maddox."

"What—what was the prince like?"

He shrugged.

"He requested your services?"

"Yes."

"Why? I mean, not to insult you, dear, but it is not as if he does not have his own royal physicians—"

Something—maybe now that he was in bed and recovering—was making him relaxed enough to say, "I am going to tell you something that you cannot ever—*ever*—tell anyone. I am serious. Not Mrs. Hurst or Mr. Hurst, even if he's unconscious drunk, or Charles or Mrs. Bingley—"

"Daniel, I understand. Out with it."

He smiled. Maybe he was still, despite everything, a little drunk. "He requested me for the removal of five stitches on his breast. A surface wound, really, but it looked bad."

"He asked this of you because—"

"—I put them in," he said. "Earlier this week."

Even with her quick wit, Caroline needed time to process this information. "You treated the Prince of Wales, and you didn't tell me?"

"I didn't know he was the prince at the time."

"Are you daft? How did you *not know?*"

"How was I to know? He was not properly attired, nor did he introduce himself, and I've only seen the prince in newspaper etchings. And the light quality was poor. So, no, I did not know who he was. I just figured he was nobility by the way he talked and the fact that he paid me extravagantly for the small work that I did. Honestly, people get so worked up over such a small amount of blood."

"Daniel," she said in total disbelief. "You are telling me that you treated the prince—"

"—Yes—"

"—And you didn't know who he was."

"I've already clarified why, I believe."

"You've not clarified a thing! Where on earth would you treat His Royal Highness for a cut? Where were his guards? His doctors? His carriage?"

Maddox groaned and straightened his glasses. "Now, this is the part of the story that is both treasonous and will not reflect well on my occupation. So for the initial reason, you cannot tell anyone. Seriously. You promise?"

"God, I promise… yes, already."

"Caroline, I'm serious—"

"I know. And you're only dragging it out now."

She was right, and he knew it. "Fine. I met the man who I learned this very night was the future ruler of England in a house of prostitution. He had been stabbed by his courtesan, who was attempting to renegotiate her price."

Caroline, who was never at a loss for words, stared at him for a full thirty seconds—he counted—until she responded, "That's the worst lie you've ever told me."

"Good that it isn't a lie, then," he said, awaiting the eruption. It came soon enough.

"What *in the hell* were you doing in a—a *house of prostitution?*"

He put a pillow over his head.

"Daniel? Daniel Stewart Maddox, I demand an answer!"

He was so ready for her reaction that he was almost relieved to hear her being angry with him. It was a strange sensation indeed. "I am a doctor, Caroline. More accurately, I am a surgeon as well, and for many years I was in need of money and went wherever I was called without any judgments made. So, because of my habit of discretion, it seems I am, sadly, quite favored by these particular... houses. And they pay me very well, so I go."

"But you've never—"

"Oh God, no. Even if I was a bachelor and I was the type... those women are all horribly diseased. I know because they describe their symptoms to me in great detail every time I pass, hoping for a cure that doesn't exist. But no, the patients I treat are men who've had too much to drink or have had heart attacks or have been stabbed."

"—Which would include the prince."

"As has been established, yes."

"And she thought she was going to get away with it?"

Since her righteous anger seemed now somewhat abated, he removed the pillow. "I suppose she imagined he would not report the incident in the interest of avoiding scandal. So either she was secretly killed, or she is very much alive."

"You did not—ask who he was?"

"No. It is not what I do."

He had a pounding headache from all of it, and he relaxed for a moment as Caroline fell into a contemplative silence, swallowing all of the scandalous and horrible information he'd thrown at her. Finally she said, "So—the invitation—?"

"—Was undoubtedly so he could see me again and judge me to be a discreet man. Which, it seems I was, because he requested my services. That, or he intends to have me killed when I go to him on Tuesday. Either one."

"You realize where this could lead?"

"My head on a spike?"

She turned back to him. "No. A royal commission."

He'd been too panicked to think of that. "It's just stitches. He probably wants me to remove them so that his own surgeon doesn't ask questions."

"Still. It is not beyond the realm of possibility. And a nicer vision than your head removed."

"Most things are."

She fell onto him, giggling. "The prince… in a whorehouse… and I can never tell anyone!"

"No, you cannot. But I suppose, it is a rather juicy tidbit."

"That is putting it mildly," she said. "You are no judge of gossip."

At this, he had to laugh. "A terrible fault indeed."

"The Prince of Wales! In a Bawdy house!"

"And stabbed by the very doxy who was with him!"

"And you did not recognize him!"

"Did I mention he was drunk, too?"

Caroline laughed into his shoulder. It was a wonderful feeling.

"Well, if he does have me jumped and quartered, at least I will die knowing we laughed about it the week before."

As expediency was key, the Darcys—all three of them—did not sit idle at the inn but began the long road south. There were places, they quickly discovered, where the spring showers had made the road so muddy that the wagon barely went faster than a man. At those places, Grégoire got out and walked alongside the path, soaking most of his robe but stubbornly refusing to return to the carriage.

"He's as bad as you are," Elizabeth said with a grin that Darcy tried hard to ignore.

At last the carriage came to a stop entirely, the wheels stuck in mud. Grégoire assured Darcy that they were approaching a drier region, but Darcy remained displeased. Elizabeth had her own concerns, but she held them back, focusing instead on Grégoire, standing alone on the hillside overlooking the valley. When she approached, he put his cowl over his head.

"Come now," she said. "I am your sister-in-law. And I'm a mess from traveling—hardly a vision of loveliness."

After a moment he relented and pulled back his hood. Elizabeth couldn't help but notice this was their first moment alone together, as Darcy was on the other side of the carriage, yelling at the teamster in his broken French. Despite the physical resemblance between the brothers, Grégoire was all humility, his gaze often averted, his posture uncomfortable. Or no, maybe he was the same as Darcy, she thought, but without the stout English upbringing. Darcy was uncomfortable around people, despite his attempts to hide it (which quite often made it more obvious), but Grégoire made no such attempts. Whether that was due to the modesty of a monk or the general Darcy lineage was impossible to discern. So she looked out at the countryside, which was quite beautiful, and not at him, which seemed to put him at ease, as he could do the same.

"So," she said at last, "you are named after your father."

Grégoire, after all, was the French translation of Gregory, unmistakably similar to Geoffrey.

"Yes," he said. "I believe that was his intention, to name all his sons so, but he was obligated to do otherwise with Monsieur Darcy."

"Yes, Darcy is named after the Fitzwilliam family," she said. "He has a cousin named Colonel Fitzwilliam. That would have led to some confusion if Darcy hadn't shunned his baptismal name." She held back a laugh. "There's a long, silly story behind it. No actual animosity. He and Colonel Fitzwilliam are great friends as well as cousins."

"I thought it might be a custom, as you are calling him Darcy and he insists I call him that," Grégoire said. "I am not familiar with English customs. I only know that Father managed to name two of his sons similarly."

Elizabeth shook her head. "You are mistaken. You are thinking of his—your—sister, Georgiana."

"No, Father said he had three sons." He turned, actually looked at her after the silence, and noticed her shock. "Have mercy on me. I assumed you were aware."

"You are sure?"

"That is what I remember. Though, I was a child, so my memory may not be clear. But—he did say his wife named Georgiana after him, out of spite."

She did not want to imagine what had occurred in the private chambers of Darcy's parents when Mr. Darcy's liaisons had come out with obvious evidence and exceptionally bad timing. Elizabeth could only think of one person who bore a similar name to Georgiana, someone whom Mr. Darcy had kept close, provided for, and left a living for… "Do not tell Darcy!"

"I am sorry—have I slandered Father?"

"No—no, he has done quite enough of that himself," she said. "But—if it is—oh, God." Had two brothers married two sisters? "Do not tell him. Please, I beg of you. Not yet, if he is ever to know at all."

"I apologize if our existence is so disconcerting—"

"No, no, it is not you, though that was a bit of a shock, but you…" she struggled to find her words, too busy with the gravity of his own, however unknown. "You are blameless. I cannot think of a man who has led a more blameless life."

"I am a poor sinner like any man."

"Not like this!" she said, unintentionally raising her voice and making sure that Darcy had not returned his attention to them. Surely he would, soon enough, now that the wagon was almost free. "I will explain it all, but please promise me you will not say a word!"

She grabbed his arms as she said this and almost shook him, and in such a stunned state as he was when she did this, he could only answer, "I promise."

"Thank you." With that, she ran off, leaving a stunned monk, and fell into Darcy's arms.

"Lizzy? Lizzy, what's wrong?" he begged. When she refused to answer, he gave a cold look to Grégoire, who shrugged unconvincingly. "What did he say to you, Lizzy?"

"Nothing. It is nothing. It was not what he said," she said, wiping away tears. "I will tell you at a more appropriate time."

"Of course," he said, helping her back into the ready carriage, but not before a stern glance at his half-brother.

She wondered, however, if there would ever be an appropriate time.

Chapter 11

APPOINTMENT WITH A DOCTOR

Dr. Maddox spent Monday mainly in fittings for the proper attire of a royal servant. The haberdasher offered to trim back his hair so that the wig would fit properly. He had to put up a considerable resistance before the man relented and managed to get a wig to fit over his bushy bangs.

His reward, he supposed, was having Caroline see him the next morning in full dress on the way to the palace. She apparently had none of his fears, or if she did, she hid them well. She was the ambitious side of the marriage, and that suited him just fine, because it took some pressure off him. "Don't be nervous. It's not as if you haven't seen him before."

"Twice now." But his hands would not stop shaking.

"He must like you."

"He will not like having stitches removed. That I cannot promise will endear me to him."

"You worry too much," she said, and kissed him on the cheek. "You're the best surgeon in Britain."

"A mild exaggeration," he said. "I love you."

"You sound so positively grave when you say it like that," she replied, and saw him off. His trip was relatively short, but he had to be led through the monstrous grounds of Carlton House, his black bag signifying his identity as yet another anonymous servant of the crown. No one paid him any heed or even inquired as to his name. He was merely made to sit and wait for some time on what was undoubtedly the most expensive chair he had ever sat on in his life. He was called and brought into what seemed to be the dressing chambers of the prince, who was dressed but for his ornamentals and his waistcoat.

"Your Highness."

"Doctor," the prince replied, without the same formality. "I suppose we should get this bloody business over with."

"As you wish, Your Highness." He gave his normal instructions for clean water and soap to be brought for him, and began unpacking his bag as the prince undressed, looking more like the person he had first encountered and not the grand host of a royal ball (and future ruler of England). But Dr. Maddox was a surgeon with a surgical task at hand, because no good doctor in England would touch their patients, out of propriety, much less operate on them. In these motions, he was comfortable, as he rolled up his considerable sleeves and washed his hands.

"I had a surgeon, once who did not believe in soap," said the prince, now sitting on a chair with his cravat removed and his shirt open.

"Not all soap is beneficial. You can usually tell its inherent qualities by the smell, unless it has been disguised by being mixed with spices and is not, in fact, soap."

"You are familiar with this?"

"I believe in cleanliness, yes." He turned his attention to the wound, removing his glasses and hanging them on his breast pocket to do so. "It has healed very well. I would recommend removing the stitches now."

"Another one used gloves instead of his bare hands."

"That I cannot recommend, unless they were new gloves," Maddox said, removing his tools from the kit. "Leather gloves are not washed, so they are exceptionally good carriers of disease." He pulled up a stool beside the prince. "This is going to be a bit uncomfortable. My apologies, Your Highness."

"At least the first time around, I was soused. I can hardly remember it."

"Putting them in is a much different experience," Maddox said, peering close to locate the first knot and then cutting it with scissors. "Excuse my closeness. I am nearsighted."

"I know," said the prince, who grunted as Maddox began to slowly weed out the snipped wire, which was similar to fishing line. "Your eyesight began to decline in your teenage years, did it not?"

"That is true," he said.

"How long before you lose it?"

The question would be outright rude from anyone else, especially from a sober patient. But this was the prince. He could say whatever he pleased, and apparently he did. "I hope very much to see my children go out."

"Yes, congratulations are in order for your wife."

Dr. Maddox was an experienced enough doctor to be able to maintain his work when he wanted desperately to pause. "You have done your research very well."

"Not me, my intelligence, of course. It's easier for them

when I hand them the card. They had practically everything on you by—ow—morning light."

"Apologies."

"No, it's my own poor countenance." There was a bit of blood from the hole where the lacing had been removed. Maddox wiped it away with a towel. "Your brother, they did not find."

"My goodness. Is he being sought after by the Crown?"

"No, just the local authorities. Still, do you know where he is?"

"No," he said, and pulled out another snipped cord.

"You are willing to lie to the Prince of Wales?" the prince scoffed, but in a playful manner.

Dr. Maddox, in his serious doctor mode, was not as playful. He was neutral, until his given task was completed. "I am willing to go through considerable lengths for the man who raised me and paid for my education."

"And ruined you, apparently."

"Gambling is a vice that has destroyed the best of men," was Maddox's quiet reply.

"But you are very well educated. Cambridge, Paris, Rome, and all the right licenses from the Royal College. You would be a fine doctor if you were not a surgeon."

"Then I would not be much good to my patients, if I was of too high a class to treat them," Maddox said before he realized that perhaps social commentary in front of the future king of England was perhaps not the best of ideas.

The prince managed to laugh though it was subdued by the experience of the stitches, no matter how carefully Maddox took them apart. "I will make no complaints about your patient list.

Though, it would not be suitable for a royal doctor and surgeon to be visiting whorehouses. Unless, of course, I was there."

Dr. Maddox stopped.

The prince just continued, "This would require, of course, a considerable shortening of your patient list, and you would have to be on the University's medical board. That could be arranged, though it might require you to attend a lecture or two. But I suppose that with your level of scholarship, you are not adverse to the idea of being invited to lectures? Especially if you were a paid guest?"

Maddox stammered, "No, Your Highness." He needed to focus. He still had a task before him—the removal of the last two stitches and then the stopping of the small trickle of blood and the bandaging of the wound. Fortunately the flesh had healed nicely and was free of infection.

"It would tie you to Town rather strictly. I know your wife has a brother in Derbyshire who is related in marriage to the Darcys of Pemberley and that crowd, but for the most part, you would be required to remain in the general—ugh—vicinity. Was that the last one?"

"Yes, Your Highness," he said, pressing the towel against the wound. "Please press down until I say to stop." He set his pocket watch next to the bowl and washed his hands again.

"Thank God for that. How long is this to be?"

"About three minutes. Time for the blood to clot," he explained. "A very simple procedure. Avoiding infection is really the most difficult thing." He turned back to the prince.

"You haven't said anything about my offer."

"It—I am working, Your Highness, and your immediate health is my first concern," he said, too shy to admit he was shocked by the forwardness of the offer. Caroline had suggested it multiple times over the weekend as a possibility, but just because he had removed some stitches? Did he want to be tied to the royal service? He would finally be able to provide for Caroline properly, not using up his savings as he currently was. It was the ideal position. "There. Let me see it, if you would."

The prince removed the towel, and no blood came up. Maddox took a very careful look, checked the cloth for anything other than blood, and then pronounced him relatively healed. All that was required was a quick bandage to keep any possible blood from staining the prince's shirt, and he was done.

"Will it leave a scar?"

"A very small one," Dr. Maddox said, repackaging his bag. "In response to your offer… I don't know quite what to say." He replaced his glasses and this time looked more generally at the prince, who was straightening his shirt.

"Most men would jump at that offer for the reasons that I have already given."

"This is true. I do not say it is not enticing. But I cannot, in good faith, refuse a patient I have been treating for some time. I can shorten my list and stop visiting those houses, but I still have those I treat who are perhaps not proper patients of a royal physician."

"And for that, you would give up a lifetime of financial security and probable knighthood at the end of it, if you didn't accidentally kill me with some prescription?"

Dr. Maddox considered it. "I suppose I would. How very foolish of me."

"Or how very noble of you. Well, my offer stands, Doctor.

Whatever your patient list may be. Infect me with cholera, though, and there will be severe ramifications."

"Of course." He collected his things and was getting ready to bow when he realized the prince was offering his hand. To shake. He was shaking hands with the Prince of Wales. He was touching him in a nonsurgical way. "Then... we are agreed."

"I will have the papers drawn up, and if they are to your liking, you may consider yourself a royal doctor, Dr. Maddox," said the prince. "My father wants his staff treating me, of course, but as his staff can't treat *him*, I'm eager to find my own."

"I am honored, Your Highness." This time, he did get his chance to bow.

The most direct route was not a terrific one to travel, especially with the state of the roads that had endured decades of revolution and government mismanagement. The Darcys spent many a night in a roadside inn, the two of them on a bed that barely fit one person, much less them both. That was the only part of the accommodations that seemed to bother neither of them. Neither did they complain about the food, which was fantastic.

Grégoire did not break bread with them during the day, instead maintaining the rule of contemplative silence during his meal, which was rarely more than bread and plain cooked meat. He joined them separately for their dinner, because then he could talk, and they quickly discovered he was most convenient for sniffing out—literally—wines. That was, after all, his main occupation at the monastery, even if he didn't partake of wine himself, except when there was nothing else to drink. He put his very discriminating nose in many a glass before they found the best wine in the tavern, and Elizabeth and Darcy tasted the finest vintages of their lives.

One night, Darcy indulged himself in an extra glass beyond his norm, and they retired early. In their tiny room, in whatever nameless travelers' inn, Darcy sat before the fire, not drunk but with his eyes red and his mood more at ease than it had been since their trip to the old d'Arcy estate.

"Darcy," Elizabeth said, taking his hand, which was warm and inviting. "There is something I would be remiss if I did not discuss, but I fear it will not be something you want to hear."

He waved off her concern with look that he gave people when he wanted them to keep talking.

"Grégoire said something to me in innocence, not knowing the ramifications. And his memory may not be perfect, please keep in mind–"

His mind seemed to click on. "What is it, Lizzy?"

"He said that you—the two of you—are not your father's only sons."

At this, Darcy began to smolder quietly. She knew this. She had expected it, but she had yet to see him in a better mood, so she decided to chance it. She detested keeping secrets from him, especially secrets he had every right to know.

Hiding his emotions, Darcy replied quietly, "And he chose to tell you over me?"

"It was by happenstance. He assumed you knew."

"How would I know? I am only just discovering this."

"Because—Darcy, because you know your other brother. Because Georgiana is named after him, and because he, too, received a generous living from Mr. Darcy while he was alive and was left one after his father's death."

Not working at full speed, Darcy's mind had to turn over the various possibilities before saying, "Impossible."

"That Grégoire said so, or that it could be?"

"It is impossible," he said with more force. "You will recall, there was a Mrs. Wickham, married to a Mr. Wickham until the day she died, giving birth to George."

"And your father kept a picture of her in his dresser in Hôtel des Capuchins. Along with a picture of young Wickham."

"Mr. Wickham did often travel with my father. Some of those things could have been his."

"I am not saying it is true. I am only saying that, considering the evidence, it is perhaps possible—"

"Evidence!" Darcy said, raising his voice slowly as did his body from the chair. "What evidence is presented before me? The accusations of a mere boy of a man, who must have heard it from my father years ago, when he was but ten?" He did not bother to hide his anger, as it was not really directed towards Elizabeth. "I will not accept such slander!"

"Darcy—"

He was already storming out of their room and down the hall, where he found his half brother in his room with his items spread out on the floor beside the unused bed, preparing himself for evening prayers. "Monsieur Darcy—"

Grégoire was no match for Darcy. He had age, but not strength or intent. He was nothing to Darcy, full of rage and an accomplished sportsman, who grabbed him by his holy robes and hurled him against the wall. "Did you say this lie to Elizabeth? Did you slander our father further?"

"I—I cannot—"

"Darcy, don't!" Elizabeth shouted, trying to pull them apart, although she was altogether unsuccessful. "Listen to me. I made him promise not to say a word. I wanted to tell you. I thought you would accept it better if you heard it from me."

"That does not free of him of my questioning!" Darcy shouted. "Do you believe my father told you that George Wickham was also his son?"

"Yes," Grégoire said meekly.

"Why would he say such a thing?"

"I—I do not presume to be in the mind of my—our—father," he said, gasping for air, as Darcy was pressing on his neck, unintentionally strangling him.

"Darcy!" Elizabeth said in her sternest voice. "Release him! He is not at fault here!"

Darcy looked at her coldly.

"Mr. Darcy," she said, returning the glance with equal fervor. "Please do unhand my brother-in-law."

He hesitated, but at least he did release Grégoire, who dropped to the ground with a thud and had to be helped up by Elizabeth. "I did not mean to speak ill of anyone, Monsieur Darcy. I thought it was common knowledge."

"What—exactly—did Father say to you?"

"I was inquiring as to my family, and he said he had a proper heir, which is you, Monsieur, and a young daughter and another son he raised as well, but his identity kept secret, for the scandal and not to hurt his steward's pride during his waning years. So, four of us, and he was named George, after his supposed father."

"And Mother knew of this? My mother?"

"I know little of her, but apparently she did, because she insisted on naming Georgiana such in spite."

It was too much. Elizabeth saw it on Darcy's face. As much as he had come to have some attachment to Grégoire, perhaps now severed, he could not begin to fathom accepting George Wickham as a brother. And Georgiana—perhaps it was having a monk in the room, but Elizabeth could not help but think that God Himself must have intervened to prevent that elopement from coming to be. How close, unknowingly, the entire family had come to terrible danger. She looked to Darcy with a look that she couldn't help but have be a piteous one, and he sighed and stepped out without a word. "Darcy!"

But he did not return the call. She did not find him in their room or downstairs in the tavern. The front door was open, and he was gone.

THE LONGEST NIGHT

DARCY DID NOT REAPPEAR until mid-morning. Elizabeth had finally fallen asleep after trying to stay up, and then, too exhausted from sobbing, had allowed herself to crawl into bed. When she closed her eyes, Grégoire was still standing vigil, but when she opened them, her husband was sitting on the bed next to her. She wanted to wrap her arms around him, and for him to do the same, but he just sat there, as if in a daze, his clothing from the day before thoroughly soaked in the morning dew and the mud from the road. Had he spent the whole night walking?

"Darcy."

He took off his waistcoat and boots, which was a considerable process, before silently climbing into bed next to her. His body alone was a comfort, the way he slid his fingers along her side before collapsing on his pillow. Clearly, he had not slept at all. She thought he might go right to sleep and continue her torment, but instead he spoke.

"I cannot do it."

She turned over so she was facing him. She wanted to feel

his breath, know he was alive and breathing, and smell his scent. They had been separated before, when he was on an errand or such, but never had she been so bothered by the absence of his physical person. "I did not ask you to," she said softly.

"I cannot accept him. Or these actions of my father, truth or lies. It is too much."

She took his hand, and he returned the grip, even tightening it in seeking her comfort as much as she sought his. "I will not ask you to. We can never speak of it again, if you wish."

"I tried—all night. It was not until the sun was rising that I realized how late it was and how far I had wandered. I cannot turn it over in my head and make it fit. On a logical level, yes. But the mind is not very logical."

"No, it is not."

"Wickham could not know. He would have pressed that advantage long ago." He sighed. "I have decided that perhaps my father was not perfect in everything he did in his life. We have enough proof of that in the next room. But this is different. I am not prepared for it. Lizzy, I cannot bear the thought."

"I hardly can fathom it, either," she said. "But that is life, and men—and perhaps, sometimes, women—err in their ways."

"You are too good a woman for Pemberley," he said, and kissed her knuckles. "I do not deserve you."

"You are not your father's son in every respect, Darcy. Don't take this burden on yourself."

"It seems I must," he sighed, turning onto his back. "But… when we return to England. For now, let us let the matter rest and talk no more of Wickham. Agreed?"

"Happily agreed," she said, kissing him on the cheek.

One other person had Wickham on his mind. Charles Bingley sat in his office at Chatton, the papers on his desk untouched. Idly he glanced out the window, where Geoffrey and Georgie were playing with Darcy's dogs, also in his care. His contemplation was only broken by a servant's entrance. "Mr. Bennet, sir."

"Of course. And have my son brought in."

The servant nodded, and Mr. Bennet appeared. Bingley rose to greet his father-in-law, who merely nodded and went to the window. Mr. Bennet had calmed considerably since the Darcys were on their way, but he had not settled into the library as he usually had during his visits to Chatton or Pemberley. He was not at ease, and there was no wonder in that, but Bingley could think of nothing to say to him that would be further comfort. What he could do, however, was provide him with his grandchildren, for whom Mr. Bennet had obvious affection.

Fortunately little Charles Bingley the Third appeared with Nurse and was handed to his father. "Please, Mr Bennet, do have a seat."

"In a moment," Mr. Bennet said. He did lean over and kiss little Charles on his blond head. Then he returned to the window, leaning one arm on it and watching his other grandchildren. "I was always a bit partial to daughters, myself. Perhaps that is why I had so many of them." He looked over. "What in the world are you reading?"

"These are some papers I've collected on the Hindi language."

"Hindi?"

"The language of the Indians. I'm learning it," Bingley said.

"I'll be sure to send Kitty to India for her studies, then," Mr.

Bennet said. So he had not lost all of his humor after all. "And don't you dare go taking my Jane to India. I have my own concerns, of course, but I would have to listen to my wife's ranting about diseases and danger for the entire duration of your travels. Though I am thoroughly accustomed to such things, so I suppose it would not be so bad. Still, my request stands."

"With three young children, you can hardly expect me to go venturing across the world, Mr. Bennet."

"My sons are always surprising me," he replied. "As are my daughters. I will say that I am certainly not bored in my old age. I have that much to be grateful for, but I do not feel very grateful."

"'These things, too, shall pass,'" Bingley quoted, though he did not know from where. In response, his son babbled in his arms.

Mr. Bennet paused before sighing and saying, "I do hope you will do a better job of raising your children than I did. Certainly, I have great faith that you will."

"I must disagree with you in the first respect, Mr. Bennet," Bingley said. "I have no complaints of any of your daughters, certainly. In fact, I am especially fond of at least two of them. And *exceedingly* fond of one."

Mr. Bennet did crack a smile, but his mood would not be stirred. "I am serious, sadly. I was—I suppose, too fond of my daughters in a certain way. I did not want to see them go. I put them out as early as possible because they wanted to go out. I did not take them to Town or go with them to public balls, where the gentlemen would have been plenty. I was not stern enough with some of them about their behavior, because I could deny them nothing, except perhaps a suitable dowry. I left it all to poor Mrs. Bennet, who became a mess because of the stress,

because I could not give her sons. That two daughters managed fine marriages beyond all expectations I can assign only
to happenstance."

"I would not agree, again, sir," Bingley said, more insis-
tent this time. "Jane and Elizabeth are your daughters in every
respect. Mary is exceedingly intelligent and was only foolish
once in her entire life, and there is much hope for Kitty. Mrs.
Wickham was a victim of circumstance."

But this pill seemed too large for Mr. Bennet to swallow, at
least for the moment. "I think of Lydia every day and wonder
how she is doing. Perhaps I may request that you *do* invite her
to Chatton, even if that brings Mr. Wickham as well? Perhaps
marriage has softened him... who knows. But I confess a desire
to see them together."

"Done," Bingley answered without hesitation. "Allow me
the time to compose the letter, and they are invited." He added,
"Oh, and please also allow me to consult with my wife, as she is
the more sensible one of us."

Finally Mr. Bennet laughed. "I think you will do well enough
in this life, Son."

When they rose from their delayed rest, Elizabeth was quick
to remind her husband that he owed someone a significant apology. Darcy found he could not disagree, and with his temper
thoroughly cooled, he sought Grégoire and found him kneeling
on the floor of his room. "Excuse me."

"Monsieur," Grégoire said, rising and closing his prayer
book. His bed was unused.

"I do hope I'm at the point beyond being Monsieur Darcy,"

Darcy replied. "I've come to apologize for my unsuitable behavior last night. My fury was designed for someone else." He bowed. "I hope you will forgive me."

"It is not for me to judge any man," said Grégoire, "but if it gives you peace, I do offer forgiveness on my own part."

"Thank you. And, as a gentleman, I am obliged to fully explain myself and my actions. It is a rather long story and a terrible reflection on our family, but you must hear it. Have you eaten?"

"No, I have been fasting."

Darcy decided it was best to not inquire as to why. "Then come. I've not had a thing since last night myself, and we will break the fast together."

Darcy put his arm around him, and Grégoire winced. Maybe he had shoved Grégoire up against that wall a bit too hard. They entered the inn together, now late in the afternoon, and took seats in the back corner. Slowly and carefully, Darcy told Grégoire the story of his youth, his experiences with Wickham, the attempted elopement, and the scandal with Lydia Wickham (née Bennet). Darcy told the tale with what he hoped was a calm voice, even lacking in emotion, and ended with the last time he had seen the person in question. On that day, he had had no desire to see him again, and now he still could barely bring himself to think of it. "Now tell me, please, if our father mentioned any other children to you, so that there may be no more awful surprises."

"None." During the entire tale, Grégoire had said nothing, his face all concentration, but looking down and not at Darcy. The Darcys had noticed the monk was often even afraid to look people in the eye. "None that he mentioned, and I do not believe he was holding back," Grégoire said.

"Then we must conjecture he had only four children, two known, and he must have told Mrs. Reynolds about the other two before his death. This, sadly, did not prevent Wickham's courting of Georgiana, as it was done in secret from all of us, including the one person who would have put a definite stop to it beyond myself. I am so rarely abroad; perhaps that explains why she now directed me to you, without saying it outright."

"I would have stayed hidden to not bring this shame on the family," Grégoire said.

That was a very Darcy family thing to say, Darcy had to admit to himself. "The Darcy family has taken a few blows over the years, as has every good and proper family, and none of this was our doing, so we have nothing to be regretful for." He said it for Grégoire's sake, as the poor boy obviously tortured himself with the very idea.

He himself had a ton of regrets, most of them involving not seeing the obvious earlier. He had grown up with Wickham, himself remarking that his father had treated him "as his own son." But he was blind to the possibility because his father, Mr. Geoffrey Darcy, was a proper gentleman in all manners. Or so Darcy had thought. But that was the problem, not this young man, who was so thrown out of his only element. "But, if you would, no more of Wickham. I—we, if you agree to return with me and see Pemberley—will deal with it upon my return. At the moment, there are more pressing matters."

"Of course," Grégoire nodded, and returned to his food.

<hr />

Bingley found Jane sitting in the drawing room, reading a letter. "Darling," she said, as he joined her on the couch. With no relatives in evidence, he sat next to her and kissed her on the cheek. "I've received a letter from Lizzy."

"Is it private?"

"No. They've not had much time to write, so she wrote it for both of them. It is for you as well, and it just arrived."

"Give me the summary. I will read it in full later."

"They are traveling to Paris to speak with the headmistress of Mary's seminary and to make sure they are not missing Mr. Mastai by going all the way down to Italy. They have hired a translator—a monk from Mont Claire. They are utterly exhausted, so the whole of it is quite brief, for Lizzy. They should be in Paris by the week's end, but the roads are very muddy and unpredictable. Beyond that, there is nothing else of major import." She handed it to him, and he tucked it into his waistcoat. "They will probably have to go all the way to Italy, will they not?"

"It is most likely. But Italy is a lovely country, and if they have good weather, they may have a pleasant trip back, after running themselves ragged getting there."

"Perhaps." Jane seemed to take comfort in the idea that the trip was good for her sister, so he said it often. "The other mail has arrived, but it has not been sent to your study yet, as I intercepted it when I saw my sister's handwriting. It is there," she gestured towards a pile on the table.

Bingley got up and sifted through the mail, retrieving a letter with a return from the Maddox townhouse and in his sister's handwriting. "From Caroline. Probably about the ball, though I don't know what she'd wish to tell me." He broke the seal and sat back down next to his wife, who leaned on his side as he read it. "My goodness."

"What is it?"

"It seems the good doctor has received an offer from the Prince of Wales to become part of the staff of royal physicians! Apparently he is better known than he esteems himself to be."

"How wonderful! But has he accepted?"

"He would be a fool not to," Bingley said, still reading. "He is still debating it, as it would tie him to Town. Caroline derides him for being foolish about it for a while here. Something about patient lists. But she says she will talk to him and he will eventually accept, which means he undoubtedly will."

"Your sister seems to have a certain—effect on him."

"What wife does not?" he said, patting her on the knee. "Though it is true that it would tie him to the Crown, and Caroline probably would have to have her confinement in Town. Which, considering Mary's confinement is but a month off hers, would be ill timed. But in the long run, it would be an exceptionally good position for him." He set the letter aside. "I will write a congratulations to them. But first, what I came to see you about."

"Pray?"

"Our proposed guest. Your father has requested it."

"He has? He has nothing but contempt for Wickham."

Bingley shrugged. "But Wickham is still his son-in-law and Lydia still his daughter, and Mr. Bennet is concerned for her. He so rarely gets to see her, and this is the only time I can think of that we could easily invite him to Chatton without having to make sure Darcy isn't outside of Derbyshire."

"What you do with your own estate is your business, Charles."

"Still, I have not been rushing to have him at my table. But you would agree that this may be an acceptable arrangement?"

Jane hesitated before answering. "If my father has requested to see Wickham, then I see no reason not to honor his request."

"Then we are agreed. I will write up the invitation in due haste." He rose to do so. "Though, if things do go ill… well, we don't have Darcy to punch him, and I'm rather terrible at it, so we ought to have a servant picked out ahead of time. One of the burlier ones. Maybe the under-gardener. Wallace is rather large. Seems like he could do the job."

"Charles!" Jane's voice was half-indignant, half-laughing.

"See? Darcy is not the only one in this family who can think up clever plans," he said with a smile before leaving his wife to her laughter.

With a relative calm reached and the most disturbing matter set aside, the Darcys were on the road again, and though much was unspoken between them, Grégoire became more at ease with them every day and they with him, odd habits as he had. They decided to push hard for Paris and rest there, because finding all the right people in such a massive city would take some time, and Darcy expressed a great desire for "proper lodgings." Elizabeth admitted to being a bit sick of the inside of their carriage as well. She had exhausted the collection of books that Darcy had purchased once they were over the Channel, and English books were impossible to come by in such remote areas. Grégoire had only a Book of Hours in Latin, but if she found a French book to her liking, he offered to read it to her, translating as he went.

She had yet to take him up on the noble offer when they found themselves stuck again, not twenty miles from the outskirts of Paris, by intolerable mud. When they were not stopped entirely, the carriage moved so slowly that Grégoire took to walking alongside the road and had no trouble keeping up with them. Their only consolation was that they were heading into a drier season and region, and this was merely a literal bump in the road.

They had, theoretically, an opening of three months to get to Italy, allowing the same to return before Mary delivered, if she did deliver at all. (This Darcy did not mention to Elizabeth and asked Grégoire not to, but he did explain the circumstances. The look he got from the monk regarding Mary's "condition" was blank enough that Darcy wondered if the poor boy knew the facts of life at all.)

They still were beyond any sight of Paris when, after a long silence during which Darcy could easily have fallen asleep if not for all of the bumping up and down, he was wrestled into full consciousness by his wife. "Darcy!" She pointed to the window.

On the grass beside the road, Grégoire was staggering, and right before their eyes, he fainted. The carriage came to an immediate stop before Darcy could attempt to give the order, and he climbed out and ran to his brother, who was lying on his side, his color gone and his breathing unsteady.

"Grégoire?" Darcy said, and then yelled at the coachman. "Get a doctor. Doctor! Uhm, *le docteur!*" He turned to his wife. "Elizabeth, please. If he's sick, let you not catch it." This seemed to stay her some distance away, and he turned his attentions back to Grégoire, whose eyes were half-opened. "Can you speak? What is wrong?"

But the monk was in too much pain to speak. That much, Darcy was able to discern when he saw the blood on the monk's back, soaking through those his grey robes.

PROPER DISCIPLINE

PARIS WAS PUT ASIDE as the coachman helped Darcy carry his brother into the coach, but not before Darcy removed his waistcoat and put it over him. Grégoire was only half-conscious and shivering, and all they could do before hurrying to an inn was to make him drink. He regained some color, but not much.

Darcy carried his brother into the shabby inn and placed him on a proper bed, removing his cowl and calling for a doctor using a dictionary he had purchased along the way. He did his best to keep the sight of blood from Elizabeth. He did not want this for her, for so many reasons, and sent her instead to gather proper food and drink for them all. At last a doctor arrived, or someone who seemed like a doctor and had a nearly unpronounceable name that Darcy didn't bother to catch. The doctor went inside and shut the door, leaving Darcy to pace outside. The wait was very short, and the doctor reemerged, Darcy demanded an assessment.

"Well," said the doctor in his broken English. "He is a monk."

"He is."

"Then you cannot expect a flagellant of his physical strength to walk the half of France. It is asking too much."

"I did not ask him to walk," Darcy replied too quickly, before he had swallowed the accented words. "You said—he did this to himself?"

"*Oui*, Monsieur."

"What—what purpose could this possibly serve? What great sin has he committed?"

The doctor shrugged. "My—limited understanding is that it is to remind oneself of the wounds of Christ our Lord, who was, of course—"

"Yes, I know!" he interrupted. "But..." He realized there was no use arguing with the doctor over this. "You have some ointment for his wounds?"

"*Oui*, but he will not take it. Let him rest, Monsieur."

He's as stubborn as... he was tempted to think, *a Darcy.* "I will take the ointment. Thank you for your services, Doctor."

The doctor nodded and handed over the jar with a contemptuous look at this rich Englishman who did not seem to understand the most basic concepts. Darcy ignored the look entirely and went straight into Grégoire's room without knocking.

The monk was on the shabby cot, back in his soiled robes but without the hood, sitting up in prayer. Perhaps lying down was too painful. Grégoire looked up and seemed horrified by Darcy's intrusion, a look of shame upon his face, perhaps because he had been discovered.

"The doctor says you should be resting."

"I am resting."

"Perhaps my understanding of your local culture is lax, but usually resting refers to lying down and sleeping." But Darcy

154

could not remain full of indignation for long as he looked at the pale, shuddering frame of the poor man he'd driven into exhaustion, however unknowingly. "Look at you. What have you done that deserves such great penance?"

On this, Grégoire was silent.

Darcy took a seat on the cot next to him. "I will not ask you to explain your illness. I know you would not expect me, as an Englishman or a heretic, to understand."

"I never said you were a heretic."

"But I do go to church on Sundays and listen to a sermon in English and perhaps a reading from the Bible in the vernacular. Surely that in of itself dooms me to hell?"

"I am not one to presuppose who is destined for hell, Darcy."

"But surely you consider yourself among the damned, else you would not engage in such penance."

"I certainly hope not. But I am weak, and the Discipline is a means of fortification."

"As we witnessed today, I would say that the two are in fact interconnected, but not in the same way." Darcy leaned over, so he was properly looking Grégoire in the eyes. "Let me be understood, Brother. If you intend drive yourself in such a manner on this journey, then I will take you no further. I will send you back to your monastery, where you can injure yourself in peace and not have the stress of the roads to put your very life in danger." He added, "I would be sorry to do it, as I doubt we would see each other again. But nonetheless, do I make myself perfectly, utterly clear?"

"I cannot disobey my abbot."

"And I cannot disobey my conscience. So we are at a standstill."

"So we are."

There was silence once more.

"If you would," Darcy said, "remove your robe."

"What?"

"If you will not take medicine from the doctor, then you must at least take it from your brother, who himself is quite ill at the idea of seeing you in such a condition. There, have *that* on your conscience. Now, pull up your robe."

Grégoire did what he was told with a grunt of pain, exposing a wounded back of raw, broken flesh. There were scars as well, running down his back, from older wounds… It made Darcy sick, but nonetheless he poured some ointment from the jar onto his hand and began to apply it to the boy's back. "There. Does that feel better?"

"It is—cooling." Though uncomfortable with the concept, after some time, Grégoire did look relieved, if not totally out of pain. Darcy wished for some of Maddox's miracle drug, if only to help him sleep. "Thank you, Darcy."

"I would offer my services again, but I never wish to do this again," Darcy said, rising. "Now get some *real* rest. For all of us." He waited, with arms crossed, for Grégoire to lie down before leaving and seating himself on the bench outside the room. Now *he* felt exhausted, if only from the stress of facing the unfathomable. What century was his brother living in?

"Darcy," came his wife's voice, obviously concerned about his awkward position of tension on the bench. "How is he?"

"Recovering," he said, finally taking his head out of his hands as she sat down next to him.

"Does the doctor have an explanation, or was he merely overexhausted? He has not been eating much."

"No." He did not clarify what part of her question he was answering. "Lizzy, he is a monk. From a very strict order."

"This I know."

Whatever annoyance she had at his reluctance to reveal the details was tempered by his unease, so she put her hand over his, even though it was so much smaller, and leaned on him. He usually went through great measures to hide his unease, and she always saw through them anyway, which at times could be very convenient, because her touch did something to settle him. "He is… a flagellant." He hoped he would not have to explain that. Elizabeth was well read. She was so good at surprising him with knowing of the existence of improper things.

She needed time to dredge up whatever memories she had of the meaning of this word. It was a moment before she answered, "They are *still around?*"

"It seems we are very far from England. And the Reformation."

"So that would explain—"

"—his exhaustion and collapse, yes. Apparently from pain."

"And the blood on his robes."

"I did not mean for you to see that."

"Which is probably precisely why I saw it."

He somehow managed to crack a smile.

There was another contemplative silence before she continued, "What are we to do?"

"I have already spoken to him about it. Perhaps not in the most… understanding of fashions, but still. We are not medieval. I told him, quite honestly, that if this was to continue, obviously to the point where he would permanently injure or kill himself on some kind of religious obligation, then I would take him no further and find another translator with less masochistic tendencies," he said. "I also added that I would regret doing so, as I would probably never see him again, if he returns to Mont Claire."

"So you do not wish him gone?"

"Hardly."

With the way she was leaning on his elbow, her expression was hard to see and read. "So you accept him, then?"

"As a backwards local with barbarous customs?"

"As a brother."

This, he could not answer. At least not immediately. But Elizabeth seemed willing to wait. She stroked his back, which was stiff from all of the riding and from the tension.

When he was soothed, he said, "Yes, I suppose. This does not mean I will willingly extend this courtesy to every child my father may have sired." Of course, there was only one known other, but his name would remain unspoken until Darcy spoke it. "Grégoire is perfectly amiable and highly intelligent, a kind, generous man who is too hard on himself—somewhat literally, extremely literally. But that is his upbringing, so I suppose it cannot be unexpected."

"Darcy," she said, "we cannot let him go back."

He had been thinking the same thing, but he was too tired to express it. He took her offered hand. "Our trip will be delayed."

"A few days will hardly make my sister any more or less with child," she said. "Or even a week. However long it takes."

He was not eager to disagree with her.

⁂

"Geoffrey! Geoffrey Darcy, you get back here this instant!"

Nurse had already given up. She had chased Geoffrey around

enough times that she was huffing and puffing, but Bingley shooed away the other servants. "He's my responsibility," he said. "Geoffrey! I meant what I said!"

But Geoffrey giggled and disappeared behind a corner. Georgie was standing there, so Bingley leaned over to his daughter. "Which way did he go?"

She pointed.

"Thank you," he said, and broke into a full run, nearly crashing into half a dozen servants before he found Geoffrey struggling with a closet door that was locked, obviously intending to hide in there. Bingley picked him right up. "There you are. Do you have any idea what you're doing to us?"

The boy, who was slowly returning to his normal coloration, merely giggled.

"Come now. It's time for your bath."

"I'm not dirty!"

"Still, you must—and I feel suddenly as though I'm a terrible hypocrite when I say this—you *must* bathe."

"I *hate* bathing."

Bingley thought laughing broke his supposed authority a bit, but he did anyway. Geoffrey was still stuck in his arms as Bingley carried him back to the nursery. "Ah, karma. Listen, I promised to take care of you, and that means seeing to your general cleanliness. If that means I must bathe you myself, I will!"

His announcement did not go unnoticed. Jane was standing beside Georgie at the door to the nursery, holding a hand over her face at the sight of it.

"Auntie!"

"Auntie will not aid you in this one," she said firmly.

"Georgie!"

Georgiana Bingley shook her head, mainly because her mother was giving her a stern look.

"Don't exasperate yourself too much on this one, Husband," Jane said, and Bingley shrugged and carried Geoffrey off.

He was not far enough along before he heard it. Two things, one in response to each other.

First, Georgie turned to her mother and said, quite clearly and with no failure of pronunciation, "*What's he going to do to him now?*"

Second, at the sound of her daughter's long-delayed first words, Jane fainted dead away.

<hr />

After three days, Grégoire was fit to travel again. His diet kept him barely more than skin and bones, and his health had not been at peak upon his injuries, whenever they were incurred. Darcy took matters into his own hands, practically force-feeding the monk bread and meat and everything that was available and making him stay in bed.

"He would do the same with Georgiana," Elizabeth assured Grégoire. "He is most protective of her."

Darcy also hired the local priest so his brother could hear Mass without rising. He did this without being asked, and when asked why, merely shrugged and said to Elizabeth, "I do not think he would appreciate me reading from the Book of Common Prayer."

What he did not share with Elizabeth, as they prepared for their journey once again, was that he had thoroughly searched the small sack of Grégoire's things and had removed the knotted-cord whip, which had several steel bits in it. The whip was stained with blood, and looking at it made Darcy sick as he tossed it in the garbage pile outside.

"It belongs to the abbey," his brother protested. "Not to me."

"I will personally pay for the abbey to acquire a new one if they press me on it," Darcy said. "You will have to find a new way to torture yourself. Try falling in love with a woman who despises you."

Grégoire was confused enough by this comment that he did not request an explanation as they joined Elizabeth in the carriage and made their way back to the main road.

After merely a day, they reached their long-awaited initial destination of Paris. With Grégoire's help and Darcy's obvious bag of coin, they were able to situate themselves quite easily in a fine hotel meant for ambassadors and people of rank. Grégoire was given an adjoining room and ordered to at least sleep on the mattress, even if he insisted on moving it to the floor. Tired from their travels, Darcy had their dinner sent up and found a British manager who would begin making the proper arrangements and acquire directions to Mary's seminary. The man, Mr. Arnold, was a former courier for the army and did extremely good work. By nightfall, they had all the information they would need for their stay in Paris.

"Look, Darcy," Elizabeth said, passing a letter to him as he devoured his own half of the pile alongside his food. "From Geoffrey."

"From Geoffrey?"

"He told me to wait until we arrived in Paris to open it."

Darcy took it and squinted at what, at the bottom of Jane's letter, was a scrawled "GD" and what was quite possibly a stick figure of a person, with blue ink scribbled all over the black limbs. "Huh," he said with laughter. "Well, at least his education is coming along. Grégoire, here. From your nephew."

Grégoire reached into his robes, pulled out his cord glasses, and tied them around his ears so that the lenses were situated so he could see the drawing. "He is—how old?"

"Two," Darcy said. "I suppose you'll put up a huge fuss if I offer to buy you proper glasses. But, ah, I'm already a step ahead of you. Would your monkish pride be insulted if I bought a pair of glasses for myself and you happened to borrow them because they matched your own eyes so well?"

His brother answered with a red face, "It is not pride. Pride is a sin."

"And so is having possessions, of course. I suppose the glasses belong to the abbey."

"They do."

"Can you read without them?"

"If I try very hard, but I hear it is bad for my eyes."

"Well, I suppose Darcy, who I never to this day knew was farsighted and required reading glasses, will have to buy himself a pair," Elizabeth said with a sly smile.

"You are attempting to undermine me," Grégoire said, but his tone was not entirely accusatory. "Why is he blue?"

"He and Georgiana—not your sister, our niece—put ink in their bathtubs. They found some amusement in it. Georgiana's father is Charles Bingley. Bingley is my brother-in-law," he explained to Grégoire. "Elizabeth's sister married him. He is taking care of Geoffrey for us, as well as Mary."

"Oh," Grégoire said. "Mary is—"

"The woman with child, yes," Elizabeth said. "My younger sister. It is confusing, because I have four, and two are married."

"Yes," Grégoire said. "The one with a child."

Darcy and Elizabeth exchanged glances before he turned to his brother. "Do you know what I mean when I say, 'with child'?"

"Yes, of course."

"Because I don't mean *a child*. I mean one *in the future*. She is in a delicate condition."

At this, Grégoire stared in blank confusion. This stare was met with roars of barely contained laughter between husband and wife.

"Perhaps before we go about our inquiries, dear husband, you should properly explain to your brother what that *means*."

"What? I assumed you would do it!"

"How could I? It would be most improper for a woman to explain it to a man, especially a monk!"

She had him, and he knew it. "This is true," he grumbled. "Brother Grégoire, I will have to explain to you where... babies come from."

This, the monk could answer. "They come from marriage."

Holding himself up by his elbows was all Darcy could do from going face-first into the table with laughter. Of the two of them, Elizabeth recovered more quickly. "My sister is not married. Therefore, we may conjecture that they do not come *only* from marriage."

"Oh," said Grégoire. He added, even more confused, "Oh."

Elizabeth got up from the table, taking her letters with her and patting her husband on the shoulder. "This one is yours, darling. Enjoy."

"Lizzy! Lizzy, don't leave me here with this—horrible duty!" But she did.

GOING TO CHAPEL

DARCY SLEPT UNCHARACTERISTICALLY LATE, so much so that Elizabeth was actually up before him and deeply suspected he might well be sleeping off the after-effects of yet another set of the best wines they had ever tasted. He had joined her in bed very late when she was nearly asleep, kissed her, and immediately fallen asleep. So, she was reluctant to wake him.

Grégoire had apparently gone to Mass, and the fact that, despite the years of anti-clerical tyranny and destruction, Notre Dame was perhaps the most splendid cathedral in the world piqued her interest. Darcy would surely never allow her to travel about the center of Paris on her own, but Darcy wasn't awake to say so and she, therefore, didn't have to argue with him about it. She left a note on the bedside table and headed out into the fine spring sun and the cobbled streets of Paris.

It was not so terribly different from Town in many ways, aside from the language, the obvious English military presence, and some destroyed or empty buildings left over from the Revolution. But she saw no guillotines and knew enough French by now to have her way pointed to Notre Dame. She had seen Westminster, but this was a different building entirely. It was taller, and with its two towers in front, more imposing. It was also filthier, still wounded from the Revolution and its attacks—political and literal—on the church.

People were leaving from Mass. As this was not a Sunday, the cathedral was not especially crowded, and she entered without any trouble. The hall was massive, with endless, uncountable rows of wooden seats, and various people still scattered about in silent contemplation before the massive altar and golden cross. Not immediately spotting Grégoire, she found her interest attracted to a rather large altar of candles, some lit and some not, in front of a painting of the Virgin Mary. Why did people from the Bible always tilt their head in such a way? People were burning candles for their lost, and she must have been there for some time, because she did not hear Grégoire approach until he cleared his throat. "Mrs. Darcy."

"Grégoire," she said. "I did not see you."

"I was in confession." Looking up at the altar and the image, he crossed himself.

"I suppose," Elizabeth said in a hushed voice, "God would be terribly confused if I lit a candle at a Catholic altar."

"God is all-knowing, and therefore, never confused," he replied. "Did you lose someone?"

"Something."

"It is not for lost items."

"Someone," she said, her voice betraying her emotion. "I've lost two children, though I was told not to think of them as that. I don't know what Darcy told you last night—"

He raised his hand. Obviously, not for a church, most of it.

"—but I miscarried, for the second time, some months ago. And though, it was not a proper baby, I still feel... as though I've lost someone."

"Then light. God will not be confused, and He is the only one beyond us who will know."

She took one of the longer candles, meant for this purpose, used it to light a smaller one on the racks without burning herself, and then put it back in its container.

"Come," Grégoire said quietly. "I wish to show you something." To her great surprise, he actually put his hand on her elbow and escorted her to a picture bearing among its images a bearded man in robes who did not seem to be Jesus and beside him, a woman. "Abraham and Sarah. Sarah did not conceive until she was just shy of her hundredth birthday. She had given up hope to the point that God sent angels from heaven to tell them she would finally conceive, and she laughed at them. Have you heard this story?"

"Briefly. I am not as versed as you are, obviously." She had, in fact, only read the Bible in its entirety once and had found the Old Testament to be full of impossible names and bizarre laws that she could not imagine anyone following. "But I do not want to wait until I am nearly a hundred, thank you."

"But you have already conceived, yes? My wording is correct?"

"Yes. But I am perhaps greedy and want more. Is that such a terrible sin?"

"I would not call it greed. I cannot presume to know a mother's longing," he said. "There is also the story of the mother of Samuel, one of the old prophets, who prayed to God for a child and then delivered one of the most important people in their ancient history."

She knew what he was trying to say and knew that, logically, his words should comfort her, but she still wanted to—needed to—cry. Before she knew it, she was leaning on his shoulder, and he was embracing her as she sobbed into his harsh wool robe. When a priest approached them, Grégoire said something in French, and the priest went away, but otherwise, the monk waited until she was spent, and slowly they made their way from the church.

"What did you say to him?"

"That you were my sister-in-law, and that he should go away," he said. "Most… improper of me."

Elizabeth could not help but laugh. It felt wonderful.

***

They returned to Darcy eating breakfast, or more accurately, lunch. "I read your note."

"And raced right to my side, I noticed," Elizabeth said, and kissed him on the head, at which he winced. So he was feeling the effects of the night before.

"I trusted your monastic escort," he said. "We should perhaps be off to the seminary. It requires only a short ride."

They had planned this out. The seminary was English, and they would not hurt whatever good opinion the seminary might still have of Mary. It was a modest building, and they applied to the office of the Headmistress, who looked a bit mystified at the trio of an English gentleman, his wife, and a French monk. "Sir and madame."

"Mr. and Mrs. Darcy," Darcy said. "My wife is a sister to a former student of yours, Miss Mary Bennet."

"Oh, yes," she said. "She left a little over a month ago. Withdrawn—she said one of her sisters was ill."

Maybe that was true on some level, but they were not here to contradict Mary. Elizabeth said merely, "She thinks she may have left something here in the dormitory, and we were traveling in the area with our guide here. May we see for ourselves? It was an important item to her."

"I do not believe she did, but you may enter, Mrs. Darcy. But this is a girl's seminary, and you will understand that your husband and escort will have to remain in the front offices."

"Of course," Mr. Darcy said in his most official, proper Englishman voice, which was all very convincing. "Mrs. Darcy, we shall wait outside for you. Take as long as you like."

There were all of the proper bows and curtseys, and Elizabeth was escorted through the dormitories to Mary's room, which was shared with another girl, from her belongings in evidence. Mary's side was empty, of course. "Not filled yet," said the Headmistress. "Because of the war."

"I see," Elizabeth said, and made a cursory inspection of Mary's side of the room. "May I perhaps speak to her roommate? I do not wish to go through another woman's things."

"Of course. I'll have Miss Talbot sent for at once."

Elizabeth did not have to wait long before a girl Mary's age appeared. They curtseyed, and the headmistress left them alone. "I am sorry to take you from your classes," Elizabeth said, "but this is a matter of some import."

"Yes," Miss Talbot said. "If I may inquire which sister—"

"Elizabeth. Commonly known as Lizzy." For she had been introduced only as 'Mrs. Darcy.' "I am second; Mary is third. I've come to inquire after her doings here."

"From England?" Miss Talbot said.

"Yes," she said with severity.

"Oh. Then, I suppose, I must mention immediately that I am not unknowing in Mary's personal affairs."

"Thank goodness I have found someone who can tell me something," Elizabeth said, her voice now welcoming but hushed. "You know why she left so quickly."

"Yes."

"Does anyone else know?"

"I do not believe so. Aside from Giovanni, of course."

"Did you know him?"

"Only of him. She met him tutoring, as she probably told you. She was quite broken up over her own indiscretion."

Elizabeth bade her to sit down, so she was more at ease. "So she was not forced."

"No, she said she was not, and I believe her. Of course, a great deal of the blame still falls on Giovanni. Excuse me that I do not know his full name and cannot refer to him properly, even though honestly, I have no wish to. I do know he offered her some—compensation."

"Did Mary say how much?"

"No. You know more of your sister than I do, but Mary took it all on herself, though I can hardly imagine she was not in some way seduced. She knew him for quite a while beforehand, some months, and she spoke of him more often than she did of any of her other students, none of whom were male."

"Was there genuine affection?"

Miss Talbot answered, "I believe so."

"But he refused marriage."

"He could not marry, of course. He intends be a priest and maybe a bishop. He has returned to Italy to continue his studies, I know not where, only that he has family in Rome.

Now the picture was becoming clearer. "So you believe he can be located through his family in Rome. Mary was not sure."

"I made one inquiry myself, after she left. She was a good friend to me, and I felt it was deserved. But when I went to his family's house, they said he was back in school." She sighed. "That is all I can tell you. I wish, for her sake, I had more to say."

"You have been invaluable, Miss Talbot."

"May I ask how she is? She was worried that her father would be disapproving."

"He was—but he loves her, and they are all staying with my sister's husband in the north, where he and my husband have estates. Mr. Darcy and I are to find this Giovanni and try to reach a settlement with him so that Mary will not be destitute. She is within the bosom of her family, who are perhaps not half as harsh on her as she is on herself."

"That is good to hear. Thank you, Mrs. Darcy. Please send my sympathies, and tell her that I hope to see her when I return to England and she can be seen."

"I will gladly do so," Elizabeth said, and they said their good-byes. As soon as she was gone, Elizabeth rushed out of the seminary to find her husband and brother-in-law sitting on the bench. "It seems we must be off to Rome. He is studying in a seminary near there, but he may retire to his family estate for the summer."

This was not unexpected, but it made Darcy frown anyway. "Then we must cut our visit to this lovely city short, my dear, and make arrangements otherwise. But first, my brother needs some glasses." In response to Grégoire's cough, Darcy said.

"Excuse me. I am apparently in need of some spectacles that may happen to fit my brother."

"Of course," Elizabeth said.

It took another day to make all of the arrangements. They would go straight south to Marseilles and take a ship to Italy, which would hopefully be a shortcut, as it would land them only a few dozen miles from Rome at most. Darcy purchased the services of the swiftest but most comfortable carriage available to take them directly south, and Elizabeth wrote and sent letters to England with details of their exact itinerary. It was late on their second day that the Darcys retired to their own room.

"On the way back, perhaps we will have time to see things properly," Darcy said. "If you wish. Or you may be eager to return to England."

"How long can we expect to be in Rome?"

"If he is there and agrees to a settlement, we must send the proposal to Mr. Bennet and he must reply if he agrees or not. So, perhaps as long as a couple of months." He frowned at his own estimation. "We will be hard-pressed to return to England in time for your sister's delivery if there is any hold-up. And there is the matter of whether we will return to Chatton to find it still standing after our son has been living there for so long."

At the mention of Geoffrey, Elizabeth drew closer to him. Now that they had a proper bed with enough room, it felt positively odd not to be forced to her husband's side the entire night, quite literally, for lack of space, and she missed the intimacy. "I miss him."

"As do I." Darcy sighed. "Perhaps he will learn some inde-pendence—the good kind. And we will be returning with a new uncle for him."

"Have you spoken to Grégoire about this or have you just decided?"

"'Just decided,'" he said. "He is wasted in that awful monastery."

"That does not mean he is meant to be a proper English gentleman. His devotion to his religion is real, Darcy."

"I am not discounting it. But he should see his father's grave, and Pemberley, at least once in his life. Surely he cannot put up an argument with that."

"If you say it in the way that you say things when you want no such argument, then yes. Which you are intending to do."

"Lizzy, you can read me quite well."

"You are realizing this just now?" she said, happily nestled into his shoulder. "But, truly, do not be harsh on him. If he wishes to be a monk, let him be a monk."

"Perhaps," Darcy said. "But maybe somewhere else—safer. Belgium, maybe. There must be a suitable monastery there. It would take some adjustment on his part but then... he would be safer. There are places where they are still destroying churches in France. Lizzy, what do you find so funny?"

"For all of your jokes about sending your sister to a nunnery," she said, "now you seek to toss your brother out of one."

"Technically half brother, but yes, there is some irony in that. Or karma, as Bingley would say."

"What?"

"I've no idea, either," Darcy admitted. "He's positively obsessed with the ways of the Indians."

"Where that interest came into his brain, I have no idea."

He smiled. "I love you."

"I admit to some fondness for you as well."

"You intentionally torture me," Darcy said. "See? All we have to do is get Grégoire a good woman with your wit, and he will have his hands full."

"I cannot quite imagine him even approaching a woman."

"Wouldn't know what to do with her, despite my detailed description the other night," he said. "I suppose I could conspire against him the same way…" But realizing where he was going, he trailed off and fell silent.

Elizabeth nearly climbed on top of him. "Darcy! What do you mean?"

"Uhm, I am inclined to keep my mouth shut at this point."

"Then I am inclined to hear what you have to say. In fact, I am positively inclined to demand it of you, Mr. Darcy."

Darcy put a hand over his eyes so he didn't have to look at her. "Very well. Again, I am at your mercy and must tell you a story that reflects well on neither person in it."

"Since we said his name would be unspoken—"

"—we shall not speak it. But suffice to say, there was a time, during my first semester in Cambridge, when a certain person who may or may not have been a brother designed upon me that I should overcome my shyness and… become a man, as he put it." Sensing from her body language that she had no objections to this story and was most enjoying it, he continued, "Rather drastic measures were taken."

"Drastic?"

"To be blunt, he purchased the services of a courtesan, got me soused, and then locked me in a room with her and would not unbolt it, despite all of my protests." He added, "I have to admit, it did the job admirably."

There was a moment of silence before they both erupted in laughter.

"You, of course, cannot employ this on poor Grégoire," she finally said. "*Brother* Grégoire."

"I suppose. If he is truly devout, then we will at least have a *discussion* before he takes his final vows and forces himself to a life without a lovely woman by his side. A very lovely woman." He kissed her. "Lizzy, I could not have done this without you."

"Save my sister? You did the job admirably once without my knowledge. You're becoming an expert on saving Bennet girls."

"That is not what I mean, and you know it," he said. "I love you."

"And I cannot imagine my life without you," she said. "I love you."

Despite the fact that they were to leave early the next morning, the strain of traveling, and the emotional turmoil the dual situations wreaked on them both, the Darcys found enough peace for themselves that night as husband and wife. By morning, they were ready for the long journey ahead of them, arms clasped tightly together.

Chapter 15

FIRE AND LIES

"I'm not going to have to shave my head, am I?"

"I don't believe so," Daniel Maddox said as he found the spot at last, a suspicious lump between brown hairs that he approached with his tweezers. "It appears merely to be a tick of some kind, not lice."

"Good," said the prince. "How did I get a tick? What is a tick?"

"Perhaps by putting your head on an unsanitary mattress. And I believe it is a type of beetle," he replied, and motioned to the servant for the bottle of whiskey. "This may sting a bit. Hold your head still, please, Your Highness."

The prince managed to do so, and Maddox poured a small amount of alcohol on the site, causing the embedded bug to pull back so he could pull it out. "Scissors."

"My hair!"

"Only a snip," he said as the servant took the bottle from him and handed him the scissors. The tick was also wrapped in hair, which he snipped, and at last he had the insect in his tweezers. "Jar, please." When it was handed to him, he deposited the tick and sealed the jar.

The prince looked around. "What are you going to do with it?"

"Try to determine the species. But you should be fine, sir. Though, if I may recommend, you should keep your head and any other hairy areas away from whatever conditions you previously subjected them to. These things can carry disease." He looked at the bottle as he replaced his glasses. That was when he noticed a man in a white undergarment charge into the room, enraptured by what he was holding.

"'And thus sayeth the Lord,' burn it with fire!" said the wiry man with white hair, before walking across the room and back again, and then out the opposite door.

While Maddox was gathering his reaction to the spectacle, the prince chuckled. "You probably should have bowed to your king."

"That—"

"—was my father, yes. But you did not recognize him, so I'll excuse it this time. And all other times that he's completely out of his head." The prince gave him an encouraging slap on the back. "You can see why they want me to rule, eh?"

"I… have no comment."

"Discreet as always. Well, everyone knows he's batty, anyway. He called me king once," the prince said, lifting the whiskey bottle from the table and taking a swig himself. "King of Prussia, to be precise."

To this, Maddox had a very hard time not responding.

When Dr. Maddox returned to his townhouse, his wife was there to greet him. "Charles is here. He's joining us for dinner."

"Is there some news?"

"No, but he had business. Or needed a break from the Bennets," she said as the servant removed the doctor's complicated and expensive wig, and he fluffed his hair back up. "How's the prince?"

"You know I can't tell you that."

"I was just curious," she said, kissing him on the cheek as she escorted him to greet their guest. Charles Bingley was in the sitting room, reading a book that Maddox did not recognize. They bowed to each other, and Maddox excused himself to change into proper attire.

"Georgiana is joining us as well—am I correct in that?" he said at his dressing station.

"Yes. But Louisa and Mr. Hurst have another engagement, so it's just us." She lay back on the chaise, and he smiled unintentionally because she was beginning to show. "So how is the prince?"

"He is fine, and that is all I will say on the matter."

"So discreet."

"It is what he pays me for," he said, and excused himself to bathe. By the time he was washed up and dressed, it was nearly time for dinner, and Georgiana Darcy had arrived.

"I've gotten a letter from Elizabeth," she said, as they gathered, and Charles put his book away. "She even sent a little picture of Calais. Doctor, have you seen it?"

"Many times," he said, as he eyed the card with an etching of the old city walls. He gave it to his wife. "Once, it was an impressive fortress of a city."

"So she says. They are going south now, I imagine, to catch a boat to Rome."

"I received a letter from Darcy," Bingley said. "They must be some way south of Paris by now."

"They are going all the way by carriage? If only there was some better way that was as quick," Dr. Maddox said. "Does Mrs. Darcy mention anything else?"

"Only that she has little time to write," Georgiana said, putting the letter away. "Mr. Bingley, what in the world are you reading?"

The book had mysterious characters on its cover, alongside English ones. "It is a book on the various languages of the Indias. Did you know there are twenty-seven?"

"Charles, if you intend to learn them all, we must find you another hobby," Caroline said.

"Yes," Maddox said. "Where this Bingley family obsession with languages comes from, I have no idea. Most perplexing."

For that he got two looks—a stern one from Caroline for undercutting the chastising of her brother and a thankful one from Charles. Fortunately, the dinner bell rang, and the line of conversation did not have to be pursued.

Over dinner, Charles announced that everyone currently residing in his household was just fine, and that Georgie had finally said her first word. "Actually, it was a whole sentence."

"My goodness," said his sister.

"Yes. Apparently she was just saving up or something," he said. "My wife was right on the floor. I would have been if I hadn't been carrying Geoffrey at the time."

"Carrying or throttling?"

"*Carrying*, Caroline," he said. "The second came later, but that is another story entirely."

"From Eliza's side, no doubt."

"I will have to correct you and say that, with all due respect to Darcy, I've known him since his college days and heard enough stories to say that he may have contributed to a certain child's personality." He decided to change the subject entirely away from sibling banter. "So, how is our prince? Or I suppose you can't tell us."

"I've never yet told you anything about a patient who wasn't a direct relative of yours or mine, and I don't intend to start now," Maddox said as the second soup course was served.

"Have you met the king?"

"As he is not a patient, there I can relent and say yes, I have met the king. Today, in fact. We were not properly introduced, because I was an anonymous servant of his son and the king was completely out of his mind when he came in the room."

"Now you have to finish the story," Caroline insisted in the way that only she could.

"It is not a very long story. He came into the room half-dressed, told me to kill it with fire—not explaining what he referred to—walked around a bit, and left."

"You saw His Majesty in his undergarments?" Georgiana whispered, as everyone was suppressing their laughter.

"I did. I didn't actually recognize him at the time, and I was not told who he was until he was gone."

"Darling," his wife said, "I must comment that you seem terrible at recognizing royals." This, she did not explain to their guests.

Bingley was staying the night, with plans to leave for Derbyshire in the morning. It was not until Caroline retired and Georgiana went home that the gentlemen were left alone, and Maddox finally got to inquire as to Bingley's sudden appearance.

"Some business, some buying of books, some pleasure," he said. "Though my sister would not be overly fond of the idea that the Bingley family is still secretly involved in trade. She thinks I am an idle gentleman. Then again, she did not marry an idle gentleman, so maybe she has warmed to the idea."

"Perhaps," the doctor said with a smile as they shared a glass.

"So I suppose her confinement will have to be in Town. I was going to invite you to Chatton. Perhaps you will not mind a semi-frequent guest?"

"Of course not," Dr. Maddox said.

"She is getting along well? Jane has been wonderful, but I think the twins have worn her out. God help me if she gets pregnant again anytime soon."

"Caroline is doing fine," Dr. Maddox said with a smile, amused at Bingley's concern for his sister. "Her only complaint so far has been that she is going to need her gowns adjusted, because she will not go about the house in nightclothes like so many women. Or, that's how she puts it."

Bingley shook his head completely knowingly. "And how is the royal commission?"

"Not particularly taxing, I must admit. The prince is actually in excellent health, and I am enjoying having London University open to me. There have been a few advances since I was last in school. And something tells me I am about to be a busy man."

"A proper gentleman has little to do with infants," Bingley

said. "Or any sort of real business. Me, I am the most terrible proper gentleman in the world."

"I, as well."

To that, they raised their glasses and clinked them together.

<hr/>

Bingley's other business, quickly dispensed, was advising Georgiana away from Chatton for a while, as the Wickhams had responded and would be in shortly. To this she had little comment, and with that dispatched, Bingley made the long journey back to Chatton by horseback, with the books being sent up behind him to arrive before his guests did.

Bingley supposed that, in another world, he would be a friend to George Wickham. Both men were excessively good at being hospitable and charming, and on the surface, they got along excessively well. (If their first meeting was stricken from the record.) If Bingley could bring himself to forget all of the past injustices this man had been party to or been the villain in, he could very well have enjoyed his company.

He was also busy looking at the Wickham children, a girl about one and a boy about three. They were named George Wickham (the third) and Isabella, and Bingley tried to keep his staring at a minimum, because he was unwilling to explain to anyone that he was looking for familial similarities. There were few to none. True, George Wickham and Fitzwilliam Darcy did not resemble each other, or the ruse (if there was a ruse at all and it was not Bingley's idle suspicions) would have been given up long ago. Darcy, by portrait, favored his mother, and Wickham his. So Bingley said nothing as he greeted them—not that he would have if the two children had been exact images of Darcy.

There were many introductions to be made, because Mr. Bennet had met neither of these two grandchildren, and Geoffrey and Georgie had never met their Aunt Lydia. When asked, Bingley merely said Jane was resting and would join them later. The Bingley twins were brought in, and there was much comparing and speculation about height and intelligence by brightness of the eyes and all that. Mrs. Bennet was in heaven, being surrounded by her grandchildren and finally getting to see her precious Lydia without going alone to Newcastle. Mr. Bennet did seem to show some affection when holding his grandson George, even if he gave the father of that child a very cold glare every time he could.

And then there was the business of Mary. They had decided to not hide her condition, as at this point it would have taken a bit of camouflage. The squeal from Lydia nearly broke most of the men's eardrums, and the three of them found it advantageous to retire to the next room, where Mr. Bennet sat happily with one of his three grandsons in his lap.

"Welcome to Chatton, Mr. Wickham," Bingley said. "It does get a bit... crazy here. Sometimes." He was just glad Geoffrey and Georgie had returned to their normal skin tones and that he didn't have to explain *that* incident.

"I can imagine. Quite vividly, actually, with all of the people in the next room. Lovely house, though. So I hear the Darcys are on the Continent?"

"Traveling, yes." Bingley did not elaborate. "They will be back in time for various—events. My sister is also approaching confinement."

"My apologies if I forget her name. Carol?"

"Caroline. Caroline Maddox, now. Her husband is a physician. They live in Town, near my other sister and her husband." In his arms, his own son began to whimper. "What is it? Do you want your mother? You're running her ragged... you know that?" He quickly passed his son off to Nurse.

"How old is he?"

"Sixteen months. And his sister is Eliza, if it all got too confusing."

"Of course. Named after Elizabeth. Isabella is named after my mother."

Well, Wickham had that part right. Probably.

It took a long time to get all the children put down or in their right places before the adults could sit down for dinner, with Bingley at the head of his massive conglomerate household. Jane joined them just in time, having regained her color, and Bingley found himself holding her hand often as Wickham did his best to delight them with military rumors. Not that hearing about disturbances in France was going to put anyone at ease with the Darcys there, but Wickham probably missed that subtlety and no one was willing to point it out.

Mrs. Bennet was delighted in having her daughter at her side "at a proper table" again (implying, however unintentionally, that the Wickham table was not so proper), and when his mother-in-law was happy, Bingley was inclined to feel some of it. Mr. Bennet kept quiet but was not as standoffish as Bingley and Jane had expected him to be, taking a great delight in hearing tales of his grandchildren, regardless of their parentage.

"And Isabel did the cutest thing the other day..."

For Lydia, it seemed, had grown into her accepted role as

a mother, at least to a presentable extent. However much she whined about money and living conditions in her letters, she did none of it at the table.

The gentlemen retired to the library. Wickham excused himself to smoke when Mr. Bennet mentioned a particular physical intolerance for the stuff, leaving Bingley and Mr. Bennet alone to share a glass of port. "How was Town?"

"Fine."

"Did you see Miss Darcy? Does she have any news?"

"Very little we do not have."

"Yes, yes, all of the letters seem to match up," Mr. Bennet said. "Sort of."

Bingley lowered his glass.

"What I mean to say, of course, is that I've noticed that the letters we're all getting are slightly different when lined up. As can be expected on some level, because Lizzy will only write calming letters to Mrs. Bennet and more pertinent material pertaining to Mary to me, while Mr. Darcy hardly says anything at all beyond their itinerary. Which, if you look at the map, has a lot of inconsistencies."

"You've—been studying this?"

"I am perhaps bored in my old age," Mr. Bennet said, knowing that was no excuse. "Or maybe I smell not quite a ruse, but something else going on. Judging from your reaction, you have your own suspicions."

Bingley frowned and leaned against the bookshelf. "I will not lie to you. I think Darcy has discovered some family business there that he did not expect to find. But it has nothing to do with Miss Bennet's situation, and I don't think there is any real 'ruse' here. In fact, I have a feeling everything will come out when they return."

"Perhaps," was all Mr. Bennet had to say to that.

STUMBLING BLOCK

THE DARCYS MADE HASTE south, as fast as the carriage would take them, often through the night, until they were all equally exhausted. The roads had dried up as the weather changed, and they made better time. Grégoire did not insist on walking beside the carriage and was eating more, so he was managing better, though he did rise earlier to hear local masses when they stopped in towns with a proper church. Despite the roughness of the carriage ride, with enough pillows, they all got very good at sleeping along the ride, and Elizabeth remarked that yes, she had seen quite enough French countryside.

As they passed beyond the reaches of real English presence, Darcy took Grégoire aside one night in yet another nameless, rundown inn. "If we are attacked, I am prepared, but I am only one man. Elizabeth's life is paramount to me, as is her honor." He did not explain what he meant by the last bit—if Grégoire missed the reference, he wasn't going to spell it out. "I'm not asking you for anything beyond translation. Obviously, I assume you are a pacifist. The church does not spill blood, does it?"

"No," Grégoire said.

"Then, at least, stay behind me, if God forbid, something should happen."

"God forbid." Grégoire crossed himself.

Darcy was more than aware of the danger of the roads. He would have had a whole honor guard for his wife, if not for the fact that, frankly, he had little faith for his and his wife's welfare in the hands of someone who fought for hire in these regions. These concerns he did not express to Elizabeth, a rarity in his case. He was responsible, as a husband and a gentleman, for protecting his wife.

His fears were not unfounded.

They were traveling through the night again, in an attempt to reach Marseilles by the next morning, when they could finally rest aboard the ship that would take them to Italy. The moon provided little light, and the coachman said there was nowhere to stop for miles, so the decision to continue onward was made for them. In fact, it was so late that Darcy was asleep with Elizabeth leaning on him when the faint sound of a pistol was heard. It was in the distance, maybe even far away enough for them to remain uninvolved, or so he judged as he snapped awake. Elizabeth and Grégoire were slower risers, and without explaining anything, he dragged the monk out of the carriage. Darcy was carrying his sword and pistol, neither of which he had ever used in his life beyond basic instruction. But he was good enough with the sword, if it came to that.

"Darcy?"

He whispered, "Elizabeth, stay in the carriage."

In the woods, there was only silence. They were alone on the road and could feel a cold breeze. The coachman said something to Grégoire, who translated. "Someone is in the woods. Several people."

Darcy shielded his eyes from the lantern light, so as not to destroy his night vision. Yes, something was out there. Someone. In fact, he could hear movement in the woods, and he needed all of his athletic abilities to know when to dodge and force his brother to the ground with him. The bullet meant for one of them hit the side of the carriage instead, bouncing off the metal of the axle.

They were approached while they were on the ground. Three men, maybe four—and obviously bandits—emerged from the utter darkness. Grégoire put himself in front of Darcy. "*Je vous en prie, nous vous voulons aucun mal!*" ("Please, we mean you no harm!")

The first man to come close enough that his dirty face could be seen in the light laughed and said, "*Jolie calèche pour un moine.*" ("Fancy carriage for a monk.")

"*Nous sommes juste de pauvres voyageurs!*" ("We are just poor travelers!")

"*Il n'a pas l'air si pauvre*," said the man next to him, cocking his gun at Darcy, who drew his. ("He doesn't look so poor.")

"Tell him if he comes any closer, I'll shoot him in the head," Darcy said, hoping his own words would convey meaning with their intensity.

There was laughter all around the carriage, but not from the passengers.

"*Restez la!*" ("Stay right there!")

The bandits all turned, because this voice did not come from them, and the clumping of horse hooves was clearly unexpected by both parties. What little the moonlight offered was the vague portrait of a man in a tall hat riding up on horseback. "*Garde nationale! Que se passe-t-il!*" ("Police! State your business!")

"*Excusez-moi, monsieur, mais ces hommes ont tiré sur nous!*" Grégoire insisted. ("Excuse me, sir, but these men have shot at us!")

The man on the horse responded by lowering his bayonet in the direction of the men he towered over and blowing his whistle to signal. "*Gardes! A l'attaque!*" ("Guards! Attack!")

"He's a policeman," Grégoire whispered to Darcy. "He's called for his men, I believe."

Whether that was true or not, the bandits were taking no chances. They scattered into the night, and the man in the tall hat did not pursue. He whistled a few more times, but no one came. Instead, he climbed off his horse, holstered his bayonet, and shuffled towards them. He had a limp and a black beard, and was, as they saw when he came into the light of the lamp hanging off the carriage, in a guard uniform of French colors. "My God," he said. "Just in time." His accent was perfectly English, probably a Londoner.

Darcy blinked, took the lantern down, and held it up as the man approached. "Hello? Who goes there?"

"When I get this damned thing off, you'll be able to tell!" the guard said, pulling at his beard. "This gum is damned itchy. I'm sure to have a rash in the morning."

"*Excusez-moi?*" Grégoire inquired, and they heard a noise behind them. Fortunately, it was only Elizabeth finally coming out of the carriage.

"Elizabeth!" Darcy put his gun back in his belt and embraced her. "Are you all right?"

"Aside from feeling quite useless, yes," she said, and

curtseyed to the man in the guard uniform, who was, at the moment, pulling off his beard. "Mr. Maddox?"

"Mrs. Darcy," said Brian Maddox, elder brother of Daniel Maddox, his cheeks red from the glue from the fake beard. "Mr. Darcy. And Brother Grégoire, I believe. We've not been formally introduced."

His bow was slightly crooked, as it had been since his injuries at Pemberley nearly two years before, when he had aided a conspirator with whom he had a large debt. This former suitor of Caroline had attempted to kill her then-fiancé Dr. Maddox but missed his target and struck the doctor's brother instead. Thanks to his quick surgical reflexes, Dr. Maddox managed to save his brother, but not the nerves in his back.

"You've..." Darcy said, stunned at both the appearance of a man he considered vaguely an enemy and the fact that this same man had clearly saved all of their lives, "... joined the French police?"

"Don't be ridiculous." Brian Maddox removed his giant hat and shook out his mane of black hair. "I won the outfit off an officer with an exceptionally good hand—literally, the shirt off his back. I don't always lose at gambling, you know."

"That doesn't quite explain why you're here, but I am grateful that you *are*," Darcy said. "Thank you. Please allow me to make the formal introductions for Brother Grégoire. Brother, this is Brian Maddox, who is distantly related to me by marriage through his brother, the Dr. Maddox to whom we write in Town."

"Pleased to meet you." Grégoire bowed, and Maddox did the same.

"If you must know the whole story, we'd best be on our

way, in case the bandits figure out that I don't have a squadron behind me. Coachman?" Maddox nodded to him. "There's an inn not five miles up the road, but you have to turn off at a certain point. I'll show the way." He climbed back on his horse, and Darcy realized they had no choice but to follow him.

The inn was warm and well lit. Though the hour was late, they were all quite shaken from their experience and not ready to sleep yet, so they joined Brian Maddox, now sans military costume beyond his gun, at a table where he ordered a round. "I have some credit here. I am a courier, and I delivered something important for them once without charge. Not really because I wanted to, but that is another story. I suppose you first wish to know what I'm doing here."

"Yes, please," Elizabeth said, because she knew she would say it more nicely than Darcy, who did not look willing to give up his old suspicions just yet.

"Well, I hope you won't tell Danny I did this, because it's precisely the opposite of what he asked me to do. He knew I was in France, or in the general vicinity of it, so he asked me to stay out of your way. Now he may have been down these roads a long time ago, but traveling here is not the same under the Emperor or whatever he's calling himself these days—first it was king, I think. Anyway, I figured I owed you a favor for saving my life by not calling the constable on me in Derbyshire, so I thought I'd see that you stayed out of trouble—or at least reached Italy alive."

"So you impersonated a guard?" Darcy said.

"Lucky I had the outfit, no? *Fortuna* and I have a love-hate relationship. I've been tailing you since you arrived, and quite well apparently, if you haven't noticed me yet. You ought to be more careful."

"We are indebted to you, sir," Grégoire said with a bow of his head.

"It's more like a debt repaid. I was going in this direction anyway, so no harm done, except to the carriage. And even that wasn't much, compared to what those men could have done."

"I prefer not to think of it," Darcy said, unconsciously putting his arm around Elizabeth. "So you know our intended journey's destination?"

"I've gotten some details from Danny in letter form, the rest from listening to you." He was not afraid of their stares. "A man's got to keep himself entertained. But I think we are in mutual agreement to keep information to ourselves about actions of both parties."

"Certainly," said Darcy. "Have you received any recent correspondence from your brother?"

"Yes. I don't suppose you know, but he recently received a royal commission. My brother, physician to the Prince of Wales himself! I always knew he could restore the family honor. His wife seems like the type of woman who would like to be *Lady* Maddox, if you know what I mean."

Darcy and Elizabeth exchanged smiles.

"How is he, by the way? I mean, besides what he writes. You've seen him more recently than I have. I know my sister-in-law is with child, so he must be doing something right."

"He seems to be doing very well," Elizabeth said. "He was very happy with his arrangements."

Brian had a warm smile on his face at this. He always was

very agreeable, but something in his face lit up when he was speaking of his brother. "That's just brilliant. If anyone deserves to be happy, 'tis Danny. But, you can fill me in later. If you don't mind, I'd like to go with you to Marseilles and catch that boat."

"Going to Rome?"

"God, no. And end up in the Tiber? There are… uh, reasons I can't go to Rome." He shrugged it off. "You know. People that I may or may not owe money. There are so many bodies in that river that they're not going to notice another one. Oops, should I be saying this in front of a monk?"

"Rome is a city, not a monastery," Grégoire said. "The Holy City, but I am not immune to tales of the past."

"A very logical perspective," said Darcy.

"Aye, he might make an Englishman after all," Brian said, and did not further explain. Apparently, he did not need to.

Dr. Maddox had a lot on his mind. He hadn't heard from his brother in a few weeks—probably a good sign—but that was really the least of his worries. His job, truth be told, was not very taxing and provided him with endless access to the University libraries, and his primary patient was in relative health, provided he didn't pick up some venereal disease. Still, several concerns weighed on the doctor's mind.

The Darcys had been gone two months now, and Chatton was, from Bingley's description, a madhouse of children and Bennets. Bingley, despite owning his own townhouse (occupied by the Hursts year-round, largely), was in town often to check on his sister, though he usually gave a more business-related reason. Maddox did nothing to stem the tide of brotherly affection. Louisa Hurst was barren and further from Charles in age, but apparently Charles and Caroline had once been quite close, and now she was to go through the most difficult thing asked of a woman. Elizabeth had miscarried twice, and Jane was exhausted from her three children.

But, in fact, Caroline seemed content when she was not losing her lunch, which had not occurred after the first few months. She was mildly annoyed as she began to retire from social life before her formal confinement, drawing nearer every day, and Dr. Maddox did his best with his new free time to keep her amused.

One morning his schedule was particularly empty, as most of his patients requested night calls and he had no lectures on his schedule. When the servant approached him about a woman at the door who would not give her name, he straightened his waistcoat and went down the stairs, opening the door again himself. "Hello—"

It was Lilly, the prostitute. Lilly, the prostitute, very obviously with child.

"Lilly!" Maddox said. "It is certainly a—uhm, surprise to see you here."

"Doctor," she said. "So sorry fer intrudin.' Can I come in?"

Or having her stand in broad daylight in front of my townhouse? "Of course. How did you find the place?"

"Asked 'round."

"Of course. Of course." He shooed the attending servants away, except to ask for tea. "I—uh, didn't expect to see you. At my house."

"Lovely place. Musta cost a fortune. Done well fer yerself, doc."

"It was a wedding present."

"Like I said. Yeh don' mind if I be sitting down on your fine—"

"Oh! No, no, of course not," he stammered, because he could hardly expect a woman—an *expectant* woman—to keep standing in his hallway. "Any seat you… uhm, like."

"I tried to come, yeh know, when yer wife's out shoppin.' 'Cuz that's what rich ladies do with their time."

"Actually, no, she's—Oh God." The very person in question was descending the steps. She must have heard the bell, and he quickly rushed between himself and Lilly, who didn't get up. "Caroline, it's not what it looks like."

Whether she'd had a proper look beforehand remained a mystery, but she certainly took one now, leaning around him to do so. "Daniel, what in God's name—"

"I'm not a 'what'!" Lilly shrieked.

"Caroline—"

"You are whatever I call you!" Caroline Maddox shouted back, and then turned indignantly to her husband. "Who is this woman?"

"Her name is Miss Lilly—uhm—"

"—Garrison," said Lilly.

"Miss Garrison. She's—someone who knows former patients of mine and current patients of mine."

"She's a whore!"

The doctor, horrified at his own indefensible position, turned to Lilly for help, to which she only replied with a shrug, "I ain't denyin' it."

"And she's with child!"

"No use denyin' that either," Lilly said. "But, I will say, the good doc 'ere's not the father, 'case you were worried."

"*Then what is she doing here?*"

"She—I don't know." He spun back to Lilly. "Miss Garrison, would you care to explain your presence?"

"'Scuse me, Mrs. Maddox." Lilly did not get up, but she made a curtseying gesture with her head. "I thought you were out. See you've also got one in the oven. Good job, doc."

Maddox was sure that either his ears were going to burn off or he was going to die of a heart attack from the stress of trying to manage this. "Please—Lilly—Miss Garrison. Explain yourself... for my sake, at least."

"Dunno if I should say it in front of a proper lady," she said, "but I need yer help."

"I must inform you that I am not, in fact, a midwife or any doctor of that sort," he insisted.

"Oh, I'll be fine. S'not what this is about. See, I figure yeh owe me a favor, what on account of you gettin' your big job with the prince."

"I hardly see how that comes into account," he said. "I think I returned the favor by not reporting you as having stabbed several of your clients and my patients."

"Did give yeh some work, though. Prolly paid for her fine dress there." She gestured towards Caroline, which, of course, set Caroline off on another huff of indignation.

"That I cannot deny. Still, I believe we are even, and though I loathe turning away a patient, I must ask that you explain what favor you wish me to grant—and do so very quickly, before my wife is further offended, which I will not tolerate."

Lilly, however, was not to be intimidated, certainly not by a quivering doctor. "I need yeh to talk to yer boss fer me."

"The prince? I doubt he is interested in talking to you or

seeing you ever again, except with head upon a—" And then realization dawned. "It isn't."

"'Tis."

"How do you even know?"

"I know!" she replied with some fury. "I keep track a these things, doc. I may be all cockney and with a Jack in the box, but I ain't stupid."

No, she was not. A little crazy and completely lacking in refinement, but not stupid. She had an ace in her deck. She intended to play it and was doing so. Unfortunately, he was to be the carrier of such a terrible message. "Why don't you send him a letter?"

"Did. No response, 'course. And I ain't proposin' that he take the kid, 'cuz I know he won't. I just need some money to tide me over, seeing as how I can't get work right now."

"I see," he said, because he did see, quite clearly, Lilly's situation. "So you wish me to risk my employment—and, frankly, my life by implying something treasonous to a royal—so you can have some money?"

"An' I know ye'll do it. 'Cuz you're all proper like, but not in the way she's proper," she said, pointing to his wife, which was a very improper thing to do. "Yer proper, right proper, because yer a decent man, all moral and carin' 'bout people. And if yeh don't do this… I got nothin.' 'Cept a royal kid I gotta feed."

Caroline meant to say something, but Maddox did something he had never done before and held up a hand for her to be silent. Maybe her condition was making her out of sorts, but she actually stopped before she said anything and allowed him to speak in a calm voice to Lilly. "While I must first discuss this with my wife, as my very life is in danger if I do this, I will consider the matter and do… what is within my discretion to do." He swallowed. "May I inquire…?"

"Three months to go, we think. Hard ta tell."

"Then we must settle the matter—if it can be settled—with all expediency. Is there somewhere I can contact you privately?"

"I ain't a very private lady," Lilly said, and apparently excusing herself, gave a half-curtsey to Maddox and Caroline without naming them. "Good 'ay."

"Good day, Miss Garrison," he said, watching her leave. As he turned, his wife was giving him the most severe look she had ever given him. "What?"

Chapter 17

PILGRIMAGE

As France disappeared into the mist, Darcy decided he was happy to see it gone. As beneficial as their long journey had been, it had come with its share of horrors—one brother he wanted and one he did not, but both ill gotten. The fact that they were visibly moving toward their initial goal put him at ease. He stood on the bow with Elizabeth, who was fascinated by the coloration of the Mediterranean, slightly different than that of the Channel. It was a shame that they would have to move into deeper waters and not see the coastline as they passed. He wished Elizabeth to see Greece with all its ancient majesty, one of the few places on his own trip he had truly enjoyed, but that was not to be.

The calm lasted about an hour. Then they made an interesting discovery: monks were apparently not made for the sea. Grégoire, not a man of great health in the first place, had no sea legs at all. Darcy quite literally carried him to the side of the boat to get him there in time before he lost his stomach. After the fifth time, Grégoire could no longer stand and slumped against the side of the railing.

"Now I very much wish your brother was here," Darcy said to Brian Maddox. "You didn't happen to peruse any of his literature—?"

"I know something about scurvy, but he doesn't have that. We've only been on the boat for a quarter of a day."

They looked at each other.

"Maybe if we kept him below…"

"Maybe if we had let him walk, like he wanted to do," Darcy said, watching his brother murmur in Latin as he fingered his rosary. "He would have arrived a few months late, but—Oh, there he goes again."

Darcy ran across the deck, which was not excessively long, and hoisted his brother up again so he could lean over the side. Brian Maddox remained in place and bowed to Elizabeth approaching him. "Mrs. Darcy."

"Mr. Maddox." She curtseyed a little unsteadily, considering the rocking of the boat. "Whatever are we doing to that poor monk?"

"What is that poor monk doing to Mr. Darcy? He hasn't had a moment's peace for a few hours now," Brian remarked with a smile. "Brotherly affection is unconditional. At least, when one is not in competition with the other. Usually it requires a great age difference."

"You are a prime example of that, if I may say, Mr. Maddox," Elizabeth said.

"My very life hinges on my own stupidity and Danny's intelligence. I won't deny it," he said. Brian Maddox was known for a former life of gambling, ruination, and being poor in a fight. "I'm very happy to hear that he's doing so well. At least now he can support Caroline on his own, which must be a great load off his mind. Me, I could hardly have the courage to bring myself to such a high-class woman. No offense meant to a sister, of course."

"It is hard to deviate from the truth," she said. "Though I cannot say I have seen much of them since they were married, as I am so rarely in Town. But, to be honest, there was some surprise in the family when we discovered she was considering a man without a great inheritance."

"Or a title. As long as he doesn't ruin it, he'll have knighthood eventually. But Danny is very good at being diplomatic to his patients."

"So that's it?" Caroline said. "You would have your own head on a spike and me a widow because of some prostitute?"

"No! Of course not! I mean, if it comes to that—," but honestly, Daniel Maddox didn't know what it would come to. He didn't know what he could say to the prince that would possibly persuade him or keep himself from being fired. "But—she is a woman in need. What am I supposed to do?"

"She is a whore, Daniel."

"That does not change her physical composition. Or the fact that she is carrying a royal child."

"So she says. Do you believe her?"

He scratched his head. "I don't know… mostly. Look, I have a moral obligation—"

"You have no such obligation. She is exploiting you—"

"So she is! What is she to do? She is desperate! Do you think women become prostitutes because they like letting men use them? Do you think they don't get horrible diseases that they eventually die of? Or get with child and are possibly killed off when they go to the married man who impregnated them? Do you think most of them have any *choice?*"

"Don't sermonize to me!"

"I am not sermonizing! I am not repeating something from a passage I read in the Bible! I'm saying this because I've seen the life, and I have a chance to help this poor, mad girl with a future child—and for some reason, I am very receptive to the pleas of expecting women at the moment."

He softened his tone, kneeling before his wife and taking her hands. "I am serious, Caroline. If you wish me to turn her away, I will. But I don't wish to. You will never have to see her again, but I want to go to the prince and tell him what damage he has wreaked, though putting it much more politely than that. But not without your consent." He touched her cheek. "I will do as you command."

Caroline seemed to be softening. Or, she seemed to be beginning to cry, either one. "I will not be a widow over this. It is not fair."

"I would not make you a widow. Or, I try my best, despite my profession." He embraced her, which was getting to be a more difficult prospect at this point. "Say the word, and Lilly's request will be forgotten."

"Will *you* forget it?"

He sighed. "No. But it will not be spoken of again."

"You're just like Darcy," she said. "Always the hero. Why can't you just be stupidly naïve like Charles? Or asleep like Mr. Hurst when someone rings at the door?"

"Charles is not naïve. He just appears to be. In—some respects."

"I know that!" she shouted, pounding him limply on the

chest. "I would ask you why you care about this woman so much, but I know you're only going to give me the most noble of answers and mean it—and then I must consent or be a horrible woman for not doing so."

"You would never be a horrible woman."

"Despite rumors otherwise. There was a reason I was unmarried until I was one and thirty."

"Well, by the same logic, since I was unmarried until one and thirty, so I must be one horrible woman as well. Though in my case, it makes sense."

This was enough to bring laughter out of Caroline, which stopped abruptly as she put her hand over her stomach.

"Are you all right?"

"The baby just kicked," she said, and Maddox pressed his hand against her sizable belly. "You can't tell it, of course."

"The gender? No. That must be a surprise saved for the end." He kissed her. "I love you."

"What good are you as a doctor if you can't even tell the gender of your own child?" she said, her mood noticeably altered from just a few moments before. "Just don't you dare make me a widow."

"Never."

"And try not to lose your commission as well."

"Then it is agreed?"

Caroline had no response but to hug him tighter. He took this as an affirmative.

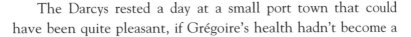

The Darcys rested a day at a small port town that could have been quite pleasant, if Grégoire's health hadn't become a serious risk. When they got him on shore, he was quite weak, but he recovered quickly with food, drink, and soil beneath him. Maddox, who knew Italian as well, hired a carriage for them and a horse for himself, and guided them until they were nearly in view of the ancient city of Rome itself.

"Here we must part ways for my own safety," Maddox said. "If you need me, send for me at an inn named Bella Notte to the east. I would point out that I am considered an excellent courier—must be all those years of running away from people that put me into such shape."

And with that, he took his horse in another direction, going north.

To Grégoire's great delight, he did get to make his proper walk to Rome, if not all the way. The path they had taken was so bumpy that the carriage had to proceed at a slow pace, and Grégoire was enough recovered to walk the last remaining miles as the Holy City appeared in the distance. At the sight of it, he dropped to his knees and bowed.

"His ardor may be decreased when he sees the reason we travel here," Darcy said.

"You are just grumpy because you know you'll never talk him out of monasticism."

He decided he was willing to give her that. "Perhaps."

And so the Darcys went down the hill and into Rome in the early summer of 1807.

***

Rome was unlike any other city. It had been built on mystic origins instead of a trading port, as London had been. Rome had seated the Roman Republic and then the Roman Empire for a thousand years, and had become the seat of the church that ruled all of Christendom before Martin Luther and John Calvin and Britain's own John Knox. Rome was full of hills overlooking the Tiber, covered with abandoned ruins and ones reused to build newer structures, so that even with all his studies on Roman history, Darcy could not point out precisely the origins of every place they found on the road. Nothing looked new, nor precisely old, and they saw as many barons and wealthy merchants as tonsured priests and nuns.

When the carriage became rather useless, they emerged into the streets themselves, which were hot and buggy but not unbearable. Darcy could not seem to ignore his brother's pleas to see St. Peter's. Darcy would have excused himself from this business, but Elizabeth expressed a more pedestrian interest in the seat of the Papery, and he wished to see it with her if she was to go.

Hands together—something clearly appropriate here, and a luxury they enjoyed—the Darcys watched Grégoire ascend and kiss each step leading to the courtyard of St. Peter, with its marble statues of the church fathers and Roman architectural façade.

"You've given him a great gift, bringing him here," Elizabeth whispered to Darcy.

"Or a favor. In which case, he would perhaps be kind enough to repay me by visiting Pemberley before returning to Mont Claire."

"Scheming, as usual."

"For everyone's good, of course," he said.

They had no words, at first, to fully describe the cathedral they entered. It was massive, and although they visited between masses, it was still rather crowded with visitors to see the wooden throne of St. Peter. And what a throne it was! It was only a wooden chair, too high in the air for anyone to sit on it now, but it had four bronze pillars surrounding it. All of the literature the Darcys had read on the wealth of the Papacy was clearly not unfounded. Grégoire bowed to the floor and was received by an attending priest, and there was some amount of groveling and blessing before Darcy could approach his brother. "We must find suitable lodgings for tonight, eventually, and your skills are needed in this. After the task is done, you can return, but I would ask this small favor of you."

"Of course. In fact, let us go now, so that I can return for Compline. He bowed to the priest, and they hurried out of the basilica.

Between Darcy's natural abilities to assess where the wealthy situated themselves and Grégoire's translation, they were able to rent a cramped, but suitable apartment that would do for the moment. Darcy kept his brother long enough only to eat something and translate Darcy's letter of inquiry as to the location of Mr. Mastai, if he was in the city at all.

With that sent, they separated, and Grégoire rushed to Compline, his exuberance carrying him all the way there. The Darcys themselves found themselves hot and exhausted, and were happy to retire. The building was centuries old and a bit drafty, and that was its saving grace.

"Better accommodations will be found," Darcy assured Elizabeth, though it was mainly himself that needed assuring. "When our business is done here, perhaps we will retire to one of those famous villas while we wait for an answer."

"Do you have a plan for asking the question?"

"Oh, yes," he said.

"Does it involve you just walking in, speaking your mind, and maybe throttling a boy younger than your brother until he agrees to a settlement?"

He smiled. "Perhaps it is not the most cunning of plans."

"Mary is my sister, and I have some questions for Mr. Mastai myself, if you don't mind. In fact, that may aid us, for if Miss Talbot is correct, Mr. Mastai may have some affection for Mary or even love her. Misplaced in his actions, but still."

"Useful knowledge to have in bargaining."

"It is not all about bargaining. Emotions are involved, Darcy. You remember emotions? Ones you feel about people you haven't even met or don't even like, but are afraid to express?"

"I am not *afraid*."

"Then you are just exceedingly shy."

"I am not shy."

"Now you are just being stubborn."

"Have you ever known me to be anything else?"

Elizabeth could not reply that she had.

⁂

They set out after Grégoire returned from morning Mass. It was hot but not unbearable, and even though Elizabeth had a brimmed hat, Darcy bought her a parasol, as well as a wooden cross necklace for his brother, to which, surprisingly, the monk did not object. The seller said that His Holiness had blessed the necklace, and as much as Darcy doubted that, he said nothing.

Rome was the Holy City, but it was a modern city as well, if a bit confused in its orientation, having never been planned out properly to be the size that it was. They soon found the residential streets quite winding and disorienting. Grégoire was invaluable, although he was horrified that Darcy was willing to put ducats in the hand of any man who seemed, through translation, to be reluctant to give directions.

They were misled and probably lied to, but eventually they found someone, a woman hanging out clothing to dry, who said she had once rented an apartment from the family, but that the family had a bigger one down the hill, and she knew little else. Perhaps the fact that this British couple was traveling with a young monk of only the most humble appearance endeared them to her enough to tell them that without outright bribery.

"*Grazie*," Darcy said, which was basically the extent of his Italian. "I did pronounce that right?"

"Yes," Grégoire said, in his own bizarrely accented English. "Down here, she said. All the way to the end."

Fortunately the route was downhill. They descended until at last they reached an old apartment house with a new false Roman façade. Darcy rapped harshly on the door with his walking stick, making no pretense of ringing the bell.

A dark woman, who was obviously a maid, opened the door, and Grégoire bowed to her, keeping his eyes low. "*Scusilo. È questa il Mastai residenza?*" ("Excuse me. Is this the Mastai residence?")

"*Sì.*" She cast a look of suspicion at the well-dressed foreigners behind the monk.

"We are looking for Giovanni Mastai," Darcy broke in, figuring the name was enough. It seemed to be. Despite his English, her head snapped up at the name.

"Tell her it's urgent," Darcy urged Grégoire.

"*Scusili. È un aspetto urgente.*" ("Excuse us. It is an urgent matter.")

"*Il padrone non è domestico.*"

"She said the master isn't at home," Grégoire translated.

"Give her this and ask if he will see us," Elizabeth said, pulling from her pocket a rosary with red beads. "Please."

Grégoire took the beads from her and held them up to the maid. She nearly grabbed them from his hand. "*Scusilo,*" and then she slammed the door shut.

"Very clever," Darcy said to his wife. "I knew I brought you along for a reason."

"Brought me along? She's *my* sister!"

He was unwilling to put up an argument, however pleasing, in the heat. Since the maid did not instantaneously reappear, they seated themselves in the little garden across the street, where a fallen imperial column made for an excellent bench and a gnarled tree created some shade. Aside from the buzzing of insects, the area was remarkably quiet, away from the bustle of the town's center. Or perhaps the Romans had the sensibility to retire in the midday heat.

Unfortunately for Darcy, he had insisted on his usual attire, though his cravat was not as complex when he tied it himself. Elizabeth had chastised him, but to no avail. Mr. Darcy was a proper English gentleman and would only be seen as one, especially on a mission of such monumental gentlemanly importance. That did not, however, mean he wasn't ruining his wool clothing with sweat.

"Dear, you're going to be ill," Elizabeth told him.

"I suppose it's my turn," he said. "You've both had a go at it."

At last, the door opened, and the maid gestured for them to enter. They were ushered into a cramped but beautiful two-story apartment. It was full of artifacts, practically crammed with them, in fact, like an unsorted collection. Every wall was lined with books. Where there weren't proper bookcases, piles of books were stacked neatly against the wall. The maid, still the only person they had seen, gestured for them to be seated on a couch in what was apparently a sitting room, if a sitting room more resembled a library, but then again, so did the hallways.

On their left was an entrance to the balcony overlooking the hills of Rome, and it provided some breeze. They were not given refreshments. In fact, they were left quite alone and wondered after a time if they were ever to be introduced to anybody, much less the right person. But then their long pilgrimage came to an abrupt end. A man—no, a very young man—entered, looking terrified with his arms folded behind his back. Around his neck was his rosary, the one Elizabeth had handed over. He was dressed simply in a seminary uniform, but without the priestly collar.

"Excuse my delay. I believe you are seeking me." He bowed, and they did the same. His English was fluent, but highly accented with the traditional Italian leanings. "I am Giovanni Mastai."

Chapter 18

THE WOULD-BE PRIEST

"IF YOU WILL EXCUSE the question," Giovanni said, "I was not told who you were, though I can only imagine why you are here."

"I am Mrs. Elizabeth Darcy," Elizabeth broke in. "And this is my husband, Mr. Darcy. My maiden name is Bennet."

"Ah," he said. "Mary's sister."

"So you know why we sought you," Mr. Darcy said in a much deeper and more obviously threatening tone. "Or have some imagination on that subject. This is Brother Grégoire, who is Mary's brother-in-law."

Grégoire bowed again.

"Then please allow me to get you some refreshments—"

But he would not have his escape. Darcy grabbed him by the collar as he tried to make his hasty exit. "While I would very much enjoy refreshments, we have not come this far to chat idly over tea, Mr. Mastai. Or is it Father Mastai now?"

"Darcy!" Elizabeth said, and would not give up her cold stare until Darcy released the boy, who gasped, once free. "We will be civil. Though, if you would, please answer the question, sir."

"It is Mr. Mastai. I have not been ordained, though it is only a matter of time." But surprisingly, there was confidence in his voice. Not only was he terrified, but he had a humble tone. "I was simply told Englishmen like to be very… what is the word, quiet and proper?"

"We are not in England," Darcy replied. "And so we must be Italians and get right to the point, I suppose. You know the only proper course of action in this situation, however delayed it would now be."

Giovanni swallowed. Elizabeth almost pitied him. "I—I am aware of your country's standards, but you must also be equally aware that I cannot do this. I have always been intended for the church, almost since I was old enough to walk—"

"That would make you quite the model of celibacy, wouldn't it?" Darcy said. "That would be expected of you."

"My family expects many things of me. Every time I have tried to disobey them, my attempt has ended in failure. Please, Signore, try to understand my position—"

Darcy was unrelenting. "Your position is apparently quite comfortable."

"You are surely aware," Elizabeth said, a little gentler than Darcy, "that my sister's position is untenable, and that while I know not your local customs, her reputation is thoroughly ruined—and she may well bring down my younger sister Catherine as well."

"'The fallen woman.' Yes, I have been told."

"Apparently not enough to affect your course of action except to have you running in the opposite direction," Darcy said.

"What was I to do? I—I cannot be an Englishman! My family would cast me off! And though I loved Mary, I could not betray all of them—" he caught their expressions. "Yes, I did love her, and still do. It is not a lie, and I will not deny it for a moment. That I should have restrained my baser instincts, yes, you are in the right. That I should have insisted that she accept my offer of compensation—"

"Compensation!" Elizabeth said, finally raising her voice. "My sister is not a light-skirt, to be paid!"

"It was the only thing I could think of. Forgive me, but do you not—I do not fully comprehend—do you not occasionally marry for the exchange of monies in England? Something about dowries? The exchange of money to signify a spiritual connection?"

"Your church would certainly know all about that," Darcy said. "No offense meant, Brother."

"None taken," Grégoire said, wisely deciding to stay out of the conversation entirely.

"But I am not false? This is true, that she must be provided for? That the child must be provided for?" Giovanni insisted. "And it is my child, so I must do it. But she refused. She was so pious, a martyr. Like Saint Mary."

"The virgin or the whore?" Darcy asked. "I would be very interested to know which biblical Mary you were considering to apply to ours."

Giovanni bit his lip. He was caught. He paced the room like a caged animal, only harmless instead of being ferocious, the way Darcy usually was when he paced. "I do not—what do you want me to say? Within reason, Signore, please."

Elizabeth touched Darcy on the arm and whispered. "Let me have a moment with him."

"With *his* reputation?"

"On the balcony. I insist."

Darcy sighed, allowed his wife to step out onto the pilaster balcony, and pointed for Giovanni to follow. They stepped out of earshot, facing out and leaning on the railing, but in perfect view of the ever-watchful Darcy.

"Some things in this life need a woman's touch," Darcy said to his brother. "Perhaps some day you will discover that."

⤙✦⤚

"My apologies—"

"It is too hot and I am too tired, Mr. Mastai," Elizabeth said. "Do you love my sister?"

"Yes. Very much so."

"But marriage is out of the question?"

"Sì. As much as... as I would want it to be. As soon as I finish my schooling, I will receive the tonsure. Only my illness has held me back from completing my studies."

"I heard it was why you were in France."

"Sì. Because of my fits. A doctor in France said he could cure me, but he was another charlatan."

Elizabeth paused. "Do you find the prospect of married life so terrible?"

"It is not my path, though my decision has not been an easy one. I was struggling with my studies when I met Mary, and she made—it all come alive. I could understand things when she said them. Still, I did not feel very pious."

"Obviously," she could not help but remark.

"But—I did love her. Or came to love her. The feeling came over me like... how do you call... a lightning bolt. And I could not control myself. Things are different here, Signora Darcy. In Italia, what we did would not have been so terrible."

"But, though we are in Italy, Mary is not. And cannot be expected to abandon her own family for you, especially since you will shortly be supposedly celibate."

"So you do see... how terrible it is. But I am to do what?" He shook his head. "Every woman I had ever met was jeweled and made up to be perfect. Mary was perfect as she was, without adornments. Humble, pious, thinking little of herself, intelligent, studious... the very ideal of the church. The Virgin Mary." He put his head down. "A terrible comparison, I know, Signora. But I cannot help it. And I ruined her. Tell me at least that she is not cast out."

"No." Elizabeth's voice was wavering, and she was having trouble hiding it. "Papa was upset, yes, but she is family, and we love her. But her position in society—that is terrible, beyond repair. There is little hope for the Bennet name when this becomes known, if that has not happened already."

He sighed again. He was obviously in anguish, maybe in tears. It was hard to tell when he looked away, which was good for her as well, because she could hide her own tears. "If I go inside and offer your husband to deliver everything in my power to give, beyond my person as a husband, he will not kill me? Because he does—appear that way."

"No, he most assuredly will not. He is just very intimidating."

He bowed. "Thank you, Signora Darcy."

"Do right by my sister, and I will be the one doing the thanking, Mr. Mastai."

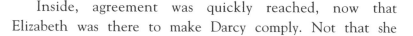

Inside, agreement was quickly reached, now that Elizabeth was there to make Darcy comply. Not that she expected otherwise, but he took one look at her reddened eyes and softened.

"Tomorrow," Giovanni said. "I can have a proposal for you tomorrow."

"I have your word of honor as—whatever you are, a clergyman, an Italian, a Roman—that you will not flee again?"

"No, Signore."

So, it was agreed. Attempts at further conversation would be too awkward, so they took their leave.

"He loves her," Elizabeth said, both sad and relieved at the same time, "but they are too far apart in too many ways."

"We will see tomorrow how much he loves her."

Their next meeting was very formal and arranged. They sat at the dining table in Giovanni's apartment with an older man who spoke little and was obviously a banker. The Darcys sat across from them, and a paper was passed. Darcy glanced at the number, kept his look of concern and impatience, and passed it back without a word.

"Oh, and for the child." Giovanni passed another paper. Darcy took a look at it, and passed it back again.

Without hesitation, he replied in an even voice, betraying neither disgust nor delight at whatever he had seen, "Mr. Bennet will, by law, receive any monies you wish to grant Miss Bennet. He may do as he pleases, though I have no doubt that he will give Mary access to the money in the fullest possible way. You may set up the trust fund for the child so that he cannot touch it. As I must deliver the check and set up the account, I will probably do so only with Mr. Bennet's approval, as I am only his son-in-law and here by proxy."

"I put my full faith in you, Signore."

"I will write to him by special courier, and we will wait to see if the terms are agreeable to him. If they are, I will take the checks immediately and return to England."

"Of course." Giovanni swallowed. "I ask only—a small favor. That you deliver a letter I have written to Mary." He removed it from his robes and passed the envelope over. It was sealed, and Elizabeth took it. "Thank you. She should know I only wish her the best, but there shall be no further correspondence, for both of our sakes."

"So it must be."

They bowed and left. Darcy was too eager to leave and Elizabeth too eager to know what figures he had seen. As they stepped outside and turned the corner, Darcy going first with his wife and brother practically chasing after him, he turned to them with a smile.

"It went well?"

"Better than my own expectations. Though I did not get my chance to properly throttle him, but I suppose I'll have to let that pass."

"That terribly much?"

"If your father accepts—and Mr. Bennet will have to have lost all reason not to do so immediately, your sister will be one of the wealthiest women in England." He whispered the sum, and Elizabeth gaped. "But first, most pressing, I must find that damned Maddox. I am in need of a speedy courier who thinks he owes me his life."

***

"So, you're not going to tell me the sum?"
"Absolutely not."

"What kind of man do you take me for?"

Darcy's blunt stare was enough to get the point across. Brian Maddox took another long swig from his mug. "You're thinking I might run off with Miss Bennet to get the money. Well, I'll let you know I have only the highest respect for the institution of marriage. Hence why I, with my low moral character, have never entered into it. Left two girls at the altar... not at the same time, of course. Though the Turks do have some strange customs."

"I don't think I even want the explanation," Darcy said, "and I will willingly rob my wife of it. Now, the letter." It sat, composed and sealed by Darcy, on the inn table before them. "How fast?"

"If I'm lucky, a month there, however long it takes him to decide, and then a month back. Two months, maybe three."

"Three months!" Elizabeth said. "It took us two to get here!"

"You're not a professional courier who is very good at riding and even running with a limp," Brian Maddox replied. "But— there is the business of me going to England. A risky venture."

"Outstanding debts, of course." Darcy did not even pretend to be surprised.

"Some have defaulted, since I haven't been spotted on British shores for two years. But some don't listen to rules, if you know what I mean. I would very much like to see my brother and the lovely Mrs. Maddox, if only in passing, but they're in Town. Where some—well, a *majority*—of my enemies are. But considering I'm otherwise offering to pay my own expenses for travel and do this actual job as a service to a family member, however distant, I'd say you'll be getting off easy by only insuring my safety while in England."

"Or I could use a proper courier," Darcy pointed out.

"Who'll pass France's embargo in that little time? He'd need a bribe for that, probably as much or more than I am asking. Which is two hundred pounds, by the way."

Darcy replied, "All things considered, I do find that reasonable. But if you don't return within three months—"

"—then I'm dead on a roadside, and you should have hired someone proper after all. Not that a proper courier would go to England and upset Napoleon. And no, believe it or not, I don't gamble. Not while I'm on duty, anyway. Or when my brother's involved."

"I have to admit, you and the doctor could not be further opposites."

"And you are in quite a position to speak of brothers."

Darcy gave a glance to Grégoire and then back at Brian. "And not a word of this."

"Of course. None of my business. Well, about as much my business as the matter of Miss Bennet, but that's none of my business anyway. I'm just delivering a letter." He smiled at them. "By the way, I have an address of a villa just outside Rome for you. You might find it more comfortable than the city itself, if you've had enough of the bugs and the heat and those awful smells."

"I might have," Darcy said. They shook hands, and Brian was gone, taking the letter with him in his rucksack.

"A pleasant man," said Grégoire innocently.

"Certainly an enigma," said Elizabeth. Darcy had no comment.

⁂

If there was one thing Brian Maddox was right about, it was Rome. It was a most unpleasant place in the summer, if one had no particular religious interest beyond sightseeing. The Darcys took their leave and rented the villa at an extremely reasonable price. It was on a hill, and on a clear day, they could even see the ocean and feel a cool breeze. It was also not far from Rome, close enough that Grégoire could walk there as often as he pleased, which was very often. They saw little of him, except when they joined him, and Elizabeth saw the Sistine Chapel and The Last Supper in all their glory, though she was surprised to find the latter was merely a painting over an ordinary square doorway.

When Grégoire had explored the city enough and spoken to enough people, he even got them entrance to the Vatican Observatory, where they saw the exact place where priest-scientists had created the Gregorian calendar used to this day. He also took them on an abbreviated tour of the catacombs, until Darcy declared that he had seen enough bones of saints to last him a lifetime, mainly because Elizabeth was looking pale at the grim sight.

They certainly had enough to occupy their time. Now at ease while awaiting Mr. Bennet's response, they toured on the days when it was not too hot and relaxed otherwise after the long trip. They were secretly glad when Grégoire spent some of his time elsewhere, probably holed up in some confessional booth, because some activities demanded privacy. Even though their time on the road had not totally separated the Darcys, they had never been fully at leisure, and some things were better enjoyed when fully at leisure, with an excellent bottle of French wine and a book that, until this point in their journey, had been carried but had gone unused.

That was not to say they were free from concerns. They both admitted to a growing impatience to see their son and their family, whom they had not heard from since Paris. The post was intolerably slow, and they could not expect to hear from them until Mr. Maddox returned, so they contented themselves with making up stories about all of the possibilities Geoffrey had gotten himself into. That brought laughter to temporarily ease the pain of separation. But other than that, and other things they couldn't change, their life was ideal. They often sat or stood on the balcony and watched the sun fade in the west.

A month after they had sent Maddox, Grégoire mentioned that it was some saint's day and he intended to spend the night in a vigil, or something Papist of that nature, and they knew they were going to be alone. Maybe he realized the gift he was granting them and maybe he didn't, but neither inquired. Instead, Darcy merely uncorked a new wine to celebrate the date and put his arms around his wife from behind. She was watching the sunset, now turning the sky a brilliant shade of orange.

"Darcy," Elizabeth said, her voice amused but still carrying a certain gravity, "I'm late."

Chapter 19

BRIAN MADDOX RIDES AGAIN

"SHAVE IT."

"What? I could never—"

"It is my recommendation, Your Highness."

But His Highness did not look pleased at the process. "So it is lice, then."

"Yes."

"Anything else?"

"Wash it first with whiskey or vodka, scrubbing thoroughly, and then with soap and water. That should do the trick."

Dr. Maddox's patient groaned. "You can tell? From that far?"

"I'm not coming any closer, Your Highness. With all due respect."

"Christ. I'll look so odd."

"I do not believe anyone will notice it. Except perhaps your wife."

"Are you serious? I haven't even seen Caroline in years, much less slept with her." He caught the look on Maddox's face before he could recover. "Oh, that's right. Your wife is also named Caroline. Well, I promise not to sleep with her, either."

"… T-Thank you, Your Highness." Maddox quickly returned to his tools and began slowly replacing them, as they would not be needed. A lower servant than he would do his dirty work, if the prince didn't do it himself. Either way, the imagery made him shudder. "But—uhm, while we are on the topic of names, I was wondering if you would remember a mutual friend of ours, Miss Lilly Garrison?" He swallowed and latched his bag, knowing he would have to face the prince for this.

"Garrison? I know a few—*Oh.* You mean, Lilly. I never got her last name."

"Neither did I, admittedly, until she showed up at my house."

"She did? The nerve of that… that whore! I mean, even for a whore, that's preposterous… showing up at a client's house—"

"I was never a client," he corrected. "I was merely the doctor on call. Even if I had that inclination, I would never subject my body to such unsanitary conditions. I might get lice."

"Well put. But then why is she bothering you?" The prince slapped himself in his bushy head. The image would have been amusing if Maddox had not terrified by the conversation and busy with that emotion instead. "Of course. Did she blackmail you?"

"No."

"Then she wants it from me. I haven't responded to her letters, or the letters someone wrote for her, so she went out of her way—I will not have my own physician so unjustly treated. Tell me, at least, that your wife was not at home!"

"It is not important," Dr. Maddox said. He needed some of that whiskey he had mentioned now, to steel himself. Shame it wasn't around. "I feel obligated to mention that she is with child."

"Feel obligated? What do you owe her?"

"Nothing. But she is a woman in need, despite her profession."

"Ah, I see." The prince, despite being on the path to moral and physical self-destruction, was a rather clever man. "She went to you because you are so noble and also had access to me, knowing perhaps you would put your own life at risk, speaking treason to the prince by making implications against the State, since I am the State, that my marriage to Caroline of Brunswick is not sacrosanct. Which would make you a great fool, putting your head on the chopping block for some whore."

Maddox mumbled, "Yes, I am quite a fool in this respect."

"Then..." The prince sighed. "What do you want?"

"It is not what I want. It is what Miss Garrison—Lilly—wants."

"Compensation, of course. Well, let me tell you something, because I know you are a discreet man. If I gave compensation to every whore or lady carrying a royal bastard, the State coffers would be empty."

"Then just this one, perhaps."

The prince laughed. "You insist upon it? Have you forgotten your place, Doctor?"

"You will refuse, and we will never speak of this again, or you will either fire me or have me killed. But yes, I will insist upon it, because I have not forgotten that a gentleman is always in the service of a lady."

"That woman is no lady. Do you remember that she stabbed me? Even when I continued to see her after she was obviously with child?"

"I am aware. But that does not change her biological composition. She is, and shall die, a lady."

The prince laughed. The folly of youth, perhaps, but they were basically of about the same age. In many ways, Prince

George reminded Dr. Maddox of his brother, not always in a good way, but he passed no judgments. Not knowing what to say, he pursed his hands behind his back to hide the fact that his stable surgeon's hands were shaking.

"You are very… I don't know, knightly. Like those old legends about going through a terrible battle for a woman's honor. Even if the woman doesn't deserve it." He chuckled. "Fine, I will send her something, but we shall never speak of this again. If Lilly ever approaches you again, tell her she is doing so against orders of the State, and that if she bothers you further, there will be no 'Miss Garrison.' Am I understood?"

"Perfectly," said the doctor, not quite believing what he was hearing. He bowed, deeper than he usually did. "Thank you, Your Most Gracious Highness."

"Your ridiculous sense of honor is going to get you in trouble one of these days, Doctor," the prince said, slapping him on the arm. "But not today. You are quite a lucky man in that respect."

Indeed, he was. He had the whole way back to fathom the length to which the prince's mercy extended. Maybe Caroline was right, and the prince just liked him and the way he mixed the proper formality of a skilled physician with actual concern, but never an improper comment until today. He had survived, career and spinal column intact.

He arrived home in time for supper and was to deliver the news to Caroline immediately when a maid stopped him and handed him a note. "We were handed this by the doorman after the post had already been delivered."

He tore open the seal of Maddox and read it.

Dear Brother,

I have some excessively hasty business carrying a letter to Mr. Bennet in the North. If you wish to catch me, you'd better head to Derbyshire immediately. Sorry for the rush.

B. Maddox

"Daniel? What's the matter?"

"Brian," he said. "He was—apparently in Town today, long enough to drop off this." He passed it to his wife, who read it quickly. "I told you he was a courier these days. Apparently the Darcys have employed him."

"Then you must go at once!"

"But I could not—"

"Don't be ridiculous. I have nearly two months. Now, go to Chatton and see that beloved brother of yours. And try not to let him talk you into giving him *too* much money."

He kissed her on the cheek. "Agreed." He grabbed his sack again and instructed his footman to have a horse saddled and ready. "Oh, and the prince said yes."

"Yes?"

"To Miss Garrison's request. Though we are never to speak of it again, and she is never to speak to me again. Those were his conditions, which I found very agreeable."

"Oh, Daniel!" she hugged him as best she could at her stage. "Congratulations."

"You were cheering for me?"

"I am your wife. I pray for success in all of your endeavors, no matter how stupidly noble. Now go and see that rogue of a brother of yours."

"I'll tell him you said that."

"You would not *dare*."

About that, she was definitely right.

❧

The company of Chatton was sitting down to dinner when the bell for the front door rang. As they had not heard from the Darcys since they left France, Bingley ran past his servants and answered the door himself. He was not expecting a thoroughly soaked and muddied Brian Maddox. "Hello?"

"Mr. Bingley," Brian bowed to his brother-in-law. "Sorry for the intrusion, but I have a letter for Mr. Bennet." He wiped his hands on his jacket, reached into his rucksack, and retrieved a formal, sealed envelope. "Express from Italy."

"Mr. Maddox, please do come in at once," Bingley said, for it was pouring, and the man was obviously exhausted. "We'll see to your horse. Do you mind if I give it to Mr. Bennet myself so you can rest a bit before joining us for dinner?"

"That would be lovely, Mr. Bingley," Brian said, and handed over the letter as the servants rushed to help him out of his overcoat and escort him somewhere where he could be properly changed and cleaned.

But Bingley wasn't concerned with that. He rushed back to the dining hall. "Mr. Bennet." He handed him the letter with Darcy's seal on it.

Mr. Bennet excused himself to Mr. Bingley's study, shutting the door behind him. Dinner halted entirely as the adult residents and guests of Chatton stood outside the door, including a very pregnant and confined Mary Bennet, listening to the silence within. Even though only a few minutes elapsed, it was an unbearably long time before he reappeared, a grave look on his face. "Mary."

She joined him inside, and the door was shut again. Jane hugged her husband, who whispered encouraging comments in her ear.

"Now, enough of all this pretense of secrecy," Mr. Bennet said, as he made his daughter sit in the chair beside him. His mood was entirely different when the door was closed. He was almost—content. "The letter is, obviously, from Mr. Darcy. I will read it to you, and then you may see it for yourself, if you wish, as you are, of course, his chief concern."

Dear Mr. Bennet,

First, I must report that Elizabeth and I are well and safely in Rome. We are eager to hear that everything is well in England, when Mr. Maddox returns with your reply.

To the matter at hand, we have located Mr. Mastai, who is residing in Rome. He has continued his insistence that he cannot move to England to marry Miss Bennet without abandoning his own family, to which he has heavy obligations, and she cannot be asked to abandon hers. Lacking other options, he has offered a settlement in ducats, which a banker has calculated to be in the area of 100,000 pounds, to go to you for the express purpose of providing for Miss Bennet. He has also asked that, upon my return to England, I supervise the arrangement of a trust fund starting at 40,000 pounds that will become accessible to the child at his age of majority. If the child is a girl, this will be her inheritance upon marriage or reaching the age of five and thirty, in accordance with British law. Mr. Mastai would do so only on the insistence that you see that the money does, in fact, go to Miss Bennet's welfare, and I assured him that it would.

If you find these arrangements suitable, please reply with haste and send our courier back, as we are both eager to return to England and cannot do so without a reply. If you want to raise argument or refusal, it is your choice to do so, but as a son-in-law, I highly advise against it.

Please give our love to Geoffrey and thank Mr. and Mrs. Bingley for caring for him in our absence, which hopefully is nearing its end.

"Signed, Mr. Darcy," Mr. Bennet finished, closing the letter and handing it to a shocked Mary, who was holding a protective hand over her sizable stomach. "Well…" He trailed off, because he could not contain his joyous laughter, which started as a chuckle and became louder as he embraced her. "It seems we are saved by Mr. Darcy once again."

"So you will accept?"

"As he said, I would be a fool not to. While I do consider myself at times foolish, in this case, I can see the obvious quite well enough."

"And it is not a terrible thing to accept money for a sin?"

"The sin has already been done, and I think any man will overlook it, even with a toddler at your feet. No obligations because you are under Longbourn's roof, no one to support… I cannot even fathom it. Though, as the custodian and official owner of this great wealth, you will perhaps allow me one discretion."

"Anything, Papa."

"I would like to take aside ten thousand or so for Kitty and set it as her inheritance. And perhaps, repair that fallen piece of the roof in the barn at Longbourn for a few pounds." He kissed her on the cheek. "Despite everything, I must say you've done well for yourself, Mary. Now, we must not keep them waiting, or I'll never hear the end of it from your mother."

She laughed. His daughter laughed, and it could only make Mr. Bennet happier, as they emerged into the awaiting crowd. "An arrangement has been made for Mary and the child, and I will agree to it, in writing, when Mr. Maddox is fit to travel again."

"Thank God! Oh, thank God! Mary!" Mrs. Bennet did not hide her enthusiasm. "We are all saved!"

"If I may inquire—," said Bingley.

"If I tell you the amount, you may divorce my lovely Jane to marry my lovely Mary, no matter how noble you are," Mr. Bennet replied, back to his usual humor, something they had not seen in three terrible months.

"Never," Bingley smiled, knowing he would hear the real amount soon enough, and hugged his wife.

Their previous dinner, while not particularly gloomy, was returned to, this time in celebration. Mr. Maddox, now dressed in borrowed clothing and still looking exhausted but at least clean, shuffled in with his odd step and joined them.

"The letter was not dated," Mr. Bennet said. "How long did it take you to get here?"

"Four weeks and two days," Brian said. "And many, many different horses."

"Then we shan't keep you up," Bingley said. "You may retire

whenever you have eaten your fill, Mr. Maddox. We are very much in your debt."

"I can't even think of debts. All I can think of is… the back of heads of horses," he said, and dove into his food.

He did retire, though, immediately following the meal. The ladies took to their own place, and there was much squealing and discussion, probably because Mary told Mrs. Bennet the amount. Bingley heard it, too, privately from Mr. Bennet in his study after a glass of port. In front of him was a writing desk, where Mr. Bennet intended to begin drafting his reply.

"My God," Bingley said.

"Yes, despite the circumstances, my daughter has done better for herself in a certain way than any of the others. I imagine knights and lords will be lining up to marry her now, after we decide how to make it known."

"Or the prince himself."

"He is married, I believe."

"I think they are estranged."

"Dr. Maddox told you that?"

Bingley shrugged. "Dr. Maddox is fastidious in his confidentiality about his patients. I had merely heard it in Town." He took a sip. "You may realize that if Mary does not marry soon or at all, if she so chooses, and she delivers a boy, he will have the name Bennet."

"I was so—overwhelmed, I hadn't even thought of it," Mr. Bennet admitted. "You're right. Goodness, five daughters and I still might have a sort of son. Not that I don't treasure my sons-in-law, mind you."

Bingley happily raised his glass to that.

"That is, of course, dependent on the gender. But my

granddaughter will certainly have enough of an inheritance that any man would overlook her history—or might not even know it. Her husband may have 'died in a war' or something by then." Mr. Bennet leaned on his hand, his thinking posture. "It may be best to cover up some of this, as indecorous as that might be, for Kitty's sake."

"Mary was married abroad, and her husband died on one of Napoleon's ridiculous campaigns," Bingley suggested. "Meanwhile, your long investment in a company in Australia finally paid off in great sum, leaving a greater dowry for Kitty, or something to that effect."

"Precisely, Mr. Bingley." They clinked glasses. "I am indebted to you, of course, almost as much as to Mr. Darcy, for putting up with us all of these months, and for the next few."

"It has had its pleasures. With her sister in confinement, Jane would, of course, have been with her anyway, so this arrangement is most convenient for me."

"Except that your sister is confined in Town."

"True. They have a target assumption of a date, so I may take leave of Chatton for that week. And now with this weight off our shoulders... Well, when the Darcys return, I will feel even better."

"Yes," Mr. Bennet said. "They have been gone so very long. That, at least, can finally end, depending on how speedily they decide to return."

A doctor was able to confirm it.

"If Mr. Maddox does not return shortly," Darcy said, "I may get to strangle someone after all, because it will be him."

Elizabeth could only laugh. She did not feel his concerns, so barely did she feel with child, and because she was so happy to be so. He was happy as well, but consumed with the pressing matter of how to return to England quickly enough and yet safely enough for her health. Riding was out.

"I will not have a French baby," he said.

"But darling, I thought you were French. Mr. *deh'Aaarcy*," she giggled, trying her best to imitate Grégoire's accent.

"I'm as French as Bingley is Irish," he said, "which, by his accounts, is not at all."

Grégoire was unexpectedly overjoyed at the news, not that he should not be happy for his sister-in-law, but Darcy did not know until that moment that Elizabeth had told the monk about her miscarriages. Or maybe he liked the idea of being an uncle. He did not, however, have any ideas of the best way to return to England, being untraveled himself until the day he met them.

"There is the other matter," Darcy said out on the veranda, in the cool breeze of late afternoon while Elizabeth was absorbed in an English book she had found in a shop in Rome, "of you returning to England."

"I cannot abandon my order, Darcy."

"I know you will not abandon your vocation, but perhaps Mont Claire could do without you... for a while. You have not taken your final vows."

"This is true."

"And... I have been considering... there must be monasteries in Austria, different from your own experiences, but the same basic ridiculous principles of celibacy and obsessive amounts of prayer."

Grégoire, well used to Darcy's taunts at this point, was unaffected by them. "It still would not be England."

"No, but it would be safer. And I would wish you in a politically safer position than Mont Claire."

"Mont Claire has Napoleon's protection. It is safe."

"You know what I mean."

Grégoire frowned. "I cannot abandon them."

"Then write them a letter that you are taking a leave of absence to visit your father's grave. There cannot be a biblical injunction against that. Have them direct their response to Pemberley, as we will, God willing, be there by the time they get the letter and respond."

"I would like to see my nephew," Grégoire admitted, "and perhaps the newer one, eventually, and my sister."

"Austria would be much better. It would be different, but more established. And Elizabeth has never seen Austria. Nor have I, in fact. When she can eventually travel again…"

"Do you think she will like me?"

"Who?"

"Georgiana. I mean—my presence, it won't upset her—"

"The idea of our father being—not who he said he was, that onus is on him, Grégoire. Georgiana is the sweetest, most loving creature in the world, and she is your age. So I imagine you will get along just fine. In fact, I believe she has always wanted a brother—one closer to her age."

He did not say, at least out loud, that he had always wanted one, too.

THE LAST JOURNEY

UNDISTURBED, BRIAN MADDOX SLEPT right through breakfast and most of the morning. He had not stirred by the time his brother arrived. Dr. Maddox had clearly been traveling most of the night in order to get to Chatton within two days. "I apologize for my intrusion," the doctor said, "but I heard my brother was here. Caroline, by the way, is fine." He was already predicting Bingley's next question as his summer coat was removed and he was ushered into the sitting room for refreshment. "He left a note. I assumed the business was too urgent for a visit."

"It was," Mr. Bennet said, and since Dr. Maddox had been a part of this from the beginning, he explained the nature of the letter and its delivery, including the settlement. Dr. Maddox did not inquire about the precise sum, unlike everyone else with whom Mr. Bennet had spoken since the wild-haired courier had arrived. The doctor was perfectly satisfied with "a considerable amount" and merely took his tea.

"Happy news, then," he said at last. "If I might inquire

how Miss Bennet is doing—though you have no obligation to tell me—"

"The midwife says she is fine," Mr. Bennet said. "She keeps her distress to herself, but I think having other children about is a great comfort to her."

"They can be charming. And I may have heard something from a bird about a noodles incident—"

"Oh yes," Mr. Bennet said. "But we shan't talk about that, right? Forbidden topic, Mr. Bingley?"

Mr. Bingley visibly colored. "No. That is over and done with and not to be discussed... *ever*."

"I will remark, though, that Geoffrey is getting most clever with his pranks," Mr. Bennet said. "They are most amusing to the people not targeted."

"*Yes*," Bingley said with some severity, and Maddox had enough sense not to further question his host. Fortunately he did not have to, because his hobbling brother joined them.

"Danny!" Brian said, with no lack of enthusiasm, and they embraced. "Look at you. I'd think marriage had made you taller, if you weren't towering over me already."

"Maybe you're shrinking," the doctor said. "How did you get back to England?"

"Well, it is an island, so the same way everyone else does— by boat," his brother said, and bowed to his hosts. "Mr. Bingley. Mr. Bennet."

"Mr. Maddox," Bingley said. "How are you?"

"I wouldn't say I'm quite ready to be back on the road, but now I can at least contemplate the idea," he said, taking a seat with his brother and helping himself to some of the rolls that had been brought out. "To answer the question properly, I was fortunate to find a man willing to pay off my still-standing debts in Town if I carried a letter for him. So, though I am not eager to go tromping about dark alleyways, I am legally free again. Besides, I must get back to Italy in all haste, so that the Darcys can return. I believe they are eager to do so. But—," and he held up a free hand, holding another roll in the other, "if I can get a ride back with them, perhaps I can be in time to see if my nephew or niece has that Irish hair."

"It's not Irish," Bingley insisted.

"I didn't say it was bad. I have nothing against the wild, savage, Papist Gaels over the crossing. In fact, it's well known that Maddoxes go *mad* over them."

The doctor just took off his glasses and sighed, and Mr. Bennet had a good laugh, all at poor Bingley's expense, of course.

"You can have more time, if you wish it," the doctor said. "The child won't be going anywhere."

"But I must be in the Carpathian Mountains by Christmas, before the hard snow sets in."

"Work?"

"You could... call it that. But you would be wrong," Brian said. "I am to be married."

"*What?*" Both Maddox and Bingley rose in response to the news.

"Sorry not to mention it in the letters. I haven't entirely decided on it, but the date is set."

"Then how, pray tell, is it not decided?" asked Mr. Bennet.

"Funny story—"

Dr. Maddox put his glasses back on and crossed his arms. "Somehow, I don't think this story is going to be very funny."

"Depends on your perspective; you see, I sort of lost myself in a bet. Now, I thought it was going to be some kind of labor transaction, but apparently, this count or baron or whatever wants me to marry his daughter, for whom he has not found a husband to his liking. And for whatever reason, I am to his liking. Now if I had known *that* and had known what cards he was holding when I raised—"

It was impossible—Bingley could not help but laugh, though he did cover his mouth when he did it, while the doctor's expression was entirely unamused. "So you are to marry a Romany girl because of a bet?"

"Not Romani. Those are the gypsies. She speaks *Romanian*. And she's an Austrian princess."

"A princess!" Mr. Bennet said. "My, my, this gets better all the time."

"Have you even met her?" Daniel Maddox demanded.

"Once… no, twice, and to be honest, she isn't so terrible at all… a real jewel hidden away in that massive castle. She was very sweet to me, if a bit shy."

"You cannot be serious."

"Oh, I'm quite serious. The question now is to never go back to Austria again or to go back and stay for the rest of my life, minus some traveling abroad. When the count—I believe he is a count—when he dies, I would inherit his estate. I could abandon it, if I pleased. So, you see my dilemma. Not that I am expecting an answer from you, though you probably would at least like to comment on my terrible habits and how much trouble they've gotten me into.

"To be honest, if I didn't appear, I don't think he would chase me. But it might break her poor heart. That's the real issue. Certainly, I've run away from altars before, but usually I thought the woman deserved it. So go on now, make your condemning response to my insipidly stupid behavior."

But the doctor had no response. He was standing there, gaping and towering over his brother but not saying anything. He scratched his head and after some time said, "... Congratulations?"

"You support it?"

"I don't know. I mean, do you know her? You only met her twice?"

"Yes," Brian said. "That's double the amount of times a couple in her country normally meets before marriage, so one could say we know each other quite well. None of this business of slow courtship through balls, dinner invitations, letters—and more dinners and more letters and going on walks—when all you want to do is marry the poor girl. Plus, she expects an arranged marriage, so she seemed mildly surprised that I was so—I don't know, *nice* to her."

No one could seem to gather any response to all this, even Mr. Bennet. It was Brian who had to continue, "But, enough about me. How is my sister-in-law?"

"She's fine," Dr. Maddox stammered. "I think I need to sit down."

"I told you I have the summer. Will you relax already? And I must go back to Italy and then come back here first. Plenty of time. What are you so worried about?"

"Your welfare and, apparently, your sanity," his brother replied.

245

In utmost secrecy later that day, as his brother rested from the long ride from Town, Brian passed a letter to Mary Bennet in the hallway, quietly and with no one around. He had barely turned around when he was facing Bingley, who was trying to look as intimidating as possible. "Mr. Maddox."

"Mr. Bingley."

"My office?"

Brian Maddox rolled his eyes but followed Bingley into his study. "So—how is my sister-in-law? Danny is too modest."

"She's fine. What was that?"

"Aren't you the noble guardian?"

"Mr. Maddox."

Brian sat down. "It was a private letter from Mr. Mastai to Miss Bennet that I was asked to deliver along with the other one. Yes, yes, I know it's highly improper for an unmarried man and an unmarried woman to post and all that nonsense, but I do think they know each other well enough for one last correspondence. Or whatever it was. It was sealed, and despite the fact that I am perfectly capable of breaking a seal and then closing it up again without the appearance of having done so, I did not read it on the way. *That* letter, anyway. One hundred thousand pounds, huh? He must be one of those old noble families. Probably traces his roots to the Roman Imperials."

"Darcy asked you to deliver this?"

"Yes. Isn't he the model of propriety or some such nonsense?"

Bingley found he could not openly contradict him. "So I suppose it should be permitted. I would certainly not want to upset Miss Bennet at this stage."

"I'm not the doctor, but I would say yes to that. Anything else?"

"Since you are here," Bingley said, "how are the Darcys?"

"Quite well, now that this is settled, or they seemed to be. They would have sent all kinds of presents, but they didn't want to weigh down my load. They are very eager to be back, I think. And you are probably eager to have young Mr. Darcy off your hands."

"How are they intending to return?"

"They had not decided. Initially, when I met them on the road from Paris, they said they might come back more leisurely, but now they may have had enough of Europe and be missing their son."

"Have they learned the language, or will they bring a guide all the way?"

Brian leaned back, his mood altered. "Odd thing for you to ask."

"Why?"

"Just, thinking that."

"Is there something you're not saying?"

"Is there something *you're* not saying?" Brian said. "God, I hate circular arguments, unless I'm winning them. Yes, Mr. Bingley, if it will satisfy you as my host, I will say graciously that I believe they intend to return with their monkish guide, and that is all I am permitted to say at this time."

"Monkish guide?"

"Yes. The young man is a monk."

"Oh," Mr. Bingley said. "Very well, then." He rose, which meant Brian was free to leave, and his guest excused himself.

Outside, Daniel Maddox was waiting, having just awoken from his nap. "What was that about?"

"Espionage, secrets, and lies," Brian said dramatically. "Is there any food about?"

Two days later, Brian declared himself well enough to leave again, and his brother did not put up an argument. With the reply and some new clothes (having thoroughly ruined the old ones), he got back on his horse, and together with his brother, made for Town. Traveling at an exceptionally fast pace, they arrived in Town two days later, and only at the doctor's insistence did Brian agree to rest the night at his house before traveling to Dover.

"You've no pain in your back? When you ride?" the doctor finally inquired nervously.

"No, none at all." Brian had been injured in his shoulder two years prior, but the nerves there affected his back and initially caused great discomfort.

"And running?"

"No pain, just that damned limp. The leg won't go in certain directions, that's all. I've gotten used to it. You already said you can't repair nerves."

"I wouldn't dare," Daniel Maddox said as they awaited the arrival of his wife, who was resting upstairs. "Surgery is a painful and dangerous procedure, even if I think I can fix something."

"Maybe that was the attraction of the count. He might think I can't run away from him if I hurt his daughter, or him, to get his fortune. Not that I would."

"Brian, you can't be serious."

"Perhaps I am," Brian smiled, making it impossible to tell if he was. "Perhaps I should settle down. I'm almost forty, Danny, and a cripple. Maybe I should recognize that God is handing me something, even if it is in the Carpathian Mountains."

He turned. "But look, if it isn't the Gaelic goddess herself. Mrs. Maddox."

"Mr. Maddox," Caroline said, descending the stairs. How she had safely managed into a beautiful gown at her stage, neither had any idea. She was still, but for her midsection, the image of grace and female form. Her curtsey, however, was excusably minor. "How are you?"

"Quite well, all things considered and that you may hear otherwise. But I must be off in the morning, sadly. I have a most important letter to deliver."

Only when things were fully explained and she was satisfied was he permitted to go to sleep, and in the morning, they saw him off in the carriage to Dover.

"Why is your brother so dutiful to the Darcys?"

"I believe the answer is obvious," Daniel Maddox said. "Besides, he has always been a man of honor when not at a card table or in a gambling den. Unfortunately, he is usually at one of the two."

After one month, many bribes, many horses, and a few close calls with authorities, Brian Maddox was back over the border and into the ancient hills of Italy. He instinctively headed towards the villa. His instincts were often very keen, except when it came to games of chance. Stopping to take a breather by a stream that must eventually have fed the Tiber and then the ocean, he washed his neck and sat in the shade. He knew if he just leaned against the tree, he would be fast asleep and lose the day, and he was not foolish or fast enough to travel this area at night.

He had lied a little to Daniel. He did, at times, have pains in his chest that a surgeon told him were phantom. He had lost weight. He had grey in his hair, coming in at the roots. He was becoming an old man before his time. Maybe settling down would not be such a terrible idea. Perhaps that very notion was why he had not gambled a penny since the day he met Nadezhda in private during their second meeting, when they were afforded some time alone on a balcony, out of sight of her overbearing, bearded hulk of a father.

Why was he turning his thoughts to her now? Wasn't he on an important mission? His brother would never grant his consent—not that he needed his brother's consent. He was a man and, besides, the older one. He just wanted Danny's look of approval for once, nodding just once in a way that said, *You have done something right. I know I'm as shocked as you are.* Only, Daniel Maddox wouldn't say it that way.

He got back on his horse and continued his journey. He made it to the villa, just outside Rome, in another two days. There he found an overeager Darcy shaking his hand and not doing the proper thing of reading the letter in private in whatever room he designated his study. He read it aloud to all present. Mr. Bennet accepted the terms. All that he wished was his daughter's happiness, of course. (And they knew Mr. Bennet meant it.)

Darcy turned unceremoniously to Brian and said, "What is the absolute fastest way to get to England without riding?"

"Without riding? By carriage."

"We could not go fast by carriage."

Brian shrugged, confused. "Then, I suppose, you could charter a boat that would go around France and take you to home. But it would be a monstrous expense and still take time."

"How long?"

He was getting alarmed by the urgency in Darcy's voice. Darcy rarely laid his emotions so bare. "Between one to two months to sail all the way around France, depending on the weather. But we would have to be lucky with the barricades."

"Can you arrange it for us immediately?"

"Of course," he said. "What is this all about? What's wrong?"

"It's not—wrong," Elizabeth said. "Nothing is wrong. I just cannot ride on a horse, and we need to return."

"Even the carriage would be a bit bumpy," Darcy said.

"Oh," Brian said. And then again, "*Oh*. Well, uhm, why don't I see about a ship then, a fast one."

"Cost is not a concern," Darcy stressed. "I will go to Rome now with the letter and see about the financial arrangements. They will probably take a day or two."

"I will return as fast as possible from the port with arrangements in a day or two," Brian said. I hope your brother has adapted to life at sea, Mr. Darcy, or we'll all be in a lot of trouble. Though, a man can survive without food for a time if he is kept properly watered."

"Don't make Grégoire sound like a plant," was all Darcy had to say to that. "You have made the assumption that I intend to take him back to England."

"But I am probably correct."

Darcy, it seemed, felt himself at a loss and only shrugged. They had more urgent business to attend to.

The Darcys, together and separately, said their good-byes to Rome. It was a pleasant place, but it was not home, not even to Grégoire, who spent the most time there. One night, he did not return at all, and Darcy stayed up in concern, long after his wife had retired. He was sitting on the stairs, knowing Grégoire would have to climb them to get to his room. When his brother did reappear, the sun was rising, and he looked exhausted. He shambled up the steps, nodded to Darcy, and attempted to make his way to his room. Darcy grabbed his bloodied robes. "I thought we spoke of this."

"The last time, Darcy. For Elizabeth."

"Explain to me, in detail, how this will help my wife."

"It is not a medical thing to be stated. It is a matter of faith, Brother, that the yoke of heaven can be pulled off one person and assigned to another." He turned around, and despite his obvious extreme discomfort, stared right back up at his towering, intimidating brother. "I would not see her suffer. She deserves only happiness."

"While I disagree with your methods, I agree with the notion, however misguided, that we both wish the best for Elizabeth. But, if this is truly the last time, then I will take your word as a solemn vow."

"I vow it." Grégoire crossed himself.

"Then," Darcy said, "let me help you to your room. That is, I believe, not part of the program."

Grégoire did not contradict him. As the birds chirped for early morning, Darcy bandaged his brother, lent him a shirt, and ordered the last remaining servant to wash out his robe with as much soap as possible. It was not until the monk was asleep on his mat on the floor that Darcy returned to his own bed, sliding next to Elizabeth, a hand on her stomach, and fell asleep. There was silence as he drifted off, and for the moment, that was enough.

Chapter 21

THE LONG WAY HOME

THE TIME SPENT ON the ship was easily the most miserable of Darcy's entire life that did not involve some emotional disaster. In fact, despite the impending confrontation with Wickham—who he had decided would have to be told—hanging over his head, he was looking forward to returning to England now that their business was concluded as favorably as it could have been, beyond even his own expectations. He had gained a brother and, in some measure, restored a sister-in-law to a position in which she could live her life. He missed Geoffrey and the Bingleys terribly, and there was, of course, the exhilarating matter of Lizzy in delicate condition again. All of this put him in a good mood—until he stepped on that boat.

For now he had two sick people to deal with, not one. Grégoire had not overcome his seasickness and did not do so over the course of the trip. Elizabeth was ill as well, and the rocking of the boat made her maternal sufferings worse. They spent most of their time sick in their cabin after the sailors tired of them rushing to the edge of the deck.

"How can you even—Grégoire, I know for a fact you haven't eaten anything in two days now! It isn't even possible! I don't know biologics, but I know that!" Darcy protested helplessly, to which Elizabeth gave a very pale smile and Grégoire just collapsed from exhaustion, to be hoisted up again and helped back onto a bench by Darcy.

His only reprieve was when the ship took port briefly in France. Elizabeth and Grégoire had time to get off the boat and eat something, out of fear of starvation, and they were somewhat restored while on land. Then they got back on the boat, and his misery resumed.

He barely had time to take his exhausted brother aside. "When we return to England—obviously, there will be some shock, but I wanted to ask if you wished to be called Grégoire Bellamont or Grégoire Darcy."

"Excuse my lack of knowledge of custom—"

"It is nothing. It is whatever you wish."

Elizabeth, barely conscious herself but aware enough to listen in, knew it to be otherwise. What Darcy was offering was to acknowledge Grégoire as a Darcy, in direct opposite of convention for a bastard son. She doubted he would offer the same thing to Wickham.

Grégoire shook his head. "I am just a humble servant of the Lord. Please, Brother, call me whatever suits you."

This was no help to Darcy, of course, and even Grégoire must have known that, but Elizabeth could not help but smile at Darcy's exasperation. She knew, in private, that his plans for his brother were comprehensive, that he hoped to convince Grégoire to at least switch to a monastery in Germany or somewhere safer than unstable France. Darcy could be as convincing as Grégoire could be stubborn, but she figured she would glean what amusement she could from the situation.

Since they were moving faster than the mail, their arrival was unannounced. They received no reception at the docks at Dover, nor at the house in Town when the carriage brought them home. No one was expecting them home for at least a month, and they could only hope that Georgiana was in Town to receive them when they arrived at the Darcy townhouse. But first there was the matter of getting Grégoire across the long, sloped plank between the dreaded ship and the dock.

"How is a man who lives on a mountain afraid of heights?" Darcy said as he practically carried him down the plank.

"Mountains are not generally directly over water," Elizabeth pointed out as she stepped onto the wood of the dock and then the cobbled stones above English soil.

The Darcys were back.

⋅⋅⋈⋅⋅

Though their desire to see Geoffrey was now immense, they could not go straight to Derbyshire. They took a carriage to the Darcy house in London. It was not practical or polite to disregard Georgiana, whom they found in the music room, at the piano. That she was surprised at their sudden arrival was an understatement. "Brother!" She ran to embrace him before the equally shocked servants could get his coat off and his manservant could be called. "Sister!"

"Oh, please don't," Elizabeth said. "Or I will be ill. Please, I must sit."

Darcy, ill only from exhaustion, said as politely as he could manage to the servants rushing to his side to greet their master,

"Please get some tea and food, and have it brought into the parlor immediately. And call for a courier." After Georgiana released him, he helped the green-looking Elizabeth to a comfortable sofa. "Sit. We are home."

In her state, she merely gestured to Grégoire, and Darcy realized the massive duty he now had, besides getting his brother back to health. "Georgiana," he said softly, "please allow me to introduce Brother Grégoire Bellamont of the Cistercians, our half-brother."

Grégoire bowed not the polite bow of a gentleman, but the deep bow of an exceedingly humble man.

"But—that means Father—"

"Yes, it does mean Father," Darcy said, knowing the sentence made no sense. "I was as surprised as you are, but he is, in fact, our father's son. He is but five months younger than you."

Georgiana looked hard at Grégoire, sizing up the young monk before her in his tattered robes and outright bizarre haircut, before running across the room to embrace him. Grégoire stiffened before accepting this and hesitantly put his arms around Georgiana.

"I've always wanted a brother," she said. "I mean, my own age." She pulled away so he had to look into her face. "Did Father really leave you so poor?"

"No, he was very kind to me," Grégoire said in that bizarre, part French, part cultured English accent. Over their travels, he had picked up on the way Darcy and Elizabeth spoke, and now that they thought about it, the change was noticeable.

"In fact, Grégoire is one of the richer men in England," Darcy said. "Father was indeed very kind. This is merely his own religious persuasion, and he is as stubborn as the rest of our family about it. But while you get acquainted, I must send some couriers to let others know that we are here."

"Yes," she said as Darcy left, leaving the three of them. Georgiana turned to Elizabeth. "You are home quite early."

"We decided rather abruptly to return by ship, which was faster than a land courier, so there was no way to send a message ahead."

"Is everything all right?"

"Oh yes," Elizabeth said as tea was served. "Just Darcy being his nervous self about getting home safely since we discovered I was with child."

"Oh! Elizabeth!" Georgiana briefly abandoned her new-found brother to hug her sister-in-law, despite her modest protests. "How wonderful! When is your confinement?"

"Oh, I'm barely two months or so along. I haven't even thought about it. I was honestly just thinking of returning home. We will discuss everything later. And Grégoire, *eat something*; you're on land now."

"Thank the Lord," Grégoire said, as he crossed himself, and the servants appeared with platters of cakes and tea. "His Holiness may be a fisher of men, but I am no seaman."

"I think we have proved that, yes," Elizabeth said, grinning to Georgiana. "He has no sea legs at all. Between him and my feminine ills, Darcy had his hands full the whole voyage making sure we didn't fall off the ship. But, tell me, how is Geoffrey? How much trouble has he gotten into?"

"I wouldn't say a *lot* of trouble that I've heard of," she said. "Or from what I've heard from Mr. Bingley, who is in Town every other week to check on his sister. Or at least, he has not said anything terrible of Geoffrey."

"Mrs. Maddox—she's must be nearing the end of her confinement now, am I correct? Oh, I've terribly lost track of time."

"She is. It would be at Chatton, but—Dr. Maddox is required in Town, and she will not leave him, or him, her. I dine there most nights. He won't talk about his royal patient, of course, but he has met the king! And he is insane!"

"The king or Dr. Maddox?"

"Elizabeth!" Georgiana turned to her newfound sibling, who was taking his food in silence. "Brother, I must explain. Caroline Maddox is Mr. Bingley's older sister, who has married Dr. Maddox, who is now the royal physician to the Prince of Wales. It is all terribly complicated when our three families get together. Chatton, I hear, is a madhouse."

"And my sister?" Elizabeth asked.

She did not have to inquire which one to get an answer. "She is quite well, from what I hear, all things considered. And Mr. Bennet, from Mr. Bingley's description, is much relieved at the settlement. Everyone is. Brother has saved the day again! Oh, now I must specify *which* brother."

It was then that Darcy reappeared in the entrance. "I've posted to Chatton and to Pemberley to open up the place. Darling, do you wish to dine with the Maddoxes tonight or just rest here? We should see them before we go, and if everyone is recovered enough, I would very much like to strike for Chatton tomorrow."

"Yes," she said. "Leave for Chatton tomorrow, please, and I am well enough now. Grégoire?"

He broke his eating to say, "Now that I am on land, I should be fine."

"And Dr. Maddox *is* a doctor," Darcy said.

A similarly exhausted Brian Maddox shambled his way to the Maddox townhouse and was warmly greeted by his brother and *very* confined sister-in-law, who had not been told a date and, therefore, were a bit, though not overly, surprised to see him.

"I suppose I must treat my hosts to some gossip, as I'm sure Mrs. Maddox would enjoy it," Brian Maddox said.

"Absolutely," said Caroline.

"But you have to promise me not to tell the Darcys I told you and to act all surprised when you hear it from them. For I know your promises are much better than mine, and I can actually count on them."

"Oh, out with it, already," she said with a roll of the eyes, leaning on her husband. Even the good doctor's interest looked a bit piqued.

"Mr. Darcy has returned to England with a bastard brother he did not previously know of," Brian said. "Though, honestly, I'm having trouble calling a monk a bastard."

This was, indeed, the kind of gossip that made Caroline Maddox (nee Bingley) most excited. She almost fell over giggling, and the doctor had to hold her up. "You can't be *serious*."

"I most certainly am. I spent a month on a boat with the seasick bugger. Though he is most pious and—young; he's younger than Miss Darcy, I believe. Don't have the exact dates. He's very much like her, but he looks like what I imagine to be a young Darcy."

"So, sweet and pious, but stubborn as hell?"

"Precisely. They've tried to talk him out of the whole monastic business, but he won't budge."

"Oh, thank God," Caroline said between laughter. "I haven't

heard an interesting thing in weeks. Louisa hardly knows any-thing... Miss Darcy is too polite to even *listen* to Town gossip... and my dear husband here, who made me this way, won't tell me a single thing about the prince."

The doctor, feeling compelled to preserve his dignity, said, "He has brown hair."

"That I know! I saw him, dear."

"Driving your poor wife batty with your discretion, aren't you, Danny?" Brian smiled, to which his brother could only shrug.

Dr. Maddox immediately called on the Darcys, who intended to stay only the night in Town, despite their exhaustion, and head toward Derbyshire after Darcy concluded some Town busi-ness the next day. He invited them to dinner, and what were apparently four Darcys sat at his table, including a young man who was most certainly a monk. Daniel hadn't seen a proper tonsure in years, even if this one was lacking some care from the journey and the hair on the top of his head was stubbornly try-ing to grow out again. That and their tales of Rome and France brought back a flood of pleasant memories.

The Maddoxes did not press too hard, for the Darcys were positively done in, and Brother Grégoire, with his strange mixture of accents, would not speak while eating and looked very intimi-dated by the number of strange dishes. Brian, in fact, was forced to tell the tale of how he came to meet them in France, though he was uncharacteristically modest about it, and Elizabeth supplied the actual details of how he'd saved all of their lives. Despite the intense interest of their hosts, the guests were released early, off to well-deserved rest. Only Darcy took a moment to corner the doctor in a hallway, which came as no surprise to Maddox.

"Is Mrs. Darcy well?" he asked mildly.

"Yes, as much as can be expected. Though the ship was a miserable experience for someone ill in the morning, a doctor in Rome advised us that it would do her no harm. My concern is with my brother."

The doctor merely nodded silently, waiting for him to continue.

"At a later date—perhaps, when we are properly settled at Pemberley, I would like him to be checked."

"For what, precisely?"

"He is a monk from one of the strictest orders. He has spent years destroying his body." Darcy didn't seem to be eager to explain it, but Maddox was not an uneducated man, and he nodded. "We are now restoring him to a decent state of health. If you would look at him—"

"Gladly." He added, "And I do recommend, if I may, that you make arrangements for him to not wear the same robe every day, as I imagine he does. It does lead to diseases of the skin. Perhaps, at least he could wear an undershirt."

"He is most intractable about his habits."

"How odd," Maddox said in a tone that meant precisely the opposite. "Well, Mr. Darcy, I will do what I can as soon as I can. Although my consultation may have to wait until after Caroline delivers, if it can."

"I believe it can. It has waited years, after all."

Maddox nodded again, and Darcy appeared relieved. That, for the moment, was enough.

The Darcys did end up spending most of the morning in

Town, as Elizabeth and Grégoire slept late, and Darcy had to make various banking arrangements. These would be finalized when Mr. Bennet returned to Longbourn, but at the moment, they stood ready, and the trust for Miss Bennet's child, if she delivered successfully, was set up.

Darcy returned to the house with a coach ready. Georgiana would be joining them, eager to be in Pemberley again and apparently eager to spend time with her newfound brother. But first, Chatton, where everyone they currently held dear was lodged.

Because Darcy would not let the carriage go at full speed, the trip took a full five days, with nightly lodging in familiar inns (with terrible wines by their new standards).

They were expected at Chatton, thanks to letters sent ahead, and Geoffrey saw them first, waiting not inside but some way down along the road, and who came running before anyone else could stop him, running straight into his mother so hard that he almost tackled her. "Mother!"

"Darling!" she said, kneeling to greet him at his level, because she wouldn't dare pick him up. "You've grown," she said as they embraced. "Oh, I missed you so much."

"It does seem so," said the smiling Darcy, who patted his son on the head. Geoffrey Darcy had gained, in the roughly six months they were gone, nearly an inch. He was nearing three years now, when his education would begin. They had missed so many precious months... it pained him, but he would not show it. "Come here," he said, when he could finally tear him Geoffrey away from his mother, and Darcy managed to lift his son into his arms. "My, you are getting a bit heavy for this. Did you miss us?"

"I wrote! Uncle Bingley taught me my initials."

"Indeed he did," Darcy said. "We got your letter." He kissed him on the cheek. "Now, please greet your Aunt Georgiana and your Uncle Grégoire."

He set him down, but Geoffrey only looked up at his father in confusion. "I don't have an Uncle Greg-war."

"I did not know it either, until recently. But, you must greet him properly." He patted his son on the back, and Geoffrey did walk over to his waiting relatives and give a proper, adorable bow to his aunt and uncle.

"Our little gentleman," Elizabeth said with tears in her eyes.

"*Finally*," Darcy said, partially in jest.

Geoffrey did embrace his aunt, or at least her legs, before turning and staring up in wonder at his new uncle. "Why are you wearing a dress?"

Darcy went to say something, but Elizabeth silenced him with a look.

"It is a robe," Grégoire said, bunching up the sleeves.

"Why are you wearing a robe?"

"Because I am a monk."

"What's a monk? What happened to your head?"

"Nothing happened to my head."

"Then what happened to your hair?"

Grégoire had stopped at a confused barber in Town and had the proper areas of his head shaved again. "It is symbolic of the crown of the church."

"Oh." Geoffrey, of course, meant it without any comprehension, and then he turned to his father and said, "Can I have my hair—"

"*No*," Darcy interrupted, "absolutely not."

"But I want to wear a crown!"

"That's treason, son. Better not let the king hear you say that."

"But Uncle Bingley says that Uncle Maddox says that the king is batty," said Geoffrey, who turned back to his new uncle. "Are you batty?"

"*I* think he is," Darcy said, and Elizabeth laughed into his shoulder.

They walked the rest of the way to Chatton. The carriage went ahead of them, so there was a crowd waiting to greet them. The Darcys had arrived.

"Now, legitimately," said Bingley, "*some* of this is my own fault."

"You owe me five shillings," Elizabeth whispered to her husband at the sight of Mr. Bingley with his hands and face dyed red.

Chapter 22

THE SAD TALE OF MRS. REYNOLDS

"IT IS NOT ENTIRELY his fault, certainly," Jane Bingley said as she embraced her sister. "But a man should look in his washbasin, before rinsing his face in the morning, to see if someone has poured ink in it."

"I wasn't even fully awake!" Bingley defended, crossing his arms and trying to look stern, which was hard to do with a bright red face that only made his hair look even more orange. "And who was responsible for that, I say?"

"Very little mystery there," said Mr. Bennet, taking his turn with Lizzy and Darcy.

"It was a surprise! For Mother and Father," Geoffrey defended.

"I suppose I will be checking my washbasin every day now. Or at least locking my door better," Darcy said, eyeing his son. "We will settle this when we reach Pemberley, which unfortunately for you, will be very shortly."

There were hugs and kisses and bows all around. And many congratulations for everyone's sake, for a great burden had come off their shoulders—except for Mary, but she was not carrying it on her shoulders. She did seem much less distressed than when they had left her. Darcy introduced Brother Grégoire, to which Bingley only said rather quietly, "The infamous guide." Elizabeth told her parents the great news, something Darcy discovered because of the shriek from Mrs. Bennet and the flurry and hugs and kisses.

"At last, at last! Oh, Lizzy, you will be a mother again at last. This time I am sure of it!"

"I do not believe she ever stopped," Mr. Bennet said.

There were trinkets to be distributed, for the Darcys had purchased things for their beloved family in Rome and had been able to bring these mementos on the ship without much trouble. Mr. Bennet and Mr. Bingley were exceedingly happy with their rare books and Mrs. Bennet with beautiful yarns, for she did love sewing for her many grandchildren. Kitty had outgrown ribbons but still loved bonnets, especially those beyond the limits of what could be found in England, and Mary was given a little book of hymns. Little Georgiana Bingley was given a doll that she would carry around for years.

The Chatton crowd—and it was, indeed, a crowd—was very unhappy at the idea that the Darcys would not be staying the night. But Darcy put his foot down and said he wanted to see Pemberley in the worst way after the long journey, and if they stayed for dinner, they could not introduce it to his brother properly. The mention of "his brother" turned some heads, for Brother Grégoire's presence had not been explained fully, but Darcy assured them there would be time for that when other, more pressing matters were settled. And so, after only a few joyous hours of reunion at Chatton, the Darcys set off on the road with the addition of Geoffrey, who was told he would receive his present when his punishment was over, though his punishment was not specified. The five of them traveled the last three miles to the great house of Pemberley.

A large audience—almost the entire staff of servants—had gathered to greet their long-absent master and mistress. They also awaited the return of Georgiana and her nephew, who trailed behind his father's coattails. What they did not expect was the last member of the party, the young monk who bowed to them deeper than they bowed to him and would have no one attend to him.

As housekeeper, Mrs. Reynolds was at the head, and she paled at the sight of Grégoire, even though he had not been identified. Darcy put his arm around the monk and approached her. "This is Grégoire Bellamont from the Monastery of Mont Claire. Mrs. Reynolds, I believe you have something to explain."

In the master study, the aged Mrs. Reynolds had to face not one, but three Darcys, as only Geoffrey and Georgiana were excluded, with Geoffrey seeming very annoyed at being pulled away from his mother. When the door was soundly shut behind them, Darcy took his seat at the desk. Above him hung the portrait of his father, looking regal and proper. "Now," he said as his wife sat next to the terrified housekeeper, and Grégoire stood, "You have undoubtedly surmised Grégoire's heritage. Though I doubt you have ever said a dishonest thing to anyone present in your life, that does not mean certain things were not made known to me, I assume under Father's instructions. But now I would like to know how you came to know these things."

"Yes, Mr. Darcy, of course." Mrs. Reynolds was shaking. "Oh, please forgive me, but your father's last wish to me was that you not know of these things until the proper time."

"Which would be now," Darcy said.

"Yes, of course."

⸙

1797

Mrs. Reynolds had to quietly admit to herself that she did enjoy her position as housekeeper. It did bring tremendous responsibility, and the status was not something she had sought greedily, but there was something to be said for taking pride in keeping Pemberley in top shape. It had been hard at times with three children in the house, one a toddler and two in their teens at the time of her elevation, and no guiding mother to rein them in. Mrs. Wickham and Mrs. Darcy had died during or immediately after childbirth, and young Master Fitzwilliam, who did so dislike being called that, was the only one who had experienced having the pleasure of a mother for his first thirteen years.

While their nurses and governesses were responsible for the children, they answered to Mrs. Reynolds as well as Mr. Darcy, who was busy and a gentleman and, therefore, not quite expected to act paternally toward Miss Georgiana in an overly interested way, though he did at times. Until the end of his days, Mr. Darcy was often busy with keeping up the estate or away from Pemberley, and while he was there, his chief concern was raising his son, the wild Fitzwilliam, who had to grow up some day to be a gentleman and master.

And grow up he did. In fact, despite their single year of age difference, Master George and Master Fitzwilliam seemed to be going in opposite directions with their lives, despite a fierce (and often, outright indecorous) competition between them at all the things boys competed about. When they were children, they competed at riding, fishing, and fencing. When they were young men, the competition turned to women, though the young George Wickham certainly had the edge there, because Mrs. Reynolds never heard a word about Master Fitzwilliam and any servants or local girls from Lambton, and she heard every word that Pemberley whispered.

When Mr. Wickham, the steward, died, Mr. Darcy took on all the responsibilities of raising and educating Wickham's son. The master was not known for being unkind, but he certainly exceeded the general expectation of generosity in doing this. By the year the boys went to Cambridge, he was actively turning his eyes away from the young Wickham's actions. Mr. Darcy said nary a word when Mr. Wickham was sent down from Cambridge, embracing him back into the estate while Master Fitzwilliam continued his studies.

The year that Mr. Darcy's illness became obvious was the year that Master Fitzwilliam returned from touring the Continent, as required by any respectable gentleman newly graduated from university and not quite ready to settle down for the rest of his life. Upon young Darcy's return, his training as future master, which had truly begun the day he was born, resumed actively and even sped up a bit when Mr. Darcy's prognosis was delivered. They learned they had a year left together, and it was well spent, so that the transition between masters would be smooth. The little boy who had once refused to bathe after jumping in a lake stepped up to his responsibilities in a way that made everyone proud.

Late fall should have been a pleasant time for everyone before it got truly cold in Derbyshire, but the angel of death hung over Pemberley. To his dying day, Mr. Geoffrey Darcy would not be idle. He was signing contracts and record books until forcibly locked in his chambers for rest. A week before the angel came, Mrs. Reynolds was called into Mr. Darcy's office—not an unusual occurrence, except that Master Fitzwilliam was not present, as he had been at every meeting for months now, and she knew of no particular topic to be discussed. Clearly the master had one; she merely didn't know it.

Mr. Darcy coughed and asked that she make sure the door was closed, and then he had her lock it on his behalf.

"Mr. Darcy."

"Mrs. Reynolds." He did not get up. First, she was a servant. Second, she doubted he could do so easily. He was leaning on the desk, propped up by an elbow, his eyes bloodshot. Had he been crying? "Thank you for coming. Do be seated."

Another strange occurrence; the good master was obviously out of sorts. He fumbled with something in his hands—a locket that she recognized as having belonged to his late wife. "I know you are a busy woman, and I will not take up much of your time and mine, which I am told by my doctors is now precious. Instead I will merely burden you with the most terrible of secrets, as it should be spoken once more before I die, and as you will come to understand, it cannot be told to my son—yet. I will also thrust upon you the trust that you will find the day to tell him."

She did not know quite what to say to this.

"You will recall the affair with Ms. Bellamont, my wife's lady-maid. You were, I believe, laundress at the time? But it must have been known all around Pemberley. I have no doubt of that."

"I do, sir, though I recall few of the specifics, and those that I do, I care not to repeat."

"Then I will summarize. Ms. Bellamont was discharged when my wife discovered she was with child, and the part you perhaps do not know is that the child was mine."

No, she did not know that. She could not fathom it, even as he said it, even as the intensity of his gaze confirmed it. The French-born maid was of excellent standing until her dismissal, working her way up the ranks of Pemberley. That she was dismissed during Mrs. Darcy's confinement with Georgiana was the most damning thing about her departure—until this point. This implied, of course, that not only had he had a dalliance with a lady-maid (not entirely unknown, but something she would have never expected from Mr. Darcy), but he did so during his own wife's confinement.

"Earlier this year," he continued, expecting her stunned silence, "I went to the Continent on business, and that business was to set up an account for my son, who was apparently named the French version of Gregory, after me in some fashion. He lives with his mother in the west of France and intends to join the church. According to the specifications of the account, he will receive a considerable yearly income for the rest of his life. No records of this account exist in England, and the account can only be altered by myself or the executor of my estate—meaning, Fitzwilliam, who obviously knows nothing of this.

"The timing is terrible, because I do not wish my son to lose both me and his esteem of me at the same time. I do not know what would happen to him or to Pemberley, but I cannot take the chance. He might go the way George went—as they are so very closely related."

He had another coughing fit, and Mrs. Reynolds rose to pour him a glass of water, for he had dismissed the servant meant to do exactly that. After swallowing some, he was able to continue in a hoarse voice. "I do not know which sin is more terrible, but there are two. George Wickham is also my son."

Her heart quickened. Yes, that made sense, on a logical level. He had raised George as a father would raise a son, beyond normal responsibilities, and his affection for his steward did not explain it beyond a certain point. Mr. Darcy had had many fights with his own son—his proper son—over Mr. Wickham, who was meant to receive a sizable living in the church upon Mr. Darcy's death. Master Fitzwilliam felt this inheritance was undeserved, and many servants believed he had every right, knowing Wickham well enough, to insist that that man deserved no more assistance from Pemberley. But Mr. Darcy would not relent, and no one could figure the reason. Now, of course, it was clear.

"I love my sons—all three of them. I have provided for all of them, partially I suppose out of guilt... guilt I should rightfully feel for being part of the worst kind of deception with Mrs. Wickham, a lovely woman until the day she died, as we never told George. He believed his son was his and named him so, and I did not prevent it. I did not have the courage to come forward and torture this man with the truth. So I am a coward as well as an adulterer. I am the worst master Pemberley has ever had."

"No, Sir—"

"Do not try to contradict me. Any good I tried to do in this life will not lift this terrible guilt from my heart. There is no absolution for me because Anne would not give it." He coughed again. Mrs. Reynolds, her mind still reeling, could not help but notice that Mr. Darcy, despite his affection for his wife, never called her by her first name in front of a servant.

"On her dying day she cursed me. She had found out about Miss Bellamont, and so she cursed me by refusing forgiveness and naming our new daughter Georgiana. The whole story had come out, and I would always hear that name—George, the name of my first sin—when I spoke the name of my own daughter, who I would have to raise alone. Anne forsook me, and she had every right and reason to. But I could not stand my son doing the same at my own deathbed—for he could hardly do otherwise, with the morality I've raised him with. Some things, Mrs. Reynolds, are worse than death." He seemed to shield his eyes from her. "Surely you will try to understand why I ask this of you."

"To be plain, sir, what do you wish of me?"

"That you tell Fitzwilliam and Georgiana at the proper time, whenever you judge it to be. For some day, they should know. Perhaps when they are settled and happy and are ready for a blow such as this. When they are, do you know of the old d'Arcy estate? The Hôtel des Capuchins?"

"I've heard of it, sir."

"I have an account at a bank near there that is funding Gregory, or Grégoire as he is called. He knows of his heritage because I spoke to him in February, but I doubt he would come to England of his own motivation. That is perhaps the best way to find him, if this is to be years away. And God, I hope it will be." He wiped his eyes with his trembling fingers, because he was definitely crying now. "I have not said a word of this to anyone but him and his mother since the day Anne died. And now, you will be the only one who will know. I will trust you with this awful burden, Mrs. Reynolds. It is the last thing I will ask of you before Pemberley goes into my son's capable hands."

She nodded and agreed, and he dismissed her. As she went out, she noticed Master Fitzwilliam, soon to be *the* Mr. Darcy, passing by with a folio. She did her best to hide her tears from him. Thankfully, he seemed not to notice.

⌘

1807

"So," Darcy said after the considerable silence that followed her tale. "Wickham is my brother. I had but one strand of hope left that it was not true. And, I suppose, if he had not attempted an elopement with Georgiana—"

"—I would have said something immediately, of course, Mr. Darcy," Mrs. Reynolds, again in tears, said. Elizabeth put a hand on her shoulder to steady her. The atmosphere in the room, though tense, was not damning. In fact, Darcy was quite cool in his own tone, not dismissive of her at all. "Immediately. Or perhaps I failed and should have said something earlier."

"None of us had that foresight. It seems fate saved us all from a sin of biblical proportions. Excuse me, God saved us from this sin," he said, as Grégoire crossed himself. "Georgiana knows about Grégoire, but not Wickham. I cannot imagine how to tell her, but I must do it."

"Darcy—"

For once, Darcy held a hand up to his wife. "I must do it. There is also the other person who knows nothing—Wickham himself. This matter must be settled with him first, as I have no idea of his reaction."

He sighed and continued, "Though I cannot say I am pleased

with this news of my own father's failings, I cannot find fault with the carrying out of your duties, Mrs. Reynolds. For you did not know of Wickham's plans for Georgiana any more than I, her legal protector as well as brother, did. You pointed me in the direction of Grégoire at a time when I was content with life and ready for such a blow. I have gained at least one brother in this." He looked at Grégoire and smiled wanly before turning to Mrs. Reynolds. "I am sorry to put you through this inquisition. Now at least you are freed from the responsibility of such a secret."

"If you wish me gone, Mr. Darcy—"

"Very much the opposite; in a way, Father was right, and I am grateful. I modeled my life after the good in him and am now reaping the results. I would not want to imagine it otherwise." He smiled. "Please see that Grégoire is situated in whatever accommodations he chooses. My only insistence is that, while in my house, he eats three full meals a day. He is very clever about his monkish habits, so keep an eye on him. Somehow we will have to find common ground between his heritage as a Darcy and his leanings as a Cistercian."

Grégoire flushed and put his head down, but he did not look entirely surprised at this. More significantly, he probably did not realize that Darcy had established him as a family member in front of Mrs. Reynolds, who would tell the servants to do so as well. Despite his own inclinations, the master had embraced him as a Darcy, and he would be treated as such. And oh, the little monk did look much like his father—unlike Wickham, who favored his mother.

Now the only obvious question was whether Darcy would show the same sympathy for George Wickham, unknowing in his parentage, and embrace him as a brother as he had Grégoire, however reluctantly. On this, Darcy remained silent.

THE WORST KIND OF CALL

THE MADDOXES—ALL THREE of them—were sitting down to dinner when the bell rang. Since the summons obviously was for him, the doctor walked past the servants, who were busy serving the meal, and answered the door, peering out into the lamplight of the Town's evening streets. "Hello?"

"Doctor." It was the madam of one of the houses he used to visit. He was quite aware of which house and had politely informed them, upon his commission, that they would have to find another doctor, so her appearance was a surprise. Besides, she had always sent a man instead of coming herself.

"Mrs. Dudley," he said with a bow. "I regret to remind you that I am no longer—"

"This is not about that," she said, climbing the steps and moving close enough to whisper to him. "This is about Lilly."

"I must also remind you, I am not a midwife."

"She has delivered," Mrs. Dudley said. "Three days ago. And now she is in a terrible way. I know you are not supposed to, and I will understand if you do not wish to be associated—"

"No," he said. "Let me get my things."

He hurried back and called for his doctor's bag and his coat, one of the shabbier ones. "A patient," was all he said, but from his clothing, the patient was obviously not the prince. Doctor Maddox excused himself and kissed his wife good-bye before joining the madam in her carriage. "Describe her symptoms."

"She has a fever and is bleeding a lot. We called the midwife back, but she could do nothing. And Lilly is in great pain."

He nodded. He had already made his diagnosis, but he would not announce it until he saw the woman. They traveled across Town, to lodgings near the old house, and Dr. Maddox followed her up a set of very creaky steps to a tiny room where Lilly lay on the bed, barely covered, with some of her blanket spotted with blood.

"Miss Garrison," Doctor Maddox said with all his doctorly formality, rousing her from her resting state.

"Doc?" Her eyes, somewhat unfocused when he brought the lamp up to see her properly, seemed to look him over as if he had arrived from heaven.

"Yes, Lilly," he said, and took her pulse and put his hand against her forehead. She had a raging fever, but the rest of her body was sweaty and cold. "Tell me where it hurts. Anywhere other than your feminine region?"

"So proper," she said. "No. Just—yeh know."

"Yes. If you wouldn't mind me doing a small inspection—"

"Plenty a men 'ave seen it, doc. Yeh know that."

"That does not prevent me asking permission," he said. Opening his bag, he removed his spectacles, which were monstrously expensive and did not work quite as well as his own eyes, but he used them exclusively when he had something he wanted to see clearly without getting in close range. He pulled up the blanket and asked the Madame to hold up the light so he could see. The smell itself was overpowering, so it was not hard to make his diagnosis. The problem was how to do it. He looked at the Madame grimly, but she did not seem surprised.

It was Lilly herself who sounded annoyed at the delay. "Out with it."

Maddox took the spectacles off, replaced his normal glasses, and pulled up a chair by her side. "The tissue in your canal is torn from the birth, and it is infected."

"From that terrible look on yer face, yeh might's'well just say it."

He did not like this part. "Childbed fever, Lilly. The result of a great struggle to bring a child into this world."

She must have known, even with some of her senses left from days of pain and fever, that there was nothing he could do. Infection could hardly be prevented, much less cured. Still, it was horrible not only to know that but also to watch the clear reaction on her face, the way she didn't question him for a magic pill or at least something to *help*.

Uncomfortable in the silence, he said, "Is there anything I can do to see to your comfort? I mean, is there anything you would like?"

"I'd like yeh to box George in the head, but I s'ppose it'd get yeh killed, and yeh deserve yer nice life with yer pretty wife."

The doctor managed a wan smile.

"S'ppose I should name 'im George, what after 'is pop. But I'm so tired." She closed her eyes. "Stay with me?"

"Of course."

"Yeh got this real calming voice, doc."

"You want me to read to you?"

"S'ppose it would be nice. Anything but the Bible, aye don' want ta hear 'bout Hell."

"All right." Fortunately, he always had a book in his bag for long visits where he was stuck with an unconscious patient. Plucking the current one out, he cleared his throat and began to read, "'The double sorrow I do tell, of Troilus, who was the son of King Priamus of Troy. In love, how his fortunes befell, from sorrow to happiness, and after out of joy—'"

The hour fell late, and his voice was hoarse when he felt the hand he held go limp and cold. "'What, is this all the joy and all the rejoicing? Is this your advice? Is this my happy situation?'" He looked up and closed his book somewhere in Book Three of Chaucer's lesser masterpiece.

He took her pulse and called for a priest. One was ready, in fact, in the other room, and as the holy water was touched upon her brow, Dr. Maddox removed his glasses to dry them from his tears. He finally managed to bring the blanket over her face and paid the priest. Exhausted, he was closing up his bag when he noticed the madam standing by his side and pointing into the next room. There was a figure there.

"Who—Caroline?" he squinted. The figure in the dark was unmistakable. Only one woman would have a proper gown fitted to the last months of her term and wear it to such a place. Unmistakably, emerging from the shadows in the unlit next room was his wife, bearing a cooing infant in her arms, wrapped in her own shawl. She looked up from it only to gaze at the scene before her. Finally, Maddox had the courage to mumble, "You shouldn't be here. It's—"

"—not proper?"

"I was going to say 'sanitary.'" He stood to greet his wife, who presented him with a newborn with a small amount of brown hair, half-asleep but still murmuring softly. He looked at the baby and said to it, "You've no idea." To what, he didn't clarify. He was suddenly tired, and not just because of the hour. He barely had it in him to question his wife as to what she was doing in this awful place; she must have gotten a look at Lilly. It was unhealthy for her here, physically and mentally, so he saved his questions. "Let us go."

"We are taking the child."

"I don't—I don't know where the orphanage is."

"I meant it more generally," she said, and with enough indignation that he had not the means to fight her, she walked off, child in arms. He was helpless but to follow her into the carriage.

"You cannot be serious," he said.

"Daniel, you know very well I am quite capable of being serious."

"But—if—," he struggled for the right words. "To state the obvious, you only have a few weeks—"

"Then I will have another infant. Oh dear, he's going to cry. We'd best find a wet nurse. And at this hour!"

"I imagine people will be awake in a few hours." Now slightly more settled into his side of the carriage, he looked hard at the infant in her arms and at the look on her face, which he could not decipher. "What—what brought this on?"

"Is that a yes?"

"You know I would not refuse you anything in the world," he said. "But—I have to admit, I was not expecting—"

"Nor I, but—look at him." The look on her face, for this

moment more important than the child itself, was absolutely and utterly *motherly*. "How can this child grow up in an orphanage? To do what with his life? Be a beggar or a thief or a dockworker at best? To never know parents?"

"Well I admit some sympathy to his situation—"

She looked directly back at him. "Can you stand two infants instead of one?"

"It is not a matter of 'standing.'" He settled back into his seat, thoroughly perplexed. "It just—I don't know. I hadn't considered it. I was so focused on… Lilly."

"Was there any hope when you arrived?"

"No," he said sadly.

"Would there had been? Had three days not passed?"

"If she had given birth in a better place, not gotten infected, then perhaps—but beyond that, there was nothing—" but, he didn't want to have this conversation with his very expectant wife. He didn't want to tell her that a queen of England had died of infection of torn tissues and there was nothing a doctor or surgeon could do for it. The idea of losing Caroline alone was terrifying. And now to be left with two children, instead of one, assuming they both survived? What would he do then?

But this was not about what he wanted—it was about what *she* wanted. He knew better than to deny a tense, expectant woman anything—especially the woman he loved, the woman who was constantly surprising him.

Despite the rising sun, they made their way home, and Caroline took the boy to the cradle meant, hopefully, for their future child. Fortunately, it was large enough for two. She set him down, and he slept comfortably, immune to the world around him.

"He can never know," Dr. Maddox said, putting his arm around his wife as he looked at the boy. He was, despite the circumstances of his birth, beautiful. "Another secret for us."

"A child should know his father."

"His father has refused contact. Now that we have his son in our house, I would not dare to press the prince again." He leaned on her shoulder tiredly.

"Does he have a name?"

It seemed odd that she hadn't asked that question before. "Lilly said something about George in her ranting, but I believe it was out of spite and was never official. Nor do I think it would be wise."

"Frederick then?" Caroline said. "I would not saddle a child with the name 'Augustus.' Unless you want him named Daniel."

"No," he said, not needing to explain why. If there were to be a Daniel Maddox the Second, he would be a true son of his once-distinguished line. "We will forever be playing a dangerous game, but I suppose, Frederick it is. What do you say to that, little Frederick? What say you to any of this?"

But, of course, the boy was sound asleep and said nothing.

At Pemberley, there was the general hubbub of the master returning. For though Mr. Darcy had spent time, even seasons, away from Pemberley during his bachelorhood, this was the first time since his year on the Continent, when he was not yet Master of Pemberley, that he had been truly abroad and unreachable. There were things to be done, papers to be signed, and of course, the small matter of the introduction of a bastard brother and the care of his pregnant wife.

Georgiana stayed with them, and Mr. Bennet joined them, for Mary still had a few weeks to go, and he, feeling his own parental burden lessened by the settlement, felt free to stop watching Mary like a concerned hawk and relax a bit in quiet. The six months of waiting had done nothing good for Mrs. Bennet's nerves, and now she was merely overenthusiastic about the nature of the settlement and a bit nervous at the prospect of two daughters facing dangerous childbirth, even if one was far off. There was much going back and forth between Chatton and Pemberley for meals and discussions, and every bit of the adventure on the Continent was told over and over again. The Darcys were happy to be back at Pemberley and would remain there until they were needed at Chatton for Mary's delivery.

There were some minor things to be worked out. The servants would not call Grégoire anything but Master Grégoire, which he was uncomfortable with, and they were equally uncomfortable with him returning their bows, however polite and humble he meant to be and at whatever length this was explained to them. Darcy sighed at the whole business and was relieved when his wife said, "Dearest, the matter will surely settle itself eventually."

It was now fall and hunting season, but Bingley was too swept up in his own affairs for much shooting, so was there less than usual. Bingley and Darcy didn't even bother asking Grégoire if he wanted to be taught how to hunt. They could assume that he did not. Darcy delighted in the dual pleasure of simultaneously teaching his son and his brother how to fish.

"Wasn't Jesus a fisherman?" he said as they sat by the lake waiting for bites.

"He was a carpenter, I believe," Grégoire said.

"Our Lord and Savior, the son of God, built houses?" asked Darcy.

"He was a modest man," was the reply.

"I heard he was a fish," said Geoffrey.

"Yes, Son," Darcy said, giving him a pat on the back. "He was a carpenter fish. Where in the world did you get that idea?"

"He is referring to the word *ichthys*," Grégoire explained. "It is the word for fish in Greek, but someone noticed that it also could be an acronym for 'Jesus Christ God's Son is Savior.' Or something to that effect. So, there are many places in Rome where you can find mosaics with the fish symbol."

"See? Your uncle is very learned, like you shall be someday," Darcy said to his son.

"He also dresses like a girl. Do I have to do that, too?" Geoffrey said, and Darcy would have been stern if Grégoire wasn't laughing.

Bingley took leave of his guests for Town, as his sister was very expectant and he wished to be there. This had been previously arranged, so he was sent off with the warmest wishes for Mrs. Maddox.

When he arrived three days later, he had a shock waiting for him. He stared for a while at the sight before him saying, "Unless I am *severely* misunderstanding the biologic process—"

"*Charles*," she said in the demeaning manner of hers, "we adopted." For she was, despite her obvious extremely delicate condition, holding a cooing infant in her arms. Hesitantly, he approached her and peered through the bundle at the brown-haired infant. "His name is Frederick."

"I don't suppose—well, uhm—congratulations!" he sputtered, flummoxed, and then looked to the doctor for help, who was just arriving from a call. "While I don't question your intelligence, may I inquire whose idea—?"

Dr. Maddox only shrugged. "Hers. And yes, perhaps ill timed, but who can say no to his wife? Besides, I rather like him myself."

"And he is—I mean his parentage—"

"The mother was a patient of mine," he said. "She died from the rigors of childbirth and the unsanitary conditions of her lodgings. The father wants nothing to do with him, and so it was this or an orphanage."

Bingley was going to go into a line of questioning that would perhaps go as far as to question their collective sanity, but he saw the delighted look on his sister's face when she held the infant and merely repeated his congratulations on their newborn son. "Twins without the effort. I should have thought of that myself, for Jane's sake. May I—" The baby was passed to him, and he looked down in wonder at the child who was apparently his nephew. "Hello, Frederick. Well, at least you won't have everyone constantly holding the color of your hair against you."

"Or your face. Charles? Care to explain?"

For indeed, the ink was still there, if fading. "Geoffrey Darcy."

"Oh," she said, because that was enough of an explanation.

⁂

"Here's the plan," Brian said to Bingley after Dr. Maddox had been forced into his study by the midwife. Unless something went horribly wrong, the doctor could not attend his own wife's labor or the birth of his child, and though this could not have surprised him, it frustrated him to no end.

"I didn't know a plan was required," Bingley said.

"If we're ever going to get out of him where that child came from, a plan is required," Brian said. "We get him soused, and then you follow my lead. You're a clever fellow. Look touched in the head when you smile, but I know you've got brains."

"Did anyone, at any point, teach you manners?"

"I think I lost them along the Silk Road. Come on."

Mr. Hurst was already there with the inconsolable Maddox. "*I'm* the doctor, damn it!" His wife's screams from upstairs seemed to wring him out like a washcloth.

"Danny, you're having a child the hard way. Sit down and have a drink." Reaching into his jacket, Brian removed a small bottle of what appeared to be water, its label in some foreign language.

Mr. Hurst immediately took hold of it. "What is this?"

"Vodka. And very fine stuff, the best I'm told. From Saint Petersburg." He took it from Hurst, popped what appeared to be some sort of cap with expertise, and poured his brother a small glass, as well as some for himself and some for Bingley, but of considerably smaller amounts. "Drink up."

Caroline wailed again, and the doctor downed his glass.

"We could make a drinking game out of it," Brian said.

"We'd all be under the table then," Bingley said.

"Well, you could probably drink our English stomachs under the table."

"I'm not Irish!" Bingley insisted.

"Pass the whiskey, or vodka. I don't care," Dr. Maddox said in a plea of despair. In fact, before long and after very few screams, he was woozy and red-eyed. "Oh God. What have I done to her? I've ruined her!"

"What are you talking about?" Bingley said. "She's the happiest I've ever seen her since she married you. Well, not precisely *now*, but until now—and probably tomorrow sometime. You've given her two children."

"And she didn't even have to have one of them," Brian said. "Patient of yours, huh?"

"Yes," Dr. Maddox slurred. "Confenti-al. Ity." He seemed to be having trouble with the words. "Discreet."

"Can you describe her?"

"Lilly… Lilly died of childbed fever. If she wasn't… if there were *sanitary conditions*…" he trailed off and took another swig from his glass, unaware that it was empty when he did so. Brian filled it again.

"So you knew her first name?"

"She—wasn' a patient. I mean, until."

"Was she beautiful?"

"I—s'ppose. I mean… I never looked at her… I never did it. I could have. But you know… not associating with her."

Brian spoke again as his brother drained his glass and Bingley closed his ears to a particularly loud yell. "Wait a minute! Was this that whore who visited you a few months ago?"

"*Lilly was not a whore!*" Dr. Maddox slammed his glass on the table. "She was, well, *technically*, she was a whore by profession. But that doesn't mean she deserved to die abandoned. She was a lady." His mood, if not already, became positively dour.

"And the father?"

"Can't—can't talk about him."

"But if he wants nothing to do with his child, and he is not a patient—"

"He *is* a patient," but it came out more like "ish." "Besides, 's treason."

Bingley and Brian stared at each other. They only knew, offhand, of one other of Maddox's patients—

"George Augustus *Frederick*," he whispered to Bingley. "No!"

"Danny," Brian said. "Are you drunk enough to tell us if the prince is the father?"

"Not enough," Dr. Maddox said. "Pour me 'nother."

Brian laughed. "All right. Mr. Hurst?"

Mr. Hurst was far ahead of them, however, and was already in too much of a stupor to respond.

"But suppose, then, we talk of Frederick himself. He's not your patient. And he is my nephew, and I am very concerned for his health," Bingley said. "Especially his blood. Would you say he is of a… royal bloodline?"

"Oh God, what have we done?" the doctor moaned. "I mean, we didn't do anything. He wants nothing to do with his son. *His own son.* Frederick would have gone to an orphanage with its terrible, *unsanitary* conditions." He raised his eyes, his glasses askew on his face. "You cannot tell *anyone*."

"That, I think, we can swear on," Brian said, raising his glass. "Mr. Bingley?"

"Mr. Maddox. Dr. Maddox. I swear never to speak of this again."

"Even to your wife! Even to your sister!" Maddox shouted. "No, your other sister!"

"Very well. Louisa shall never hear it from my lips."

"Oh, thank God," Dr. Maddox said, and put his head down on his desk.

He was not roused again until very early in the morning, long after Bingley himself had fallen asleep on the couch, and it was Brian who shook his brother awake. "Come on."

Still half-asleep and feeling the effects of the night before, the doctor was led up the stairs and into his wife's bedroom, where he was seated on the armchair beside her and a baby was placed in his arms. He stared at it numbly, barely aware in his stupor that he was holding his new daughter.

※

Frederick and Emily Maddox were christened together nearly five days later, when Dr. Maddox finally judged his wife's health had returned enough for a short trip to the cathedral. The girl, with her very Bingley orange hair, was named after her maternal grandmother. In attendance, with everyone caught up in Derbyshire, were merely the Bingleys, the Hursts, and the Maddoxes. Jane had come down to be there for her niece and nephew, as Charles would be leaving almost immediately after the ceremony and they would ride back together. Louisa and Mr. Hurst were named godparents, lacking the abilities to be parents themselves. Afterward, they all returned to the Maddox house so the babies could be settled in their cradle, and many presents were given to two children who were totally unaware of the events surrounding them.

Excusing themselves after an early lunch, Mr. and Mrs. Bingley were back on the road to Chatton, assured that the doctor would join them when they sent for him or when Caroline was ready to travel, whichever came first.

"*Two* children," Jane said in the carriage, leaning into her husband. "For the work of one."

"I know. Why didn't we think of that?"

"Charles!"

He took her hand. "Are you thinking what I am thinking?"

"I am looking forward more to the idea of more children, should they come to be. But that is all for God to decide, as our new brother-in-law would say."

"Well, if a christening makes you so maternal, you may very well have another to enjoy very soon."

"I never said I stopped loving our children! I just would prefer that we have them at a convenient time and in a convenient order!" She nestled into his shoulder. "Oh, if only life were so simple."

"It would certainly be less interesting."

Chapter 24

The Last Bennet

Maddox did make it to Derbyshire in time, because Mary was a week late, and with him came Caroline and their two children. "As long as your brother doesn't loot us out of house and home while we're gone, we should be fine," Caroline said as they stepped out of the carriage.

"I think Brian will do just fine."

"That's what I'm worried about."

Caroline would not leave her infants, and Bingley welcomed them both, saying that with his children nearing their second birthday, Chatton was becoming eerily quiet. Of course, there was some shock among the less-informed of his guests about the Maddox children, who were not actually twins and did not look a bit alike, as tiny Frederick had brown hair, unlike his sister or his parents as babies. Dr. Maddox just shrugged at any question-ing about the peculiar timing of the adoption. Though happy to be back in her grand gowns, Caroline surprised the Chatton crowd with her overwhelming affection for her infants, having taken to motherhood with unexpected vigor.

"It's positively endearing," Jane said to Lizzy when she came in. "And a little bizarre."

While being late to deliver was not an abnormal occurrence, each day that Mary was late created increasing tension, and she was even harder to corner than normally.

When Elizabeth finally did, it was in Mary's room, which was all set up with a cradle for the baby. Mary was staring out the window, fingering a beautiful locket that Elizabeth did not remember seeing before. "Mary? Are you all right?"

"I am fine."

"I meant it more generally." Elizabeth gasped. "Oh! I completely forgot!" she added. "Miss Talbot sends her regards. She says she very much wishes to visit when she returns from the Continent."

Mary turned around. "She does?"

"Yes, very much so. In fact, she was instrumental in locating Mr. Mastai, so we owe her a great debt. Though, I will say, she was not a gossip. I did have to pry the information out of her." She joined Mary by the window. As her condition increased, Mary had been keeping her distance from everyone, shriveling away from contact. "She said there was genuine affection between you and Mr. Mastai. He did say most truthfully that he loved you, whatever the circumstances that resulted."

"I know," Mary said. "He wrote that in his letter that Mr. Maddox delivered. Giovanni was never once insincere, so I don't doubt it now."

"Did he give you the locket?"

"Yes. So the child will know its father, even if some things cannot be." Even though there was heaviness to her voice, it was not filled with sadness. "I love him, but it is not as though I cannot imagine life without him. I would be so desperately lonely for all of you in Italy, even if he quit the church. And he would be adrift here, as Grégoire is, even though he is half-English."

"Grégoire will not stay," Elizabeth said. "Darcy will find a monastery to his liking somewhere and he will leave us, but he will visit. But you're right, in that he is a blood relative with no other standing family, so his situation is entirely different." She sighed. "Some people apparently do wish for the contemplative life."

"Giovanni does not. He will hardly be a monk, and he has obligations," she said.

"Mary, there are others out there. In fact, you will find many a man in England who has not promised his life to the Catholic Church."

"But this is not about me," Mary said. "Not entirely. I should not be so selfish." She stroked her stomach. "Nine months is so long. I was so miserable with worry, and now I realize I have something to look forward to." She smiled. "Excuse me, Lizzy, but I must sit."

"Oh, yes," Elizabeth helped her into the armchair. She was surprised Mary had been standing that long. "Please."

"Did you fancy Rome?"

"It had its spectacles, but it was terribly hot and had a rather bad stench in the late afternoon," Elizabeth said. "I would not want to spend more time there than I did. The food, though, was amazing. It is better to live outside the city in a villa. Mary?" For she noticed her sister had gone pale. "Mary!"

"It—is probably nothing. But please, I would appreciate Mama being in a different room from me when you tell her."

Mary suffered through nearly two cruel days of labor, to the point that her health became a serious concern, and Dr. Maddox was called in to take a look. "I think the child is merely taking its time. Everything appears fine, Miss Bennet."

"*You useless*—" and then Mary let loose a stream of Italian unknown in nature to the crowd of women that surrounded her, for Mrs. Maddox had opted out of being at her side. From Dr. Maddox's reaction, what she had said was not particularly polite. He left red-faced and did not return.

He was correct in his estimation, for without any complications except the exhausting length of the labor, Mary delivered a healthy baby boy, whom she immediately named Joseph, the allusion being obvious. Dr. Maddox insisted that she drink more than she was inclined and be washed, but he made no other important medical notations.

Without anyone to admit him, Mr. Bennet knocked on the door, asked to see his grandson, and took the seat beside his daughter. Little Joseph Bennet wailed in his grandfather's arms as Mr. Bennet wiped the baby's chin. Elizabeth emptied the room of everyone but the mother and the grandfather, and she was about to excuse herself, but she thought the look on her father's face was too memorable. He loved all of his grandchildren, but this look was positively radiant. Mary was partially asleep and could only have been minimally aware of anything, much less her father's gentle laughter and tears of joy as he held the boy he would raise under his own roof, the boy who would take his name, his legacy. Of all the girls, only Mary had given that to him.

Elizabeth did excuse herself, but neither person noticed. She ran right to her room and found Darcy inside, being dressed for the celebratory dinner. She gave his manservant a look, and as he bowed himself away, Elizabeth ran to her husband, who towered over her more than usual on his dressing stand, and hugged him.

"Lizzy?"

"Nothing. I'm just—so happy. For Mary," she said. "And Papa."

"I must admit myself that my opinion of relations beyond marriage has been raised considerably over the last few months."

After Mary was out of danger, Mr. Bennet and Mr. Darcy made a trip to Town to settle all of the accounts, and Mr. Bennet went from there to open up Longbourn from his longest absence since the birth of Jane. Some of his servants had found other work, he discovered, and together with his son-in-law, he saw about hiring new ones and fixing the roof. Mr. Bennet was in such a good mood that he even traveled back to London with Darcy so he could escort his returning family home.

"You could do some renovations," Darcy suggested.

"Only if Mary requests. It is, after all, her money. Though, I doubt she or I are equipped to deal with it."

"It should be properly invested," Darcy said. "I would be happy to offer the services of my steward, who is most trustworthy. In addition, the trust fund for Master Joseph—Mr. Joseph Bennet—will mature considerably in the seventeen years before he gains access to it. It may be as much as fifty thousand by then."

"Fifty thousand pounds," Mr. Bennet said in disbelief.

"They will be waiting in line, once they hear of Mary's inheritance, however obtained and whatever baggage it brings."

Mr. Bennet could not seem to fathom it all. He shook his head. "Mary does not seem the marrying type, or at least, is not willing to put herself on the market just yet, certainly. Maybe in a few years. My pressing concern is Kitty, who herself is now a prize, to be honest, with ten thousand pounds. Perhaps I should buy her an apartment in Town. She and Georgiana do get along well."

"They do. And Mrs. Maddox's temperament has improved tremendously since her marriage."

To this, Mr. Bennet only smirked in reply.

When they returned to Chatton, preparations were under-way to somehow get all of the infants back to their homes, for everyone had had enough of newborn squealing, except perhaps Lydia, who had finally arrived to greet her new nephew. Joseph was christened in the same chapel as his cousins, as the vicar gave Grégoire a disapproving look for just existing in that bizarre medieval way of his.

After a luncheon, Darcy and his brother excused them-selves while Elizabeth was still absorbed in her new godson and nephew. They had something to do at Pemberley that concerned no one else.

⁂

"Is there something we should say? At this point?"

Darcy and Grégoire stood on that bright fall afternoon in front of the gravestone of Geoffrey Darcy, who had died on that very day, ten years before. In the graveyard behind Pemberley, no one would disturb them.

"I'm not a priest and, therefore, cannot say a Mass," said Grégoire. "Nor do I have the implements to do so."

"He was… a wonderful man."

"A loving father."

"An excellent gentleman. In… most respects. He did everything in his power to steer me correctly. And you are a hopeless cause anyway."

Grégoire smiled.

"He did do what was in his power to… bring us together." Darcy knelt beside the grave. "He taught me everything he knew. Except how to deal with Mr. Wickham."

"No one told me I was invited."

They turned to the approaching figure, the person in question. Just getting off his horse, still in partial regimentals, was George Wickham.

George Wickham did not consider himself a selfish man. By definition, that would imply he thought only of himself, and he did not. He had many other people on his mind. Granted, he wasn't always handing out money to others, but he liked to interpret the word to mean he never thought of other people—which he did, quite a lot. For one, his wife was a talker, though he blamed Darcy for that one. Not for making her the country horse that she was, but for forever tying her to him in some kind of sadistic plan of revenge for some perceived slight. He had also been responsible for turning Darcy into the man he was, quite literally, in one night with a fancy lady in Cambridge. *And I paid for that out of my own pocket! Never asked for it back! Ungrateful little brat!*

All right, so he envied Darcy of Pemberley and Derbyshire. The most prim and proper of men, except when he was drunk or locked in a room with a whore *while* drunk, but honestly, most of the stories Wickham couldn't tell most of the stories he knew out of fear of self-incrimination. Darcy had had one dirty evening after Wickham left Cambridge and that he had heard of in passing, but he never knew the full story. The only one who knew it was Charles Bingley, the First Mate on the Darcy Ship and stupidly, stupidly loyal. Emphasis on *stupid*. He would never get a word from him.

Since becoming Mr. Darcy of Pemberley, Darcy had been the most upstanding and proper man, to the point that Wickham wondered the precise height and width of the stick up his arse. Darcy waited until he was nine and twenty to marry Elizabeth Bennet, that courtship behind guarded with such traditional Darcy secrecy that not even that squealing, gossipy wife of his could account for it. Wickham had tried to learn the truth of it himself on the wedding day, only to be rewarded by having his last remaining fine suit stained with cow droppings when Darcy reacted to his presence by pushing him out a window and into the manure pile below. Darcy would have nothing to do with him, and that was that.

But not everything on Wickham's end could be severed. While technically they were brothers-in-law, Wickham was never permitted entrance anywhere near Pemberley, even when his wife was, and she so rarely was that it was barely worth trying. And he did miss Pemberley, he begrudgingly admitted to himself when he was drunk enough to do so. It was not just the money practically dripping from its ancient walls, either. The happiest years of his life had taken place there, even after the death of his father, when Mr. Darcy had taken him in and treated him like a king. His son did not show the same kindness. Yes, he'd given him the worth of the living, but surely Darcy had enough intelligence to know he'd lose it all and come crawling back? Why couldn't he just shut up and beg his way back into Pemberley? The plan with Georgiana had been a last resort. The plan with Mary King had been the last resort of a… last resort.

Maybe he should have taken the church living. Celibacy was not expected of a vicar. But then he would have to deliver boring sermons. Caught between a rock and a hard place. As if Darcy ever found himself in that position.

Wickham was nibbling on that piece of gristle—and an actual piece of gristle—when a letter arrived from Lydia. She did love to gab, but sometimes that was to his benefit, especially when it involved the Darcys. And this time, it was. When Lydia had gone to Chatton to see to the birth of her unmarried sister's bastard child (scandal enough, but not worth a penny in Newcastle), she had also been introduced to a monk who was Darcy's bastard brother. It seemed the senior Mr. Darcy, whom they both had regarded so highly, had had his own little extramarital dalliances.

Perhaps that was why, Wickham pondered as he sped to Pemberley, Mr. Darcy had been good enough to turn a blind eye to all of the maids he fired for mysteriously becoming "with child" as soon as Wickham learned of the bounty of feminine delights. The old fool was no fool, but he was apparently not practicing what he preached. Mr. Darcy would have made a terrible vicar, as well.

With that consolation, Wickham expertly bypassed the guards and the field workers. He would not be admitted to Pemberley itself. His only hope was to catch Darcy visiting his father's grave on the anniversary of the senior Darcy's death. If not, at least Wickham would visit the graves of his own parents, as the private graveyard had a section for the beloved Wickhams. He hadn't been bothered in years—in fact, he couldn't think of a time he'd seen the stones since the one for his father had gone up, and he'd never known his mother—but it seemed as good a time as any.

To his great luck, Darcy was there. He was not alone, but guards did not flank him, either. Beside him was a young man in grey monk robes and sandals, his long string of beads hanging off his rope belt, and his brown Darcy hair in a ridiculous tonsure. The hair style probably had been implemented to make the balding abbots feel better about their hair loss. But the familial resemblance was undeniable, especially when Darcy put his arm over the monk's shoulders as they mourned their father, a rare gesture of affection that made it all the more affectionate.

A pang of jealousy struck Wickham. When they were boys, he and Darcy had been friends, even like brothers. When they were very young boys, before all the jealousy and rivalry set in. This stupid Papist had missed all of the taunts, the spars, and the rides, and instead had the same affection bestowed on him that Darcy probably showed Georgiana. He looked that age, too.

They had not noticed him, but when he was mentioned in their conversation, Wickham felt obligated to announce his presence. "No one told me I was invited," he said.

Shock and alarm described Darcy's reaction as Wickham dismounted and approached him.

"Darcy." Wickham bowed and turned to the monk. "And I do not believe we have been introduced."

He did believe, unless Darcy chose to lie outright, that the scandal would be revealed now, in front of the grave of the man who had wrecked the family. Or had potential to. Surely Darcy would put up a sum of money just to keep Wickham's mouth shut about a stain on the house of Pemberley.

By his estimation, a *great* sum of money. And he intended to get every shilling of it.

Chapter 25

THE DARCY BROTHERHOOD

DARCY LOOKED AT HIM with levels of barely controlled rage. Wickham was more than familiar with this. While Darcy was a mystery of a man to everyone else, Wickham knew him better. And one of the surest things he knew was that the man knew how to keep grudges. When Darcy intruded on his absconding with Lydia, Wickham was fairly sure (at the time) that it was more about getting his revenge for Georgiana and doing that white knight thing he loved so much to do.

Only later Wickham found that Darcy's actions had been more about maintaining Lydia's sister's social standing so Darcy could marry her, which was not a huge surprise, either. Darcy cared about social standing. He would pay a lot of money to protect a family's honor, an astronomical amount to protect his own. And here Darcy was, cornered with proof of his own father's indiscretions in the form of a church mouse, and all he could manage was a deeply intoned, "*Wickham.*"

"I suppose I'm not going to be introduced. Well, I don't know your name, but Lieutenant George Wickham at your service." He bowed politely, taking off his regimental hat.

"Brother Grégoire," said the monk, bowing in innocence. "Grégoire Bellamont, sir."

"Bellamont? Wasn't that… wasn't that the name of one of Mrs. Darcy's maids? From when we were young. Fitz?"

"Yes," Darcy growled. "Your attempts at civility are tiring. Yes, he is our half-brother." *Of course*, he was referring to himself and Georgiana, who was not present.

"At least I was trying. Live and let live? Forgive and forget? Isn't that one of your people's teachings, *Brother* Grégoire?"

"Yes," said the monk, or more accurately, the pawn, overshadowed by the two much larger players with more moves. His accent was partially French. Darcy must have picked him up on the Continent like a souvenir, then brought him home because of some ridiculous honored notion that a son should see his father's grave or some such nonsense. "We are all poor sinners."

"Well, I only know two people here who are poor," Wickham said. "And it seems the Darcys are responsible for that."

"You are mistaken by his pious appearance," Darcy said. "Unlike you, Grégoire has not squandered his inheritance gambling."

"Inheritance?" Wickham laughed. "You call three thousand pounds to buy me off when your father passed away an inheritance? Do you know how long that lasted?"

"And the ten thousand to settle your gambling debts and provide you with a living in Newcastle. The thousands Father spent raising you, educating you, and sending you to Cambridge. At least you had the decency to be sent down in the first semester, since all you were going to do was—"

"Brother!" Grégoire interrupted, a look passing between him and Darcy that Wickham could not observe from his viewpoint.

So the monk was to be his advocate? He was going to make this even easier? "Tell him."

"Tell me what?" Wickham said, curious.

Darcy sighed, and it was not a sigh of annoyance. Wickham knew Darcy's frustrated sighs well enough. This was almost sadness. It crept into his voice when he spoke, more civilly this time, directly to Wickham. "It seems... you are my half-brother as well."

George Wickham blinked. "Are you daft?"

"Surely your scheming mind can work your way around that one," Darcy replied, stepping closer to him in front of his father's grave. "I admit Father had me fooled, too, while he was alive. But why else would he raise you 'as his own son' and give you a living that you proved over and over again was undeserved? A living in the church, of all places! His last attempts to hope to reform you, even when that was beyond hope. How many maids did he have to dismiss? How far did you spread the Darcy seed around?"

To say that Wickham was flabbergasted was putting it mildly, but he knew that Darcy could be as tricky as he could. "You are a fool if you don't think I see your strategy. You are trying to draw me into your own little family scandal so that I cannot ask for money for my silence, and you apparently would go as far as slandering your own father to do so."

"Despite my lack of desire to believe it, your father was, in fact, my father," Darcy said. "So the only person slandered here, beyond him, is your mother, who was married to Mr. Wickham at the time, which is a sin above Father's own... dalliances with his wife's lady-maid."

He was getting angry. Wickham was not at his best when he

was angry. He didn't like being angry either, especially when he was trying to get money from people. He could not think of a way—no, he had one. If Darcy was to up the scale, so would he. They were alone. The setting was perfect.

"Darcy, you have slandered both my parents to a point that is unsuitable, and as a gentleman—and you may laugh at the idea if you wish—I must defend their honor. I challenge you to a duel."

Darcy gave him one of those perfectly clear "You can't be serious?" looks of his and scoffed.

"I am serious," Wickham said. "Most serious."

"I cannot shoot a—brother."

Maybe Darcy really did believe it. Well, Darcy was a fool, or he was playing some game beyond Wickham's own. "Then to first blood. I will be at the disadvantage, as you are better with the blade than I am, so accept my poor lieutenant's spare in place of your expert rapier. Just so you don't cut me to pieces immediately."

"You have two? On you?"

"Of course. I am, despite my own intentions, in His Majesty's service," Wickham said, returning to his horse to retrieve the blades.

"Darcy." Wickham heard Gregory, or whatever his fancy name was, in the background. "You cannot fight on consecrated ground."

"It appears I do not have a choice. Wickham?"

But Wickham was a step ahead of him, literally. As he spun around, he carried two blades in one hand and his pistol in another, whereupon he fired and shot Darcy.

"My hand! You bastard, my hand!" Darcy fell to his knees, clutching his wounded right hand. Grégoire, ever his attendant, ran to his side and looked at the wound.

"It has gone straight through," he said, removing his cowl and tearing off a piece of the linen to wind around Darcy's hand.

"You could not expect me not to even the playing field," Wickham said. "You are too good on your strong side for almost any man in England who is not a professional fencer."

"You bastard," Darcy groaned. "You ignorant, stupid son of a whore! And this time, I mean it literally!"

"You're not doing it correctly, you damned monk," Wickham said, approaching them. Grégoire did not put up much of a fight as Wickham pushed him aside, pulled loose Darcy's cravat, and wrapped it tightly around the wound. The bullet had apparently gone right through his hand. "An excellent shot, if I do say so myself."

"You bastard," Darcy snarled as Wickham tightened the bandage and tied it off. "If I call for my servants—"

"They won't hear. And if you send your 'brother' for help, I'll shoot him. Now." He released Darcy's hand. "Let's establish the terms. Since I've already drawn first blood, we'll have to go for second. If I succeed, I want an apology and a proper living. How much does Gregory have?"

"Don't tell him," Darcy said to his brother, but Wickham merely cocked his pistol, and Grégoire looked terrified.

"Three—three thousand a year."

"*He* gets three thousand a year? What does he do? Did he buy his way into heaven?" Wickham said in disbelief. "Then those are my terms. State yours."

"You take a post in the Indias, preferably in a hostile area."

"Self-imposed exile, yes? With a little possible death thrown in to free up Mrs. Wickham so she can properly remarry? Very noble of you. She may be a cow who squeals like a pig, but you know, she does have her positive qualities. I bet Elizabeth would never—"

"*Wickham*," Darcy interrupted. "My sword."

"Then the terms are agreed?"

"Yes!" Darcy must have been aware that he was bleeding badly despite the bandages, and would lose energy with that, so time was on Wickham's side. "Grégoire, stay back, but if he tries to shoot you, I'll run him through. And Wickham, you would be shooting your own half-brother."

Wickham was indeed beginning to wonder if the story was true. After all, Darcy would be the last person in the world to want to admit any relation whatsoever to him. As a bastard, out of wedlock, Wickham could never make a claim on Pemberley or any part of Darcy's various land holdings, but he could reasonably demand more money than he was currently receiving from pay and his wife's income. But that would mean his father had been hoodwinked, and that Mr. Darcy was one of the worst kinds of men. And then, he realized, there was the matter of Georgiana. If he was half-Darcy, then he had almost—No, he was not ready for that yet.

There was an order to things.

Darcy knew he was at a loss. He could fight with his less-used left hand; that much was true. But he was older now and out of practice with his months of traveling, and he had been wounded on his left side not even two years before. And there was the small matter of his bleeding, throbbing right hand as a major distraction. Was he good enough now, in this state, to beat Wickham? The man was a military officer, even if he had never seen active duty. He must have trained.

As Darcy took the sword in his hand, he contemplated just giving in to Wickham's demands. They were outrageous, true, but the money was no more than what Grégoire received, and surely some of it would go to support Lydia Wickham and her children, who were his niece and nephew on *both* sides and were of his bloodline, at least by a quarter. They deserved not to live in poverty, even if Wickham did.

But no—he had been challenged, and his honor demanded that he defend himself for as long as he could stand. However, he doubted that would be very long. Slowly and carefully, he adjusted his hand to the blade's unfamiliar hilt and took his stance. "I would shake on it, but it seems I am without a free hand." His voice came out tinnier than he would have liked. Perhaps he would not speak much.

"Brother, *please*," Grégoire pleaded with him by his good shoulder, which once had been considered his bad shoulder before an injury forced Darcy to switch sides. "Not in front of Father, on holy ground."

"If your estimations are correct, Darcy, there is no more deserving a witness," Wickham said, gesturing to the gravestone of Geoffrey Darcy.

"He is right, perhaps," Darcy said. "For once in his life. Stand back, Grégoire, and we shall finish it."

It was not quite their old childhood games. As they touched tips in some kind of gesture of respect, even though there was none, Darcy wished it were merely a game. Was it the blood-loss

induced haze, or were the memories of his younger days of playing with Wickham choosing to come back to him now for some
nefarious purpose? This was not the way he wanted things to
happen. True, he had put off planning a confrontation, but he
could not think of a way for it to go more horribly wrong. And
he had just jinxed himself by thinking that.

Wickham struck first. Darcy knew he would do that.
Wickham did not have the patience or the intelligence to do
otherwise. He thought he was a snake, lying and waiting for his
prey, but though he had many serpentine qualities, he was more
like a charging boar of smugness and ferocity. He came at Darcy,
who responded with an easy parry, but only because he knew
Wickham. He knew he would have to strike back, before the
blows started falling heavily. Parry, parry, parry. "Damn it, hit
me, Darcy! You know you want to run me through!"

Trying to incite him. Wickham was good at that, and Darcy
had to admit that he was not in the best of moods to begin with
and would have to calculate that in. He could not drone out
Wickham's calls altogether, but the pounding in his ears was
helping him out in that respect. His blood was up, and Wickham
knew it, and the reverse.

The "second blood" they drew would not be a gentleman's
prick. Both men knew that; it did not have to be spoken. So he
had to parry and parry on auditory and physical fronts. Deflect.
Protect. Himself. Grégoire. Pemberley. Elizabeth. His son and
his future child. Everything was at stake here, and he was not a
gambler. He was not comfortable with those high stakes.

But Wickham was. He was brazen, continuously trying to
draw Darcy out, continuously attacking to wear him down. Either
strategy could easily work. But Darcy blocked. He blocked again

and again until it became like a dance, like a dream. Wickham was darkness, and he was light. He was truly the knight in shining armor. The Lady in the Water had given him a magic sword, and he could pierce Wickham's black heart.

He was probably hallucinating. Loss of blood, of course. He squeezed his hand, but that just made the wound bleed that much worse. There were cries from Grégoire to stop, stop this madness, but he barely heard them. Then there was a blur in front of him, all grey robes, as Wickham thrashed, pushing him back against another tombstone. Darcy comprehended that the blade would have gone to his heart, not a gentlemen's duel wound but a killing blow, and his arm may or may not have responded to the brain's call to parry. But that was irrelevant, because Grégoire had tackled Wickham, and they were rolling around on the ground. There was a gunshot, and the little monk slumped against the stone, trailing blood behind him. *Had Grégoire been using the Discipline again?* No, Darcy remembered taking that away. And now he was having that conversation again with Grégoire.

"I will personally pay for the abbey to acquire a new one if they press me on it," he had said, was saying again, at least in his mind.

No, better to imagine he was back at Cambridge, fighting a match against a worthy opponent. That he could understand. His opponent, not properly guarded and masked, was picking himself off the ground. He was open. He knew, within the lines, he could not drop his guard. He had violated the rules. There would be punishment, and Darcy would deliver it.

Darcy's blade went right through Wickham's uniform, then his flesh, and then his organs and bones. He could feel it. Darcy could hear it and feel the tip break through the other side, as if an extension of his own hand, his left hand, but still his hand.

"F-First—first blood," Darcy stammered as Wickham, still standing because he was probably in shock. Darcy pulled back his weapon, out the same way it had come with a burst of blood. "Second, technically."

But hatred would not die so easily. Wickham raised his pistol, but Darcy dropped his sword, and with both hands—and very painfully—managed to lift the gun so the shot went off into the sky, leaving only a small ball of smoke to cover their faces with gunpowder. Wounded, angry, and flailing, Wickham tackled Darcy and bashed him in the lower back with his sword hilt, unfortunately made of steel. Both men went over together and rolled to the grass, where they managed to separate.

Being off his feet felt immeasurably good, even if he could barely breathe and his back was still figuring out which nerves to activate and his hand was still bleeding. Beside him, beyond the pounding in his ears, he heard Wickham's ragged breaths as he tore open his jacket and shirt, soaking his hands in blood in the process.

Then there was silence, except for the sounds of Derbyshire on a pleasant fall afternoon, when the leaves were at their best color, and the birds were chirping their last before heading south for the winter.

"Darcy?"

"Hmm?"

"You… you meant what you said?"

He had to gather a bit of strength to respond. "I don't… properly remember everything I might… have said. Remind me."

"We are brothers?"

"So it seems." He picked his head up just a bit—a painful endeavor—to see Grégoire still slumped against the tombstone, his eyes closed but breathing. He looked the other way, to Wickham covered in his own blood, and craned his eyes above. They were, appropriately, in front of his mother's and father's stones.

"Then we are... terrible at it."

"At what?"

"Being brothers."

"So it seems." His brain wasn't processing a lot. He was resting in a pool of agony, but the resting part was wonderful. "Cain and Abel."

"Unless we... both die."

"Cain never died."

"Yes he did."

"No he didn't."

"Did."

"Didn't."

Despite everything, Darcy found himself laughing. He found Wickham joining him, until they were both too exhausted from the process. That did not take very long, and then they were quiet again.

"I love Elizabeth," Darcy said. "I want those to be... my last words."

"I love... uhm..."

"... Money?... Gambling?... F-Fratricide?"

"My... best qualities."

It was getting late. It was still early in the afternoon, but it felt so very, very late.

"I didn't... mean for—I just wanted money... Darcy."

"I know."

"I didn't—kill Gregory… did I?"

"Grégoire."

"Whatever."

"No… I don't know… I can't—get up."

He heard George slowly rise to his feet. It was a concentrated effort, and when he stood, he was hunched over, one hand desperately clutching the wound in his chest as he towered over Darcy. "If I don't survive… I'm sorry about Georgiana," he stopped to grunt, as if his very insides were shifting around in him. "I didn't know."

"I didn't either," Darcy said. "Where are you going?"

"To get… some help." He tried to straighten up but failed. "Agh!" He made his way to his horse, where he leaned on the animal and tugged weakly on the stirrups. Finally he was able to climb into the saddle. Darcy saw little more than a shadow. He was seeing little more than shadows and darkness now. "Darcy."

"George."

As the shuffling of the hooves of the beast disappeared into the distance, Darcy sighed and let the last of his strength flow out of him.

REQUIEM

IT WAS LATE IN the day, and Elizabeth Darcy realized she and Georgiana needed to be home for dinner, but first she had to find her son. This, of course, was no easy task. The Bingley twins were running now, and she had to carefully sidestep them to avoid their collision in order to find her son somehow on top of a very large bookcase.

"I don't even want to know. Come to Mother."

Geoffrey eagerly obeyed, though she was glad to put him down when she had him safely out of danger. "Now don't bump into your cousins. Really, someone should be watching them."

But the entrance of Georgiana Bingley, who ran up to him and whispered something in his ear, distracted him enough.

"Coming!" said Bingley, either having heard Elizabeth or following his fatherly instincts. "Eliza! Charles!" He picked up his daughter, handed her off to her namesake for the sake of convenience, and then scooped up his son. "Now! What did I say about running in the house?"

Elizabeth looked down and noticed her son was tugging at her skirts. "What? What is it?"

"Georgie wants to tell you something."

"Well, she can very well tell me herself. I am her aunt."

"But it's our secret. No one else saw it."

"Georgiana?" Bingley looked at his daughter. "What is it?"

"I was going to tell Geoffrey," his elder daughter said. "There's a red horse on the road."

"A red horse?"

"It's a horse, and it's all red."

Elizabeth and Bingley exchanged glances. "Can you tell us where you saw it?"

She nodded eagerly.

"See, just delayed," he said, referring to her speech. "All right, you're both very good children for telling us. Let's go." He handed his son off to Nurse, who had appeared behind him, and Elizabeth dropped her niece off as well before they followed Georgie through the hallway and out the front doors of Chatton. She broke into a full run, and Geoffrey kept pace with her.

Not far down the road, they saw it. It was indeed a horse, shuffling aimlessly about, masterless and not tied to anything. Its saddle and back were covered in blood, obviously not its own.

"Regimentals," Elizabeth said, looking at the markings on the saddle.

"Wickham," Bingley guessed. "He was here a few months before. I recognize it."

"Lydia is inside."

"I mean Mr. Wickham. Yes, he was invited, and it's a long story. But—where is Wickham?" He turned to his daughter. "Go back to the house and tell the servants to get Dr. Maddox here at once. And take Geoffrey."

"But I want to see!" wailed Geoffrey.

"Go with her," Elizabeth said in the sternest possible voice, which was quite stern. "*Now!*"

By the time they were off, Bingley had already found the trail of blood. It led down the road towards Pemberley, and they ran to follow it until it curved off the road. There was the obvious spot where the rider had fallen off and then a smaller trail leading into the tall grass. Resting in the foliage was a wounded George Wickham. Bingley stepped forward first and turned him over, which did not rouse him into consciousness. Bingley took the pistol in Wickham's belt and smelled it. "It's been fired."

"Oh God. Darcy!"

"I know." Fortunately, people were arriving, and Bingley slapped Wickham until he woke. "Where's Darcy?"

"Darcy... what?"

Elizabeth took the pistol from Bingley's hand and cocked it at Wickham's head, so that there could be no mistake about her intentions. "Where is Mr. Darcy, Wickham?"

"Oh." He put a bloodied hand to his head. "Yard. Graveyard. God, I hope... I haven't killed him."

Bingley had to hold Elizabeth back from physically attacking Wickham as Dr. Maddox arrived with Jane and servants. Maddox knelt beside the patient with his bag and pulled open the shirt, but Wickham angrily tore him away. "Get going, you glass-eyed son of a whore!"

"You need medical attention, Mr. Wickham," Maddox said sternly.

"I'm not here for me! I didn't... come all this way... I'm regimental; I know wounds. Forget me, and find Darcy and his pet monk before they both die!" He cried out as if something inside was bothering him and turned over to hack blood into the grass.

"Doctor," Bingley said. "He's telling you to go." He turned to a servant. "Horses! We need horses! And a carriage for Elizabeth! Now, man!"

"George!" Lydia Wickham had finally caught up with them. "Dr. Maddox—"

"Let the doctor... go about... his business," Wickham coughed. "I'm no loss to you, anyway."

It was only three miles to Pemberley. They left Wickham with his wife and the many servants of Chatton to help him back to the house, but he would not be carried inside. A strange sense of dignity presided over him as he asked to see Georgiana Darcy, and with Mr. Bennet giving him a stern glance, she was brought forth, having been unaware of the proceedings so far. "Mr. Wickham!"

"Georgiana!" he reached out, but his hands were unable to catch anything. He had lost all coordination. "I'm so... I'm so sorry. I didn't know. I wouldn't have... I did love you, but not... Thank God, not as a woman. Just a little girl that I loved." She finally offered him her hand, and he kissed it. "Sister."

"Darcy isn't here to say it, so I shall," Mr. Bennet said. "Don't bother this poor woman any longer."

"I'm not... I wasn't told..." he closed his eyes and then opened them again. "All this time... I was a Darcy. I should have..." He leaned over and coughed on the ground before straightening up again and leaning on the front steps. "I should have acted... like one. Forgive me." He swallowed. "Please forgive me."

"I—forgive you," Georgiana was confused but not ignorant. She already had one bastard brother, so a second was not terribly hard to imagine. And he seemed so sincere. "George."

He smiled. "Go to your brother... the one who acted like one."

With Mr. Bennet's nod of approval, she called for a carriage and was off to Pemberley, but not before granting Wickham a kiss on his forehead. As she disappeared down the road, he slumped further onto the steps and refused offers to be carried inside.

"George," said Lydia, the only one now at his side, at least closely. "What have you been up to?"

"Terrible... unforgivable things. But... I have been forgiven... by the most wounded person of all." His grim smile faded, and he leaned into his wife. In her embrace, George Wickham died.

Darcy's first impression back in reality was the uncomfortable notion of being wet. Cold and wet. Where were his manservant and his properly heated bath?

But the discomfort did the job of waking him admirably.

"Darcy," Elizabeth said desperately, wiping his face. "Can you hear me?"

The ground that he had found so comfortable was now hard and uninviting, yet he could not find the strength to move. In fact, he could barely open his eyes and focus on the two figures in front of his face, the sky behind them. One was his lovely Elizabeth; the other had the easily recognizable spectacled face of Dr. Maddox.

"Mr. Darcy," he said, "if you can, I need to you to lift up your arms and your legs. It does not have to be all at once or very much, but I need to see you move before we attempt to get you on a cot. Do you understand?"

He did try desperately to say yes, but it came out incomprehensibly, between his limited ability to speak and his parched throat. He did succeed in barely lifting his limbs, which was enough for the doctor to have him moved. Elizabeth kept whispering things to him, but what he heard seemed to go right through him. Only when he was back on a bed in Pemberley, and properly given food and drink, did he become aware of the pain, specifically when Maddox unwound the blood-soaked bandage around his hand. "Ow!"

"You're going to need stitches, but I think I can save the hand," the doctor said, turning it over and looking at the still-bleeding exit wound. "The bottle, please. On your left."

Someone, somewhere, was helping him. Were they asking Darcy questions? He wasn't entirely aware. He managed to ask, after his own mouthful of horribly tasting medicine, "My brother—"

"Grégoire is patched and will be sewn shortly, but he is comatose."

"He was—he was shot," Darcy said.

"Then it didn't hit. You might have heard a shot, but his injury is head trauma from landing against a tombstone."

"Will he wake?"

"I don't know, Mr. Darcy. Now take some deep breaths, and try to relax."

Relax? Yes, he could manage that. After all, wasn't he dead and this was purgatory?

It was late in the night when Dr. Maddox was finished with both of his patients. Aside from the servants, no one bothered him. Elizabeth held Darcy's other hand, but he was largely unresponsive, and what details they managed to glean from him of the events that occurred earlier in the day were contradictory. The real story, obviously, would not come forth until someone recovered.

Around midnight, a sobbing Georgiana Darcy and a teary Lydia Wickham arrived with the news that Wickham had passed on to the next world and that arrangements were being made, but there was some question as to where he would be buried.

"Elizabeth," Georgiana said. "You can decide this as Mistress of Pemberley."

"If it can possibly wait until Darcy wakes and we have the whole story, or he can make the decision himself, then it will," she announced, and everyone heeded her decision.

"Why didn't someone *tell me?*" Georgiana said, giving no explanation as to what she was alluding to. It was too obvious.

"Because—because Darcy was waiting for the right time."

"And he thought *this* was the right time?"

Elizabeth, exhausted from a long night of worry, could only manage, "Your brother is not perfect, Georgiana. Do you wish to hear the latest from the doctor? Because I do."

A tired Maddox was taking tea in the sitting room. He rose and bowed to the Darcys. "Mrs. Darcy. Miss Darcy."

"Doctor, please don't trouble yourself. How are they?"

"I can't quite decide who is the more complicated case," Maddox said. Elizabeth noticed that his usually steady surgeon's hands were shaking as he held the teacup. "Brother Grégoire—excuse me, this is going to be graphic, if you want the whole of it."

Elizabeth gave a nod to Georgiana, who replied with obvious frustration, "I am sick of being left out of everything! To think, this could have all been prevented in the first place if Brother had said where he was going, or who Wickham was, or we had been told by Papa..." she broke off. "I want to know everything. Please, Doctor."

Maddox swallowed and continued. "Brother Grégoire is comatose."

"What does that mean?" Georgiana asked eagerly.

"It means he is asleep and cannot wake up, to put it very simply. But if he does not wake in a few days, he will waste away. Not that he was... healthy to begin with."

"I know," Elizabeth said, hoping to spare Georgiana from that at least. In his inspection, Dr. Maddox must have seen what Darcy had said were extensive scars down the monk's back. "Please go on."

"The coma is a result of head trauma. Beyond that, there is not much I can say. As for Mr. Darcy..." He took another sip and put the cup away. "The hand is not connected to a lot of major organs, and if it becomes infected, he can afford to lose it, as horrible as that would be. If he escapes infection, he may not fully be able to use the hand again. I tried to do what I could, but so many of the nerves had been cut by the bullet—" He sighed. "There is also the matter of his back."

"His back?"

"He must have been struck, because he is bruised extensively there and, in his moments of lucidity, has complained of pain in his gut. If he has internal injuries, the symptoms will surface in the next few days and drastic measures may have to be taken."

"Drastic measures?"

"With your permission, Mrs. Darcy, an apothecary at Cambridge is the closest place to Derbyshire that I know with the right tools and ingredients, and I will apply for all of them immediately."

Elizabeth nodded numbly. Maybe it was the late hour, but she could think of no other response.

The funeral of George Wickham took place two days hence, when his children could be retrieved from Newcastle for Lydia's sake and comfort. Darcy was awake but still not himself. He was feverish and his mind dulled by pain, but the story they managed to gather from the scattered details in his brain was eventually sorted out. The fight, the revelation, the duel. Things flying out of control —and all within sight of the tombstone of their mutual father.

Jane was shocked that two brothers had unintentionally married two sisters, whereas Bingley shrugged his shoulders and said nothing. A few days before, many of them would have been openly or secretly glad to see Wickham gone. Even now, the fact that Darcy and Grégoire's lives still hung by a thread did not endear him to them, but he had, to some degree, given his life so that his brothers might be discovered in time, and that, in and of itself, was commendable. Even Elizabeth shed a few tears as she watched from the window of Pemberley as the priest said the final blessings and the coffin was lowered into the ground.

When the funeral was over, Elizabeth joined her husband, patting him on the shoulder. Darcy had to be carried to the funeral in an armchair and said nothing and, at times, may very well have been unconscious or asleep during the brief service. His request was, of course, honored. He was Master of Pemberley, and he could bury people where he damn well pleased. So, instead of next to the Wickhams in their private corner of the steward section of the cemetery, George Wickham was buried beside his father, Geoffrey Darcy. He retained in death only the last name he had used in life, marked on his grave while the stone was still under preparation. In a moment of silence, they all fell under the spell of wondering about the mixed legacy of George Wickham-Darcy.

"*Réquiem æternam dona ei, Dómine.*"

Darcy and Elizabeth turned to see Grégoire Bellamont-Darcy shambling up the hill to the grave. His head bandaged, and clad in the white bed robes in which the servants had dressed him, the dazed monk crossed himself. "*Et lux perpétua lúceat ei. Requiéscat in pace. Amen.*" ("Eternal rest grant unto him, O Lord. And let perpetual light shine upon him. May he rest in peace.")

"Amen," said Darcy as he crossed himself.

Chapter 27

SYMPATHY FOR THE DEVIL

THE NEXT DAY, DARCY's health had not returned. Though his hand was healing, the pains in his body would not relent. He had trouble taking food, and sleep was nearly impossible. He was, however, still Darcy, a man who was affronted when anyone, even his doctor, stormed into his room with a chamber pot. "Why didn't you tell me?"

"Tell you what?"

"As your physician, Mr. Darcy, I must know all of your—proper functions." He did not have to say that the chamber pot, which had just been carried out by the manservant, was filled with blood.

"Do you know... all of the prince's... proper functions?"

"I know his every venereal disease, yes."

Darcy blinked.

"Now, will you please tell me: is blood coming from anywhere else on your body?"

"No."

"You are including *everything?*"

"*Yes.*" Darcy, at least for the moment, seemed to have his senses about him. "Why do you ask?"

"Because I am trying to… conjecture if an organ has failed."

"And if it has?"

Dr. Maddox passed the pot off and did not respond as he washed his hands. "I need to see the spot again."

Darcy groaned and turned on his side so the doctor could have a look at the bruise on his back. Not his only one, but the largest, so much so that he had circled it, like a butcher preparing to carve up meat. "So it is that horrible?"

"I have to ask you this question, Mr. Darcy—Are all of your affairs in order?"

"That horrible. Yes. What good would I—Ow, stop it!— would I be if I had left for the Continent without doing so?"

"I'm not even touching you!"

"Well, it feels as though you are!"

Maddox was used to stubborn patients, but usually he was able to deal with them by assuming their stubbornness was derived from their medical trials and not their personality. With Darcy, he could not make that assumption. "Do you feel a stabbing pain on your side? Here?"

"Yes! Now, by God, do something about it!"

"Darcy," he said softly. "I am afraid to kill you."

"I would prefer your brews to a slow death, Maddox."

Dr. Maddox was too flustered to respond.

Most of the materials Maddox needed he had already sent for or were available in Lambton, so the treatments began.

"Drink this," Dr. Maddox said, offering a hazel mixture of something to Darcy, who was barely capable of sitting up.

"What will it do?"

"If your kidney is inflamed, it may lower the inflammation and save your life," the doctor said. "Also, it will make you very ill." He watched Darcy grimace. "I thought you would prefer not to be surprised."

"Is there anything else to be done?"

"I could bleed you to death," Maddox said. "That is the conventional wisdom."

"You are such an optimist."

He pushed the glass into Darcy's hands. "Drink."

A cloud of gloom fell over Pemberley, though everyone tried to keep a cheery face for Darcy himself, who managed with his very small bits of strength to give them annoyed looks at their intentions. Fitzwilliam Darcy would not be fooled. Between doses of the various tonics, he spent a long time talking to Bingley with his steward present, and there could be no doubt as to what they were discussing.

Darcy insisted, despite advice otherwise, to see the others at least sitting up in a chair beside his bed. His son was set in his lap. "Are you going to die?" But even with Geoffrey's regular lack of tact, his voice was outright terrified.

"Hopefully not," Darcy said, playing with Geoffrey's hair. "Ow, don't hug so hard. Please, for Father."

"Am I supposed to be Mr. Darcy now?"

"No. When you're much, much older and I'm a doddering old fool."

"Was Mr. Wicked really my uncle?"

"Mr. *Wickham*. And yes, he was."

"Then why did you hate him?"

Elizabeth must have seen the look on Darcy's face, the way he slumped in his chair, because she came rushing. "Geoffrey, don't. Your father has been through a lot with Wickham. I'll tell you when you're older. Now, don't wear your father out."

"Yes," Darcy said. "You'd best get ready for bed. Then you can come in and say good night."

"All right." Geoffrey kissed his father on the cheek and then scrambled off to be escorted away by Nurse. The moment he was gone, Darcy sprung up far enough to get to a bucket. All he had drunk all day was barley water and some thin gruel, along with hourly doses of what the doctor said was "nitrate of potass." Either way, the mixture was making him increasingly ill, and his only comfort was a hot towel placed over his back when he collapsed.

Wiping the tears from her eyes, Elizabeth tried to maintain her composure. "I assume Bingley will be responsible for Geoffrey's welfare if anything happens to you?"

"Yes. I apologize for passing over your father."

"It could hardly be expected of him. Bingley is younger, better with money, and in Derbyshire."

Georgiana wanted a private audience. She hugged her brother and, between sobs, managed to say, "I'm so sorry."

"For what? You've done nothing wrong in your life."

"For tearing you and Wickham apart."

"Georgiana," he said, "those seeds were planted before you were born. You were merely a link in the chain. And if anything, you have broken it."

She smiled wanly.

On the next day, Grégoire appeared. He bowed and took his seat. He looked a bit ridiculous with the bandages wrapped around his head, but no more ridiculous than his normal hairstyle, Darcy supposed. Maybe now his hair would grow out. "Do you have any sins you wish to confess?"

"May I remind you that your poor brother is a believer in the Church of England?"

"That does not make my question invalid."

Darcy considered. "All right. But—we don't exactly have a booth here."

"I suppose—we could put up the dressing screen from Elizabeth's room."

"How did you know Elizabeth has a screen in her quarters?"

"I—I just *assumed*—"

Darcy admitted he liked watching Grégoire blush. "Just have them bring it."

The screen was set up as a makeshift confessional barrier, and Grégoire took a seat on the other side. "I should point out that I am not, technically, a priest."

"And I should point out that I am not, technically, a Papist."

"Very well." Grégoire cleared his throat. "Do you have any sins to confess?"

"What if I am a perfect man?"

"There is the sin of pride."

"Very funny. Should I begin at the beginning? It will take an awfully long time if I cover everything *you* consider a sin."

"What do you consider a sin, Mr. Darcy?"

Darcy sighed and shifted on the bed, which did nothing to lessen his pain. "When I was a boy, I was very unruly, very disrespectful to my elders. And Wickham... we got into terrible trouble. Well, not so terrible—boyhood pranks and the like." He smiled. "I can remember some good times."

"So you did care for him."

"Yes, at times. It just—became more vicious. As we grew older, we fought." He laughed, but it was more of a cough. "By Cambridge, I had given up on him. I could not follow his lead. Oh, and while this is confessional, I should mention I slept with a prostitute after he paid for her services so I would… enter into manhood, which you should try some time, by the way."

"I am just your confessor now, Mr. Darcy."

"You don't know what you are missing," he said. "So… when Wickham was gone, when he was sent down, I was lost. I descended into the same debauchery he so enjoyed, only I was subtler about it. Then I met Charles, my last year, and desired to keep him away from the path where Wickham and I had strayed. But I was not always a good friend to him."

"How?"

"I misled him. About Jane, when she was just Miss Bennet. I drove them apart."

"But they did find each other again, not of your own design. And they are very happy."

"Actually, I apologized to Bingley and pointed him back to her."

"So you have repented thoroughly. Hardly a terrible friend."

"And I was cruel to Elizabeth. My first proposal was most insulting."

"Proposal?"

"For *marriage*, Monk. The thing normal people do."

"Respect for the church is also an important virtue."

"Depends on the church. So… and then there was that night—but I can't tell that story."

"If it was a sin, you must."

"Well, we didn't *really*... I don't remember what we did after the third bottle. But... enough. So there was my father."

"Yes. What of him?"

"I fought with him, at the end, over Wickham. Now, looking back, how much it must have pained him that I wanted to disown my own brother."

Grégoire said merely, "He did not tell you... therefore, you could not have known. While you were, I suppose, disrespectful in some fashion, you did not dishonor him in that. Did you not model your life after him? Did you not listen to his wisdom?"

"I have tried... every day of my life. With the one exception that I have been loyal to my wife since the day I first saw her eyes across a ballroom."

"But yet, you cannot forgive your father?"

"No. Is that a sin?"

"Forgiveness is a virtue, hatred a sin."

"I don't *hate* him. I just—do not comprehend his actions. He was so virtuous and yet did such great sin."

"We cannot all be saints, Mr. Darcy."

"Are you asking me to forgive my father?"

"I am not asking. But I think it would bring you comfort to begin to let the past be the past."

"Yes, the past." Darcy frowned. "There is the matter that I killed my own brother."

"Did you not do it to save my life? And your own?"

"That does not change the fact that I did it."

"So it seems there are two people you must forgive, if you are to find peace, and one is yourself," Grégoire said. "At this point I would say, 'my son,' but that feels odd."

"Indeed."

"You have lived, by all accounts, a virtuous life as a good gentleman, a father, a husband, a friend, a son. The amount of family that surrounds you even now is… overwhelming. They have forgiven you, if they ever thought you were in the wrong in the first place for your actions with George. Now you must forgive yourself. You cannot take this self-torture with you now."

"You are the expert on self-torture," Darcy said.

"I will not dignify that with an answer. Darcy, you know what I mean. I am told George died begging forgiveness. For you, from your family, it has already been granted, and God grants it now, but only if you forgive yourself."

"That… that you cannot ask of me."

"I am perfectly capable of asking. The reply is up to you."

Neither master nor mistress got much sleep that night. Darcy, because he was in such pain, and Elizabeth, because it was hard to sleep while clutching him so tightly and yet still trying not to hurt him. "So you shall know," she sobbed, "if you die, I will kill you."

"I must point out that that is technically impossible."

"Then I will have your tombstone signed with that awful nickname where Fitzwilliam should be."

"I will have to do my best not to die, then," he said, but despite it, they could not lighten the mood. The rest of Darcy's night was spent going back and forth between the chamber pot and the bucket.

In the morning, Darcy was dizzy and feverish and so nauseous that his manservant had to physically make him drink his morning linseed and barley water.

Holding up a glass, Dr. Maddox said, "Drink." He seemed cruel and unrelenting.

"My God. What is that?"

"Do you really wish to know?"

"Yes!" Darcy shouted, and then shook his head to try and clear his senses. "Excuse me. I am not sleeping well."

"I am sorry, Darcy." Dr. Maddox passed him the glass, and waited for Darcy to drink before answering him. "It's castor oil, mucilage of gum acacia, fennel water, and tincture of jalap."

"Terrific." Darcy lifted the glass. "Do I even want to know what this is going to do to me?"

"No."

Darcy laughed; at least the doctor was honest.

⌘

Darcy could not tell if the pain was dissipating in his back. It seemed to be better when leeches were applied over the area, as unsettling a feeling as it was while the treatment was occurring. His days and nights seemed to be irrelevant. He shut his doors to visitors, as he could not hold even the briefest conversations without needing to excuse himself. If the tonics were determined to force everything out of his body to free him from inflammation, they were certainly trying.

There were times when he was too dizzy to focus his eyes, and not just at night. He pushed Elizabeth away—he didn't want her to see him like this. He couldn't sleep in his bed without her, but he couldn't sleep anyway. He would just collapse somewhere before the bed, and the servants would lift him up and make him drink. Beyond that, nothing.

Darcy did not truly fall asleep. He was familiar with the

feeling of drifting into a feverish haze. The pain did not leave him and at times could be intense, but it was distant and he wasn't sure it was real. He felt between worlds, not literally. Some part of his brain knew it was all the power of days of this regimen to rid his body of inflammation.

"So logical."

Darcy sat down next to Wickham. The fire in front of them was roaring. He had a special affection for the ancient fireplace in their shared dormitory at King's College. It was older than Pemberley, dating probably to the foundations of the college, and it had a very medieval feel but yet still kept them warm in the cold winter months. The armchairs had been restored many times, and with two young hounds, given to him by his father for Christmas, nipping at his shoes, his regular homesickness was somewhat abated.

"Excuse me for adhering to reason," Darcy said. Sitting back did not relieve or affect the quite literal stabbing pain in his back.

"Darcy?" said Maddox. "Drink this. No, it won't make you sick. It's just water."

"What?" said Wickham.

"Nothing," said Darcy.

"Oh. Whiskey? Single malt."

"Anything decent?"

"I have standards, Darcy. They might not be as high as yours, but trust me when I say this is a fine whiskey. Have a glass."

Darcy picked up his glass and allowed Wickham to pour. It was tasteless and very fine at the same time.

"You know what it reminds me of? Guess."

"I prefer not to think about what occurs in your mind, Wickham."

"You think me more perverse than I actually am. Which means you must think me a regular Nero."

"Have you actually been studying your books? Can you actually *read?*"

Wickham ignored the question. "Loch Lomond. Remember, when Father took us to Scotland?"

"Oh, no. I had a terrible fever and did not go. You went with Father and Mr. Wickham. And that must have been... Georgiana was not born."

"No, I don't believe so. Father let me have just a bit of whiskey at the distillery."

"Which father?"

Wickham just laughed. His face was lit up from the fire, and when he smiled, he did have the appearance of being charming. He had perfected it over the years; Darcy was outright jealous of his social ease. The future master of Pemberley could barely manage a grin in public, and only when he had overheard a snippy remark.

"All right, try this. New Year's. We were—I was eight, you were nine."

"Oh God! Was it *that* New Year's? The one where you convinced me to stay up past our bedtimes and drink half a bottle?"

"It was more than half, and it was your idea."

"Certainly not!"

"Remember, this was before you had that stick up your arse and were actually a bit of fun."

Despite himself, Darcy chuckled. "Ah, yes. And we suffered for it."

"We had to hide it from Nurse—"

"She thought us ill for having terrible headaches. We had to stop her from bringing a doctor in."

"Ha! That was hilarious!" but he was cut off by a moan he could not prevent.

"Is it terrible?"

"I am told I have only a small chance of surviving."

"Then you'd best drink up."

Darcy did not contradict him, no matter how unsubstantially the alcohol affected him. "Why are you being so kind to me?"

"We are brothers, are we not?"

Darcy, again, could not contradict him.

"Were we not always, however unintentionally?"

"We were certainly terrible at it."

"Sibling rivalry is a long-standing tradition in almost any family. Especially one where the cards are so stacked against one." Wickham circled the glass with his hand and took a sip. "Though, I suppose, now that I think about it in hindsight, I would have made an awful Master of Pemberley."

"On this I feel I can soundly agree."

"I would have despised all of that responsibility. I would have had trysts with the maids after marrying some girl who was pretty and only after me for my money, instead of your sensible marrying of Elizabeth Bennet; thereby creating the same crisis that we all had to endure, even the little monk."

"His name is Grégoire."

"So French."

"His mother was."

"Ah, yes. But I imagine I would have left so many that we could have had a proper battle instead of a duel, with tactics and everything. Two armies of bastard sons."

Despite it, Darcy had to chuckle.

"God, Darcy, you are—well, I might say, pleasant when you're delirious."

"That stick is still there, Wickham, or I suppose I should say, *George*." He stared down into his glass, finding it hard to focus his eyes. "Father always wanted me to call you that."

"Father always wanted me to call you Fitzwilliam."

"You opted instead for insulting nicknames... in front of women, too."

"You know my mouth hurt for weeks afterwards from that? That was the last time I ever got between you and a girl with pretty eyes—Oh, I am wrong. But the second time, you defeated me soundly without even punching out one of my teeth, so an improvement on both sides. And you got to keep the woman."

"As I am currently in the most pain I have ever been in and am quite sure you are merely a side effect of its hallucinative effects, my heart does not go out to you."

"My heart *is* out. I think I left it on the road somewhere."

"Thank you for that lovely image, Wickham."

"We could have gotten along quite well, don't you think?"

"What, if you were not a gambler and a promiscuous man who stole the honor of what I must assume was an endless number of ladies, and I were not a proper gentleman with no patience for such improprieties?"

"If I had loosened up less and you had loosened up more, perhaps, we would have been at least bearable to each other. And do not hide for a moment behind this 'proper gentleman' business!"

"Are you implying I am not?"

"I think he's coming around," Dr. Maddox's voice came in, booming in the room, though Wickham didn't hear it and continued undisturbed.

"You are a gentleman. I will not deny it. But you take it to extremes because you are… disabled."

"Disabled?"

"You are afraid of people, Darcy."

"I am not afraid of anything!"

"Perhaps a better word," Wickham said. Darcy had forgotten that he could display a high degree of intelligence. But he was, after all, the son of Geoffrey Darcy. "Uncomfortable."

"What do you mean?"

"People that you do not know. People that you *do* know, but lack the means to play that social dance, and I do not mean a literal dance, as you are quite accomplished in that respect despite your lack of practice."

"I think I've just been insulted and complimented in the same breath."

"It was not so much an insult. I was not saying you are stupid or mentally ill, but behind all of that propriety and stiff posture is a real man, waiting to get out. Or perhaps, you show him to Elizabeth. She is then a very lucky woman, because you can be quite pleasant if you wish to be, even likeable."

"So," Darcy said. "We have a man with no scruples but excellent social abilities, and the very opposite. And one killed the other."

"It has not been established quite yet whether I returned the favor. It depends on your brother-in-law. You could not find a doctor with proper eyes?"

"He has an excellent record and has saved my life before."

"I can't quite decide if that is good or bad for me. I did not mean to kill you, Darcy."

Darcy sighed. "I cannot honestly say the same thing."

"If I had not attacked Gregory—"

"Still," He shook his head; that, he could manage to do. "My hatred was too deep for me to forgive, even when considering one of your mistakes was made by accident. Had you approached Georgiana more formally—"

"—Mrs. Reynolds would have said something." George Wickham, of course, did not have this information. Or maybe he did; Darcy didn't question it. "And while that would have changed our lives, it would have prevented the intended marriage, certainly." He said in a softer voice, one that actually sounded concerned, "You know I never compromised her. Or even came close. I never laid a hand on her, except to escort her around Brighton."

"I know."

"But that does not unburden me—even with her forgiveness. Some things cannot be forgiven, however unintentional."

"Or perhaps they can," Darcy said. "You said she did."

"Yes."

"Then I must follow in her lead," Darcy said. He raised his glass so he did not have to say it. "I feel as if… a terrible burden is off my shoulders."

"Maybe they amputated them while we sat here in front of this pleasant little fire."

"Be serious."

"See, we are opposites. Like you and Bingley, only he meets

your stringent requirements of virtue. Otherwise, we are partners in a strange friendship."

Darcy raised his glass. "To brothers."

"To brothers. And brothers must forgive and forget. Both of us."

"Even for the most heinous of crimes?"

"As we both fall into that category, with attempted incest and fratricide, we must overlook them if we are to forgive each other at all."

"Done, then."

They clinked glasses, which shattered, along with his world.

⁕

"Darcy? Mr. Darcy, can you hear me?"

The picture came back into definition, instead of the haze before him. Dr. Maddox, his manservant, and his wife were across him. He had collapsed on the floor next to his bed. So talkative to the dead, he did not feel up to putting together an answer for the living.

Maddox touched his forehead. "His fever's broken. On two?"

They hauled him back up on the bed, onto fresh sheets, and changed his shirt again. It felt wonderful to be clean and dry. "Thank you," he mumbled after Elizabeth offered a cup of coffee, of which he managed only a few sips.

"Do you feel ill?"

To his own surprise, he shook his head.

"How is your back?"

He fumbled to touch the spot with his own hand. "It feels—better." He couldn't find any pain at all. He looked up hopefully at Maddox. "Can we stop now?"

"Yes," Dr. Maddox said, his own voice bordering on joy-ous delirium, from Darcy's limited sense of perception. "Yes, we can."

Darcy nodded and turned his head on the pillow, instantly asleep.

EPILOGUE

D<small>ARCY'S RECOVERY TOOK OVER</small> a month. The Maddoxes would return to Town officially after Christmas because of the doctor's various requirements there, although Dr. Maddox did return briefly to see Brian off on his adventure in the Carpathian Mountains and to check on his royal patient. Darcy was no longer in the prime of youth and had been injured twice in the duel, so he was pained for a long time, so much so that Maddox began restricting the dosage of medicine.

"I will not turn your husband into an opium fiend," Maddox said to Elizabeth.

He was frustrated with the results of only one aspect of the proceedings, which was that Darcy's hand had lost some of its capabilities. Though it was hardly frozen or limp, its flexibility was limited, to the point that his normally perfect script was illegible.

"It does match Geoffrey's almost perfectly," Elizabeth said, smoothing out the hair of her flustered and grumpy husband.

Aside from his own recovery and his wife's increasing girth,

Darcy had few things to worry about. In fact, the only thing he could think of at the moment was Grégoire, the monastic secluded from his monasticism. As much as he enjoyed being with his newfound family, and as much as his humility prevented what would have made Darcy outright furious at the stares he got for his appearance, he was not settled in England. He probably never would be, Darcy eventually came to realize (after much prompting from Elizabeth). And in Ireland, where they still clutched onto their Catholicism, the monasteries had been dissolved. Despite his youth, Grégoire was a relic.

Doubling his pain was a letter from the Monastery of Mont Claire. The Abbot wrote in long and lengthy Latin, and whatever it said, Grégoire paled at it and disappeared. When he did not return for lunch or dinner, they sent a party out and found him lying on his father's grave, staring up at the sky.

Darcy called the men off, set the lantern down, and sat down beside him. He barely noticed that Wickham's tombstone had been finished and installed. "I would build you a monastery if I could."

"You cannot."

"What did the Abbot's letter say?"

"I don't care to repeat it and slander my Abbot." He sighed, clutching the cross from Rome. "Well, I suppose he isn't my father abbot anymore."

"So you were cast out?"

"Yes."

"On what charges?"

"He made various assumptions about my activities and behavior on the road."

"Was he correct?"

"Partially... I did ride in a carriage when I could have walked." He laughed. "I suppose that is a bit ridiculous."

"A bit?"

"He also wrote that he knew when I walked out the door that I would give in to the temptations of wealth and flesh."

"But, you have not."

Grégoire turned his head without sitting up. "Am I a changed man since I walked out of the cloister?"

"I don't see you in a gambling den with a whore on each side, no. In fact, my barber has complained to me about your insistence on trimming your hair in such a fashion that he finds backwards and ridiculous."

"What did you say to him?"

"That if he every complained again, I would dismiss him."

There was silence in the cold winter night.

"When I am well enough," Darcy said. "I will take you back to France or even go as far as Spain to find you a proper abbey."

"I cannot ask you to travel for me."

Darcy replied, "You have no idea how many people have told me not to do things for them. I've never listened to them, because I am a ridiculously stubborn man, and somehow I always get thanked in the end. Or shot. Sometimes both."

The brothers shared a laugh, and Darcy escorted the little monk back to the house.

He had convinced Grégoire to winter in Pemberley, if only to see his new nephew or niece in the spring. On this, at least, Grégoire was convinced, and they arranged for a more abbey-like arrangement for him in the private chapel, which was still medieval in character. Mrs. Reynolds even located the old altar furnishings behind a dusty wooden screen, unused since the

Reformation, and Darcy dubbed the room beside the chapel "Pemberley Abbey."

The families all gathered at Pemberley for Christmas, since Darcy was still slowly recovering and it conveniently was also the birthdays of the Bingley twins. When they realized someone was missing, the Maddoxes made their apologies for Brian's absence.

"He's gone where?" Darcy said, not having been informed in all the commotion of his situation.

"The Carpathian Mountains. In eastern Austria, I believe." The doctor did not look excessively happy about it.

"To be married to a woman he's met twice."

"And is royalty," said Mr. Bennet, still highly amused. "The foreign princess."

"I would say that I've heard crazier things from Brian, but this may actually be the thing that would qualify him for Bedlam," Dr. Maddox said, unconsciously looking with concern at his wife, who cradled their daughter. "I can't say I was happy about it, but I have no authority to stop him."

"Her name again?"

"God, it's impossible to pronounce. He's only said it a few times. Actually, he's been rather quiet and shy about the woman herself."

"Hmmm," Caroline Maddox said, "When do men get quiet and shy about women?"

"I don't get quiet and shy about women," Bingley said.

"That's because you're a social twit," Darcy said. "The correct answer is apparently when they're in love."

"*Twit?*"

"Yes, that was what I was looking for, Darcy," Mrs. Maddox said. "Don't you agree, Mrs. Darcy?"

"Did he really call me a twit?"

"Absolutely," Elizabeth said, "especially when they're deeply, passionately in love but cannot bear to show it."

"I know it's his house, but still! Darcy!"

"What?" Darcy said, pretending to be broken from a reverie. "Bingley, I can only be assaulted on one front at a time, and here I have two women, so will you please just take my side?"

"Against my sister and your wife? Do you think me mad?"

"Well, everyone needs to have a mad brother," Jane said.

"I've already got one. Sorry, Mrs. Bingley," Darcy said, ignoring the fact that Grégoire had tossed an olive in his direction, "and so does Dr. Maddox. So really, the Bingley family is lacking in brothers who won't listen to reason unless you look around the other way and count Bingley himself."

"Look, I don't have to take this—"

"Does anyone know the hour?" Darcy looked at his pocket watch.

"Why do we assume our Lord was born precisely at midnight?" Maddox said. "Seeing as how the sun sets faster in the east, isn't it already midnight in his birthplace?"

"Don't mix logic and religion, Doctor," Mr. Bennet said, "or you'll get something quite combustible."

"Cheers to that," said Grégoire, and raised his glass as he crossed himself.

Darcy made further inquiry into his future health, beyond his new dietary restrictions and his struggles to learn to write with his left hand.

Despite Maddox's insistence that they did not have to pay

him for his services, he did receive a new set of the latest medical compendium from the University of Paris in the post several weeks after his return home.

But that was not the only gift the Maddoxes received. For a while he wondered if the prince would ever bring up the subject of Frederick Maddox, because his royal intelligence surely knew of it, but the prince did not ask and Maddox did not offer up the information. He thought he had escaped the matter entirely until Frederick's first birthday, when a new boy's cradle arrived at the house with no return address. The fact that it was of expensive Continental construction with Dutch wood engravings and gilded edges made him suspicious, as he had already received his son's gifts from those who both knew the real birthday and were fantastically wealthy—and that list was very short.

On the other side of the family, the Bennet household was full of joy—and a lot of wailing. The Widow Wickham had two rowdy children, and until she remarried—which, knowing Lydia, would be as soon as she could take off her black mourning for Mr. Wickham—they would remain at Longbourn, which had undergone some minor renovations. And then there was baby Joseph, with whom everyone was much happier when he was sleeping through the night and not waking the whole household, especially because Mary refused a wet nurse and took all responsibilities on herself. So Longbourn was filled with children again.

If anyone had any questions as to how Mary had appeared with a child, Mr. Bennet insisted that not only had she sworn off marriage for the moment, but that she had taken in an orphan child while in France. She was simply too attached to the child for him to separate them. Any amount of social digging could discern this was an outright lie. It was also known that Mr. Bennet had come into a massive fortune, and however questionable its origins, one did not speak too unkindly to a man with such a fortune and three unmarried daughters, even if one was wearing jet and one had a child—at least, not within listening distance.

Kitty was sent to Town to be more forwardly on the market. Mr. Bennet did not have to buy her an apartment, even though he was thoroughly capable of doing so, because Georgiana quickly invited her to come live in the massive Darcy townhouse that was barely in use beyond herself and her own staff. As Georgiana Darcy was the most proper of ladies, she would be an excellent influence, and she would put Mr. Bennet's mind at ease. He imagined that if a gentleman so much as tried to walk up the front steps without good cause, Mr. Darcy would magically appear in Town on a cloud of smoke and escort him back down the street with a pistol.

The winter was cold but short, and it was an anxious time for the Darcys, but in a happy way. By her confinement, Elizabeth's chances of miscarriage were slim. In fact, she was perfectly healthy aside from the normal trials of being with child, so there was no reason to expect a bad turn.

On a chilly spring day, when the roads of Derbyshire were wet with melted snow, Elizabeth Darcy delivered a child after a day of cursing Darcy, everyone of relation, everyone who tried to aid her in the trials of labor, and mankind as a whole. Her vocabulary, Jane had to admit to her husband later, had improved in a very fascinating way due to her many travels since her last labor, and Jane had learned a good deal.

"Well, I'll clearly be spending any future labor of yours drunk again," Bingley said, patting her on the back.

The child was a healthy, beautiful baby girl with brown hair and what Darcy immediately noticed were "Elizabeth's fine eyes." He had the misfortune of being allowed not more than half a glass of wine a day, and so he had spent the long hours in his study pacing endlessly and occasionally cursing at the dogs as they followed him around. His usual calm demeanor only returned when presented with his child in front of an exhausted Elizabeth, who had the further suffering of her first child leaping on the bed to get a good first view of his new sister.

"What's her name?"

"They don't come with labels, darling," she said. "But I have decided that she should be named Anne, so that your father can have something to do with that lovely bracelet without giving it to Mrs. Fitzwilliam, which at this point would be downright odd."

It took Darcy a moment to recall it. "Yes, of course." He handed the baby back to Elizabeth's eager arms, weak as they were, and ran out of the room quickly, returning with a small gold bracelet—the one they had recovered from the drawer of Darcy secrets in the Normandy estate. "My darling Anne," he said. The child, barely awake, did not have the wrists yet for it, but he let her grasp its hoop with her tiny fingers.

Anne Jane Darcy was christened in the little chapel in Pemberley, and despite his insistence on a lack of ordination, they insisted that Grégoire have the honor of doing it as soon as Elizabeth was well enough to attend. After a rushed portrait could be made so he could have one of each of them, Grégoire Bellamont left for the Continent to trade in his grey robes for black ones and become a Benedictine novice.

Brian Maddox had seen the abbey in Austria himself on the way through and sent his approval to all of Darcy's exact specifications. They would even let Grégoire travel to visit his family in England, as they were not French and not so isolationist. He was allowed to leave Derbyshire only with a promise to write and to return to see his niece and nephew, and with a wooden staff he had carved from a tree branch, he quite literally walked out of Pemberley.

"Stubborn to the end," Elizabeth said as they watched him disappear down to the road.

"He'll hit the ocean eventually, I'm sure, and then he *will* have to ride," Darcy said. "But he'll probably walk across Europe, too… obstinate monk."

"Truly a Darcy."

"I think we have living proof, right here and now, that I am no monk," Darcy said, and kissed her as Anne gurgled in her arms. "You know, you were not required to name her after my mother," Darcy said, with no dispute in his voice.

"Oh, but I did. She did me the great favor of having you and putting up with you during your worst years."

"If you think I was intolerable as a child, then you know nothing about University," he said. "But that is another story."

"Darcy! Are you hiding something from me?"

"It is not so much hiding as leaving out various things which do not bear repeating."

"When do I get to go to University?" Geoffrey asked, looking up at his father.

Darcy replied. "Never. Also, Anne's never going out. It's the Abbey for both of you."

"Father!"

"I hope you like chores and prayer. Long, boring hours of prayer, and wearing a dress."

"No! You're not serious!"

"I'm being perfectly serious. And not just the top of your head, some orders shave their whole head. You'll be bald before you're fifteen if I convince them to take you that early."

"Darcy," Elizabeth whispered. "Stop torturing our son."

"Well, if he can do it to me at three in the morning, I should occasionally be able to do it to him," her husband replied.

"Then I should have my rights to torture you as well."

"Lizzy, you have been doing it since the night we met," he said. "Now I'd best catch our son before he sets up a trap for us."

"*Us?* I was hardly involved beyond defending him. You are the mocking father here, Darcy. Now run along and catch him before he gets himself all muddy, and I have to see to his cleaning myself. You know Nurse can't get him clean."

"Yes, *Mrs. Darcy*," he said with a stiff bow, and just as he was about to break off in pursuit of Geoffrey, he turned back again and kissed Elizabeth. His son had a good head start before he could begin the proper chase down the path, but Darcy decided it was worth it.

THE END

HISTORICAL INACCURACIES

SCREW YOU, WIKIPEDIA!

When I wrote the first draft of this story in 2006, I was no stranger to history but a big believer in the power of the Internet as a research tool. This book was also the first story that ventured out of England, requiring more research than the previous book. The result was me writing myself into some pretty disastrous corners of historical inaccuracy. Some mulligans were required to resurrect the story.

All of the monasteries in France were dissolved in 1789 and turned into public houses and storage facilities. Many monks decided to remain in France on a subsidy, but they eventually either moved abroad, left the clergy, or became priests. The tonsure and clerical dress were practically outlawed. In 1804 to 1805, Napoleon allowed a few Catholic ministers to form monastic houses, but he later changed his mind and had the houses dissolved by the end of the decade. Mont Claire doesn't really exist, nor does the monastic house there, though it could have briefly existed in 1807.

Giovanni Mastai-Ferretti was never officially involved with a woman, though there were unconfirmed rumors of a relationship in the 1810s. He did have epilepsy and picked up French at some point early in his life, but he never fathered a child with a fictional Jane Austen character. Honestly I think it would have been pretty impressive if he did.

The *Kama Sutra* had yet to be officially translated into English, which is why the book is never named in the text. During the late eighteenth and early nineteenth centuries, British soldiers living abroad translated many Indian texts into English, so a manual of that sort could have been one of them.

George IV probably fathered several children out of wedlock, but he was never caught visiting a brothel.

Finally, all of my own characters (and Jane Austen's) are fictional, so none of the events in the book ever happened.

ACKNOWLEDGMENTS

FIRST OFF, THIS BOOK would not exist without Jane Austen's genius, as it is a sequel to a sequel to her immortal *Pride and Prejudice*. To be very thorough, these events could have happened, but only in some kind of alternate universe where night is day and we're ruled by crab people. I wouldn't want to live in that universe, without Jane Austen, though I have heard some good reviews about the crab-based administration.

Brandy Scott goes next, and she's going to be in every book, so why don't you all just get used to it. I don't know why this woman does so much editing for me of her own free will, but who am I to question the majesty that is Brandy Scott?

Deb Werksman at Sourcebooks keeps buying books from me, so she deserves a round of applause for her boundless enthusiasm for new authors, which is pretty hard to find in the book industry. Susie Benton and Danielle Jackson also put a lot of hard work into this book, as did the terrific production team and everybody else at the company. Sarah Ryan did some excellent copyediting.

Kate Menick has been an invaluable agent and very support-ive friend. I hope this book does insanely well and she gets some money from it. That's not the only reason I hope the book does insanely well, but it's up there.

Once again, all of the loyal readers at Fanfiction.net and the various sites where I also posted this story were the people who got the story written, as this was all long before I had any dream of publishing it.

The following people deserve many thanks for helping me with research: Diana Bryant, Rene Garen, Sharon Lathan, and Michele Young.

Many people offered their help with the translations into French, even without being asked. Thanks go to Copperstring, nienie, and some other people who responded via email and that I've not been able to track down. User Story 215 provided some invaluable medical wisdom.

To my parents, who went far beyond what I would expect to make sure everyone we knew not only knew about my first book, *The Darcys & the Bingleys*, but also purchased or received a copy from them. I don't think a reference to Jane Austen characters ever appeared before in a synagogue bulletin.

To my grandmother, Helga Franklin. When I was very young and still played on the carpet with toys, she sat with me one day while I told her all of the stories I'd made up for the vari-ous action figures. She said to me, "Where do you come up with these stories? You have so much creativity." It was not the only time she said that, but it's been the most meaningful to me.

For all the publishing and legal questions I have thrown at her, I would like to thank my boss, Diana Finch.

To the good people at the New York Public Library, thank

you for never noticing when I seemed to be photocopying an entire history book that cost too much to buy. I would say the same of the library staff at The City College of New York, as I can remember copying a number of ancient and massive out-of-print books there.

I'd like to put my brother Jason in here. I want to say something about "love" and "support" but that's too clichéd, even for a brother. We all know he loves and supports me. I heard he actually talks about my book to girls at parties. My book. It makes my heart melt.

Thanks to Shir Lerman for moral support. Current roommates get a freebie on this one.

And finally, all praise goes to the Holy One, Blessed be He, for creating 613 commandments to follow and not making a single one of them mention whether I could crib off Jane Austen or not. I checked.